To the Crew of <u>The Hague</u>
She Was the Cabin Boy—
but Behind Closed Doors . . .

"What—are you going to do?" I whispered.

"What I've seen you wanting me to do. . . . Take off the clothes."

"Roger, not this way! Oh, please! Not like a—"

"You want to be courted? Like a lady? You want me to say you're the most beautiful woman I have ever seen and handle you tenderly? You want me to say I'm in love with you? What do you take me for? You're a runaway, a stowaway, escaped from Newgate, dressing and living as a man! You're no sweet, innocent maiden . . ."

"No . . . please," I whispered.

"You want it," he growled. "And so do I."

Books by Saliee O'Brien

Beelfontaine
The Bride of Gaylord Hall
Captain's Woman
Shadow of the Caravan

Published by POCKET BOOKS

Captain's Woman

Saliee O'Brien

PUBLISHED BY POCKET BOOKS NEW YORK

This novel is based on events in the life of the female pirate, Mary the Red. For purposes of clarity and story-flow, the author has taken license in the sequence of dates and events.

Another *Original* publication of POCKET BOOKS

POCKET BOOKS, a Simon & Schuster division of
GULF & WESTERN CORPORATION
1230 Avenue of the Americas, New York, N.Y. 10020

ISBN: 0-671-81287-4

First Pocket Books printing December, 1979

10 9 8 7 6 5 4 3 2 1

FOR CAPTAIN CARL BROWN

PROLOGUE
LONDON
1714

Chapter 1

I stood in the great lower hallway of Hunter House and watched my distant, money-hungry kinsman, Sir Cecil Hunter, gallantly escort his exquisite raven-haired wife, Lady Gwen, down the broad, curving staircase. Behind them Tom, the bootboy, struggled with the last of their fine bags. He'd come to serve my recently deceased grandmother two years ago, a healthy, happy lad. But in the past two months, since Sir Cecil had arrived from France, Tom had grown scrawny and haggard. Sir Cecil was sole heir to all the Hunter estates, houses, monies and investments. He came to a halt at the outer door and focused his attention on me, his thin lips touched by a smile. Tom and the butler, Jones, began to transfer the clutter of bags outside to the carriage. I stood my ground, expressionless, trying to hide my dread and dislike of my kinsman and his lady.

Sir Cecil watched me keenly, his curled wig gleaming almost as black as his own hair which I, on demand, had dressed several times. He frowned and his sharp brows dipped, as he drew himself to his full, needle-slim six foot height, openly bored by the need to inspect his estates, despite the money they were worth.

"I shall expect you to keep an eye on the servants while we're gone, Read," he said to me in his thin, demanding tone.

A shiver went down my spine. After his tour of inspection, what would happen to me? I couldn't possibly stay on here. There was no place for me. I was educated, I had aristocratic blood in my veins, but I knew that unless Sir Cecil chose otherwise, my fate, when I left Hunter House, would be no better than Tom's. Tom had already been given notice.

"You understand, Read?" Sir Cecil asked. His pale eyes shimmered perhaps with anticipation. I knew exactly why he was throwing Tom out. It was because he meant to dally with me next. So far as he knew, I was only a young man of nineteen, and of no real importance in his household.

He waited for my reply, his look piercing.

I made a small bow. "I shall look after your interests, sir."

"I may be gone as long as a fortnight. There is the manor house to rearrange, farms to inspect. And the country gentry will entertain us. However, I expect all here in London to be perfection when I return."

As I murmured assurance, Lady Gwen nodded coolly and they went out the door. I watched Sir Cecil help his lady up and follow her inside. The carriage started briskly away.

I fled upstairs to my room. I had a fortnight, fourteen days, before he would begin on me. The past two months he'd made me increasingly uneasy, to the point where I felt an inward trembling which I found hard to control.

My grandmother had married Sir Stephen Hunter, a man old enough to be her father. His young son, Hilary, who was my grandmother's exact age, took umbrage at the marriage and left home. Neither Hilary nor his son, William, ever returned, but William's son, Sir Cecil, had now come to take possession of all the heritage. My own father, Bruce, was the second son and, even had he lived, would have inherited nothing. Nor had I claim to any of the Hunter wealth. It was all in the hands of Sir Cecil, and there it would remain.

Since his arrival, Sir Cecil had been engrossed with Tom, concealing his behavior from Lady Gwen by playing the tender husband. But when poor Tom grew worn and haggard, Sir Cecil began to look at me boldly during meals. His objective was clear and I understood it fully, for poor Tom had confided in me, pleading for help that wasn't in my power to give, confessing and describing the master's way of using him, a depraved practice of which I'd had no knowledge until now. For the past week Sir Cecil and I had been subtly fencing, very politely on the surface, but under it lay his seething determination and my own resolve to thwart him. I knew that his finesse would be replaced by aggression. Men like him took what they wanted, even by force.

I couldn't just leave, because I didn't have any money. I was, however, educated to be a tutor. My hope lay in that field, but it would require help from Sir Cecil. If he refused, my one thread of hope—if I dared use it—was something I'd heard Lady Gwen say to him as I neared the open library to fetch a book.

"This Tom-folly is to stop," I heard her say. "It's unnatural, it would disgrace us if . . . We have our position to consider. Get rid of the boy. Forget this aberration."

"You know how to make me forget, Gwen."

"That's as unnatural as the boy! Oh, Cecil, what has happened to you?"

That was all I heard, for I scurried away to avoid eavesdropping. Now, as I stepped into my bedchamber, I was distraught. I had twice the problem Tom faced, and couldn't think how to handle it. Either way, whether I repelled my kinsman or he overpowered me, he could throw me out, leave me homeless and jobless. And when he found out my secret, I knew I would be doomed.

Distressed, I went to the mirror and studied myself. My auburn wig, which my grandmother had ordered me to wear, was flawless, hiding my wealth of rich red, madly curling hair. My arched brows were nearer auburn than red. My lips were red—passionate, my grandmother had warned—but they could be firm and determined. Though I was only five foot, eight inches tall, my one hundred thirty pounds were well distributed and, in my brown durant breeches and tan frockcoat, I looked what I professed to be—a mannerly, educated young gentleman.

In reality, I was a nineteen-year-old girl, and my name was not George Read but Mary Hunter, daughter of the long-deceased Bruce Hunter and the deceased Fanne Read, village seamstress. Fanne had been hard-working, beautiful, red-haired, hot-blooded, and with depths of tenderness few mortals possess.

My father, not yet presenting his wife to his blue-blooded mother, had gone adventuring on the sea. During a time of sore need, my mother decided to go to London and ask my grandmother for help. Knowing that the aging Lady Victoria disliked girls, my mother cut my hair, dressed me in boy's clothes, and had me pretend to be a boy. Delighted to meet a grandson, Lady Victoria gave us a crown a week, without which we scarcely could have survived, and demanded a yearly visit. I was fourteen when my mother died and Lady Victoria took me into her household, told me I'd be known as George Read, protégé, and hired tutors to instruct me.

Oh, how I hated to live like a boy! I had to be ever on the watch. I had to walk like a boy, hold my shoulders like a boy, lower my naturally low voice still more, sit as a boy sits.

Often I had thought I could no longer endure it. I vowed I'd tell the truth. But then some sort of strength formed in my young breast, and I held back the words. My grandmother was fond of me; she was educating me. I studied history, languages, calculation, literature, as well as riding, shooting, and fencing. When I turned nineteen, she was to have given me a letter of recommendation and I would get a post as tutor. Only she'd died suddenly, and I had no letter.

Thus life had forced me to live and be educated as a boy, and I had reluctantly accepted this, rather than hurt Lady Victoria, who was kind to me, even loving. But always, every day, I had longed for the feel of skirts around my ankles, for the freedom of my own hair. I hungered to sew and dance and sing and play music. To have a handsome young man, a sweetheart, who would become my bridegroom. Instead, I was forced to continue the masquerade or, after hurting my grandmother, risk being sent packing, unable to make a living except, perhaps, back in the village as barmaid. And there I'd be fighting off the worst types of men and no decent man would choose me for wife.

In the village, when I was a young girl, I'd often wished I was more like Janie, my friend, who was freckled and plain as sand. The men had been after me then. I'd laughed off their remarks and slid away from their hands.

Now, staring into the mirror, I evaluated myself. According to my grandmother, I had my father's patrician features and hot blood. I had my mother's flaming hair, her white skin, her passionate mouth, and her hot blood. Even though I stood dressed as a man, I could see both of my parents in myself and knew I had a double portion of their dangerous handsomeness and their even more dangerous hot blood. I would, when I could resume my true role as girl, tone down my looks, but I'd still be pursued by men. And I was already being pursued, despite my boy's guise, by Sir Cecil.

It was an unbearable situation.

"Like what you see?" asked a thin, slow voice. I whirled.

Sir Cecil was in my doorway, leaning against the jamb. He looked at me with those pale, penetrating eyes, and his lips went to threads as he smiled. His chin sharpened, too. Women fawned on him. That I'd seen at dinners they'd given here. The women flirted with their eyes, seductively, smiling very slowly into his face. He took it as his birthright. I'd heard Lady Gwen say women had always spoiled him.

Even at thirty, which should be an age of discretion, he wore his male, polished attraction like a robe.

Kinglike, he took it for granted that any woman he favored would succumb, that any lad—

"You seem surprised, even troubled," he said. "I thought you'd gone."

"We did start. It struck me, suddenly, that it was vital I have the conversation I've been planning to have with you now. So you can ponder it in my absence."

I waited.

"It took only a clever ruse on my part to inspire Lady Gwen to return and change her travel costume." He lifted his shoulders. "I can manipulate any woman . . . or lad. As you will learn, George."

Never before had he addressed me as anything but "Read."

I met his look, deliberately keeping myself calm. He couldn't harm me in just the time it would take Lady Gwen to change. But he was aware of my underlying fear, and he took open pleasure in it. He was so sure of himself. Some women would have forgotten they were wearing mens' clothes, would have felt delicious shivers, if he were to look them over so lingeringly.

He needed, I understood abruptly, frequent new conquests so he could reassure himself of his male powers. He treated his wife gallantly, indulging and fussing over her enough to keep her contented. When she made an issue of something, he gave in to her. For the moment. I knew, from my grandmother, that they hadn't married entirely for love, but also to merge her fortune and his heritage and to pour a double strain of blueblood into their future children.

"Now," he said, "our talk. I have a duty to you. I've neglected to ask whether you're content here."

"I've always found Hunter House pleasant, sir."

"I've been learning things about you," he continued, "I've uncovered some astounding things. Things not mentioned in correspondence with Lady Victoria's lawyers."

He couldn't know I was a girl! How could he have found out? Even my grandmother hadn't known.

"There's a bit you neglected to tell, George."

"I didn't consider it necessary," I responded, feeling my way.

I was amazed at my own calm tone, but I wasn't going to be cowed by something that wasn't my fault. Since he had no way of knowing I was a girl, then he must have uncovered the truth of my parentage, and I wasn't ashamed of that.

"I've known the degree of our kinship," he said. "Your father was the second, much younger son of Lady Victoria and old Sir Stephen."

"He was."

"A splendid line. One of the oldest, with the bluest blood. Your mother, on the other hand . . . "

"She was a seamstress. She was married to my father."

"Very convenient explanation."

"My grandmother accepted it."

"But she didn't accept the mother, only the grandson. And by her own rules."

"My grandmother loved me."

"She couldn't have done otherwise. You're very handsome, George. Very . . . appealing. Provocative. You were delicately reared and well tutored. The seamstress' urchin disappeared, replaced by a cultured young gentleman. She meant for you to remain such."

"She meant for me to be a tutor. She was going to give me a letter of recommendation."

"Surely you want better than tutoring, George!"

"It was what we planned. Only now . . . "

"Yes?"

"Everything's changed. You've learned of my mother's blood. You'll want me to leave."

"My dear lad! Have you leave, indeed! My lad, my handsome, fine lad, my only wish is to help you!"

"The way you helped Tom?" It was out before I knew it.

His eyes narrowed. "Tom's a different situation. Thank God, he'll be gone when I return."

I stared at his casual ease, stunned at my own temerity, but I just couldn't help what I was thinking. If the Devil himself came to earth, he couldn't be worse than Sir Cecil. Because he was wealthy, a blueblood, he assumed he could make toys out of waifs like Tom. And because he was a handsome, compelling male, he thought he could enslave anyone, woman or lad. My cheeks burned, I was so angry.

"Is this what you came to tell me? That you know of my mother's blood?"

"Partly. And to let you know I have plans for us. So you can ponder, as I said, and anticipate."

"I'll anticipate nothing!" I flared.

"Ah. I knew you were a blazing flame."

"I'm not like that! I'm not the kind . . . "

"You're one apart, the finest. Splendid. I knew the first day. I wanted you to become accustomed to us. To appreciate that all you enjoyed with your grandmother is still here. And more . . . now that I can devote myself to you after visiting my properties."

"You'll be wasting your effort, Sir Cecil."

"Oh, no. I don't forget the hot blood in your father. Or in your mother. You're not the clean-cut, proper young gentleman you pretend to be. You've got fires in you as hot as those in Hades."

He came to where I stood at the mirror, stopping only inches away. He was so close I breathed the spicy soap he used. He was dressed in brown plush breeches and pleated tan coat with buttons on the front. His elegant clothing intensified the male air which enveloped him.

"We're going to be very intimate, you and I," he said.

"You're wrong, Sir Cecil!"

The thread of a smile, his eyes filled with amusement. They had smudges under them, almost puffs. Dissolute, I thought, but my blood was fast and I was trembling inwardly. I despised him and I was frightened of him, not only that he'd find out I was a girl, but because his nearness caused an uncontrollable thrill.

"Please," I said, "leave me alone."

"Impossible. You don't want me to. The education, the manners, the unusual intelligence, don't alter fact. You've got that hell-hotness."

"No!" I cried, fists clenched.

"You're handsome as a god, too fine to waste yourself as a tutor. I'll give you a position as my secretary. You'll help run my estates. You're going to be happy. You have no idea how happy."

Casually, he put his hands on my shoulders. Before I could step back, so benumbed was I, he let them fall.

"You're starving for me, George."

"I'm not! I . . ."

"That's what you say now. But in a fortnight . . ." He stepped to the door, looked along the hallway. "Still with Read, darling. Do join us."

Earlier she'd been wearing black. Now she'd changed to dark blue silk and tiny diamond earrings, as beautiful as I'd ever seen her. Her hair was dressed tall, and I wondered who had done it for her. Occasionally, knowing that I'd always dressed Lady Victoria's hair, she called upon me to do hers.

Now she gave each of us a quick glance.

"Have you given Read your final instructions, darling?" she asked.

"Just, my dear. Ah, how beautiful you are! Come, let us be on our way again."

I went weak with relief.

He bowed, gave me a thin smile, offered his arm to Lady Gwen and they left.

I closed my door. He wouldn't return again; he'd accomplished his mission. I believed he'd truly and deliberately driven away the first time, fully meaning to return, partly to wield his power over his wife but mostly to shock and frighten me. Oh, there was no evil of which I didn't suspect this kinsman! I sat on a straight chair for a very long while, empty of any feeling but that of being trapped.

I appreciated how fortunate I'd been for my grandmother to educate me. If only she'd written that letter of recommendation, I'd now have a tutoring post. I'd be earning wages of which I'd save nearly every penny, have a couple of small boys to teach, my own bedchamber, good food, neat clothes, even if they weren't dresses. I could be working toward the day when I could afford to make the change and live as the girl I was.

But now, if I couldn't get a tutoring post, I'd have no way to earn money. And if Sir Cecil found out I was a girl—if I lost my chances that way—What can I do, how can I explain? I asked myself. Oh, dear God, what can I *do?*

Chapter 2

They had been gone for twelve days, and for twelve days I'd lived in suspense, safe for the moment, but knowing it wouldn't last. Tom was gone. Sir Cecil would return, what he meant to do would be done, and I still didn't know where to turn.

It was mid-morning now. I was sitting on a bench in a far corner of the rose garden, a book open on my lap, but I wasn't reading. Instead, as the sun brightened the masses of pink, climbing roses, I thought of the life which had brought me to this pass.

I'd been a happy little girl, back in the village. I remembered a tall, laughing, black-haired man in seagarb tossing me into the air, catching me, nuzzling into my curls. "Red," he murmured, "little red-head!"

My mother, surrounded by dressmaking work, laughed. "Please!" she cried. "Her name is Mary!"

"She's a beauty, like her mother! The two of you will steal my mother's heart!"

"But you said she hates girl-children, Bruce!"

"Not Red! She won't hate Red. One look, and she'll be won over!"

"And when will that be, my darling?"

"When I get back, my love! When I present my wife!"

"It may not be so easy. She'll have every right to feel that my background . . . "

"She'll fall at your feet, drown in love! When I get back!"

Only, he never returned. No letters came for a long time, then one did arrive, which my mother seized with eagerness and read through slowly, for she'd had little schooling. Another seaman had written the letter, telling of a storm at sea, of my father's being drowned. My mother wept bitterly, and when I began to weep too, she dried her tears, tossed her red curls and dressed in her prettiest gown.

"In t-time, Mary darling," she cried, "we'll have fun! I promise, oh, I do!"

And fun we had, despite the sadness sometimes in her eyes. We lived in a room cluttered with lengths of silk and satin and velvet and cloth of gold, where chattering ladies came to be fitted and had long discussions over where to place a velvet bow or how far a neckline dared be cut. They brought me dolls and toy dishes and fruits. And there was always laughter, the smell of fine fabrics, a feminine, gala excitement.

When material was left over, my mother fashioned lovely, simple dresses for me. When I wore them I felt almost as pretty as the ladies, and the men who came to visit said I was pretty, and they brought me toys, too. My beautiful, warm, lively mother loved me, and she loved her work. After that time of weeping, she loved the men who showered her with attention. She was natural and giving, and though some called her bad, I knew that wasn't true. As I grew older, I helped her dress to go out, and we discovered that I had a talent for arranging her hair, so that became my special, loved privilege. I liked all this. I liked the men too, teasing and calling me Red, Mary the Red, and black-eyed little beauty. Gaily, as I blossomed, I danced away from any man who tried to put his hands on me.

The destruction of my contentment started during a lean period in our circumstances. I wasn't much over four, but I remember my mother coming in that afternoon, coughing so violently she could hardly walk, her clothing plastered wetly to her body. She'd been calling on ladies with samples of brocades, but hadn't found even one who was ready for a new gown.

She was very ill, dragged herself up to feed me, fell back onto her cot, sent away the men who knocked at our door. I remember that some of them offered her money, calling it a loan, but she thanked them and refused, saying she didn't need it. When she grew better, she began to sew again, her fingers shaking on the small garments she was making in my size. I always loved a new dress and was excited, but soon discovered that she was fashioning not a dress, but a pair of blue velvet breeches and matching coat.

The day she put the new clothes on me for the trip to London, she cut off the curls, that reached beyond my shoulders, and left me shorn like a boy. I hated the ringlets; I hated the velvet breeches and coat and cried and tugged to pull them off.

"No, darling," my mother said, holding my little hands so I couldn't twist at the hated garments, "no, precious. We've got to do this. We're going to see Lady Victoria, and she hates little girls, but likes little boys. When we go to see her, your name is George. George Hunter. Now don't forget, luv. When we come home, you can be a girl again, I promise."

My grandmother was old, white-haired, tall, wrinkled. She was very cool to my mother but friendly with me. "You're a handsome lad, George," she said in her stiff manner. "My own hair was red as yours, one day. You have your father's features . . . yes . . . precisely." To my mother she said coldly, "I suppose you expect me to do something for him."

"Only if you want to," my mother replied, as coldly and proudly as my grandmother. She was in straits, and had humbled herself to make this effort for me, but she wouldn't beg.

"What do you call yourself now that my son is no longer alive?" my grandmother demanded.

"Mary Read, as before."

"And the boy?"

"G-George Hunter."

"That won't do. His name must be the one you use. Call him George Read. It will save him embarrassment not to have his name different. Am I not correct?"

Ashen, my mother nodded.

"By birth he is Hunter, granted. But now that Bruce . . . and my deceased husband's firstborn has established a line of succession . . . " She gestured. "I'll give you a crown a week for George. You're to bring him once yearly so I may see his progress. Be a good lad, George. Remember that I expect perfect conduct and correct manners. You may take him now and go," she said to my mother, and the interview was over.

Oh, how I hated those visits! How I loathed the new breeches and coat each year. I found breeches unnatural and uncomfortable and protested having my hair cut. And how I hated the deception! But it had to be done, and I endured, for my mother was never well again. She could take only an occasional dress to sew, and even that drained her strength. There was seldom a man now, because her beauty paled and she became thin, her once-ready laughter gone because it sent her into awful, prolonged coughing, with blood increasingly present.

With her last breath, she begged me never to let my grandmother know I was a girl, to go to her at once, to be, in future, careful around men. Weeping, I held her in my arms and promised. After she was buried, I whacked off my hair, put on a breast-binder, dressed in boys' garb and walked all the way to London. It seemed my whole world had crashed.

My grandmother, by this time very old and lonely, took me in, announced I was a distant kinsman, and lavished money and attention on me. She grew fond of me, and I of her. I had to bite back the truth of my sex when she bemoaned the fact that I, son of Sir Stephen's second son, had no right to any Hunter assets. At any rate, she did what she could for me. She filled the town house and the country manor with tutors and tailors, the latter of whom I hid my sex from by wearing breast-binder and underdrawers during fittings.

Thus the seamstress' daughter became a blue-blooded gentleman. After a year it was hard to remember I'd ever been anything else and I enjoyed life, except for the hated male part I had to play and the deception of my grandmother.

Five years of my life, thus, were rich and full. It came to an end with my grandmother's death. I stayed on, awaiting the arrival of the heir and his wife. Lady Gwen found my presence distasteful. Sir Cecil eyed me often, but spoke no word of my future. I waited, my objective being to give them time to settle into their new life before they had to deal with mine.

I knew I had to obtain employment. I had every qualification to be a tutor if I could get a recommendation. Since I had only a man's wardrobe, it was out of the question to seek a post as governess. In any case, I'd move out of Hunter House soon. With the few pounds I'd saved from my allowance and by selling some of my fine clothing, I could rent a cheap room and try for a teaching post. I'd have to meet with success almost immediately, because my money would last only a short while. I could, of course, sell all my fine clothes, replace them with modest dresses and try to become governess or nursemaid. But here again, I'd need a recommendation, and in view of Sir Cecil's plan for me to be his secretary, this wasn't promising.

Hunter House had been my refuge. And I was going to lose it whether or not I let Sir Cecil have his way with me.

The sun stood at noon as I left the garden, carrying my book. As I came into the front hallway, Warren, the young footman, came up from the sitting room the servants shared belowstairs. A likable boy, he had a wide-lipped, smiling mouth, ruddy cheeks, and long brown eyes darker than his wig.

"I was startin' to wonder 'bout you," he said. "Cook's got our meal ready. Have a nice read?"

"I'm afraid I only sat."

"It's a holiday to have the new master an' mistress away. Less strain. They're quality . . . but *demandin'!* Will you be eatin' with us?"

"I believe not, Warren. I'm not hungry. I'll go to my room and read." What I meant to do was think, to somehow find a way out of my predicament.

"Take a rest, George. Ain't good to use the brain reckless. If you get hungry, let us know."

I smiled at him and moved on. Although I was above the servants, I did not hold myself above them. I always ate at their table in preference to a tray in my room when my grandmother wasn't well. I'd never acted superior to them, but rather had felt guilt for deceiving them. Consequently, I was liked by all. Jones, the butler, looked upon me almost as a son. Mrs. Wabash, the housekeeper, took extra care that the upstairs maids kept my chamber perfectly, and Cook sent up something special when I had a tray. Tom, the erstwhile bootboy, hung around me and Barney, the coachman, liked to discuss horses with me. Without their friendship, I should have been lonely, because my grandmother rarely came out of her rooms. I longed to chat with the maids about girl things, but that was out of the question due both to my male protégé status and the fact that all of them, even plain little Dorrie, made eyes at me.

My room was at the end of an upstairs wing, with

guestrooms between it and the stairway. Thus it was isolated, and gave me privacy.

I locked my door and sighed in relief. I loved this room in London, where we'd spent so much time. As my grandmother grew older, she wanted to be near her doctor in the city, and we stayed less and less at the country estates.

This chamber looked over the back of the rose garden. The furniture was old but well cared for, and it was comfortable. Though the sun was right over-head, one streak lay across the good but faded carpet, paling and growing narrower by the second. I took off coat, breeches, and shirt and hung them in the ward-robe. I took off my wig and put it on its stand, closed the doors, took the pins out of my hair and let it fall in waves and ringlets. I kept it shoulder length because I so longed to be myself, to be a girl. I removed the square-toed mens' slippers and knee stockings, leaving only the despised underdrawers and the wide breast-binder. These I got out of fast, first the binder, and stood gratefully sucking in deep breaths of rose-scented air; every moment I had to wear the thing I could only half-breathe. Then I got out of the underdrawers and put on the nightrobe worn by men, thinking of silken nightgowns with longing.

I brushed my hair, watching it spring and curl back upon itself, the redness dazzling. I looked nothing like the reserved, proper George Read with his neat wig and costly garb. Sir Cecil wanted George Read. Would he want me if he saw me now, I wondered—a girl, not a lad—and then I bit my lip with concern. I left the dresser and moved to the bed and lay, staring at the ceiling, full of worry.

The late sun was gone. Shade deepened within my room. I thought about Sir Cecil, the man. I loathed him. Yet, despite what he'd done to Tom, he was un-deniably attractive. I remembered how his hands had felt on my shoulders. I remembered his impressive height, and deep-buried feelings stirred in me.

Pondering what he'd said about my parents' hot

blood, I wondered if I truly did have it double-strength in my own veins. I was a virgin, had never considered the possibility of sleeping with any man. I was clean and pure, yet even though I despised Sir Cecil, I could understand why women were attracted to him. If he forced me, if he took me by main strength, would I be as frantic as I thought? Of course I would! Pure girls simply couldn't be *had* by devils like Sir Cecil Hunter, who lusted after lads!

Hours had passed. No matter how I delved, thinking through everything, I could find no solution to my dilemma.

The evening breeze moved the curtains at my windows, held them out like gauzy wings, let them fall. Because I dared not be out of men's garb longer, I took off the nightrobe and stood while the curtain lifted once more. The breeze felt comforting to my naked body. When the curtains fell again, I dressed in the hated garments, put on my wig, took one last look into the lamplit mirror to see that all was proper.

I was about to start for the stairs when I heard someone moving along the hallway. Instant panic took me. I knew that long, quick stride, the way those red heels rang on the wooden floor. I sprang back into my room. My pulse was thundering. He'd returned sooner than the fortnight!

Outside, the long twilight lingered. The room was filled with a mixture of it and the glow of the lamp. He stopped at my door, tapped.

I backed away, shoulders straight. "C-come in," I called.

The door opened. He stepped inside, locked it. My breath hooked in my throat.

"George . . . lad."

"I . . . you . . ."

"You knew I'd be back," he said, and smiled. His lips became threads. He was arrogant, needle-handsome, compelling.

"Lady Gwen disliked the country intensely. It gave

her violent headaches. I brought her back early, at her own request. Didn't you hear the carriage?"

I shook my head. I must have dozed, sleeping through any sound of their arrival. Dare I take hope because Lady Gwen was in the house? Would that stop him from doing the foul, unspeakable things he'd done to Tom? Then I recalled that Lady Gwen had been here when poor Tom was defiled, and a shudder ran down my spine.

"No?" he said. "Then you've been sleeping. You're rested and fresh. Splendid. I've been here over an hour, most of which time I spent settling my wife in bed and giving her a tonic which eases pain. She'll sleep for several hours—for which time I've planned exquisite sport for the two of us. It's marvelously remote, this chamber. Any sounds we make can't be heard."

He was keen and excited. He'd never looked so fine and handsome. He wore scarlet nankeen breeches snug at the knee, a blazing gold velvet pleated coat, a yellow vest, a linen cambric shirt gathered at the neck, and a scarlet cravat. He removed his wig and tossed it onto the dresser. His hair was rumpled, glossy. With his etched features and that smile, he was breathtaking.

I began to tremble. He saw this immediately.

"Surely you're not afraid of me, Georgie?"

"Please. Leave me alone."

"You won't say that ten minutes from now."

"I've never been . . . never done . . . "

"Not even with a servant lass?"

"I . . . I'm not like what you think. I've never . . . with a man . . . "

"And not with a girl?"

"No . . . never!"

"Don't expect me to believe that."

"But it's the truth!"

He gave a laugh. "I'm an experienced man. I've known all along what you are. The proper manner, the education, the clothes, even the trace of blueblood, never deceived me. Now. Remove your clothes, Georgie."

My heart leaped. He moved toward me, eyes holding mine. He stopped, almost touching me. I tried to plead, but my tongue was thick and wouldn't move. He looked me over, missing nothing: the snug fit of my coat, the tidy fit of my breeches at the knee, the shape of my stockinged legs.

He put out a hand and jerked off my wig so sharply the pins came loose and my hair tumbled, curling wildly, to my shoulders. His breath sucked in.

"That hair! It's a sin to hide it!" His voice thinned, almost to breaking. "I've known my share of lads . . . lassies, too . . . and women. But never one so comely. It's ridiculous for you to wear a wig." Then he shook his head. "No. The hair is for me, only for me. You'll continue with the wig, Georgie."

He kept calling me Georgie. I hated it, yet it was a girl's name, and I was . . . Oh, God, he didn't know yet that I actually was a girl! What would he do when he found out?

"Take your coat off, Georgie."

"No. I won't."

"Then I'll do it for you. My pleasure."

"Don't touch me!"

"You won't say that an hour from now. If you really are the virgin lad you say, you've untold delights ahead."

I went mad with fear. I was all fear. I made a try for the door, but he caught me and yanked me to him. I fought. He laughed and, despite my struggles, pulled off my coat, my shirt. He almost paused when he spied the breast-binder, but then he ripped that away and my breasts sprang free, and he gave one sharp laugh, like a bark. On and on he laughed, all the while keeping my twisting and kicking under control. He wrestled me around so my breasts were crushed to him. He rooted his lips through my hair, along my cheek, to the side of my neck. My flesh seemed to be on fire.

"What a surprise!" he murmured. "I think you're a

luscious lad, and you're actually . . . " He held me out, in a vise, while I struggled.

"We have hours ahead of us, Georgie; I've a double-prize in you. The juicy lad I anticipated proves to be also a nubile girl. Both claiming to be virgin! I'm going to teach you exotic things! When you experience them, you're going to be the happiest little playtoy in the British Empire! First . . . ah, first, I choose to have you be your natural self. First I shall teach you to be woman!"

He put those thin lips on mine and kissed me so long that my burning flesh turned into helpless, molten lava spreading through my body. He put one long-fingered hand around my breast, and again I was helpless under sensations I couldn't resist. I had to make him quit. I had to do it before I, too, turned depraved!

Sure of himself, he dropped his arms. His lips were half-smiling. This, for some insane reason, caused that new, unconquerable sensation to grow in me.

"Take off your breeches, Georgie."

"No!"

"Very well. Still my pleasure."

Hooking his fingers into the waist of my breeches and underdrawers, he tore them down slowly. His face showed him to be beside himself with barely controlled anticipation. Nothing existed for him but his discoveries about me.

He threw aside my garments, yanked off my stockings and slippers, and held me clamped in one arm. I was too weak, for the moment, to resist.

I was nude.

He stroked my breasts. I froze, both at what he was doing and the effect on me. As soon as I could move I'd run, naked or not. Then my breasts did something I'd not known they could do. They grew hard in his hands and the nipples stood up. Weakness swept me as he leaned to kiss one nipple, then the other.

Somehow, I leapt suddenly back and kicked with all my remaining strength. But my bare foot made little impact on him and yet it sent a pain shooting from my toe to my knee. He cursed, grabbed my waist. We crashed to the floor. I screamed, but he clapped his hand over my mouth, and his laugh filled my ears.

"So this is where you want it?" he purred.

He held me to the floor. The carpet dug into my flesh. I tried to get up, but he slammed me back. I tried to knee him, and he slapped me. My ears exploded; I could see a dazzle of light in my head. I lay sobbing.

"Such delight, little wench-lad . . . such variety!"

"No!" I screamed. "No!"

"Go ahead, Georgie. Scream. I love it."

Then he was covering me, smashing me, pinning me down. I writhed, and it delighted him. He crushed my screams with his mouth, kissing me so fiercely that every part of me quickened. He got to his knees, straddling me, and he was smiling. Sobbing, I tried to buck him off, but it was useless. He opened his breeches, and then he held me pinioned beneath him.

"No!" I breathed in agony.

He purred. He hung over me like the Devil from Hell. I whispered pleas. I tried to get my hands free; he held them so that pain went to my shoulders. Panic swept me, and my whole body trembled. And yet it burned, too. Burned with a wicked fire which he had lit.

"Now. Wench-lad. Little slut! This comes first!"

He gave a stabbing movement and I screamed as he entered me. Tears coursed my face as he thrust fast, with deliberate intent. I was screaming inside now, silently, and still I struggled, and then it seemed that my whole self flew into hot fragments. I held to him as those blazing shreds whirled. On and on they spun, and the world itself hung motionless in the sky and sang a new, shattering music.

Chapter 3

Still by his order, I sat and stared at Sir Cecil, spread-eagled naked on the bed. It was deep night. Outside was ink-dark; inside there was lamp glow. Twice he'd tied, gagged and locked me into the room and gone to tend his ailing wife; twice he'd returned. This torture would never end. I loathed him. I'd never detested anyone before, and felt that I never should again.

He had used me violently, time after time. He had compelled me to return passion for passion and I hated him for that most of all. He'd forced me to slowly put on my underdrawers, breast-binder, shirt, breeches, and coat, watching every move with lust. He even ordered me to pull on my stockings, step into my slippers, put up my hair and set my wig in place. When I finished, he didn't touch me, but gazed avidly, those etched, wicked features glittering with delight. Then he ordered me to undress, taking off the wig last. He assaulted me still another time, and when it was finished—while I was recovering from the explosion he'd roused in me this time, he spoke.

"This is a pleasant change for me, Georgie."

"My name is Mary!"

"I prefer Georgie. Yes, a delightful change, after my wife's refusal—after a diet of inferior lads. Later, lovely toy, I'll initiate you into another game, one you'll go wild over."

I didn't answer. I thought about Tom and the other unfortunate lads this devil had tormented. I knew exactly how he had used them; he'd described it to me, in detail. The very idea made me sick to my soul.

Still, my inner self had hardened in these hours; I'd discovered a deep, strong resolution in myself which I'd never suspected. I vowed now that I would never again be defenseless. Every ideal had been destroyed by this man. I hadn't a friend in the world. I was on my own. I had to do everything for myself or perish.

"I believe," he said, "I'll save the new pleasure."

I glared at him.

"How does that strike you, Georgie?"

"I think you know!"

He laughed. "Anticipation, Georgie. Ah . . . anticipation!"

"Anticipate, then. Your wife won't always have a headache."

"Stolen hours, playtoy. Sweeter for being stolen. You'll be my secretary, remember, and when I feel so inclined . . . well. Gwen will undoubtedly sense it . . . she always does . . . but I know how to deal with her."

"You actually think I'll stay on! After . . . While . . . "

"What else?"

"I shan't do it."

"That's a bold statement from a nude girl."

"I'll not endure such conditions."

"I'll force you."

Fear pierced me again, but I steeled myself. My determination grew.

He got up and stretched like a cat, slim, strikingly male, but his nakedness, dazzling as it was, left me unmoved. The breeze stirred, struck through me, and I shivered. I was chilled to the bone, felt I'd never be warm again.

He came and stood in front of me. "You're the loveliest creature I have ever seen. The most passionate. You were striking as a young gentleman, but now there's something more . . . the glow of an awakened virgin. I knew you were a hot creature, Georgie. Now I've proved it. Even to you."

"That's what you think!"

"Don't say you didn't love it. You were born to romp."

"You really do intend to keep right on?"

"Indeed I do."

"I've told you. I won't stay on. I want . . . "

His brows speared up. "You're in a position to dictate what you want, Georgie?"

"Yes," I said evenly, "I am."

"You're quick to rebel! Where is the proper Mr. Read with the smooth manners?"

"He has gone, along with my innocence!"

My voice was cold. I stared at him, showing how much I hated him. But he seemed amused.

"You're behaving foolishly, my love," he warned. "With no money, no post . . . "

"I'm forced to do what you want?"

"Correct, luscious one, and you'd better remember it. This is becoming tiresome. You'll do what I want, when and in any manner the whim strikes me."

"I'll not be your plaything!"

"Of course not. You'll be my secretary. A position of value."

"That's just a ruse!"

"I assure you, there'll be legitimate secretarial duties."

"I'll not be your mistress!"

"What insane thing do you want to be, then?"

I knew exactly what I wanted. And I blurted it out. "I want you to tell your wife that I'm leaving to take a post as tutor. I want you to write me a letter of recommendation . . . not for George Read, tutor, but for Mary Read, governess. My grandmother died before she could write the letter she meant to write. Do that, and you'll never have any trouble from me."

"And if I refuse?"

"But you can't!"

"Only I do. Absolutely. What action can you take?"

Suddenly I knew. Oh, I knew, but I wasn't going to forewarn him!

"You're boring me, Georgie." He dressed. "I'm

going to Gwen now. I'll meet you here at noon." His tone was smooth, yet there was raw threat as he went on. "In the meantime, think carefully. When I return, I'll expect a sensible decision from you."

He unlocked the door and left. I could still hear the echo of that raw threat and it frightened me. But I was going to stand my ground.

Even though I was exhausted from the indignities to which he'd subjected me, I lay awake the remainder of the night. I couldn't sleep. When Dorrie rapped with my breakfast tray, I told her to leave it outside, but I never touched it.

Outside, the coachmen and grooms were talking, voices low. Birds sang in the garden; the breeze wafted my window curtains, bringing the scent of roses. It was a beautiful morning, a time for lovers to go hand in hand. But it might have been thundering and lightning and streaming rain as far as I was concerned, for I knew the Devil would return at noon. I knew he could do worse to me than he'd already done, that he could use me as he'd used Tom. No, he won't, I determined. I'll dig his eyes out first!

I arose, brushed my hair, watching the curls spring and burn their brilliant red. I studied the woman in the mirror. There was a new firmness in the chin, in the no longer innocent mouth. The black, lustrous eyes were underlaid with watchfulness. The shaken, defenseless nineteen-year-old girl obliged to masquerade as a man had disappeared, and the woman who gazed back from the mirror was more attractive. There was an allure, a sensuousness which now limned the patrician features. Mary Read had cast out George Read and gained strength.

I went to the wardrobe to select an outfit. Soon I'd be wearing dresses. I pushed aside the dark colors and reached for the bright green velvet breeches, the gold velvet coat, the cambric shirt with full sleeves gathered into wrist cuffs. I put on the breast-binder, my red-heeled shoes, and an emerald cravat. I pinned up my hair and set the wig over it. Even then, in the bright colors, the high flush in my cheeks, mouth red and defiant, I subdued my flamboyant handsomeness but a trifle.

Suddenly I tore off the wig, brushed my hair again, drew it back, in waves and ringlets, to the nape, tied it with narrow black ribbon. The effacing kinsman was gone forever. No longer would I hide my looks with drab colors. After today I would no longer hide my allure in mens' garb. Beauty was my new tool, to be used along with my education. Plus the lessons I'd been taught by Sir Cecil.

I knew exactly how I was going to proceed, and felt no shame. During my grandmother's lifetime, such an idea would have horrified me, but I'd grown up in a few awful hours. I fully appreciated now who I was: the legitimate daughter of a seamstress and a blueblood of the realm. I belonged neither to her world—due to my education—nor to his, because I could not inherit. Sir Cecil's treatment had made it imperative that I leave, and my education made it impossible for me to return to my mother's way of life. Now I had to use my wits.

I loathed Sir Cecil, but he had, in his evil way, taught me that in order to survive, I must never again be at the mercy of others. I'd fight, do anything, to get along. But I'd pay for value received. Nothing would cause me to deviate from this.

He arrived at noon, looking tall and elegant in blue breeches, red coat and vest of silver cloth. He wore a silver cravat. He noticed my lack of wig instantly. His lips threaded, then twisted into his peculiar smile.

"First rate, Georgie. The outfit, the hair. I'll say I've ordered you to leave off the wig and dress brightly as my secretary."

"If I had a dress, I'd be wearing that!" I cried.

His pale eyes traveled along my form. "There's not a woman in the Empire who can rival your beauty. And you're all mine."

"I'm not! Not at all!"

His brows speared. "I warned you, Georgie. I assumed you'd see things my way."

"You're wrong."

"Then I shall have to resort to extreme measures, little wench-lad. I have no choice but to expose you as an imposter . . . a lad, of course . . . posing as Lady Victoria's grandson. Unless . . . "

"Unless?" I whispered, angry, but dry-throated.

"You become my 'male' secretary."

"And if I refuse?"

"There are legal punishments for imposters."

I stared.

"You still refuse, little wench-lad?"

"I certainly do!"

"I ask you to reconsider, my love."

"I've done my considering. And I'm not your love."

"Girls and women don't leave me. Or lads."

"This one will."

"I could drag you to the bed, but that would be only a fleeting victory. No. Not even to demonstrate my artistry with a lad. I'll use, instead, my knowledge of love-making."

"I'm going to your wife, Sir Cecil."

"For what purpose, pray?"

"To tell her everything. My posing as a lad, the letter you won't write, what you did to me. Your threats."

His smile twisted. "Shall I take you to her, love? She's fully recovered."

"Yes . . . and you can stay in the room!"

I didn't trust him, but this was the only way open to me. I'd have to be alert, counter his every attempt to make me appear the fool, to keep him from discrediting me.

The musical notes of the lunch gong rose in the house.

Again his smile twisted. "What a pity! Lady Gwen needs lunch after her illness. Then she must rest a bit. I'll arrange an audience for you with her at . . . three o'clock, shall we say? Come to the library at that hour."

He strolled out. When I knew he was safely downstairs, I got my bags off the top of the wardrobe, put them on the bed and began to pack. I did it carefully, folding each garment neatly. I was very calm, not at all frightened, though I dreaded what I must tell Lady Gwen. However, there was no question of breaking her heart; I'd heard her speak in a manner which revealed that she knew of his wickedness. Actually, my interview with her was a sort of favor; she'd be ridding her home of her husband's latest playtoy.

Dorrie brought another tray, and I took it in, giving her no chance to spy my packing. I ate hungrily, set the tray in the hall, resumed working. Then I strapped the bags and put them near the door, my bit of money safely in one of them. I was going to leave the moment Lady Gwen demanded that Sir Cecil write me the letter of recommendation, which I felt confident she would do.

I entered the library on the stroke of the clock. No one else was there, and I looked once again at the solid, rich luxury of the room in which I'd spent so many hours. Two walls were solid books. Brown armchairs flanked the outer wall, in the midst of which were set double glass doors. The remaining wall held a white marble fireplace and more books, with other armchairs set about. There was a flat-top desk in the center of the burgandy carpet and there were brass lamps. Over the mantel hung a painting of Lady Gwen.

Now, wearing her favorite shade of green, black hair dressed high, she came into the room, followed by Sir Cecil. She was sheet-white, and her lightly rouged lips had a tendency to quiver until she pressed them together. I felt sorry for her, but could not swerve from my purpose.

Sir Cecil was utterly without expression.

She spoke. "I'll not ask you to be seated . . . " She broke off, her light blue eyes sad.

"Under the circumstances, my sweet," Sir Cecil said easily, "you're right not to do so."

My pulse quickened; the hairs on the back of my neck stirred. Had he told her some lie, some malicious fabrication, putting me in the wrong, painting me as evil?

"Lady Gwen," I blurted, "I have things to relate, all true. First, I'm not a man, but a girl. My name is Mary Read."

She inclined her head, glanced at my flaming hair. It seemed that she already knew; I watched the pulse in her throat, the lift of her chin.

"My wife knows all, George . . . Mary . . . whatever you call yourself," Sir Cecil said in his thinnest, coldest tone. "Did you really think, wench, that I'd subject her to such a shocking revelation from your lips? Did you think I'd permit her fine sensibilities to be tortured? As you planned?"

"It wasn't meant as torture! It was . . . "

"To use both of us. To shock my wife with the fact that you're a wench in men's clothing, that I unmasked you and, being a man easily led, had my sport with you. She knows your terms, your evil intentions, and . . . Tell her, sweetheart. Tell her what our decision is."

"We'll not give you a recommendation," Lady Gwen whispered. "My husband . . . men are . . . they have . . . pressures . . . which a wife must understand. And forgive." She turned to him. "Cecil, darling, finish it, and let's be done."

"I've called in the authorities," he told me. "I'm entering charges against you. The men are in the morning room. Move. We're going to them."

Chapter 4

Mind awhirl with what this devil was up to now, I moved out of the library. Sir Cecil and Lady Gwen followed me, her skirts making a silken, rustling sound. I knew this couldn't be happening, not to me. Nothing could happen, for I had right and truth on my side. If Sir Cecil and Lady Gwen wanted the authorities to find out what had been going on in this house, that was their problem.

Two plainly dressed men were seated in the morning room. They sprang up as we entered.

"Permit me to introduce these men, darling," Sir Cecil said to his wife. "They help to enforce our laws." He indicated the square-shouldered, half-bald one. "This is Mr. Ryan . . . and this is Mr. Clarke. They've come in response to my note. This, gentlemen," he continued, indicating me, "is the individual in question."

Clarke bored at me with hard, colorless eyes, looking as though he'd like nothing better than to hit me. Ryan stared at my hair, as if I'd broken some law because it was red.

"What have I to do with these men?" I asked, forcing calm and becoming instantly alert.

"Shut up, you!" Clarke snarled.

Sir Cecil looked pleased. This devil was up to mischief, and I had only my wits for protection. My wits and the truth.

Sir Cecil glanced at his wife. She nodded.

"I'll repeat what I told you earlier, gentlemen, so my lady can hear. Thus you'll appreciate how serious my charges are. Two months ago I came into my heritage at the death of my step great-grandmother, Lady Victoria Hunter. I found this . . . individual . . . in residence, purporting to be the legitimate grandson of Lady Victoria."

Ryan and Clarke were listening intently. Sir Cecil put his arm around Lady Gwen. She looked at me. There was victory in the look. I knew then. My heart seemed to roll. Sir Cecil watched me with those penetrating eyes, a thread of smile twisted, then was gone. He'd personally arranged the "interview" for me with his wife. This trick was the result of lies he'd told her.

"Yesterday," he went on, "when I arrived home with my wife from our estates, I discovered that the 'grandson' is actually a female disguised as . . . you see for yourselves, gentlemen. Mary Read, she confessed to be and then, even though I'd uncovered her deception, she brazenly let me know that her intent was to seduce my innocent wife! Certain depraved females, as you know, inflict themselves sexually on pure females, which is what this person was intent on doing to my wife! When I informed her that I knew all, she tried to blackmail me. She said she'd accuse me of defiling her, demanded that I give her a large sum of money, or she'd tell my wife that I had . . . seduced her."

"That's a lie!" I cried. "Only a part of it happened, and then you forced me!"

Clarke stepped over and slapped me across the mouth so hard that I fell back against the wall. I blinked away angry tears, hardened my chin, and glared around the room, numb from the blow. I didn't even understand the full meaning of Sir Cecil's lying charges.

"The charge is blackmail, sir?" asked Ryan.

"That, and intent to seduce my wife."

"What've you got to say, wench?" Ryan demanded.

Summoning all the dignity I could, I met his eyes full on. "I deny everything. The true story is a very long one."

"I'll wager it is!"

"And not what you've been told! My own mother dressed me as a boy because . . . "

"Sure she did!" Clarke scoffed.

"We'd best take 'er in, sir," Ryan said.

"Thank you, gentlemen." Sir Cecil's smile was very thin. He worked some coins out of his vest and gave some to each man. They were overwhelmed. "I suppose you'll take her to Newgate."

"That we will," Ryan agreed.

"Be very firm with her."

Ryan got his meaning instantly. He grinned and nodded. "We'll be no rougher'n she makes it 'erself, sir." He stepped up to me and gripped my right arm so brutally it hurt. Clarke took my other arm in the same manner. When I tried to pull free they clamped mercilessly and I had to desist.

"I knew I could trust you," Sir Cecil said. "She's high-flown, remember. You can instruct her on proper Newgate conduct."

"We'll do that, sir," Ryan declared.

Sir Cecil made a small bow to his wife, then preceded us to the front door. The men hustled me along, hurting my arms, and almost before I knew it, we were outside. Sir Cecil remained standing in the doorway.

My bewilderment had gone now, my throat was dry, my tongue brassy. I was terribly afraid, in panic, but I wouldn't show it and give that devil satisfaction. I glanced back and he was expressionless. The sunshine was warm, but gave no comfort. The men jerked me viciously and I almost fell, but they dragged me along.

"We got us a rare 'un today," Clarke muttered.

"Sure did," Ryan growled. "Le's take 'er somwhere an' make 'er strip. See the evidence." He looked at me, face lustful. "We'll do it 'fore we reach Newgate. Recall that alley we passed . . . deserted like?"

They kept dragging me toward a big, enclosed carriage, though I did my best to walk properly, wits sharp, ready to jerk free and take to my heels. We reached the carriage. A pair of gray horses stamped impatiently; the driver was on the high seat.

Clark opened the door and Ryan threw me inside so hard I came up against the far door, striking the side of my face. Even as I shot my hand out to open the door, Ryan was inside, clamping his big, hard arm around my waist, crushing me to him. When I tried to wriggle free, he squeezed me so violently that there was a moment when I couldn't get my breath.

"You act nice," he snarled. "Me'n Clarke, we don't enjoy bein' treated mean."

Then Clarke got in. He slammed the door shut, and the prison carriage began to move. There were two facing seats, faded curtains hid the windows, and every inch stank in the dark interior.

Gradually, my eyes adjusted, and I could see Ryan's lewd face. He stared at me, his eyes full of lust. " 'Ere we be!" he chortled. "On our way!"

"Prisoner thinks she's too good fer such as us," Clarke drawled.

Ryan made a great show of surprise. " 'N 'er a imposter an' woman seducer, an' a woman 'erself! Them's 'angin' deeds, accordin' to me!"

"She'll 'ang," Clarke agreed with relish.

"Seems a pity she won't get none of whut she dressed like a man fer."

"We're good at whut she needs."

"You ever done it in a alley?"

"Don't 'member as I 'ave."

"I'll go first then, an' you watch how."

I made another lunge for the door, but Ryan only grabbed me again, cruelly. I fought, trying to pull away. He held me so I couldn't move, and Clarke slapped me on the face, over and over, sometimes across my mouth and head, until I felt I was on fire.

The carriage bounced over the cobblestones, throwing us around. Clarke stopped hitting me after I tasted blood, and then Ryan put his foul, open mouth over mine. He kept it there, saturated with tobacco, straining me to him. I thought he was going to break my spine; my lungs were bursting. He finally took his mouth away, grinned at my open revulsion.

The carriage stopped. Clarke opened a door. "This's it, eh? An' I've got 'er slapped silly. She'll be no trouble. Coast's clear."

"We'll take 'er down them steps into that 'idey-'ole," Ryan said.

It took both of them to drag me out of the carriage. I twisted, yanked, kicked, tried to bite. I screamed to the driver for help but he looked the other way, and I knew these beasts would give him a coin as a reward. Once on the ground, I fought desperately to slip their hold, but Ryan got me under one armpit, Clarke under the other, and they dragged me, face up, heels trailing, for a distance, then down slimy rock steps and into a dank, dark cellar-like hole.

They dropped me on my back. Instantly I rose up, but Ryan knocked me flat, fell onto me and ripped and tore at my breeches. I clawed his face, tried to scream, but he chopped the edge of his hand on my throat and I lay choking, unable to draw breath. He bared me ruthlessly, began his attack, grunting and talking and rutting.

"She's a woman . . . no lad 'ere . . . all juicy wench!"

During this horror, Clarke chortled and cursed, and to this salacious background, I felt the horrid rise of passion in my body, deep and degrading, much worse than with Sir Cecil. Oh God, the wonder flashed through me, what girl am I? To feel at a time like this any drop of response!

And then it was Clarke's turn, and it was Ryan who cheered him on, and again there rose in me the hurting, heavy, evil passion to answer his. In these moments I would not have cared if I had died. During the hours that Sir Cecil had used me endlessly, I'd believed I knew what it was to be defiled. But now I really knew.

Chapter 5

They each had another go at me.

And each time I suffered the degrading, filthy response, the self-hatred. By this time I was naked, some garment was bunched under me, others gone in the blackness. I still, however, had on my stockings and red-heeled shoes. I lay on my back, exhausted, bathed in sweat, quivering in terror and revulsion. I had to get away. I couldn't survive any more of this; I dared not be thrown into Newgate. I forced myself to breathe deeply and regularly, trying for strength.

The panting of the men filled the hole.

"She's a rare 'un!" Ryan gasped. "We got time for 'nother bit?"

"Could take time," Clarke rasped, "but she's got me drained. You get extry, but be quick 'bout it."

Dimly I made out the figure turning toward me, saw it make ready to kneel between my shaking limbs. Instinctively, I kicked him in his male part, my shoe striking hard into it.

He fell aside, doubled over, howling.

As Clarke rushed to him, I scrambled to my feet, snatching up the garment I'd been lying on as I did so.

"What's wrong?" Clarke yelled.

"The . . . damned . . . wench . . . kicked . . . !"

That was all I heard, for I was streaking up the steps to the alley. The driver spotted me, and as he came down off his perch and Clarke pounded up the steps, I went fleeing for the street, clutching the garment around me.

I turned the corner, sped along the walkway. Thank

God there was no passing carriage; pray God there'd be no person out for a stroll, no one to see me from the window of one of the mansions! My breath sliced into my lungs. I heard no pursuit, but this didn't deceive me; they'd come, in their prison carriage. Unless I found a hiding place instantly, they'd overtake me.

Here was an ivy-covered wall surrounding the gardens of a great house. I sped on, close to the wall, ivy brushing my naked shoulders. Now I heard wheels on cobblestone. I managed to run even faster. Ahead was an iron gate set in the wall.

With one last surge, I flung myself against the gate. It fell open and I fell with it, then scuttled, on hands and knees, clutching that one garment, to the growth of hedge lining the inside of the wall. I plunged into the space between and cowered, trembling and waiting, expecting with every stabbing, quivering breath, to be discovered.

The carriage rumbled past. Then another and another. Hands shaking, I fumbled at the wadded clothing on which I'd lain while those beasts ravished me. Thank God! I'd had the wonderful fortune to escape with my shirt, which was made long and covered me halfway to the knees!

Huddled there, first making certain no one in the nearby house might glimpse me, I got into the shirt properly and buttoned it with shaking fingers. It was torn, but it served.

My breath still shuddered in and out and it still hurt. I couldn't stay here. Suddenly my wits clicked and I knew what my next move had to be.

Ryan and Clarke would comb this neighborhood; they'd drive up one street, down another. They dared not lose a prisoner; they'd be dismissed. Gradually, they'd widen their search—had already, pray God!

Keeping between hedge and wall, the soft cambric of my shirt stroking my legs, I stole to the gate and peered up and down the street. Two carriages passed, both private and drawn by high-stepping pairs, a gentleman in one, two fancy ladies in the other. All walk-ways were deserted.

I made my move. With the way momentarily clear, I had to run as I'd never run. My very life depended on it. I made it to the alley, and ran to the end, back into the hidey-hole. This was my only hope, this slimy, foul darkness. I willed them to be so stupid they'd not realize I'd have to come back for my clothes.

Unless they'd taken my things with them!

I dropped to hands and knees and began to search. Creeping and listening, always listening, I felt along the damp stone floor. After an eternity, my fingers touched cloth; it was my breast-binder. I continued to grope, again touched cloth, velvet this time. I learned by feel that it was my coat. On I crept, listening al-ways for the faintest sound of prison carriage, for softly walking feet, and I discovered the breeches, even the underdrawers and the cravat.

Hastily, I dressed. I took off the shirt, put on the breast-binder, got into the shirt again. Not daring the time for underdrawers, I thrust one foot and then the other into the breeches, fastened them. I combed my fingers through my hair, tied it back with my cravat, folded narrow. Last I put on my coat.

I was ready. Impulse told me to leave this instant, to put miles between myself and this alley. Instinct held me there, whispered that my bright green breeches and gold coat would identify me to Ryan and Clarke even if they were streets away. All they needed was a flash of my colors and I would again be running for my life.

Thus I crouched in the darkest corner of the hidey-hole, listening, always listening. I waited for darkness. And during those hours I decided what I must do. It was daring, but I had to dare. I had no letter of rec-ommendation, my bit of money was in my luggage at Hunter House. I possessed only the clothes I wore. I had to get out of London; I had to get out of England or I would be hanged.

Blessed darkness covered the city. The prison carriage hadn't returned. As far as I knew, Ryan and Clarke were still searching for a naked girl; probably every officer in London was searching for her. I ventured up the steps, into the alley. Waited, listened. Nothing. On tiptoe, keeping to one side of the alley, I ran to the street. No pedestrians were abroad, no carriage approached from either direction.

Tremulous, I stepped onto the walkway and moved along as though I had every right to be there. Should someone emerge from a house or should some carriage other than the one from Newgate pass, I'd appear to be a young man on his way to a respectable destination.

I did pass others, and carriages did go by smoothly as I made my way across London toward the waterfront. As I left the better part of the city I walked faster, resisting the impulse, as I had from the first moment, to run. Now the houses weren't so fine and there was an occasional cart in the traffic, an occasional wagon, and I caught the odor of whiskey as I passed some rough-dressed men walking with exaggerated care, as though to prove they had no need to reel or stagger.

I hurried past shops boarded up for the night, shabby places dimly visible from street lamps. Now I was much closer to the waterfront; there were more people, and I walked sedately. There were drinking dens, filled with dim, smoky light, all noisy and crowded with rough men and women.

Suddenly I came face to face with two painted street women in soiled, gaudy dress. When I would have passed, they barred my way.

"Hey, Sadie!" squawked the haggard blonde. "Wot we got 'ere?"

"We got us a pretty lad, loose from 'is mansion!" chortled the raddled, dark-haired one.

"Wot'll we do with 'im, Sadie?"

"Please," I said, keeping my voice at low pitch in accordance with my male appearance. "Ladies . . . "

"Ladies, 'e says!" screamed Sadie. " 'Ear that,

Marge? I say we take 'im to Horatio's an' set up the drinks. An' after that . . . "

" . . . git a room upstairs, the three of us! 'ow's that sound, pretty lad?"

Each put a hand on my arm, clinging. I pulled away as courteously as possible "Sorry," I apologized, "But I . . . I'm meeting somebody."

They screeched and made lewd jokes about the manner in which they assumed I was going to spend my time, but made no effort to delay me. I continued on my way, holding my pace, weaving in and out of the night people. There were sports, rigged in cheap imitation of current style; there were women garishly dressed. There were seamen ashore for the evening, entering the drinking places in groups, pairs, singly. Many of these escorted a cheap-looking girl or woman.

Next I passed dark warehouses, rows of barrels, kegs, packing cases and bales. Now, for the first time in my life, I was at the very waterfront. I stared. It was a clutter of vessels of every kind, masts reaching into the night sky. Ships rode at anchor as far as I could see, and I felt my eyes widen. Except for pictures and a bit of reading, I didn't know a sloop from a schooner. I knew nothing whatsoever about a ship, but I had to find out.

Mustering my courage, I went up the gangplank of the next vessel. I asked a seaman, about to go ashore, where I'd find the Captain. The fellow glared at me by the light of a ship's lantern.

"Can't you see?" he growled. " 'E's yonder, an' in a nasty temper." He charged on and I walked, with a fiercely assumed air of confidence, across-deck to the captain.

He was in sea uniform, standing under a lantern, glaring ashore. Despite my desperate situation, I couldn't speak right out as I'd meant to do, because inside I began to quake at my own temerity. I could only stare up at the big, dark Captain with the iron jaw and wait for him to become aware of me.

At last he did. "Who're you?" he snapped. "What do you want?"

"To go to sea, sir," I managed, making my voice low.

He looked me up and down. His nose jutted and he had angry eyebrows.

"Where was your last berth?"

"I . . . nowhere, Captain. I'm going to sea for the first time. I like this vessel, sir. I'll do my work. I'll learn. I'll be an able seaman."

And I would be. I'd have to. I was forced to be a seaman. And remain one until I could, with the money I'd save, establish myself in another country as a woman.

"You've been in a fight," the Captain said. "Your face is bruised and cut. It's swollen."

"Yes, sir. I . . . had a fight. But if I can fight," I plunged on, "I can learn to be a seaman."

"How many fellows dressed in velvet do you think I hire onto my schooner?"

The question was a blow, a numbing, verbal slap in the face. Why hadn't I thought of that? It was indeed odd that a lad in velvet would apply for a berth on a seagoing vessel.

"Well?" he snapped.

"I've got everything I own on my back, sir," I said recklessly.

"You mean you're a runaway."

I was a runaway indeed, but not in the manner which he assumed.

"I'm alone in the world, sir," I said. "I've got my way to make. I'll get seamen's clothes, trade these, and I'll work longer and harder than any man aboard."

He scowled, shook his head. "When I sign on a crewman he's got to be a man, not a fop who's been in a brawl. Or a chap from a high-born family. Off with you before I call an officer and let him find out which!"

"Thank you, sir," I managed. Then I hastened

across deck, down the gangplank, and into the darkness.

Quelling the instinct to run, I walked away, past other vessels, at a measured pace. I followed the line of seagoing ships and smaller craft moving at anchor. I listened to their creaking sounds, to the quiet lap of water.

Why hadn't I thought, earlier, of trading my fine clothes to a seaman? Now I eyed each one I passed, but they were broader in the shoulder than I and had longer legs; they'd never be able to wear my clothes. It would take a lad, and I met no lads.

After thought, I gave up the idea of trading clothes with a seaman. If I approached the wrong one, he'd be as apt to call the law as make a deal. He might think I was in trouble, needed disguise, and, if he wore my outfit, would himself land in jail.

Thus I couldn't change my appearance. Nor could I go to another captain. He might call officers on the spot. Even if he didn't and I tried various captains, I'd lay down a trail for my own capture. I'd find myself dragged to Newgate in spite of all I'd undergone to escape.

On I walked, vessels on one hand, rat infested rows of cargo on the other. There was only one way open, one way to escape London.

With this in mind, I walked slower, looking over each ship. There was little activity aboard, but on most I located a sentinel moving about.

The moment I spied the big, sturdy vessel with the solid-looking masts and the gun-ports, I liked her. My eyes flew over her, gulping her strength, which made her a thing of beauty. Her name convinced me she was a merchant ship.

"The Hague." I whispered, coming almost to a standstill.

Some of her crew were coming off, laughing. I stepped into black shadow, stood against a packing case.

My heart was going, going.

"Matey!" shouted one. "We get women tonight! Sailin' at dawn!"

"To the West Indies," shouted another. "Women there!"

"An' they like a Dutch ship, too!" laughed a third one. "They've told me so!"

They walked on. Their voices died away.

I stared at *The Hague*. She was to sail at dawn, for the West Indies, far, far from London, far from Sir Cecil, far from Newgate. I watched the deck. The sentinel made his rounds, moved out of sight.

It was then I made my move.

On shaking legs I strolled to the gangplank as though I had every right. I went up it, heart pounding. At the top I darted for a flight of steps leading into the body of the ship. Down another flight I went, and another, and found myself in utter blackness.

Hands out, I went on slowly. I had to find a place to hide, before someone came below. My hands touched wood. Carefully, I felt it over, learning, finally, that here were stored packing cases from the bottom of the ship to above my head.

This, then, was where cargo was loaded! Somewhere in here there'd be a spot into which I could wedge myself. There I'd stay while the ship put out to sea; there stay as long as possible. Then and only then, I'd approach the captain and surely he'd give me something to do. He wouldn't throw me overboard.

I went on, deeper into the cargo. There were a few aisles between stacks of kegs, barrels, cases. Only a few, for the cargo was packed solidly.

My eyes strained uselessly to accustom themselves to the inky blackness. If only I could see! I crept on. And on. Something scurried across my foot, and a shiver cut through me and I almost screamed. I wondered how many rats there were, wondered if they'd attack and bite. No matter. Despite my fear of vermin, I'd endure them. The important thing was to get away.

It was when I thought I'd crumple in spite of everything that I found a hiding place.

It was a short slit branching off the aisle along which I'd been groping. I had to turn sidewise to move into it, lined on both sides with barrels. It seemed an impossible place, but I continued sidling deeper, wanting not to miss a space large enough into which to tuck myself.

But the slit never widened. I went sidling back. As I stepped again into the aisle, my trailing hand unexpectedly struck not barrel or packing case, but empty air! I explored at once.

It was a space large enough to hold two barrels. I went into it, sank down and let myself tremble. And then I examined my refuge by feel. It was very near that larger aisle, only one stack of cases between them. On my other side were the barrels. There was even room for me to lie curled up, and I was so bitterly tired that I did so at once.

But I mustn't sleep. I can lie down, I thought, I can sit and even stretch my legs into the aisle. If I'm careful, and if I'm very, very lucky, no one will find me!

PART I
THE PIRATE SHIP
1714

Chapter 6

There was no way to get comfortable—the wood was so hard, and I was sore and battered—but the feeling of being hidden was sweet. Only now had I won respite from the horrible hours with Sir Cecil, the ordeal in the alley, my panic-stricken flight. Only now could I let go—trembling—and hope I wouldn't be discovered.

I was so thirsty and so hungry. I'd had nothing to eat or drink since lunch, and it was now late at night.

The ship swayed at anchor. Timbers creaked. Rats squealed and scuttled, but they didn't find me, not yet, thank God. I quaked, then braced myself. I would bear whatever came. These rats weren't as bad as the human rats I had left behind.

Time went so slowly. The boards grew harder. I sat up to ease my soreness, leaned against the packing cases, wrapped my arms around my knees, rested my chin on them. Finally, I heard sounds of the crewmen coming aboard. It was very late. They were shouting and laughing. Then, when all was quiet, I assumed that each seaman was in his nice, comfortable berth. The boards were even harder now, the rats noisier.

The night crept on. My hunger sharpened, and my thirst. Foolishly, I let my mind dwell on water, on roast duck, on vegetables, on milk, then sternly wrenched it to fact. There was no telling how long I'd have to go without food and water; I'd not think of them again, for it only made things worse. I would survive.

My real problem would be weakness, but perhaps

that didn't matter since, aboard ship, I couldn't flee. I felt unexpected tears, but I forced them back. I simply would not cry. That would be the day! I hadn't endured degradation at the hands of three men to be bested by a clamoring stomach!

At last the ship came alive. It was a new day. Life was stirring on the waterfront, and my life was beginning anew with it. *The Hague* filled with men's voices, with the creak of timbers. I knew that sails were being hoisted, that they'd snap in the wind. Dawn would be replacing the stars. Other ships, too, would be setting sail.

The moments crawled. I sat erect, tense, aware that my breast-binder, which I'd put on so hastily back in the hidey-hole, had come loose and was creeping toward my waist. Later, when we were at sea and the crew was fully occupied, I'd take off my shirt long enough to adjust the binder.

Eventually, the long rise and fall under me told that we were underway. The crewmen shouted, laughed, roared, and this assured me it was really true. I was actually started toward my freedom!

I sat with pounding heart, sat endlessly, trying by feel to recognize when *The Hague* entered the open sea. The sun must have risen, hurtling into the sky like a fiery ball and centered on this vessel. It became steaming hot. I began to sweat, salty wetness covering my face, soaking my hair, drenching my velvet garments.

Every second was an hour. The hours did pass, for I heard a breakfast gong and a noon time gong. We'd been on open sea for some time, I knew, for the ship rose and fell with the long, swelling waves.

I wanted to creep out of my hiding place, seek the captain and plead for a berth, but practicality told me it was too soon, that he could hail a passing vessel, put me aboard, send me back to London. No, I had to wait until we were too far asea for him to do that. I refused to dwell on the sudden thought that he could turn me in at the first port; I'd got this far and I meant to go on, all the way to the West Indies and eventually to a safe country, regardless of what I had to do. Nothing, absolutely nothing, would extract too great a price.

When the supper gong was beaten. I was desperately hungry and my mouth was so dry I could hardly swallow. Water, was my main thought, water! Which I couldn't have . . . I mustn't complain, not even in my thoughts!

Now that the crew was eating, I decided to try to cool off a bit. I struggled out of my damp coat, out of my damper shirt. Hot though the stuffy air was, it felt cool to my drenched skin. I took the breast-binder from around my waist; I fanned my breasts and back with it. I stood up and fanned my whole upper body. This was the most delicious coolness I'd felt in a long time and, recklessly, I kept fanning, unaware of all else.

I didn't hear a footfall. I didn't glimpse the ray of lantern light. I didn't sense a presence. The first I knew anybody was there at all was when a low, male voice swore, "Damn! If it ain't a stowaway! And a woman, at that!"

I tried to snatch up my clothes, but the man struck my hand aside, and the breast-binder fell to the floor. I stood with my back pressed against the packing case, while the man's lantern cast its yellow rays over me and over himself.

He was exactly my height, and his light brown eyes were on a level with mine. He was young, not over twenty-three, and he had thick, sun-dusty hair faded in streaks. He was freckled and tanned, square-built and muscular, and his mouth, lips parted in a stunned but avid smile, held kindness.

His eyes moved over my breasts, my hair, my lips. He missed nothing, and I didn't miss the fact that his instinct was to want from me the same thing the others had taken from me by force.

"Please!" I cried, reaching out for that kindness I

had seen in his lips. "Don't tell! I've got to sail on this ship! I can't be sent back!"

"Why'd you stow away?" he demanded in a low tone, lantern never wavering, nor his intent look.

Desperate, I gave him truth. "I was educated to be a tutor . . . "

"Tutor. Ain't that a man?"

"Yes, but I . . . Circumstances forced me to dress as a man. There's not time now to explain."

"Go on."

"A kinsman . . . violated me . . . and when I demanded that he give me a letter of recommendation as a governess in . . . in restitution, he threw me to the law for posing as a man. He lied and said I was t-trying to seduce his wife. And then the beasts who came to take me to Newgate . . . " Unexpectedly, I began to weep.

"Three men took advantage?"

"Yes!" I whispered, angry at my weeping.

"And you thought you'd stow away and be a seaman?"

I struck away my tears. "Not at first," I told him. "I tried to get taken on a ship, and the captain said I was a fop and hinted at calling the law. So I . . . " I broke off, spreading my hands.

"So you sneaked aboard here. And want the captain to give you a berth. You, a girl?"

"I'm nineteen! I learn fast, and I'm strong! When I'm . . . dressed . . . nobody takes me for anything but a man! I'll show you!" I leaned down to pick up the rest of my clothing, but he caught my wrist.

"Look at me, girl," he said.

I looked, extremely uneasy.

"If I keep your secret, help you get a berth, will you . . . ?" He broke off, waited.

My heart became leaden. Of course, kind though his lips appeared, this man wanted the same thing Sir Cecil and the Newgate men had taken. My chin firmed. I'd determined to do anything at all in exchange for freedom. I met his eyes square on.

"I'm Mary Read, known as George Read. What's your name?"

"Karl van Buskirk. One grandfather from Amsterdam, one from London. Decent men. I try to be decent, too."

"I'll give you what you want," I said softly, woodenly. Why not? Sir Cecil had taken my virginity; Ryan and Clarke had raped me like animals. Now I was, of my own free will, trading my body to Karl van Buskirk for silence.

"Put something on," he muttered. "Then come along."

I put on the shirt, carried coat and binder, followed him along an aisle. I had almost to run, so fast did he go, but I didn't mind, for he was taking me to a safer place.

He stopped in a corner formed by cases. It was like a tiny room. There were two rolled blankets, a hook for a lantern, some books. He spread the blankets on the floor, one on top of the other.

"Take your breeches off," he said. "I can't stay long, not this time." He hung the lantern up and fumbled with his breeches.

"W-why do you have this place?" I stammered, to delay the fatal moment.

"To read. Think. When the heat's not too bad. The others've got no patience with a tar who reads. Come on, Mary . . . off with 'em."

My skin was blazing. I must have been fiery with blushes. I pulled off my breeches.

"Lay on the blankets. I'll be quick."

The blanket was rough. He knelt over me promptly, spreading my legs so that he was inside them. He entered me with one hearty thrust which, surprisingly, didn't hurt, and then he began to move—lusty, eager, hungry for what he was getting. I had every intention of lying motionless, of letting him have his way and be done. But I felt a new sort of passion rise in me, one that was clean and honest and eager, and I could not lie still but met him thrust for thrust and then, miraculously, I seemed to be on wings and helplessly responded with honest passion.

He rolled to one side, holding me. "I'm damned!" he panted. "Never . . . had a girl . . . like you! No wonder those others . . . "

"It wasn't the same with them," I said, and it hadn't been. The overwhelming sensation which Sir Cecil had called to life had been evil incarnate; the shameful, degraded feeling I'd suffered with Ryan and Clarke had been filth. This had been clean and sea-swept like Karl himself.

"How was it with . . . them?" he asked.

"Evil. Filthy."

"And this?"

"Honest. Clean. And with my consent."

He kissed me then, his lips warm and firm. "You're quite a woman, Mary Read."

"Call me George. Please."

He laughed, stood up, adjusted his breeches. "Stay here. You'll be safe enough. I'll come back soon as I can."

"Could you . . . bring me something to eat, and water?" I whispered, holding my shirt to hide my nakedness.

"How long since you ate?"

"I've lost track."

"I'll bring what I can. And I'll leave the lantern. Chances are slim anybody'll come this far in."

He was gone.

I put on breast-binder, shirt, and breeches, leaving off the coat. I was twice as hot and wet now, since the lovemaking with Karl. I lay on the blankets, longing for the food and water he would bring. It had been so long since I'd slept. Starved though I was, choked by thirst, ashamed and regretful over my shameful response to the intimacies of four different men, I fell asleep through sheer exhaustion.

Karl woke me. I didn't know whether it was an hour later or ten.

"Mary," he whispered, "wake up. Don't ask me to call you George, not when we're alone. I've brought you what I could to eat. And water."

I sat up, rubbing my eyes. My hair tumbled about my face, the cravat having come off while I slept.

Karl was smiling at me, and despite what he'd done to me earlier, despite the fact that he'd made me respond the way no girl should respond to a stranger, I found myself liking him.

"What time is it?" I asked.

"Breakfast. I filched what I could when the cook didn't see." He produced a hunk of cheese and a goodly portion of wonderfully smelling bread. There was also a firkin of sweet, cool water.

"Thank you!" I cried, reaching for the water.

"Shh," he warned. "Nobody comes down here much, but we've got to be careful. And go easy on the water . . . don't make yourself sick."

I sipped obediently, then set the firkin down. I held the loaf in my hands. It tasted so good, and so did the cheese, which was aromatic and mellow. Between bites, I sipped more water. When I'd finished, when every crumb of bread, every bit of cheese was gone, and I had only half the water remaining, Karl looked at me anxiously. "Was it enough? If you're still hungry, I can try . . . "

"Oh, no! I've had enough. I don't know how to thank you, Karl."

That male look came to him, and he gazed at me as hungrily as I had stared at the food only moments ago. "You know how," he whispered. "And now I've got time to spend . . . if you're willing."

Alarm and warmth sprang in me. Alarm at what he wanted, warmth because he didn't have a thought of evil in him. I liked him, despite the bargain we'd made. What lay between us was fair exchange—my willing favors in return for this hiding place, food, and water.

He watched me. He smiled uncertainly, and the

smile was so filled with concern that I found myself returning it.

"You're not afraid of me, then, Mary?"

I shook my head, worked at taking off shirt and binder. His eyes brightened and his mouth shook when my breasts sprang free and then, clumsily, he pulled off my breeches and entered me.

It wasn't exactly the same. It was cleaner, sweeter, better. Almost gratefully I felt the rise of that hotness in my depths, gladly moved beneath him, and when he moaned in release I was moaning, too.

Afterward we lay quiet, his arms around me, his breath on my cheek. "Do you hate me, Mary?"

"Why should I hate you?"

"For asking you to *pay* for the little I've done. For wanting what the others wanted."

"Of course I don't hate you!" I whispered. "They ... This is clean."

"Clean!" He seized the word. "Mary, believe me, I don't care what's happened to you. It was against your will; you fought and were raped. I've got no intent of rape. It's that you're so wonderful that no man could look at you like this with no clothes, and not go crazy with wantin' you. I don't know if I can make you understand, Mary ... "

"George," I whispered.

"It's a sin to call you that. When you're so much a woman!"

"But I've got to live as a man until I can manage as a woman," I said. "Can you get me ashore at some port, Karl? Then you won't be blamed if your captain finds out about this." I indicated our corner.

"It ain't real safe," he agreed. "None of 'em's ever showed up when I'm here, but that's not to say they won't."

"Then the sooner I go ashore the better."

"What can you do there?"

I told him the whole story, beginning with the time I was a child and my mother dressed me as a boy, progressing through my becoming grandmother's protégé, including the arrival of Sir Cecil and Lady Gwen, ending with rape, arrest, and escape.

He lay quiet. "Putting you ashore's out of the question. Getting you a berth's still the best way."

"All right," I agreed. "But I know nothing about ships. I'll do anything to learn to be a seaman . . . scrub, climb masts, work in . . . where the food's cooked . . . "

"That's the galley."

"Just so I get the chance to learn. My education was all in man things, so I can do it. I fence, spar, things like that, as well as study books."

"You'd live in the crew's quarters, sleep there?"

"D-don't the men have just a berth and sleep in their clothes? I read that in a book one time."

"They sleep in their clothes."

"Then I can go to the Captain?"

"Not until we get farther out to sea, and not until I tell you about ships. I'd say another twenty-four hours. Captain Courtney . . . Lord Roger Courtney . . . runs a tight ship. He'll put you to work if he don't find out you're a girl."

"And if he found out?"

"Hell'd break loose. I don't know what he'd do. Lock you up, turn you over to the law at the next port. He don't tolerate foolishness. So now let me explain about ships and tomorrow we'll see me takin' you to him as a stowaway lad."

"Thank you, Karl."

"Now. *The Hague's* a sloop and very fast. She carries a crew of seventy and she's fitted out with ten guns. She's a merchant ship. The crew eat in the mess in relays."

He talked for a long time, answered every question I could think of, and I tried my best to remember it all. Then he began to kiss me, slowly and warmly, and next he stripped both of us. Our naked bodies pressed together, moved as one, clung. And even after that, before he had to go on deck, we knew the closeness and the delight still again.

"I'll bring more food if I can," he said, dressing. "Think you can last it out?"

"Easily. Karl. My friend. I can get along on one meal a day if that's all you can manage. And with nothing before we see the captain if there's the least chance you'll be caught."

"Cook's used to me comin' into the galley and grabbin'. He curses, but he's proud when somebody likes his cookin' well enough to filch. Between meals, he can be meaner'n a wild animal, because he's busy plottin' his next meal."

"Be careful," I urged. I hated to see him go, to be alone, not knowing whether some other crewman, one lacking Karl's kindness, might discover me.

He seemed to have the same thought. "I'll not leave the lantern this time, Mary. It ain't really safe. With me on deck, if one of 'em comes below and sees the light back here, he'll investigate. When I'm not on deck and they see light, it don't make any difference because they know it's me."

"It doesn't matter," I assured him.

But when he'd gone and I was alone in the blackness, I was frightened by it and, presently, by the scuttle and scratch of rats. By gnawing. So far I'd escaped having one of the horrible creatures run across my foot. But suppose one should do that, or worse?

Sternly, I put my mind on Karl. How unexpectedly he had come into my life! But no matter how I looked at it, to let him take me as I did, to respond to him, was morally wrong. Yet, how could it be wrong? He was protecting me, feeding me, giving me water. He had instructed me about ships, and was going to take me to the captain and try to get me a berth. And I didn't really have any other choice.

The rats grew noisier. I endured, feet square on the blanket, knees under my chin, making myself as small as possible. I began to shiver.

If only I could have the lantern!

You're being foolish, I scolded myself when my

chin began to tremble. What has happened already is far worse than a few brainless rats scampering through their brainless lives. Get hold of yourself; wait as you have to wait.

I crept to where Karl's books were stacked. There were a dozen of them, and I loaded my arms and carried them to the blankets. Here I arranged them in three stacks, ready to throw, one volume at a time, at any rat that might invade my territory.

The hold grew hotter and hotter. I sweated, dreaming of baths. Once more time crept by so slowly, and besides the rats, there was only the blackness which bore on me like a wet, heavy blanket. My thirst was so great it was a struggle to take only one sip of my remaining water at a time, to resist gulping it all down.

I considered taking off my clothes again. But there were the rats and, even more dangerous, the chance that some crewman might stumble onto me and discover that I was a girl. I'd never be found out again—I vowed I wouldn't.

After an eternity of darkness, I saw a glimmer of light. My heart began to pound. It was Karl.

He hung the lantern up, and gave the new firkin of water into my eager hands. I drank thirstily.

Karl sank down beside me. He stroked my sweat-soaked hair. "Really hot," he said, and somehow his words were comforting and seemed to help.

I nodded.

"I couldn't bring food. Downer was in a temper . . . threw a cleaver at me. Cursed, and he's got some choice words. And I couldn't sneak anything from the table without them seein'."

"It's all right," I murmured, although my stomach was convulsing with hunger. "Tomorrow . . . "

"You'll eat before tomorrow. But first, I've got things to tell you. I . . . damn it all, Mary, to start with, I took you for my man's needs. But now I am afraid I'm beginning to love you!"

I stared at him, aghast.

"I know it's sudden, Mary. But I want it settled."

I didn't know what he meant, but then he went on. "Do you love me the same?" He looked at me, hard and long. "You don't . . . do you?"

I shook my head. He was my friend, my savior, but I couldn't love him. Neither could I lie to him.

"I'm sorry, Karl, but no. I cannot."

"Maybe I could show you. If you could put up with my rough ways, you bein' raised among gentlefolk."

"I couldn't, Karl," I told him sadly, giving him my heart's truth. "Now or never. Only as a friend."

"I'll ask again," he said, tone uneven. "If you won't get mad."

"I could never be angry with you, Karl."

Oh, how I wished I could learn to love this honorable man! But the answer was clear. He was a friend, nothing more.

He patted my hand reassuringly.

After a moment he said, "I had a word with Captain Courtney. He's in a good mood, so I spoke up. Asked for some time with him, and he told me to come to his cabin."

"You told him about me?"

"Not a hint. Come. Do whatever straightening up a woman does, and let's go."

I tidied myself, ran my fingers through my hair, clubbed it at the neck, using the folded cravat. I put on my coat, buttoned it neatly and was as ready as it was in my power to be.

"My face," I said to Karl. "Have the bruises healed?"

"It looks fine. All well. Come on."

But I held back, even though his hand was on my arm. "What are you going to say Karl . . . that you've found a stowaway? Please don't let him know you've hidden me! Don't get yourself into trouble!"

"I'm just going to take you into his cabin, tell him I found you in the hold, introduce you. Don't be afraid. Things will be all right. He's not a cruel man;

he's a gentleman. He'll have to deal with you, one way or another."

Pulse racing, I let Karl take me swiftly through the hold. I was nervous about meeting the Captain just yet. I would have preferred to wait until tomorrow to make certain we were so far asea I couldn't be put off the ship.

I whispered this to Karl.

"We're far enough out," he whispered back. "With the Captain in a good humor, it's best he finds out about you now." And then he hurried me away.

Chapter 7

We passed three of the crew. They stared and muttered. Karl hurried me along faster. At the end of a passageway, he rapped on a door.

"Enter," called a voice that was clear and strong. It sounded neither friendly nor unfriendly, only assured.

Karl opened the door, urged me inside. The Captain was sitting, back to us, writing at a desk. His hair was auburn, clubbed at the back with a narrow black ribbon. Even seated, it was evident that he was tall, wide-shouldered, slimly and strongly built. He wore a blue uniform with gold braid.

"I'll be with you in a moment," he said. "I'm bringing the log up to date."

"Aye, sir," Karl said.

I made no sound, for he didn't know I was there.

Along one side of the cabin were berths, two of them, one above the other. They were curtained. Opposite them were cabinets and drawers. There was a shelf of books held in place by rods of gleaming brass. The table was in the center, bolted to the deck, as were the chairs drawn to it and the one in which the Captain sat. The desk was a hinged shelf. All the wood was beautiful, highly polished mahogany. The brass, including bracket lamps, was polished until it blinded.

Now the Captain pushed his log book toward the back of the desk and closed the shelf, hooking it with a brass fastening. Then he got to his feet and turned, saying, "All right, van Buskirk, what can I do for . . ."

His deep blue eyes landed on me. His auburn brows moved, almost bent in a frown. His nose was straight and strong. His lips, which were pleasantly shaped, now clamped and a small white line sprang out around them. The eyes blazed over me—my damp, flaming hair, gold velvet coat, green breeches, red-heeled shoes, the emerald cravat with which my hair was clubbed.

"Well, van Buskirk. What have you here?"

"A stowaway, Captain, sir."

"Where did you find him?"

"In the hold, sir."

The blue eyes came onto me.

"What's your name?"

"George Read, sir."

"Age?"

"Nineteen, sir."

"Why did you stow away on my ship?"

"To become a seaman, sir."

"Why didn't you ask for a berth?"

"I tried that with one ship, sir. But the Captain wouldn't take me because of my clothes, sir."

"Ah, yes. You're not from working people."

"I have no people, sir. They're all dead."

"Why are you dressed this way? Did you steal the garments, buy them at some hole-in-the-wall . . . were they given to you?"

He was trying to be just, actually he was giving me an opportunity to lie. But I couldn't lie to this man with the auburn hair, the deep blue gaze. I had to give him truth as far as I could without letting him know I was a girl.

"I earned the clothes, sir. My grandmother had me educated as a tutor before her death, and she bought my clothes."

"Why aren't you in a tutoring post now?"

I could feel Karl's tenseness behind me, sense his fear that I'd betray myself. I drew a long, slow breath, and then I replied.

"I lost my post sir. Without a letter."

"Why did you lose it?"

"My . . . the master took a dislike to me because I wouldn't let him . . . " I broke off, cheeks flaming.

"Wouldn't let him what? Speak up, lad."

"Take his pleasure with me, sir. I demanded a letter of recommendation, he denied it, called the men from Newgate with a lie. I got away."

The brows met on the nose. "That's a wild tale. Do you expect me to believe it?"

He must believe, had to believe! I couldn't bear for him to think I'd lie, that I'd look right into those blue, blue eyes and tell an untruth! Not to him, on whom my whole future rested.

"What I've said is the God's truth, sir," I replied, somehow keeping my lips from trembling.

"You're on the run, that's easy to see, whether from wicked master, Newgate, or both. Or from your family, taken by a lad's yearning to go to sea."

"I truly have no family, sir. And the sea's the only way I can think of! If you can bring yourself to pardon the fact that I sneaked aboard sir, and if you'll give me a berth, I'll learn whatever tasks I'm put to and do them well. I'm very strong, and I learn fast."

"You're aware that I can turn you over to the law at the first port."

"Yes, sir. I throw myself on your mercy, sir. To let me prove myself. To let me live free, for I have committed no crime."

I saw a look of—understanding perhaps—come into his eyes. But then it was gone, and I knew it must have been a trick of light. At least the white line was gone from around his lips, though he was still frowning.

"What to do with you is the problem," he muttered. He looked at Karl. "Van Buskirk."

"Yes sir, Captain Courtney?"

"You're of a height with Read. Have you enough clothes that you can outfit him?"

"That I have, sir," Karl said, and I could tell he was having a hard time keeping delight out of his voice. "Enough for two sets. I bought new in London."

"Good. Give Read your old garments."

"Aye, sir."

"See to it that he sponges before he changes."

"Aye, sir."

"My name," the Captain said, turning to me, "is Captain Roger Courtney. You're to address me as 'Captain Courtney' or 'Sir'. Being educated, you'll know which term to use according to the occasion."

"Aye, Captain Courtney, sir," I agreed, standing at attention.

"It happens that my cabin boy married and stayed ashore just at sailing time, Read. That's the only berth open. This is a position of responsibility. You'll keep my cabin ship-shape, fetch my bathwater, care for my uniforms, serve my meals, run such errands as needed. Think you can manage?"

"Aye, Captain Courtney, sir."

"You've taken care of your own garments?"

"Frequently, sir. I know how, I believe, to serve you well."

Though I spoke in a low-pitched, assured tone, I was in turmoil. I had no idea how I kept my voice from quivering, knees from buckling.

"That we shall see. I believe there's a berth for him, van Buskirk? The one the last boy used?"

"Aye, sir. It's just over my own, sir."

"Report to me here at breakfast gong. With my tray."

"Aye, sir," I agreed, overwhelmed. With Karl ushering me, we left the cabin properly.

Karl showed me my berth. He opened his sea chest and took out the clothes. An occasional crewman passed. I heard one mutter, "I ain't goin' to give a tit to no stowaway." The man with him growled agreement. I bit my lip, troubled.

A burly fellow with muscles like rope passed, giving me an ugly glance. Karl snorted. "That's Grider. You can bet it's all over the ship we've got a stowaway. Get up there, pull your curtains, and I'll bring a pan of water and soap."

I scrambled up into the berth.

He thrust a set of clothing up and I took it.

"When I come back with the water, throw down your other stuff," he said. "I'll pitch it overboard."

Longing for a real, tub bath, I sponged my body thoroughly, huddling in the berth. The breast-binder, of course, I had to put back on. Karl's soft old shirt was too broad in the shoulder and too long in the sleeves, but these I turned up at the wrist, and belted in both shirt and breeches as tightly as I could. There was nothing for it but to wear my own red-heeled shoes.

Karl rummaged in his sea chest until he found a piece of black cord, which he gave to me, along with the use of his comb. I pulled it through my hair, pulling it to the nape of my neck, clubbing it.

When I came down, Karl gave a low whistle. "You sure look different!"

"Do I look like a seaman, do I?"

"Almost. With that hair . . . " He grinned. The grin was replaced by a look I could have sworn was one of desolation.

"What is it . . . what's wrong?"

"You wouldn't want to hear."

"Yes I would, I do! Please tell me!" I put my hand on his arm.

"It's . . . I thought maybe you'd be willin' to meet

me in the hold sometimes. But not now. You being cabin boy."

My heart jerked.

Karl was my only friend. I'd given him my body, true, but he'd protected me. He'd even practically offered himself as husband. But since talking to the Captain, all thought of what Karl wanted had vanished.

"Don't be a goose," I said.

He took it the wrong way. If I'd hit him in the mouth, he couldn't have looked more stricken.

"Karl," I whispered. "I didn't mean . . . "

"I'll not betray you. And I'll not make you meet me."

"But I want to!"

"Out of pity, is that it now?"

"Out of friendship and affection, Karl. Please. I truly want to meet you!"

He lost the stricken look. "It's my fault, Mary. I see now how you meant it."

When he would have taken me to the galley for food, I declined. I didn't want to rouse the cook's everlasting hatred by asking to eat between meals. I did ask Karl if there was an extra sea chest I could use, and together we searched, even going into the hold.

We found a battered chest which Karl carried to the berth. I placed my neatly folded change of clothing inside, then he closed the lid and pushed the chest underneath his berth, beside his own.

"You can use my comb until we get to a port," he said.

I thanked him and said no to his offer to take me on deck and introduce me around. I said I'd meet them at supper, which was soon enough. I suggested that we go to our nook in the hold, if he wanted to, him being off duty and my own duties not yet begun. He was delighted, and we hurried to our hidden spot.

Wrapped in each other's arms, we had a long, sweet encounter. Karl told me again that he loved me, and I stroked his cheek and wept that I could not return such love as this. He kissed my tears away.

When he went on deck, I got into my berth and lay, trembling and hungry. Trembling in shock that, for the moment, I had succeeded. I was really on my way to freedom.

Karl took me in to supper, the first sitting. The mess had two long tables, benches along the sides, all bolted to the deck. Seamen lined every bench and, as I entered with Karl, every one of them stared at me.

Karl introduced me. There seemed to be nothing but probing eyes, disapproving faces, unheard of names—Vannice, the captain's mate, Beld, Grider, Warner, Klaxton—on and on. I nodded to each, meeting his look, my jaw so stiff it ached.

After I'd sat down between Karl and Vannice, the men began to talk among themselves. Suddenly Vannice raised his mug—Karl had told me the crew were allowed one drink each night—and proposed a toast.

"Safe sailing and safe landfall!" he said.

The mugs were lifted, the contents downed. They made one big thump as they were set back on the board table. I stared into mine. I'd never tasted so much as a sip of whiskey. If I drank this, whatever it was, I might get so drunk I'd do something that would betray myself.

"Drink up, you . . . 'Red'!" yelled one of the men right at me.

"That's the stuff!" shouted another. " 'Red'! After his flamin' hair!"

"Right!" bellowed still another. That was Grider, he of the rope-like muscles. "If he can stow onto our ship and get to be cabin boy, he's 'Red', and he can drink what we drink!"

The others took up Grider's cry. One yelled that I needn't expect to be tit-fed, that they were crew, not wet-nurses.

All the eyes were boring into me. I stared at my mug.

"Drink," muttered Karl, even he. But he was speaking for my own good. The other men didn't want me aboard.

I lifted the mug, set my lips to it, held my breath, drank. One swallow, two, three, four. Fire slid down my throat, blasted into my stomach. I had to cough, but I would not. The whiskey had brought tears into my eyes. They stung. I'd die if I drank more, but down went swallows five, six, seven, and on to the end. At last I thumped my mug loudly on the board, felt my mouth open despite trying to hold it shut, and sat gasping.

The men roared. It was taunting, cruel laughter. They shouted remarks about a cabin boy not man enough to hold his drink. This went on, with me choking, trying to get a full breath of air without their knowing, pretending not to notice them at all.

"Eat," muttered Karl.

I seized a spoon and attacked the food on my plate. There were potatoes, I believe, and cabbage and beef with gravy. I ate as fast as I could, swallowed, ate, swallowed, to put out the blaze which flared in my stomach and through my body, even into my head.

"He sure-hell ain't used to whiskey!" chortled one man.

"Then he ain't used to the sea!" shouted another.

"He'll have to prove hisself," called one from the other table. "Stowin' on, fast talkin' the Cap'n into makin' him cabin boy! He's got a cut of work in front of hisself, Red's got, turnin' hisself into a seaman! Red the fop! His hair makes him that!"

Miserable, burning from the whiskey, shaking inwardly from the roughness of the seamen, half-choking, I downed that meal both to put out the fire of whiskey and because I was half-starved. I listened to the crew grumble and curse and complain and criticize, all of it directed against me. All but Karl, who kept muttering, "They'll get over it. You'll show them you're as good a man as any. They're rough, but you'll be all right, Red. Little Red!"

Chapter 8

The breakfast gong had sounded when, carrying a heavy tray, I tapped on the door of the Captain's cabin. When he bade me enter, I saw that the little green drapes had been drawn back from the portholes and sun shone through to glitter the polished deck. The berths were empty, the pillow on the lower one dented, sheet and sturdy green cover shoved back.

Captain Courtney stood at a mirror, back to me, shaving. "You're late!" he said sharply. "When I give you a specific time, I don't mean a second or two after, but on the stroke! Remember that!"

"Aye, sir."

"Set the tray on the table and get out. I'm not in a permissive mood."

"Aye, so I see, sir," I remarked, not knowing, before the words were out, that I was going to utter them.

He was cleaning soap off his face. He turned. His brows met on his nose. "Did any of my crew give you the idea that I permit even a hint of insubordination, Read?"

"No, sir."

"It was your own idea to be late?"

"It was my idea, sir, to be on the stroke. I miscalculated. It won't happen again, sir." I set the tray down and made ready to leave. I couldn't tell him that Downer, the cook, had delayed me by not having the Captain's tea ready.

"You think me too strict, perhaps?" Captain Courtney demanded.

"It's not my place to think one way or another, sir."

"That's right. You do think, however. I see it in your eyes. You think me a stern, hard captain who drives his crew like slaves. Well, understand this, Read, as part of your training. Men at sea have to be kept busy; a ship must be in top condition every moment. The Captain prevents his crew from becoming lax, even fighting among themselves, by demanding that every task be done to perfection. The result is a crew fully occupied, tired enough to sleep in their turn, and a smoothly run vessel." He paused.

I'd turned, as he spoke, out of respect because he was my captain. Those blue eyes were blazing.

"I understand, sir," I said. But I wondered. What kind of slave-driver was he? Karl hadn't spoken against him. But then, if this strong-faced man had his crew under his thumb, none of them would dare to gossip about it.

"I trust you do understand, Read. Or should I call you 'Red'?"

So he knew even that!

"Red will be fine, sir." It would be protection for me. Hopefully, the crew had already forgotten the name George Read. Consequently, in port, they'd not make connection between Red, cabin boy, and George Read, wanted by Newgate, should there be broadsheets out.

"As a crewman, you'll continue to eat with the others. You have a berth and your whiskey at night. I'll work you hard, but that's the lot of the seaman."

"Aye, sir."

"I give shore leave when I can. Some captains I could name order a shift to stay aboard the whole time. I don't always do that, though I've had it thrown in my teeth I'm too lenient. Hell . . . why should I try to convince you that I run a proper ship?"

"Why indeed, sir?" I murmured.

He gave me a sharp glance, as though he were undecided whether a reprimand was in order. He frowned, then his face smoothed.

He took off the robe he wore and I saw that he'd

pulled on breeches and boots, but his chest was bare. His body was slim, and smoothly, powerfully muscled. At mid-chest, auburn hair formed a cross extending perhaps the length of my hand in both directions. It was a natural growth. The sight was disturbing and I lowered my eyes, wishing I didn't have to pretend to be a lad, wishing I could hate him for his assurance and almost-arrogance.

"Is there something else, sir?"

He motioned to the cupboards. "Get me a shirt."

I opened a door, reached for a shirt.

He stopped me. "Not that one. The next one."

I drew it out, closed the narrow door, held the fine cambric garment while he thrust his arms into it. When I would have buttoned it for him, he brushed my hand aside.

"A cabin boy isn't a valet! Just hand me my clothes. Don't try to dress me."

"Aye, sir. Do I leave now, sir?"

"Wait." He finished with his buttons, tucked his shirt into his breeches and, ignoring me, stepped to the table and glared over his breakfast tray. "I don't suppose you know how to cook," he said.

"Aye, sir. I know a bit."

And I did know. My mother had taught me the basics, and, while I was with my grandmother, I'd hung around the kitchens, watching how things were made. I'd thought that, when the day arrived that I could live as a girl, I'd cook to my heart's desire. I considered it an art, the taking of meats, vegetables, sugar, spices, and creating delectable things.

"Good," the Captain said. "I'll instruct Downer that you're to prepare my meals. If I like your food, that will be added to your duties."

"Aye, sir. Is cooking regular duty for a cabin boy?"

"Not that I'm aware of. It will be now, I hope. In port, incidentally, I'll see to it that you have better clothes."

After he dismissed me, I went to the mess for my own breakfast. I slipped into place between Karl and

Vannice, ignoring the way the men across the planks glowered through their eyebrows at me. It didn't last long, for they bent their faces almost to their plates and gobbled the food before them.

Later, with the Captain on deck, I went to his cabin. Here I made up his berth, smoothing the sheets that still smelled of his clean body, pulling the canvas-like top cover tight, anchoring it under the mattress so it looked more like a couch than a berth. As I ran my palms over the cover, I wondered about the strange, unfathomable man who had taken a stowaway as cabin boy. A man who was unaware that, under my seaman's garb, I was a fully developed woman. I wondered, too, if he had a wife, fiancée, a mistress.

I took his tray to the galley, returned to the cabin and rubbed with a cloth every inch of polished wood and shining brass. Only when it sparkled more brightly than before did I stop work.

Now I didn't know what to do. I was hesitant about going on deck and being in the way of the unfriendly crew. I dared not go into the galley until I could assume the Captain had told Downer I'd be cooking his meals.

At a loss, I went to the only spot I could call my own, the upper berth. There I lay dreaming up a meal for which the galley should have supplies, planning how to conduct myself so as not to enrage Downer. And above all, striving to think what food would best please the Captain.

Who does he think he is? I thought, suddenly angry. He has a beautiful cabin all to himself, he orders a crew of seventy, and now he's too good to eat the same food the men—and I—eat. However, in honesty, my stomach did feel heavy from greasy potatoes, and I supposed the Captain's felt the same. And the crew, as well. Maybe, if I could get Downer to tolerate me enough, I could influence him to use less grease.

Eventually, I ventured into the galley. Downer, a brawny man in a dirty apron, seemed to be covered with black hair. He was muttering a deep, rumbling string of curses as I came in, and that was before he saw me. His wide, hairy face was sweating, his shirt was sticking to his back, and his big hands were everywhere at once, stirring, cutting, moving pots.

His helper, a skinny lad even younger than myself, was scurrying about in response to an occasional profane bellow from Downer. How could I ever get so much as a slice of bread out of this place? One swipe of that big, fast hand would flatten me.

Now he saw me, and surged to a halt. "Yer Red!" he shouted. "The ninny the Captain thinks can cook better'n me!"

"Aye, I'm Red, sir. The Captain . . . "

"Hell, I know! An' he knows I don't like it! Use that shelf an' that stove section. Keep the hell from underfoot! Don't ask my helper fer nothin' . . . he's mine!"

I ventured a glance at the hurrying lad. He was caught up in work, but didn't seem to be frightened.

"I'll need supplies, sir," I said with spirit.

"Find 'em fer yerself. Stay out'n our path."

Furious at Downer, even more furious at a captain who prided himself so much on running a tight ship that the galley was a hell-hole, I managed to assemble what I needed. It was hard to keep out of the way of the other, rushing two. Quickly I noticed there was efficiency to their rushing; I remembered they had seventy mouths to feed. The galley had to be this busy before meals. I'd seen no evidence of feverish attention to duty among the crewmen, nor did Karl seem to be worked to a frenzy. Yet work, and work hard, they all did.

I found a nice piece of beef, which I broiled. There were green peas, *The Hague* being fresh from port, and garden vegetables still at hand. I cut small red radishes into flower shapes, made fluffy rice topped with butter, and baked tall biscuits. For a sweet, I put a small, covered dish of honey on the tray, covered all with a napkin to keep it warm, and hastened to the cabin.

I tapped at the Captain's door. He called to enter. "You're on time," he remarked as I came in.

"Aye, sir," I said, and put the tray on the table.

He lifted the napkin, examined the food with interest. "It looks . . . and smells appetizing," he commented.

I was startled. It was the first compliment he'd paid me. The first time he'd been anything but displeased. I would have sworn that he'd never speak this way.

"Thank you, sir," I murmured, face hot.

"What are you serving me tonight?"

"Beef, green peas, rice. Tall biscuits."

"You spoil me, Red."

He looked at me, and there was something like admiration in his eyes. Pleased with his meal, a morning's duty behind him, he didn't seem nearly so stern and unfeeling. The exacting manner was gone, and I sensed a warmth that hadn't been there before. He seemed about to say more, then his eyebrows met on his nose.

"You'll see that I have such meals in the future."

"Aye, sir."

"The men, too. I'm ordering Downer to observe that you cook without grease and for him to do the same."

My heart warmed. Now the others wouldn't have such heavy stomachs! Nor would I.

"Go now. I'll set the tray outside when I'm finished."

Taken aback, I left the cabin. He was an ice-monster. He was totally without feeling. I'd imagined that instant of warmth. Roger Courtney was incapable of any real, human feeling. All he wanted was to run a tight ship. Well, let him run it!

As I went to the mess for my own greasy meal, I felt my eyes sting with tears. I swiped them away viciously, enraged. He thought I was a lad. I was his cabin boy, his lackey, nothing more, and that was the way I wanted it. "I hate him!" I whispered. I hated him with my entire heart, and I was glad he didn't know I was a girl, glad that it had been Karl, not he, who had found me half-naked in the hold. Glad it was Karl, not Roger Courtney, who'd bedded me!

As the crewmen ate, slurping, talking with their mouths full, it was all I could do to sit there and eat enough to avoid drawing attention. *The Hague,* Karl had murmured when I first sat down, was at her fullest, fastest speed, all her canvas filled with wind, and she was beating further and further out to sea.

I wondered if beating out to sea meant that the vessel slid down forever as she now did, hung for a space in the depths, then climbed back up. But I didn't ask Karl; I'd not display my ignorance before the others.

"The weather's gettin' rough," Karl said.

Vannice put in his bit. "Sky's gray. Waves are getting taller. We're in for a blow."

"Blow, hell!" bellowed a rough old seadog from the other table. "It's a full hurricane we're headin' into! We got hell ahead!"

Karl took me on deck. I had to cling to the side of the companionhead to keep from falling. When we stepped out, the wind tore my hair loose, and I barely caught the cord with which I tied it. The deck was alive with crewmen on the run, pulling ropes, changing the angle of the sails, charging from one task to another without let-up. All was confusion, but ordered confusion, through which cut the Captain's shout at intervals, snapping out directions.

I found myself appreciating the worth of the sloop, remembering things Karl had told me about the vessel. Even I could see she had great breadth of beam; he'd said she had a perfect draught and a correct waterline. I knew, from having seen her in London, that her painted sides were snowy white. Hull, I thought, that's the hull. There was smoothness to her meticulously greased masts and a majestic beauty to her white rigging.

I kept watching the crew. Fast though they moved, order prevailed on deck with every rough, foul-tongued seaman at his post, springing to the next when needed. Suddenly they didn't seem so foul, but rather strong and experienced, ready to deal with whatever the raging sky might hurl down upon them.

Karl was among them, having ordered me to stay here. I couldn't find him among the fast-moving men, but knew he was one of the best and felt proud of him.

Clouds continued to rise in the already darkened sky. They came with stunning rapidity and soon spread over the existing ones, making everything like the dusky forerunner of night. They seemed to be agitated by some dreadful commotion. Thick, dark masses seemed to revolve. Angry lightning began to leap from them. And, on the heels of the lightning, thunder rolled in, and then the rain drove down, drenching all. The sloop made a long, long dive, sliding down the side of a great breaker, hung in watery void, climbed precipitately up the next breaker.

I didn't want to be alone here. I wanted to be near Karl . . . or Roger. The Captain, I meant. I corrected myself . . . Captain Courtney. I let go the companionhead and started forward.

Almost immediately I lost my footing and crashed into a sturdy body. Whoever it was caught me by the arms only to steady me, as if I were indeed a lad.

It was Karl.

"Watch me!" he cried above the noisy rain, the thunder, the blast of lightning. "Watch my feet! You've got to dance against the sea!"

Terrified, feet spread apart and braced, hanging on-to the companionhead, feeling the deck beneath me dive as though headed for the bottom of the ocean, feeling it rise as though to wing into the blackening, streaming, flashing sky, rain enveloping me in a constant veil, I watched Karl. Each time the vessel dived into a trough, he danced to one side; as it climbed out, he danced to the other side. He seemed to keep time to the plunge and climb of the vessel as if it were music.

Now I tried the footwork, and it helped. I had some difficulty with the sloop's upward leap but managed, though I still clung to the companionhead. Presently it came more easily.

"I've got to go!" Karl shouted. "You'd better go to the cabin!"

"No!" I shrieked into the hurricane. I was a crew member. I'd not go below and cower the way men expected women to do. I'd signed on as a man, and a man's part I would play.

Karl pressed my shoulder, then went away, back to his tasks.

The wind kept blowing, in great fury now, sweeping from over the vast ocean, hurling foam and towering waves over the deck, over the seamen struggling with sails. The sloop trembled and quivered as the sea leapt higher around her. Once she wallowed under its onslaught, but righted herself and held her own against the storm.

Clinging to sodden wood, dancing, rain swathing me, I gloried in the sloop, in the raging sea, in the storm, in the tough, relentless men battling it. I gloried in Roger Courtney who was somewhere unseen, shouting his orders, directing the battle.

I peered intently through the dark melée, searching for him. Dimly, at last, I found him in the midst of the action. They were taking in all the sails now, lashing them down. They began to run out the anchor so they could lay to and ride out the storm.

The Captain was having trouble. All his men were fighting sails and rocking seas. There was no one to help him with one billowing sail which he was struggling to furl.

I rushed to him, keeping to the dancing. I nearly fell at every step, did fall across his arms as he heaved on a rope. The wind ripped at the sail, threatening to tear it off and away.

"Grab hold!" he yelled.

I gripped the hard, slippery rope, my hands above his. It cut into my palms, but I hung on, legs spread, pulling with all my might. Once I heard the labored breath of my captain, then it was swallowed into the roaring wind. The shouts of the crew were thin, scarcely audible above the booming thunder and exploding lightning.

The spar, sail flapping, began to give. Was it supposed to give? I didn't know, could only hang on. The wind was king of the sky, he flung his robes of rain over us, roared with his thunder, laughed his stabbing cackle. He pushed us in the direction opposite that for which we fought, and then he spun the rope through our hands, but we held onto it. Roger was thrown against me, his arms encircled me, his hands now above mine on the rope. We were melded together.

There was a sharp splintering. The spar came at us. I had one glimpse as the spear-like, broken spar fell like a broken arrow. I sprang aside, almost fell. Captain Courtney was the target of the spar's point, as he placed his back to it, dancing with the ship's motion to keep his footing.

Head down, I hurtled across space. I struck him in the small of the back. He sprawled on the slippery deck. I landed on top of him, clutching for his shoulders, and at that instant a pain glanced along my own shoulder, splintered wood ripping down along my ribs and away. Rain enveloped my bare back, folding itself over me like a wet, moving garment.

"Get . . . off . . . me!" shouted the Captain.

I struggled off, holding to him. I pushed up, facing him. I was sitting, rain sluicing over my naked breasts. Lightning flashed in the sky, illuminating the deck, where the men were fighting to save their ship and their own lives, shining on my breasts.

I even glimpsed the Captain's face. The white line was around his lips.

"Of all the damned, deceitful . . . !" he yelled. "Let go of me . . . hang onto the spar!"

Shaken by the thundering storm less than by his wrath, I grabbed the spar. The sloop lurched, tipped, seemed about to turn over, righted herself, rocked. Lightning snapped and hung again, like a giant lantern. Captain Courtney was tearing off his coat.

He threw it into my face. "Cover yourself!"

Somehow, holding to the spar, I got the sodden coat around me, my arms into the sleeves, and buttoned it over my breasts. My shoulder hurt and so did my side. I could feel them bleeding.

I knew when the anchor had taken hold. *The Hague* seemed to go into her own frenzied dance on the turbulent ocean, as those of us aboard braced ourselves.

Lightning stabbed and stabbed. This is worse than before, I realized. We're going to be shaken to pieces and drowned right on deck! I slid a glance around whenever lightning stood out; the men were hanging onto anything they could just as the captain and I were doing. I thought I saw Karl, started to call to him, when the demon wind hurled rain at us, nearly choking me.

I began to cough, but I still held onto that spar.

Fingers gripped my bleeding arm. "You damned little . . . ! On your feet! We're going below!"

It was the Captain. He yanked me up and shoved me along, pressing my injured arm, hurting it. "Dance!" he shouted. "Damn you . . . dance!"

I went into that terrible dance, feeling, with every step, that I'd be hurled to the deck. Captain Courtney danced beside me, still hurting me, still pushing me heartlessly along toward the companionhead. We fell, got up, went on, dancing madly.

He was tearing my arm from its socket, was pushing harder, faster. I found myself half-falling down the steps, along the passageway and into the cabin. The little room was swaying like a thing apart from

the ship. Momentarily, I closed my eyes. My stomach
began to lift and fall, but I couldn't be sick, wouldn't
be sick, not in front of this man!

He had lighted a ship's lantern and now he fastened
it to a hook. His shirt was sodden, sticking to his body.
His hair streamed water. He glared at me, face as
white as the line around his lips.

"Damn!" he swore. "What kind of hussy *are* you?
Passing yourself off as a man, sleeping with the
crew ... What's been going on aboard my vessel?"

Miserable, shaken, realizing he didn't even suspect
that I'd saved him from being hurt by that broken
spar, terrified both of him and the hurricane, I could
only stare at him.

I was as angry as he was, enraged because he'd
hurled the coat into my face, because he was accusing
me of lewd conduct with his crewmen. Yet I was also
terror-stricken as to what he could do about me, if we
survived the storm. In port, at his word, I could be
packed off to London and Newgate. At this moment,
white with rage, he didn't look like a man with a drop
of mercy in him.

"Take off that coat!" he yelled.

"No! I won't!"

"Or I'll do it for you!"

I took it off, furious, trembling, trying not to fall.
In spite of my effort, I did fall once. He didn't help
me up. Not him. Instead, he was stripping off his wet
clothes. That cross of hair was dark and wet. Water
dripped from it and ran down his belly. He toweled
himself, put on a dark red robe.

My teeth were shivering, no matter how I stiffened
my jaw. Naked, clinging to the berth post with both
hands, I waited. He threw a towel at me, then a robe.
I dried myself, scrambled into the robe. It was red,
exactly like his.

He sat down on his berth, still white with anger,
and watched me. Once I'd fastened the robe so that it
revealed nothing, I clung to the table.

The vessel pitched and tore at her anchor. Timbers

creaked, the lantern swung crazily, making the dark daylight in the cabin crazy.

"Now," the Captain said at last. "Go to your berth. Get into dry clothes. On the double! After the storm lets up, I'll deal with you. Right now, I'm tempted to lock you up. You've been nothing but trouble."

"You liked my cooking!" I retorted, goaded beyond all patience. Oh, how I'd like to scratch his eyes out, to rake my nails down that arrogant, bossy face!

"You should cook . . . you're a woman. A woman who . . . When you see van Buskirk tell him to find you a coat."

I was about to go, when a knock sounded at the door.

"Enter!"

Vannice came in, clothes running water, puddling on the deck. He stood long-faced and reluctant to speak.

"What is it, man?"

"It's van Buskirk, sir. I thought you'd want to know."

My heart stirred. Karl! Kind, loving Karl! Why should Vannice have to report something about him? Karl was one of the best seamen on board.

Vannice swallowed. He looked fearful.

"What about him, Vannice? Did he get hurt?"

"Not that, Captain, sir. He was washed overboard. We couldn't . . . We've lost him, sir."

My heart snagged, then pounded. It hurt, exactly as if someone was pinching it. My only friend, my dear Karl! He was gone forever. Dead. I was bereft. Moreover, I couldn't weep for Karl, not now, in the presence of these men. I had to hold back unmanly tears.

The Captain didn't speak. That white line sprang around his mouth, whiter than his still-white face. At last he asked. "Did the bitch . . . were there any other casualties?"

"No sir. None."

"Divide van Buskirk's duties among others."

"Aye, sir."

"Any extent of severe damage topside?"

"No more than you saw, sir. We can ride it out."

"Keep a sharp watch. You may go now."

"Aye, sir."

When I'd made my way to my berth, cleaned away the blood from my shoulder and along the ribs, I put on my clean shirt, hoping the blood had stopped and wouldn't stain the garment. I wanted no one to know of my wound. I had no breast-binder now, of course, but the shirt was full and should hide my breasts until I could find something to use for a binder.

Roger—angrily I realized how often I'd thought of him by that name and forced myself to call him Captain—was dressed in a fresh uniform when I got back to the cabin. His hair was as smoothly combed and clubbed as though he were going ashore, not waiting in the middle of the ocean for a hurricane to blow itself out.

"Sit at that end of the berth," he ordered.

I obeyed.

He sat at the other end, each of us holding to an upright. He said nothing. I said nothing. He hadn't had time, yet, to decide how he would deal with me as a woman, probably wasn't even considering me, not with the wind still wild and at least one broken spar on his vessel. I knew that could be fixed; Karl had told me they carried extra spars. Tears smarted in my eyes for Karl, and I blinked them away.

I watched the tight-lipped Captain. I dared not speak yet—to reason, argue, plead. I pressed my lips together to keep from crying out, from explaining. I dared not risk making him angrier than he already was.

So I just sat there, heart aching for Karl. The pitching of The Hague had lessened. I no longer had to hold on so tightly. But the storm of grief for Karl grew. I remembered his kindness, his clumsy gentleness, the love of which he had spoken. And regretted with all my being that I'd been unable to return that love.

Abruptly, without the formality of a knock, the cabin door burst open. A seaman, clothes streaming, shouted, "Pirates! Two ships of 'em!"

Chapter 9

"On deck with you!" snapped Roger. "Tell Vannice to meet me on the gundeck!"

As the seaman left, Roger grabbed a dry coat and literally threw it on, barking orders at me. "You stay in this cabin! Get bandages ready . . . tear up towels . . . sheets . . . anything white!"

"I won't! I won't stay here while you . . ."

"You'll damn well do what you're ordered to do!" He thrust a pistol into his waistband, yanked his musket out of a cabinet. "I'll have no woman on deck!"

"I'm a crewman! It's my right to defend this ship! It's my duty! I'll not toy with bandages while our men are being killed . . . while . . . !"

"It's my order, damn you!"

"I'm trained as a man! I can use any hand weapon!"

He was thrusting a second pistol into his waistband.

I tried for it, and he slapped my hand away so hard it went numb.

"When you can help . . . with the wounded . . . I'll send for you!"

I flew at him again, trying for the pistol. "Give it to me!" I screamed. "I'm not going up there unarmed!"

He pushed me so hard I reeled backward, past the

table, and fell onto the berth. I was up and going for him as he reached the door. I saw what he was doing —jerking the key out of the lock—and knew what he'd do next. So, the treacherous, swaying cabin to the contrary, I ran at him.

And lost my footing and fell.

And heard the key turn outside.

I fell against the door, beat my fists on it, screamed his name. I demanded that he unlock the door and let me out this instant.

The pitch and rock of the cabin was the only reply. He was gone, up the companionhead, onto the gundeck. He was at his captain's post, ordering his vessel made ready to withstand attack, making sure his gunners were in place, his musketeers at the ready, checking to see that every man had pistol and knife.

All but me. I, who had been trained in marksmanship, sparring, fencing, the use of knives! I, who could fight as well as any man, was locked into a cabin simply because that arrogant captain had discovered that I was a woman!

I had to get out of here, take my place with the men. Though I knew it was useless, I threw myself against the door. It didn't even strain with my assault. I leaned against it, mind racing.

Now sounded a low boom from beyond *The Hague*. Shouts came from the decks. I knew what was happening, for Karl had explained the way of privateers. One cannon shot had crossed our bow from one of the attacking vessels, a warning that we were to be boarded and there'd be no bloodshed if we surrendered.

I listened, trembling with suspense and frustration. Another cannon boomed, this one from our ship, telling the privateers we would fight to the last man.

Frantic to get out, I examined the hinges of the door. They were iron, solid, and the pin was so snugly fitted I couldn't detect any space no matter how searchingly I ran my finger around it.

Another cannon shot came from beyond us; there

was no impact. Probably the second privateer sending her own warning shot. *The Hague* returned this shot promptly. The next shot struck us at least a glancing blow, for *The Hague* shuddered and rocked. Then there followed a salvo of musket fire both from our decks and the attackers'.

I half-ran, half-fell to Roger's desk, opened it, got the thinly-bladed knife he used for opening things. With this I returned to the door, sat on the deck, and set to work on the bottom hinge. I tried to insert the point of the blade; it slipped. Tried again, and again it slipped.

Muted musket fire, shouts, the boom of our big guns filled my ears as I worked doggedly at the hinge. The handle of the knife rubbed against my rope-burned palm. I kept on.

It was no use. There was no getting the pin out. And even if I did, there was nothing to stand on to reach the top hinge because everything was bolted to the deck. And suppose I did unbolt a chair—I'd have to bolt it in place at the door, and there was no tool with which to do so. Besides, it would all take too much time. I had to get out *now*.

A key! my mind screamed. Oh, you fool! I dropped the knife.

Sounds of fighting grew as I sped about, looking for the spare key Roger must have somewhere. I searched his desk. There was a key, and I want stumbling to the door with it. The key didn't work. I flung it away and ran to the cabinets. I looked in every drawer, disarranging the neatly stacked garments, finding nothing, my suspense and anxiety at a peak.

I had no idea of how things were going topside, didn't know whether the shooting was from vessel to vessel or if the pirates were rowing their longboats at us from two directions, and the shooting was between them and *The Hague*. I didn't know if our men could kill the pirates as they boarded, or—I didn't know anything, except that our ship was under attack and I was locked into the cabin of a stubborn, overbearing Captain whom I hated with every inch of my being.

I yanked open still another drawer. And there, in plain sight, I found another key. And this was the right key. It slid into the lock, turned as though oiled, and I opened the door.

Coatless, I shot into the passageway. It was jammed with crewmen making for the decks, loaded with weapons. I lunged up the companionhead in the crush, aware that the time I'd been locked up had been much shorter than I'd thought. The men scattered, some making for the top deck, others running for the cannons. A few hung up lanterns to lessen the gloom resulting from the hurricane.

I stood just outside the companionhead, rain drenching my fresh clothes. I could see only vaguely in the dusky light and the occasional brief flares of lightning. I looked frantically about for Roger. It was at his side I must fight. No matter how angry he was at me, or how much I hated him, my first loyalty was to him, and nothing, no pirate, no musket nor cutlass was going to stop me.

Unable to locate him on the gundeck, I climbed to the topdeck. I saw evidences of his speed and efficiency everywhere. Our crew had worked swiftly, were still at it, preparing *The Hague* for battle even as battle raged. From the hold came heavy cloth wrappings, which were quickly draped and hung over bulwarks, fife rails, and all wooden sections. The light sails, which had been lowered during the storm, had been replaced by heavier rain-soaked canvas which would prevent fire, should the sun come out hot and blazing. The running rigging was doubled, and some of the standing rigging was replaced by chains to hold against flying shot. Extra tiller ropes of rawhide were put near the helm; oakum plugs were lined along the rail, ready to fill shot holes in the hull. Blankets were spread and hung over the powder magazines.

Extra muskets, pistols, cutlasses, and pikes were stacked near all the battle stations. The grenades, square bottles filled with powder and pistol shot, were ready, as were the stinkpots, jars full of sulphur to be lit and tossed onto enemy decks. Along the rail, too, Vannice was presently placing the culverins, which were broad-muzzled blunderbusses loaded with spikes, nails, and pieces of glass.

I kept watching for a knife among the weapons, berating myself for the one I'd left in the cabin. But first I had to locate Roger.

The wind had dropped to a breeze, but it was strong enough to fill our sails. Maybe Roger planned to make a run for it, outdistance the privateers, save his cargo and his vessel. But he wasn't at the helm. I looked everywhere among the men finishing preparations and the musketeers firing over the rail. Finally, when I returned to the gundeck, I spotted him at one section of guns, and went directly to him. He shot a look at me as he turned to the gunners, barking out orders.

The enemy cannon boomed. *The Hague* gave a long, shuddering lurch. The spars swung, creaked, and sails flapped so violently they could be heard on the gundeck.

Roger chopped down his hand in signal. Our cannons let out a broadside. But the pirates were now on us with longboats. They came swarming aboard, overflowing the gundeck, onslaughts of them, crouching low, racing for the topside. Our men were firing musket and pistol, taking fast aim, reloading. Some pirates, armed with pistols, returned the fire. Others had muskets and some had cutlasses and knives.

Roger was firing steadily, first musket, then pistol, reloading. I would have reloaded for him, but he shoved me aside. I stayed right there near him, ready to be of use.

Men fell, enemy and crew alike. The pirates were throwing themselves bodily, knives out, onto our men who returned blow for blow. At one split second, Roger and I glimpsed a pirate who had just driven his knife into the back of one of our gunners. Together, we bore down on the pirate, and I helped to hold him, while

Roger dispatched him with his knife. I tried to claim the knife from the body of the man the pirate had killed, for I was still unarmed and of little use. But Roger pushed me away. "Little fool!" he growled. Whirling, he gave the gunners the signal for another broadside.

As ours thundered out, another broadside from one of the privateers sounded, throwing its deadly balls of lead. We suffered no direct hit, thank God. I wondered then, in the fear and blur of battle, why the privateer would fire on us when her own men were on board.

The privateers must be firing short, to terrify and cow us. They had no intention of killing their own men.

"Reload!" shouted Roger. "Fire!"

The cannons drew back, belched and roared. There was an answering broadside, closer this time. Deck fighting continued, fiercer, bloodier. Blood spurted, flowed, mixed with the ever-present rain.

Roger was facing the gunners now, and I moved to stand behind him, shielding his body with my own. He could deal with any pirate he could see; now, if one tried to run him through or shoot him in the back, the missile would have to pass through me first. He was on the alert, pistol in one hand, knife in the other. He turned from the gunners every second, ready for any pirate. But it would take only one unguarded second for him to die.

The deck was a bedlam of belching, smoking cannons, of musket clatter, slicing cutlasses, flashing blades. Wounded men screamed, their throats or bellies slit, their stiffening faces twisted and their eyes bulging. The smell of blood and smoke filled me, and the deck ran rivers of blood.

Overhead, on the top deck, the same murderous struggle, the same screams and musket-clatter, made a lid of tumultuous noise that clamped down over the clamor here, intensifying it. I saw a crewman try to get to his knees; a pirate buried a knife in his throat, yanked it out and whirled straight for another of our men who fell, his blood mingling with that of the others.

The first crewman's knife lay just beyond me. Careful of balance, I scurried the two steps, grabbed the weapon and, ears throbbing with noise, death, and fear, sped back to Roger, armed at last. I held the knife at the ready, on the watch for any attack on my captain.

Everywhere were dead and dying men. The pirates kept boarding us by the dozen, and still we fought. Our cannons spoke, but the pirates came without end, flowing onto our ship like a river in flood. Our own numbers were dwindling, each man fighting up to his last agonized moment.

Repeatedly, I was knocked to the deck. Once a pirate came at me with his knife and I drove my own into his heart before he could touch me. He fell at my feet. I gave him one numb glance; I didn't want to kill; this was the first life I'd ever taken. But Roger must be protected. On Roger's skill, on his wits, depended all the lives of our remaining crew. I gripped my knife, driving it into more than one pirate, and I stabbed and wounded, not knowing whether I killed. Fear was lost as the exhilaration of battle was born. An excitement in me, a frenzy, spiced with the glory that I was fighting shoulder to shoulder with Roger.

All at once, a huge pirate came at Roger from behind. I sprang to shield my captain, but I slipped and fell to the bloody deck. I scrambled up, knife ready. The fellow came hurtling, swept me aside, knife going for Roger's back. Gripping my own knife with both hands, I drove for his chest, but the blade sliced across his arm, deflecting his aim and the knife went upward, piercing Roger, as he whirled, near the eye. Sobbing, enraged, before the beast could again draw back his arm, I drove my knife into his shoulder, felt the impact in my whole body as the tip struck bone. My enemy bellowed, got my hand, flung me away so violently that I was thrown nearly across the bloody deck.

I made it to my feet, stumbled toward Roger. Even as I struggled through the clash of straining, fighting men, the noise of hell in my ears, I saw Roger wipe the blood from his eyes and swing his knife up. The pirate, my knife protruding from his shoulder, dodged Roger's stab and plunged his own blade at Roger's chest. In a continuing motion, he yanked the blade out and drew back his arm, his aim now straight for the heart. Roger was still on his feet, knife ready, blood glistening on his coat.

I dove for the pirate's knees, throwing him off-balance and then lunging forward to grab the knife. I gripped his hand, tried to wrest the thing from him. Instantaneously, another blade flashed, passing my face by not more than an inch, and buried itself in the pirate's back.

I managed to get to my knees, and look up. There was Vannice, now catching Roger in his arms, lowering him to the deck. He eased off Roger's sodden coat, tore off his own coat and his shirt as well. I snatched the dripping white garment, tore open Roger's shirt and wiped his bleeding chest.

"He's dead!" I cried.

I couldn't bear it for him to be dead. I couldn't bear to have failed him, to be without him.

But Vannice held his fingers to the Captain's throat. "Not dead, boy. But bad hurt. Keep sopping that blood. This fight will soon end and . . . The pirates've got us bested. Never seen such a band of cutthroats. Watch what you're doing, boy! You hampered the Captain being underfoot and him with a battle on his hands. Now at least wipe up that blood fast as it comes."

"W-what will they do to him?"

"The pirates? Nothing. Not now."

"Their captains?"

"Their captains will see that our captain gets proper, decent handling. I'm going to see to that."

"But why will they . . . why should they? The pirate captains are thieves . . . killers . . . all of them!"

"Shut your mouth, boy. I know captains, be they pirate or otherwise. I'm surrendering *The Hague* and all cargo to these fellows."

"You can't surrender! You're not the Captain! Only the Captain has that right!"

"I've got it now, boy. Understand that. It's my right and duty as mate, with my captain too bad hurt to take command . . . unconscious now and only the devil knows how much longer . . . and it being necessary that somebody take command, to surrender. Under terms. Or just give up, which Captain Courtney would never do. I'm going to deal with those fellows. When we get the Captain back to life enough so that he can talk, him and the pirates, they'll make their bargain. So you keep your mouth shut. And don't go telling you saved Captain Courtney's life. All you done was throw the pirate off balance. It was my knife that killed him. Don't you try to claim the glory."

"I won't," I murmured, desperately sopping blood. Would it never cease? What did I care about who had "saved" Roger as long as he was alive?

Chapter 10

Vannice left us. I hovered over Roger, shielding him, wiping blood. He was still breathing, but I was afraid. The breathing seemed to increase the bleeding. I was lost in a haze of fear for him, of all his precious blood flowing, robbing him of life.

Dimly I sensed that the din of battle had lessened. The cannons no longer boomed, nor did the muskets clatter. Then came a time when no man shouted; the only sounds were agonized groans. Then I knew the battle had ended. Even the breeze had dropped to a gentle, raining brush of air, and the vessel no longer pitched, but rode the big swells easily.

After an eternity, Vannice was back.

"This is him, Captain Fox," he said to a pirate who towered above him.

"Not dead, is he?" roared Fox.

"Not him, Captain! He's a tough one, Captain Courtney is!"

I glanced up again, stared briefly.

The pirate Captain was tremendous, taller than any man I'd ever seen, and broader. He had a big black beard, which was plastered wetly to his face, and beady black eyes, which glittered. His black hair, reaching beyond his shoulders, was running with rain. His full shirt clung to his great torso, as did his full-cut breeches. Around his waist was a rain-darkened red sash, the ends of which fell below his knees. On his feet were leather boots whose wide cuffs, half the height of the boots, rose almost to his breeches. In one hand he held a cutlass; its blade was gory. On his face, as he glared down at Roger, was an expression of murderous triumph.

He fastened his attention on Vannice. "As mate, do ye surrender this vessel and all her goods an' men to me and Cap'n Mixer of the privateer *Rover?*" he demanded in a bellow.

I looked quickly at Roger, but he was still unconscious.

"Aye, sir," Vannice said. "That I do, with full right, in the name of Captain Courtney."

"And yer decision," Fox bellowed on, "is to have yer own crew . . . what's left . . . kilt? And yer ship took over by men from *Crossbones* and *Rover?* Or is it to git yer crew's help and run *The Hague* with us, as a privateer?"

"I speak for the crew. Any man of them, including myself, chooses life and piracy to death."

"What about him?" shouted Fox. He nudged Roger's arm roughly with his boot.

I gasped, tried to push his boot away, but he stood there, solid.

"He wants money as much as the next man," Vannice said. "He told me he signed on as Captain of this vessel because he stood to make a commission besides wages. One thing, Captain Fox."

"Speak out!"

"With our crew running *The Hague* . . ."

"If we've not kilt so many we have to put men from the other vessels aboard to fill out. We dump all dead overboard, yours and ours both."

"Regardless. I can speak for my crew and captain. They'll enter piracy; they'll join *Crossbones* and *Rover*. But our men'll want our own captain."

"If he's of the mind. If he lives."

"I can vouch for both things," Vannice said grimly.

Fox glared at Vannice, who met his eyes unflinchingly, then nodded. "We'll let it stand that way, for the time being," he said.

With that settled, Vannice insisted that Roger be taken to his cabin. Fox roared and four burly pirates came running.

"Take him below," Fox commanded. "Put him in his cabin. Out of the way!" he yelled, booting me, the toe of his boot slamming into my scraped ribs, knocking my breath away.

Two pirates lifted Roger, one at his shoulders, the other at his feet. Vannice led the way. I followed, trying to keep the shirt-bandage over Roger's chest wound, heedless of my own shoulder wound from the hurricane, which had begun to bleed again.

Fox roared for me to get away or he'd throw me overboard, so I had to fall back. I prayed wildly, convinced that if Roger weren't already dead, he'd never be able to survive this rough handling.

But he did survive. He was breathing when they dropped him onto the berth and stomped away. I knelt beside him, hastily pulling my wet shirt loose so it wouldn't mould my breasts, then lifted a wet and bloodied lock of hair off his head wound. He was so hot that his skin, even rain-drenched, seemed to burn my fingers. My breath snagged.

"He's burning!" I told Vannice.

He laid a hand on Roger's brow.

I hurried to the cabinet, got clean towels, ran back. I cleaned away the blood from his forehead, revealing a long, rather deep gash which ran from the hairline to an eyebrow. Then I tried to stop that blood from his chest . . . and couldn't.

"We've got to get his clothes off," I said.

I was already sitting on the edge of the berth and now put my hands under Roger's shoulders and heaved him up while Vannice stripped off his shirt. He groaned as I lowered him to the pillow and began, with a fresh towel, to clean the flowing blood away from the wound.

He opened his eyes and looked at me, but I knew that he didn't recognize me, he didn't know me at all. I rested my hand on the clear portion of his brow. He tried to speak, but no words came and his eyes filled with anguish.

"It's all right," I whispered. "You're going to be all right. The ship's going to be all right."

I bent over him, wiped away the blood welling from his chest. There was blood in that cross of auburn hair, and I washed that away. There was not only the stab wound, but a cut near his shoulder about three inches in length.

"Boots and breeches off now," Vannice said.

I nodded.

Roger cried out as Vannice began to pull on one of the boots. He flung his arm wildly, hitting me across the face, knocking me off the berth.

"Hold him down, damn you!"

Secretly yanking my shirt away from my breasts again, I sat on the edge of the berth, put my hands on Roger's shoulders and bore down as hard as I dared as Vannice tugged at the boot. Roger fought wildly, trying to knock me away, but before the second boot was off, he had fainted.

When Roger finally was stripped, I wet a cloth in water Vannice had ordered brought, and bathed and dried him. I had to work fast, tending the chest wound all the while. Through all of this, he showed no reaction. I kept blotting blood, cleaned the cut at his shoulder and the one above his eyebrow. These weren't too serious; it was the deep stab in his chest where lay the danger. There was no way to tell what the blade had done deep inside. I sopped the wound, bathed it, glancing now and than at the strong, unconscious face, willing him to live.

Vannice watched, helped when he could.

Finally, I bound the chest wound, then covered Roger with a blanket.

"This all you're going to do for him?" Vannice demanded.

"I don't know anything else to do, sir. Except to keep him clean, try to bring his fever down, feed him."

"You don't know some poultice?"

"No, I don't," I said, so worried that I kept impatience out of my voice because it would require energy I didn't have to spare. "Bleeding washes out a wound. I've heard that said by a doctor."

"Well. Keep him clean. I'll be back when I can."

After Vannice left, I sat on the berth gazing at Roger, stroking his arm, certain that even in his black unconsciousness, he would know that someone was looking after him, willing him to live. He lay very still, his labored breathing the only sign that he really lived.

Still watching him every second, I took off my own wet clothes, toweled myself, bandaged my shoulder, slipped on one of his robes and began to search for men's clothing I could wear. I'd been lucky that Vannice's entire attention had been on Roger and that he hadn't noticed my shirt occasionally clinging to my body.

At the bottom of a drawer, I found a pair of heavy breeches and a plain blue shirt, better than the garb the crewmen wore, but not so unlike it as to be outstanding. I put the garments on. They were much too big, but I managed. I retained my wet footwear; there'd be no substitute for that.

I sat on the berth, watching over Roger. The wounds were scarcely bleeding now. Sitting thus, trembling, watching that unconscious face, not knowing whether he was going to live or die, a new feeling rose in me. And it was then I knew that I was in love with Roger Courtney and hadn't even suspected it.

Now I realized that I'd been drawn to him from the first. Had I known it then, I should have told myself that it was the same attraction I felt for Karl when we were together in the hold.

When does attraction become love? I wondered. For I did love this man. Just sitting beside him, even in this desperate situation, made me glow. And this feeling ached and tormented me with guilt. How could I feel so filled with a sweetness I could scarcely contain, while he was so near to death? So this, was love —this shaking, hurting, frightening, sweet misery! This was what woman gave her man—gave in tenderness as now; gave in passion when the man was strong and well!

Fact crushed my brief glory. I glanced at the breeches I wore. Before the world I was a lad, a cabin boy. Such a man as Lord Roger Courtney would never love a girl who masqueraded as a man. Oh, how I hated that deception, now more than ever, because already it had made this man turn from me in disgust and anger.

He moaned, flung out both arms, kicked at the blanket, made the bandage slide off his wound. Tenderly, I replaced it, drew the blanket up enough to cover his manhood, my eyes lingering on it, on his perfect body, on the wonderful, unique cross of hair. He lay quiet.

The cabin was stuffy and smelled of blood. I went

to the porthole to let in the fresh air. The timbers groaned, rain was still falling, a mere patter now, and the breeze had strengthened. The ship was at anchor, riding the swell.

"Genevieve," Roger said weakly, "where are you?"

I stared, stricken. His head was rolling back and forth on the pillow. His eyes were closed.

I took his hands. They clung to mine, and he began to mutter in delirium. " . . . must get . . . money . . . Genevieve . . . thousands . . . pounds . . . they borrowed . . . save the estate . . . wait for me . . . do anything . . . money . . ."

Tears crept down my cheeks. "Yes, darling," I murmured, "everything's going to be all right. I'll wait." My heart quivered; my tears increased. I had found love only to learn I had no right to it. If he heard me at all, he believed I was another girl, Genevieve in England, not myself. But who was I? Only the cabin boy at whom he was so angry.

Hours passed. Vannice looked in twice. I alternated between Roger's wounds, and speaking to him in his delirium, playing the role of Genevieve. Always he muttered the same things: " . . . debt . . . money . . . Genevieve . . . wait . . ." I promised to wait, hating the unknown girl about whom he raved, aware that even if I'd been able to meet him in my true womanly self, his heart was already taken. This was the bitterest thought of all.

I started to cry again. Suddenly anger took me, and I dashed away the tears. Even now, if I could throw away mens' clothing and dress as a woman, I'd give that Genevieve something to worry about! Love would endow me with such beauty and I'd display such warmth and tenderness that Roger, whom Genevieve had permitted to sail away, would be drawn to me despite himself!

Eventually he slept without muttering. Then, near dawn, he began again. He also began to sweat heavily, and this I bathed away. He tossed, his face twisted, and I stroked it, whispering tenderly, trying to calm him. He quieted, and I drew a quivering breath. Maybe now he'd fall into restful, healing sleep.

Instead, he sat abruptly erect, towels falling, eyes open and unknowing. He grabbed my arm so hard that I flinched.

"Got you . . . damned pirate!"

"I'm not a pirate! I'm . . ."

"You boarded . . . saw you . . . and the others . . . took my ship . . . ! But you I'll kill . . . have . . . that . . . satisfaction . . ."

His manic eyes were full of hatred, and he grabbed my shoulder, right on the wound, hurting me, and he shook me. I saw, too, he was bleeding again. "Roger!" I screamed. "You've got to . . ."

"Kill you . . . pirates . . . money . . . title . . ."

I struggled with him. He was delirious, had no idea of what he was saying or who I was. I was hurt and frightened. He'd been so weak before but now he was filled with the strength of two men. Suddenly his hand shot up and he began to choke me. I tried to scream and he pressed harder, shouting viciously, and I thought he was really going to kill me. Blood thundered in my ears, and I could no longer see his face. Finally I gave a strong twist, tore free. His effort had opened the chest wound and blood was seeping out.

I backed away. From across the cabin he stared at me in amazement. He became aware of the bleeding, frowned, looked at me again.

"Red! What happened?"

"You were . . . delirious."

He stared at my neck, which I knew was marked. Quickly I buttoned the shirt to hide it.

"I choked you? Yes I did. Because you were a pirate, not honest even about that, a woman . . . I should have finished the job." Though his voice was gentle as a kiss, I knew that he still had no idea of what he was saying.

As abruptly as he'd sat up, he fell back, unconscious. I bathed, bandaged his chest securely this time, pulled the blanket to his waist. I touched that cross of hair. I lay beside him, ready to meet his every need. His head moved, touched my own bandaged shoulder, was still. From his breathing, I could tell he was in a normal sleep. I stroked his arm, touched the muscles of his side. I lay tasting every moment, knowing I might never again feel him against me, would not be able to put my hand on his hair and caress his cheek.

He slept quietly. Morning came. As first dawn showed, I carefully got off the berth so he'd not rouse and find me there.

On his back, naked because he'd kicked off the blanket, he slept. I adjusted my clothes, made certain the shirt's folds really concealed my breasts.

I lifted the towel off his brow. The wound was open and clean. Fresh air and sunlight would heal it. I unbound his chest and found that those wounds, too, were clean and not inflamed.

It was then that Vannice knocked and entered. Roger opened his eyes. He was aware, and—thank God—he was in his own mind!

"What happened?" he demanded of the mate.

Standing at the foot of the berth, Vannice told all. He related how he had taken the authority to surrender to the pirates. "Our crew votes to turn pirate," he continued. "They vote for you to captain us. We lost fifteen men. It was Fox and Mixer—*Crossbones* and *Rover*—boarded us. I made the deal with them, pending your agreement. It was that or lose our ship and all hands aboard killed."

Roger pondered. He frowned.

"There's money in privateering," he said.

"Aye, sir."

"More than in a merchant ship."

"Aye, sir. True."

"Privateering's the dirtiest, most dangerous business of our times," Roger said. He pondered. When he spoke again, it was with decision. "So. We turn privateer and make our fortunes. Tell Fox and Mixer I agree. See to it that a new spar is put up to replace the one we lost in the hurricane and do whatever else is needed. Tell Downer that Red'll be there to prepare my breakfast."

He was hungry! That meant he was getting better!

"Aye, sir," Vannice replied and departed.

Roger looked at me. "How did you get out?"

"I found the other key."

"Why did you fight . . . keep getting in the way?"

"I'm a crewman. I was protecting my captain."

He managed a weak, angry glare. "Don't be afraid," he said curtly. "I can't turn you over to the law in port now whatever you are, man or woman, honest or criminal. I'm a pirate, and so are you."

"Aye, sir."

"I'll be over this . . ." he gestured at his bandages —"in no time. As to you. From now on, you'll sleep in this cabin."

"B-but why? I'm supposed to sleep in the crew quarters."

"And have one of them find out you're a woman? This isn't for the protection of your precious virginity, understand. It's because pirates are a superstitious lot and think it's bad luck to have a woman aboard. It's so I can run a tight ship."

Chapter 11

After *The Hague's* repairs were begun, *Crossbones* and *Rover* stood by, and made repairs of their own. Fox and Mixer came to verify Vannice's actions, and it was decided to name Roger's vessel *The Skull*. The other captains knew of a merchantman laden with silk, and were impatient to get our convoy of three in shape to pursue and take that booty.

I nursed Roger, cooked for him, delighting in the fact that he ate everything I prepared. He stated openly that food gave him strength, so I had to do no coaxing. Also, it seemed that the loss of blood he'd suffered had truly washed out any infection for, aside from just a bit of redness, the wounds gave no undue trouble. The one on his brow was going to leave a scar, but even this the sun would dim.

He treated me exactly as if I were a man. He ordered me to get poor Karl's new clothes and wear them, which I did. I believed that, when he regained his strength, he'd take me as the others had done, ravish me in his own fashion. I found myself both awaiting the moment and sadly dreading it, the mixed feelings warring in me because I loved him so.

When I climbed to the upper berth at night, fully clad, he paid no attention to me. One day he said he'd never before permitted a cabin boy to use that berth.

I waited, increasingly confused and tremulous. He was stronger now. Surely his man's hunger would tempt him and he'd take me. I looked forward to this nightly, only half-ashamed because, to be in his arms, to comfort his desire, would be an expression of my love. Maybe it was the wounds. When they were completely healed—I tended them, amazed at how fast they healed.

Vannice came twice a day. He reported that the twelve pirates assigned *The Skull* from the other vessels were handy fellows. Friendly, too, fitting right in. "Even if they are cutthroats," he finished, under his breath.

"We're cutthroats ourselves now," Roger said.

"Not you, sir."

"Myself included. I'm in it for the money. I'll do what I have to do. However, I mean to arrange with Fox and Mixer to take our booty with less gore than we had aboard this ship."

"I don't know how you can influence them, sir. Besides, we fought back."

"Some will, of course. But I mean to persuade Fox

and Mixer that we'll take more prizes with planning and strategem than with sheer force."

When Vannice left, I ventured a question. "How can you keep those pirates from brute force? They like to kill, to smell blood, to . . ." I shuddered.

"Don't be squeamish. If there's anything I can't endure, it's a swooning woman."

"You forget I'm not a woman now!" I flared. "I'm a seaman! I didn't swoon when we fought those killers! I've never swooned in my life!"

He gave me a straight look, and I glared. Oh, how I hated him in that moment! Oh how I yearned to dress as the woman I was! I longed with passion to live what I was—vital, vibrant woman—but could not. And all at this time because of Roger Courtney, on whom I was dependent for my very existence.

My anger wouldn't be denied. "You *like* being a pirate!" I accused.

"I appreciate the advantages, certainly. I would have begun as a privateer if I'd had the funds to buy my own vessel. It's not too difficult to be commissioned by the government to go out against enemy vessels, easier still to take a merchantman now and again and enrich yourself. Now that circumstances have given me a vessel, I'll get the money I need faster."

"That's stealing!"

"Not at all. Privateering is legal. We sail into port and sell our booty. Necessity in the form of Fox and Mixer . . . force me into privateering, but I'm not sorry. A successful privateer is to be respected, for he follows a dangerous life. He survives many battles such as the one we survived."

The day he was well enough to go on deck was one of rejoicing among the crew. There were fifty-five of our original crew alive, and every one of them was eager for the new life.

We sailed in convoy one morning at dawn. I wanted to go on deck, learn to be an able seaman, but Roger forbade it. He ordered me to stay in the cabin, cut up a sheet and make myself some breast-binders, though he didn't call them that. What he said was, "Make something to flatten yourself with."

"You can't even go on deck this way," he added. "The wind would press that shirt against you and every one of them would see the truth."

His eyes were on my shirt. They probed until it seemed they were tracing the curve of my breasts, including my hardening nipples. The white line stood around his lips. He was angry because I was a woman and a bother. I'd loved him more each day, waited for a sign of tenderness from him each night. All I meant to him was an obstacle to be dealt with, an interruption in his new career.

"Put my sheets on the upper berth," he said from the door. "And yours on the lower."

"But why? I've been sleeping in the upper . . ."

"With the ship at anchor. Now, in rough seas, you can fall out."

"I slept in an upper with the crew! The ship wasn't at anchor then!"

"Don't argue, you little spitfire! I'm not going to have you break your leg or some other female thing. Then the truth would be out. I could even have a mutiny on my hands, three ship loads of it!"

He slammed out before I could say another word. I knew he was right, but did he have to be so bossy? What was wrong with me, that I had to fall in love with a lord-turned-pirate who was determined to make me pass myself off as a man? Even with him, in private. He'd seen me half-naked. He was a strong man, filled with masculine needs. Why hadn't he taken me as the others had done? Even Karl, my only friend, had done so. And why did I, a decent girl at heart, keep wanting him to hold and touch me? Did he treat me so because of Genevieve? I seethed. I hated that female, her name, the fact that Roger loved her. I raged that I had no chance against her because he made me live like a man.

Brooding, I made two breast-binders, sponged myself at the wash basin, put one of the things on and fastened it. My instinct was to yank it off, throw both of them out the porthole, put on a shirt and belt it so tightly that my breasts would be unmistakable. Instead, I put on the shirt over the binder.

I spent the day polishing the paneling, cooking Roger's meals, washing his dishes. That night when I returned to the cabin, Roger was working on charts. He glanced up. Inadvertently, I smiled shyly. He scowled.

"Get undressed," he said, "and into your berth."

My pulse lunged. Was he, after all, going to take me? I was all atremble. I couldn't speak, couldn't swallow. Despite his bald order, I was so helplessly in love with him, and this was the first hint of possible interest, that I couldn't even lift my hands to unbutton my shirt.

"Well, Red? What is it? Surely you've undressed before?"

"Not on this vessel. I slept in my clothes."

"So I've noticed."

I got into my berth, started to pull the curtains.

"What in hell are you doing?" he demanded.

"G-getting ready to . . ."

"Don't be a little ass. Behave as the man you're supposed to be. Strip as I do, sleep bare, as I do. It'll help you pass as a man, give you the feel of being man. You don't dare betray yourself."

I stared. Far, wild hope said he might be doing this because he was attracted to me—in spite of Genevieve. I began to unbutton my shirt, fingers unsure. Then I stopped.

"I won't! I refuse!"

"If you don't," he said grimly, "I will."

Boiling, I continued with the shirt. He watched face impassive. I got the thing off, hung it on the chair across the table from him, removed my battered, red-heeled shoes, and my stockings. He didn't miss a thing.

I was still furious, but now at myself. If he meant to take me, I hadn't the strength, or the wish, to resist him. What I wanted, growing weaker on removing each garment, was his arms, the brush of that auburn cross of hair against my breasts, the pulse of his mouth on mine, his body in mine meeting the glory which waited there. I knew I should feel ashamed of these unmaidenly thoughts, but I was no longer a maiden and at this moment would trade my entire future for one night of love with him.

I ventured a look at him. His expression hadn't changed. I unfastened the binder; my breasts sprang out and up, nipples tall. I took off the breeches and was nude. His blue eyes were on my nakedness, wandering the flowing curves of my burning body, lingering on the flaming heart of love between my thighs.

He didn't move; his probing gaze never stopped. Tension sprang up between us. It made me hold myself so erect my knees trembled.

Would he approach me now? He had more right than any of the others, except Karl, who'd had equal right. His lips tightened; the white line appeared, vanished.

"You're very beautiful, cabin boy," he said. His eyes flamed. He reached out, took my hand, pulled me to his chair, to my knees. "You're even lovelier than I suspected." He put one hand on my bare shoulder, where the wound had healed, and with the other pulled the cord from my hair so that it tumbled to my shoulders. "Now. You're all woman, Red."

On my knees, I went into his embrace. His hands slid down my back, over my buttocks, and his head bent to me. Trembling, I waited for his kiss. Before his lips touched mine, he drew away and laughed, soft as breath.

"You're willing to trade your favors for my discretion? Was your crime in London so bad? I hoped you were clean, that circumstances really had gone against you, that you'd give your body to no man for any price!"

"Oh, you beast!" I cried, trying to pull free. "What do I have to say about anything? You can blackmail me, you can r-rape me . . . you don't have to take my wishes into consideration!"

"Quiet!" He pulled me closer. "Do you want Vannice to show up and hear you? Do you want to betray yourself?"

"Maybe I should!" I taunted. "Then you could have me thrown overboard and be rid of me and all the trouble I make!"

He glared down at me, eyes a fierce blue.

"I'd not impose my . . . needs . . . on you if you were the only woman in the world," he said.

I stared. He'd admitted needs!

He smiled in a mocking way and the smile, despite the mocking quality, lit his face with male beauty. "You heard, little Red. However, I have no intention of making love to you tonight." He ignored my stunned look and continued. *"If* the time should come when I seek delight with you, it will be of my own choosing. Now get into your berth. And draw the curtains."

Quick to obey lest he see how hurt I was at his rejection, I scrambled into the berth, drew the curtains, pulled up the cover. He'd never understand, even if he'd let me explain that I loved him, that my disappointment wasn't for the lack of intimacy, but because he held only scorn for me.

I pretended to fall asleep in case he should part the curtains and look in. But I lay awake long after he'd climbed, naked, to the upper berth and himself slept, breathing steadily. And I wept, crushing my face into the pillow, wept bitterly for a love he had spurned.

Chapter 12

He didn't even glance at me next morning. I was fully dressed when he leapt down from his berth, stretched his magnificent, nude body like some great, graceful cat. He strode to a porthole and gazed out on the sun-sparkled, gaily leaping ocean, as I'd done earlier. These waters were in a gentle clime where winter never came, and he'd told me our convoy would make this part of the sea its theatre of operation.

As he looked out the porthole, I moved my eyes over him. His long, smooth muscles were very strong, his belly hard and flat, his shoulders broad, hips slim. That auburn cross of hair was like a jewel. It matched, in color, not only the hair on his head, but that from which rose his manhood, strong and proud even now, untouched by desire.

He turned, hand out for the underdrawers and shirt I had ready for him.

"Thank you, Red. Incidentally, Vannice let slip yesterday that you saved my life."

"W-what do you mean?"

"Oh, from his account, *he* did the saving. But I learned that you tackled the pirate and threw him off balance and Vannice killed him. Thanks. You're due a reward."

"I want no reward!" I snapped. "Keep your money!"

His eyes narrowed. "You *are* a spitfire! Very well. I'll keep my money. About rewards, we'll see."

"If I could be a woman openly. That would . . ."

"You know your life depends on posing as a man.

Otherwise . . ." He gestured. "One of the pirates would see to it you met your end."

I glared, not so much about the costume in which I must continue to masquerade, as the way he'd treated me last night.

When he'd dressed, he told me to polish the brass, to clean and press yesterday's uniform, wash his underdrawers, cook his meals. I was so furious I ached to claw his face.

Now he was punishing me for being a woman. He was forcing me to wear the mens' garb I hated so fiercely on the pretext that superstitious pirates must not know I was a woman. Well, that might be sound, but most of all he wanted to exercise his power over me because I was a trouble to him. I asked again to go on deck and work and again he refused. And I knew that when the convoy attacked a prize, he'd make me stay below, all because I was a woman!

A dozen times, as I worked, I determined to have it out with him; a dozen times gave up the idea. I had no logical arguments; I had no rights. I was a stowaway; I had deceived all aboard into thinking I was a man. Roger had every reason to keep the superstitious crews of three privateers from knowing my true sex. And he wasn't blackmailing me into bed either.

That this should make me so angry was a puzzle. I should admire him for being less animal than the others. Miserably, I wondered if my shameful response to the other men—Sir Cecil, Ryan, Clarke, Karl—had been my woman-self trying to get free of the imprisonment of living as a man.

All day these thoughts troubled me. They might well be true. Yet, the longing I had for Roger went beyond that. This was a woman's true and recognized love. Even to be alone in the cabin with him, no matter how he spoke to me, was a privilege. And, though I lashed out, I would not have given up sharing the cabin with him.

That night after supper he again ordered me to bed.

I wasn't sleepy and wanted no repetition of last night.

"It's my duty," I said, "to help you to bed first."

"I notice you don't call me 'sir' any more," he observed.

"No. You won't let me learn to be a proper crewman. Which I could do and be cabin boy at the same time. I'll call you 'sir' when others are present."

"And now you don't want to follow my orders."

"I've followed your damned orders all day! I've polished and cooked and . . ."

"I don't like for women to swear, Red."

"I'm not a woman . . . I'm 'Red.'"

"What the hell *is* your name?"

"Mary. Mary Read."

"How did you start . . . this?" he demanded, indicating my garb.

The more he talked so, the hotter burned my anger. "It's none of your business! I'm doing your work, I'm wearing these horrible clothes, I'm . . ."

"You're a damned beautiful woman, Mary. On second thought, don't strip. Not just yet."

"I'm not going to strip at all, you lecher!"

A smile touched his lips. "What is a 'lecher,' Mary?"

"A filthy beast who forces a woman to take off her clothes and watches like . . . like an iceberg . . . then makes her sleep naked when she never did it in her life!"

"A 'filthy beast' like me."

"Exactly! Oh, if I could only make you know how I hate you this minute, Roger Courtney!" There! I'd called him Roger to his face again, which infuriated me even more. "And how I despise these breeches . . . how I hate you for forcing me to feel . . . such terrible ways!"

Even as I raged, I loved him. He just stood, calm, looking me over. I fell silent, my fists at my sides to keep from flying at him and raking my nails down his cheeks. Then I winced that I could have such a thought—to mar the perfect man I'd nursed back to health.

Into our silence came a knock. "Bring it in!" Roger called.

Two crewmen carried in a bathtub and put it near the table. Other burly fellows brought in wooden buckets of steaming water and poured them into the tub before they left. Roger went to the door, locked it, turned.

"I always carry a bathtub," he said. "It can't be used often because of the fresh water entailed. Now. Your 'lecher' has a new project for you, Mary Read. Your reward for tumbling that pirate and saving my life."

"I don't know what you're talking about!"

"Beautiful women love to bathe, to keep themselves sweet and clean."

"You . . . you . . ." I sputtered, bewildered.

"Also, at the same time, I'll test myself. See if I can keep my hands off all that beauty. Undress, Mary, and get into that water. The men think it's for me, of course."

"You want *me* to take a bath?" I gasped.

"Surely you don't have an aversion to bathing, Mary. Not after what I just said."

"I have an aversion to being watched! You get out of this cabin!"

"No cabin boy gives his captain orders." He straddled one of the chairs, rested his hateful chin on the back and said, "Take them off. Get into the tub. Do it yourself, or I'll do it."

Weeping unexpectedly and stormily, I undressed as fast as I could. I almost dove into the water, then gave a yelp when it burned me.

"Caution, little one. Don't be so impetuous. You should have tested the water."

Lips clamped, I endured the stinging heat. Gradually I became a bit accustomed to it. To my great satisfaction, the water reached to above my waist, and I'd crossed my arms over my breasts when I gave that yelp.

"Mary. Look at me."

There was amusement in his eyes.

"You forgot your soap and wash cloth. Now you'll have to get out of the tub and fetch them."

"I won't!"

"Very well. I shall be your attendant." He brought the things, resumed his place on the chair. "Now you can bathe. Enjoy it, Mary. It can't happen often, because the crew won't cheerfully cater to my personal demands. If they knew it was for the cabin boy . . ." He shook his head.

I began to bathe, enjoying the feel of sweet-smelling lather. It seemed like years since I'd had a real bath, so many men had used me since, and all I'd been able to manage had been sponge baths, that I grew not to mind, very much, that Roger was watching.

I glanced at him secretly. His mouth was tight, eyes intent. When I asked for it, he poured the extra bucket of hot water into the tub and I leaned back, luxuriating. I even washed my hair.

Finally I realized I didn't have a towel. If I got one for myself, I'd track water over the spotless deck which I'd later have to wipe up, and in Roger's presence. So I asked him, keeping my tone cool but polite, if he'd give me a towel, and, wordlessly, he did.

I dried my hair, then myself and finally wrapped the towel around my body and tucked it in. Roger watched my every move. I watched for a gleam of warmth to come into those blue eyes, yearned for him to take me into his arms so I could lose my fingers in that auburn hair. I longed to feel his tall, strong maleness, for just one smile, to again light his handsome face with beauty.

What he did was turn it away. Was it—oh, was it reluctantly that he turned? My heart went fast; my throat trembled.

He said, "You've got to have heavier breeches and shirts before you come on deck. These . . . if a man looks closely, he sees a curve of hip that can be woman only."

That, then, was his reason for keeping me below! I

was so relieved, so ready to grasp any straw of kindness, that I dropped my towel and got naked into my berth and pulled the covers up almost naturally. He could put himself to bed. I watched as he emptied the tub into the buckets and set everything outside.

"They'll think you did this," he said.

"Umm," I murmured sleepily.

I could scarcely believe this. He'd done my work; he'd spoken kindly. For an instant I thought I must have been dreaming.

"You must have a dress," he said. "You must know how it feels to wear one."

I fell asleep with that offhand remark in my heart. I dreamed of parading before him in silks, velvets, furs. Once, half-waking, it came to me that his watching me naked wasn't lecherous at all. When I was naked, he'd looked at me admiringly, had said I was beautiful. He'd not touched me. One day that wall of ice, for which surely the girl Genevieve was responsible, would crack and he'd be mine.

But next morning, though I dressed early and waited, full of hope, for him to waken, I was dealt a blow. Nothing had changed. He snapped when I asked what he wanted for breakfast, saying he was too busy to eat. He did give me some information, but only so he could order me around.

"We sighted our prize after dark and cut our speed for the night," he said. "We're going to attack now, from three directions. After we take her, we're sailing for Havana with the booty. You're to stay in the cabin until we set sail from Havana. Is that clear?"

"Yes," I replied stiffly. And, after he'd left, whispered, "Darling."

Uneasy, afraid for Roger's life, I stood at the cabin door and listened. He hadn't locked me in today; I was trusted. *The Skull's* speed kept building.

I waited, tense and anxious, for our convoy to attack. It seemed hours went by and still I waited. The time came when I held the door ajar so I could hear better.

At last a cannon shot boomed out from either *Crossbones* or *Rover,* and I knew it crossed the bow of the prize as warning to surrender. Another cannon boomed, this time from *Skull.* I began to shake. This meant that within seconds Roger might be in another horrible, bloody battle, and I was forbidden to be at his side. I was denied the privilege of fighting with him. I almost went running to deck anyhow, but, because he'd trusted me, remained where I was.

There came, eventually, the rattle and clatter of musket fire. This continued for some time. Then it stopped abruptly. There were shouts of men, and then comparative quiet. After a long period of this, I sat on my berth, trying to convince myself that the chances Roger had been wounded, much less killed in so short an engagement, were slim. The prize had been overwhelmed and had surrendered, I assured myself.

Nevertheless, I paced the cabin. Hours passed. The time came when I'd ordinarily be cooking Roger's noon meal. He must be snatching a bite from Downer. Anxiety almost won, and I actually got as far as the steps, then turned back.

I waited just inside the cabin door, listening. Our men were bringing goods aboard, stowing them in the hold. I wondered how they'd find room, since we still carried our original cargo, but they didn't lade much, probably just overflow from *Crossbones* and *Rover.*

By mid-afternoon we were underway, riding the swell, beating along the sea. I wondered how closely we sailed with the others, Havana-bound. I couldn't see either vessel from the portholes.

I thought about Havana. If *Skull* anchored at the dock, I could slip ashore, jump ship. I'd find some kind of work as a man, perhaps as a cook, and labor until I saved enough to make the change-over and live openly as a woman. At that time, with a suitable wardrobe, I'd forge a letter of recommendation as a governess.

But then Roger came back, immaculate, not a hair out of place, and I faltered. How could I run away from him? How could I bear to live in Havana, knowing he was aboard *Skull,* sailing the seas, seeing beautiful women in every port, returning, eventually, to Genevieve? No, my instinct cried, stay with Roger!

"So. You followed my orders for once," he said. "Thank you for that. The operation went smoothly. Two shots across the bow and the captain surrendered after only token resistance. We turned him loose."

"But I thought . . . When they took *The Hague* . . ."

"They wanted her because she's a sloop and fast. A privateer must have speed, so she can overhaul the prize and get away. This merchantman was too slow."

"Then . . . you don't scuttle ships and drown the crew?"

"We're not that bloodthirsty, Mary. If a merchantman wants to go his way when we've finished, why not? He may find himself our prize a second time."

"It's so . . . cold-blooded."

"Privateering is legitimate, remember."

"But *Skull* isn't commissioned!"

"She will be, if I can accomplish it. If not . . ."

"You'll be a common, bloody pirate! Stealing and selling your loot . . ."

"Don't call names, Mary. Go to the galley and eat. And while you're there, reflect. You're a member of *Skull's* crew. You yourself are as bloody a pirate as you say I am. You can't escape it."

I can jump ship! I thought rebelliously. I can get away! But even as I thought this, I knew I could never leave him.

Chapter 13

We dropped anchor outside Havana and boats ferried our cargo ashore. Thus, even if I'd planned to, I couldn't jump ship. I was locked in again, for my own protection according to Roger, but he knew I wanted to see this city and obviously suspected I might escape. He took both keys.

This action gave me hope. If he felt no attraction to me, if I were nothing but trouble to him, why would he refuse to let me go ashore? Why would he lock me in? I was unquestionably a burden to him. If he wanted to be rid of me, he'd give me opportunity to jump ship.

Happily, I looked out the portholes, trying for a glimpse of the tropic city. This was a failure; we were lying so all that met my eye was a vista of sea, dotted to the horizon with vessels.

When at last we sailed, Roger unlocked the door and came in, arms filled with packages. He dumped some onto my berth and tossed others into the upper berth, his expression a mixture of coolness and triumph. From his pocket he drew a velvet box, which he dropped onto the table.

"There!" he exclaimed. "Now you can be a woman! Inside this cabin, with the door locked."

"What are you talking about?" I demanded.

"Open them," he said, gesturing at the packages. "See how they fit."

Confused, I opened a package. When the paper fell away and I saw the blue satin dress, I sucked in my breath.

"Do you like the color . . . the material?" he asked.

I stared at the gorgeous blue, stroked the gleaming satin, the fine lace. I held the gown to myself for size and knew it would fit. "I love it, Roger!" I breathed.

Warmth came onto him. "You'll find what you need to wear with it in the other bundles. Put everything on."

"Now?"

"Immediately. I went to some trouble. I'm impatient to see if I succeeded."

I tore away paper, lifted out undergarments of fine white cambric, daintily embroidered, slim satin slippers which matched the dress, pale silk stockings with clocks up the sides, embroidered in gold thread.

Roger straddled a chair and watched. My face was burning. I'd been right about his keeping me aboard! He felt interest in me, or he wouldn't have made me strip, wouldn't have watched me bathe, wouldn't have bought these costly garments! Surely now—after all, he was a strong, healthy man. He couldn't go forever without a woman.

If once, just once, he'd hold me in his arms! The love I had for him would seep into him. Given that much, I'd win some of his affection and, that accomplished, get him for my own.

Thus hopeful, I got out of sea garb quickly. Then, with leisurely movements, I put on the dainty undergarments, drew on the delicate stockings and the satin slippers.

"Why, Roger!" I exclaimed. "They fit exactly! How in the world . . . ?" Sitting on the edge of my berth, I looked at him in question.

"You have small, narrow feet. I got you some sturdy boots to wear with your pirate gear, too. You can throw the red heels overboard."

I was so excited that, suddenly, I could hardly breath. He'd noticed me even more than I'd dared to hope! He'd observed my very feet so closely he could buy slippers exactly the right size!

Going to the mirror, I used Karl's comb until my hair glistened and fell, springing and curling, to my shoulders. Its redness had never been more dazzling, and the intense blue of the gown would increase the crimson.

I lowered the dress over my head and felt it slide richly down until only the toes of my slippers were visible. The low, square-cut bodice was boned, the tiny waist pointed, the snug elbow-length sleeves ruffled with lace. The stomacher was covered with lace. I pulled the gown together at the back and started to lace it up with the silken blue cord.

"I'll do that," Roger said.

His fingers were on the cord. He was clumsy at first and the clumsiness delighted me, for it told that he wasn't experienced in helping women dress. I didn't want him to be experienced. I wanted to be the first woman, the only one!

"Now," he said. "Move about. Let me see you."

Delighted, I complied, the slippers light as air, the feel of satin and lace delectable, the richly moving skirts, wide with panniers at the sides, graceful. The top skirt was divided in an inverted vee over a petticoat covered with lace.

"It's perfect!" I cried. "I don't see how you . . . !"

"I've studied your body, Mary. I have an eye for size. In the shop they tried to sell me a corset, but I said you didn't need it."

"As you know, I've never worn one of those things!" I laughed. I moved about, showing off my finery. I laughed in joy over the clothes, over the close feeling with Roger, over being alive and a woman for the first time in my life.

"Your hair is like fire with that blue. And your skin is whiter against it."

He'd even noticed my skin! It had grown tanned when I was on deck some, but he'd kept me below so much the tan had faded.

He took the velvet box from the table, opened it, held it out. On white satin lay a strand of gleaming pearls.

"F-for me?" I stammered.

And him with such debts to pay! Spending so much on me! There was genuine kindness in him.

He laid the pearls around my neck, fastened the clasp. He turned me to face him, but immediately dropped his hands from my arms.

He looked me over. "You're a natural beauty," he said.

For some reason his voice was icy.

I could only stare, my own love open for him to read, wondering why he hated me. Almost, I thought, his arms had lifted. And then did not.

His eyes narrowed. "How does it feel to be a woman?" he demanded.

"It makes me wish . . ." I broke off.

He knew what I meant. "You can wear this when we're alone. You can play at being a woman."

If he'd slapped me, he couldn't have hurt me more. Or made me angrier.

"I was going to thank you for being kind!" I said, speaking as icily as he had ever done. I backed up to him. "If you'll trouble yourself to unlace me, I'll put on the clothes I'm supposed to wear. I have no desire to play-act, but it seems that no matter how I dress, I *have* to play-act!"

"As you wish!" he snapped.

I scrambled out of the finery. So angry I scarcely realized I·was naked, I hung the clothes in the cupboard, pulled off the slippers and stockings, put them inside, slammed the door. Clad only in the pearls, which I'd forgotten, I grabbed my sea garb, got into my berth, yanked the curtains shut.

He laughed coldly. Then there was silence.

In the cramped berth, I struggled into my breeches. The vessel climbed a swell and I had to brace myself, breast-binder in one hand. As *Skull* dropped down, I lost my hold and the binder went sliding away across deck. Furious, not only at Roger but at my own carelessness, I streaked out to retrieve the thing. Flaming with hatred of men's clothes after having worn women's dress, angry that now Roger could see me, I neither heard the rap at the door nor saw that he was sitting at the table, back to me. I heard his voice, but not the words.

Too late, I both saw and heard. A voice spoke. It was that of Grider, the seaman I disliked most; it was his roar and no mistake. I looked up. His eyes were riveted on my breasts. I clutched the binder to them.

Roger, alerted by Grider's roar, by the grin on his big mouth, glanced around and saw me too. "Red!" he snapped. "Berth!"

I dived behind the curtains.

"Explain yourself, Grider," Roger said. "Why did you come here?"

"The mate. He sent me, Captain, sir."

"Come in. Shut the door."

"Aye, sir."

"Why did Vannice send you?"

"Downer, sir. He's swearin' an' wantin' Red to do his cookin'."

"He'll be right up. Because it's what I want. Not for Downer's convenience."

"Aye, Captain, sir."

The words were right, but the tone gloated.

I was trembling, fumbling into binder and shirt.

Roger said, "You saw that my cabin boy isn't a male. Keep your mouth shut. Unless you want to walk the plank."

"Aye, sir. I will that."

"If you hear a word from some other crewman, heed this. Your captain doesn't credit the pirate superstition that a woman aboard is bad luck. Fifty-five of our men are new pirates and haven't got that set in mind. Right?"

"Aye, sir. Right."

"The crew we took on from Fox and Mixer may believe that rot."

"Aye, sir."

"As to Red, he . . . mind you, I say *he* . . . isn't a

true woman. He's lived male all his life. He's brought us no ill luck. True or not true?"

"True, Captain, sir."

"Now that he's a good cabin boy, he's to train as an able seaman. With you helping."

"Aye, sir."

"Hear this. If word gets around, I'll know where it came from."

"Aye, sir."

"If the *Crossbones* and *Rover* find out, I'll know the source. It's they you need to fear most . . . they'd land us on some island to starve, and burn *Skull* to the waterline."

Grider swallowed, making a loud sound.

"Red stays."

Silence. Not even a gulping swallow.

"Go now."

"Aye, sir . . . aye, aye!"

The door opened, closed.

I came scuttling out of the berth, furious.

"You didn't even tell him I serve only as your cabin boy! You didn't explain! You said I'm not a true woman!"

"I'm Captain. I explain what I please."

"He'll talk!"

"If he does, I'll deal with him. And others. I blame myself for this, Mary."

"They'll think I'm . . . that you're . . . !"

"Let them think and be damned."

"You don't care that they'll say I'm your . . ."

I couldn't speak the word. Shame, anger, and fear beat in me. Shame that I wanted him to be that of which I accused him, anger that he didn't care about my reputation, fear of the crewmen. Then fury swept me that, so long as his pirates didn't make trouble, they were free to entertain any evil thoughts they wished.

He now took down the packages he'd thrown into the upper berth. "I've bought pirate clothes for you. Two sets. They'll hide your form. Too late for *Skull*, perhaps, but not for the others."

"I hate you!" I cried.

"Shut up, Mary. Stow your pearls in my top drawer. Change clothes."

I undid the clasp, laid the pearls in their box, put it into the drawer. I took the bundles he gave me, got into my berth behind the curtains, and tore away the wrappings. One package held the two sets of clothing —full cut, good blue breeches of heavy cotton, good white shirts with big, gathered sleeves, also of sturdy cotton. The other held two pairs of black stockings and a pair of black, shining leather boots.

I wriggled into one set of clothes, bound the wide blue sash I found around my waist, pulled on the stockings and boots. These fit as perfectly as the blue slippers. This time, instead of being pleased that he knew my size so intimately, I burned with rage. He was the most hateful man alive, showering me with satin and pearls, then telling me to shut up, not defending me to Grider.

Suddenly my lower lip quivered. In my blind anger I'd forgotten him! Roger, the man I loved, the one I'd give my life for, had a real problem on his hands. There was real danger that his crew would soon know I was a woman and make trouble with which he'd have to deal.

When I pushed back my curtains, he was in pirate rig. His breeches were fire-red, as was his shirt, both made full. His wide sash was glossy black with a white skull in front, a replica of the flag our vessel now flew. He wore soft black boots almost to the breeches, and had strapped on personal weapons—cutlass at hip and half a dozen pistols slung on belts crisscrossed on his chest.

He looked like a different man, more handsome, the scar on his brow adding character. He looked dangerous. And he was dangerous. I'd seen him fight. He didn't know what fear was. My heart shrank at the dangers into which he was heading. Boldly, deliberately.

"Now we dress the part," he said.

"I didn't know you were a fop!" I snapped. It was either that or plead with him to somehow, despite the other two ships, make a run for it and give up privateering before he got himself killed.

"Call it what you will," he said. "We've changed the look of the vessel. The crew has dressed the part now. Nobody will recognize us or suspect that we're *The Hague,* missing at sea."

"You're proud of it!" I accused. Maybe I could shame him into giving up piracy and thus save his life.

"Not 'proud,' Mary. Now, get to your duties. I'm so hungry I could eat the mainmast."

"You expect me to stay on in this cabin, with the crew . . ."

"You can't bunk in crew's quarters now. You're Red, woman pirate. You're also to learn to handle a pistol."

"I already know how! I learned that, and fencing . . ."

"Spare me. Just do your work, be ready to use this . . ." He tossed a small pistol on the table—"which I suggest you keep in your waistband at all times."

I snatched up the weapon, found it was loaded, jammed it into my waistband and without another word stormed out of the cabin, along the passage, and into the galley. Downer swore at me, using such filthy words I was convinced he hadn't heard about me. Still, he was such a vile creature he might be more profane simply because he did know about me.

Oh, how I hated all men! I slammed utensils onto the fire, determined to cook Roger the best meal yet.

That he ate what I gave him without comment, enraged me further. We didn't talk all that night. He didn't watch me undress though I stripped as though I were a man, went naked into my berth and pulled the curtains. Now what was he up to? When only he knew my sex, he'd watched me strip. Now, when the entire crew might know, he acted as if he'd lost all interest. I turned and tossed, angry at him, longing for him, worrying over what future trouble I might cause him.

He ate his breakfast in silence.

When he was ready to go on deck, I spoke. "What do I do? Stay in the cabin? Or can I come topside and begin my training?"

"Topside, by all means. We'll do no hiding. Brazen it out."

He'd flung me a challenge. Well, I'd take it up.

I went to mess, and did feel safer in thick pirate garb than I had in Karl's lighter weight clothes. To look at me, none could tell I wasn't a man.

Except that some of them knew. I saw it in sly glances, heard it in guffaws they pretended to smother. There were four of them. Grider had confided in his intimates, of that I was convinced. The others didn't seem to know.

After breakfast, pistol in waistband, I got a wooden bucket, filled it with water, collected soap and scrub brush and went to a spot beside the companionhead where those same four men were scrubbing. I'd face them boldly, show them I wasn't afraid. I rolled up my sleeves, knelt, swished my soap around until I had suds, dipped my brush, began to scour as hard as any of them.

"Look what we got!" jibed one.

They guffawed, and began passing bald remarks.

"Show's Red's a man!" said another.

"One rip of my hand'll show diff'runt!" grunted a third.

"Whut'll it show?" chortled the fourth.

"Whee . . . !" they all mouthed.

"I won't say it loud," muttered the first. "Don't aim to walk no plank into the ocean! Red's fer the Captain!"

One of them dropped his brush, sprang up. "Th' hell with that! Captain, he's busy on th' topdeck! I aim to have me a taste of whut he feeds on!"

I kept on scrubbing, not touching my pistol but

ready to run, gambling that the fellow was all talk. I knew that his name was Crouch, and had thought he looked more like a mean brown bear than a human.

He was coming at me. The others stood. I scrambled to my feet, brush in hand, slipping on the deck I'd just cleaned, the soapy smell rising with me.

Before I could slam my brush into his face, Crouch had me by the arms. He gave one a twist, and my brush went flying. His teeth showed—very wide and yellow, also wide-spaced.

"Let . . . me . . . go!" I gritted, yanking.

He pushed me down the companionhead. I tried for my pistol. One of the others, following, knocked it away. I heard it clatter somewhere.

They shoved me slowly down the steps, a tide of men. No one had seen us, for no one was interfering. I wouldn't scream for help, like a woman.

I tried to crash a fist into Crouch's nose, but he pushed me in a half-turn and dragged me along side-wise. I twisted. He pulled me further. The others trod close behind, cursing in delighted whispers.

The more I fought, the harder Crouch gripped me.

"Lively . . . ain't ye?" he panted.

After the companionhead steps, he yanked me down the steps into the hold. I kicked and slugged. Just inside the hold, I'd fought him almost to a standstill.

The men closed in. They made a wall around me with their bodies; they encircled me, with rough, low exclamations.

"I like a wench with life," said Crouch. "Real sport. If yer a wench dressing' man, pleasurin' any tar can get his hands on . . . ain't no better'n a London whore . . . even if th' Captain has took a fancy to ye."

"He'll kill you!"

"No he won't. 'Cause when we get done . . . if yer a wench . . . an' we got reason to think ye are . . . we'll toss ye overboard come dark . . . an' he'll never know who done it!"

"Can't never prove nothin'!"

"Can't make ever' man walk the plank, neither!"

Almost, I tore free. Then Crouch's bear-like paws crunched harder. He wound his arm around my waist, clamped me. His other hand shot down the front of my shirt, into the binder, clutched a breast. He snorted, the most evil sound I'd ever heard. It held filth, glee, arcane triumph.

They pushed me, fighting desperately, deep into the hold. At last they stopped. I was panting for breath. But so were they.

Crouch still clamped me. I twisted so violently he had to fight even harder to keep his hold. "Still plenty of life! Ain't that nice?"

I kicked up and to the side with all the force I could muster. The heel of my boot crashed into his male part. He yelped, swore, grabbed for his injury.

One of them hurled me to the deck.

I screamed.

What happened then was lightning-fast. A great, beefy hand clapped over my mouth and nose and I not only failed to scream again, but couldn't breathe. I tried to bite, but the hand forced my lips against my teeth so that I was biting my own inner lips.

They waited, panting, listening.

Nothing.

"Hell," said Crouch. "They can't hear nothin'. We'll go to the end of the hold. Where extry supply boxes an' barrels are."

The one with his hand over my face used the other hand to grab my collar, his knuckles boring into my skin, hurting me. Another grabbed my collar, too. They dragged me roughly, though I fought. I was bruising painfully.

I never let up fighting, trying to bite, to scream, to get loose. A new set of hands grabbed my feet and pushed while the men dragging me pulled. Some other hand was on my mouth now. My chest was heavy, bursting. Then everything went black.

Dimly, there was light. There was a lantern. I could breathe, but I couldn't scream, for there was a gag in my mouth, cutting the corners of my lips, the knot digging at the base of my head. I tried to move my feet, my hands. They were bound.

"We got us a fighter," someone muttered. "Grider might of made a mis-take."

"No mis-take." That was Crouch. "He's comin' 'round. I'll show ye."

Slowly my eyes adjusted. I recognized the pirates. Crouch was the only one I knew by name. There was a grizzled one, a black-browed scar-faced one, and last a young fellow, lean as a strap.

"Untie them legs an' arms," Crouch ordered the grizzled man. "An' you," he said to the black-browed one, "ungag our pris'ner of love."

They guffawed, did as Crouch told them.

I caught the full, foul odor of the grizzled man. He was quick; the ropes fell away. The gag was yanked out, cutting my mouth. I almost screamed, in spite of Crouch's threat to kick me.

"Hurry up!" urged the lean fellow. "Show us whut we got!"

Ruthless fingers grabbed the front of my shirt, tore it away. They groaned in delight, and then the hand was ripping off my binder.

"Look at them tits! She wus too purty to be no man! We shoulda knew!" chortled black-brow. "An' sleepin' in with the Captain! He didn't give us no shore leave in Havana, an' I ain't had me a woman sence . . ."

They began to shove at each other, each wanting to be first.

I lunged to my feet. Someone gave me a wrench and I was clamped to the putrid body of the grizzled one. His stink enveloped me. While the others urged him on, he bore me to the deck, began to yank at my breeches. I fought, twisting and writhing.

"Yer to behave, un'nerstand?" he said, foul breath all but choking me. "Don't ye scream, or I'll knife ye an' it won't matter, 'cause we're goin' to throw ye overboard." He gripped my hair, holding my head down viciously. "Answer me, bitch!"

I managed to dip my chin slightly, which was all I could give in the way of a nod. These animals would do what they said. If I endured, I'd have a bare chance to come out of it alive.

My breeches were gone. The grizzled beast was tearing at his own breeches.

I went suddenly, quiveringly taut.

I felt a presence, though I'd not heard any sound except for the pirates. Someone was near, at the edge of the blackest part of the hold, among the barrels.

I listened deeply, sensed a cautious movement, faint as breath, inching nearer.

It was Roger there in the darkness. No one else would steal up so noiselessly. Any pirate would make himself known and demand a turn at me. I had to warn Roger. They'd kill him, too. They'd even mutiny, take over *Skull*. And it was all my fault. Because I'd carelessly let Grider see me in the cabin, I'd put Roger into this ill-fated position.

The foul beast was ramming into me, then was yanked off roughly. Roger's fist crashed into his face, and he pitched to the deck, his head making a loud noise. I shot up to a sitting position.

Roger had whipped out a pistol and was holding it on them. "One step," he said from his teeth, "and I shoot for the heart." He reached out, yanked the pistol from the lean fellow's waistband, dropped it into my hands. "While I reload, Red will shoot for the next heart."

They'd already raised their hands high. Roger prodded the grizzled one to his feet. "Put on your clothes!" he barked.

This the fellow did, and with haste. Roger then herded the four in front of him—with me following—and in this manner marched them to the cabin set aside for prisoners.

At the door, the grizzled one tried to run.

"Keep your pistol on them, Mary!" Roger cried. He thrust his own weapon into his waistband, and darted both hands around the grizzled one's neck in one swift, flowing motion. I kept my pistol trained, unwavering. Roger pressed the pirate's throat with such brutal force the muscles under his full shirt were evident.

The fellow grunted; tears ran out of his eyes. He was like a painting of terror. Roger shook him, choking without let-up. The face turned red above the beard, and the eyes bugged out.

Suddenly Roger threw him into the cabin so hard he fell on his back. Murderously, he shoved the other three inside and locked the door.

"Vannice!" he shouted up the companionhead steps. "Come down here!"

Shaking, I thrust the pistol into my waistband.

Vannice arrived, on the run.

"I've got four bastards locked up here," Roger told him. "Bring Grider and lock him up, too. The charge is insubordination. The first island we sight, set them down on it with supplies to last until some vessel picks them up."

"Aye, sir," Vannice said.

"S-suppose no vessel . . ." I began.

"If you prefer," Roger snapped, "I can make them walk the plank." He took my arm, hustled me away from Vannice, lowered his voice. "They would have killed you. I'm gambling the five are the only ones who know about you. By keeping them locked up until the moment they row themselves away, they can't spread the information. Which means no man aboard, except myself, will know about you."

I nodded, miserable. It was a wonder he didn't put me on an island too, the trouble I'd made for him.

"Come along!" he snapped.

He started along the passage and I followed. At his cabin he opened the door. I was trembling inside, still deeply frightened. The look on his face as he turned was not at all friendly. Although there was no white line around his lips, I knew that he was filled with anger.

"Inside with you!" he snapped.

Chapter 14

I stood against the cabin door, trying to still my inner trembling. Roger looked at me keenly. I couldn't speak. I felt guilty, even though I'd done nothing to lure the men. I knew exactly what Roger was thinking. It would be useless to try to explain how important it had seemed to prove myself a good seaman. Even, to cast doubt in the pirates' minds about my being a woman if Grider had talked.

"You had to flaunt yourself," Roger said.

"That's not true. And you *did* tell me to go on deck."

"Which was wrong. The men aren't entirely to blame. For the present, you're to stay here until I tell you it's safe to come out."

Then, without another word or look, he left.

I felt the drag of the anchor, ran to a porthole. There was full view of a lush, green little island. There were sounds of a boat being lowered. I waited.

Now I could see the boat, with five men in it. They were rowing for the island. One by one I picked out the four who had dragged me to the hold, and I recognized Grider, who had talked.

I watched until they landed. I spied *Crossbones* and *Rover,* beating slowly along beyond us. Roger would have informed Fox and Mixer of insubordination; luckily none of the four was from their vessels originally, so they'd not press Roger for particulars.

I gazed on at the island as *Skull* again set sail. The five who had been isolated in the midst of the ocean stood looking toward the vessel. In spite of what they'd almost done to me, I felt a pang of sympathy and said a little prayer that, very soon, they would be taken aboard another ship.

When the island was only a dot, hardly visible, Roger came into the cabin.

"Do you really think they'll be rescued?" I asked.

"Undoubtedly. There's no reason for you to worry about them. You're fortunate they didn't kill you and throw you to the sharks. I'm satisfied none of the crew knows about you. Which means they don't know those fellows were bold enough to take the Captain's woman."

"But I'm not . . ."

"You make a lovely boy in pirate garb. Take it off."

I stared, astonished at his order.

That line appeared around his mouth, and the blue eyes deepened in color, filled with a relentlessness that swept me with misgiving.

"What . . . are you going to do?" I whispered.

"What I've seen you wanting me to do. A man can put himself through only so much to prove to himself that he can resist. Take off the clothes."

"Roger, not this way! Oh, please! Not like a . . ."

"Do you want me to do it?"

I unbuttoned the shirt and removed it, pulled off boots, stockings, breeches. He watched. My hands shook. I took off the underdrawers, reached around in back, unfastened the binder and dropped it.

I stood, breasts hardening, nipples erect. I could see his anger. The line around his mouth whitened. He took off his red shirt, the full sleeves billowing, tugged off boots, breeches, until he was naked.

Tears flowed down my cheeks. It was all wrong this way, so businesslike and coldly angry, with no feeling except that angry passion impelling him to do what love—or even warmth—should have inspired.

"Get on the berth, Mary."

"Roger . . . ! Oh, please . . . !"

"The berth. Sit on it."

I shook my head.

He reached me in one stride, gripped my arms, hurting me, backed me to the berth and sat me down, hard. When I refused to meet his eyes, he pulled the tie-cord off my hair, tousled it so that it curled in every direction. He buried the fingers of one hand in the thickest part and tipped my head back, forcing me to look up at his face, on which the lips had lost that white line and were set in passion.

He sat beside me then, took me in his arms and kissed me, a hurting, ruthless kiss, as he would kiss a hussy. Rigid in his arms, I felt no response. He drew back, probing into my eyes.

"You did want this," he said angrily. Accusing.

"Not . . . not this way."

"You want to be courted? Like a lady? You want me to say you're the most beautiful woman I have ever seen, and handle you tenderly? You want me to say I'm in love with you? What do you take me for? You're a runaway, a stowaway, escaped from Newgate, dressing and living as a man! You're no sweet, innocent maiden . . ."

"I'm a woman who feels, and wants feeling in return!"

"When I ordered you to sleep naked, did you protest, did you display any modesty? When I ordered you to bathe before me, did you know I was testing you as well as myself?"

"No! That's not true!"

"Did you refuse? No. You slept naked. You bathed. You hid behind my orders, pretending to be reluctant, and, while you were acting thus, you were tempting me, seeking to make me forget any other woman exists!" His brow darkened. "Even now, when I came to check the hold and saved you from the trouble you got into and ordered you to undress, did you tell me to go to hell? No. Here you sit, naked. And this time I'm not resisting."

Again, before I could speak, he kissed me. His lips were hot. They forced mine apart. His tongue came into my mouth, found my own tongue, and a spasm of delight went down my spine. He held me close, his thigh against me, my left breast pressed against that cross of hair. I trembled, fighting the spasms which kept going down my back, forcing myself to hide all my pulsing sensations. But it was useless. My body responded even as my mind wept that it was wrong, that it shouldn't happen like this, not with Roger, not with anger, without tenderness.

"No . . . please!" I whispered.

"You want it," he growled, " and so do I!"

He pushed me down. Even I could tell how hard my breasts had become, could feel that the nipples were very tall. His fingers came onto one, sending wave after wave of delight everywhere.

Without warning, he fell upon me.

I was only a body to him, something into which to pour his need. I began to fight, trying to throw him off and onto the deck. I fought him hard, and then I became fully occupied with fighting myself, the rivers of ecstasy racing in my blood like fire, singing in my ears, trembling my lips, consuming me with a flame, with woman's love for this man, love which he didn't want. When he thrust hard and fast within me, my arms went around him and held him closer, my fingernails dug into his back, that cross of hair brushed across my breasts.

Finally there was only my burning urgency and his.

He groaned my name. "Mary!" he called me and crushed into me mightily. And I tried to take it, to hold and keep it. He held me tightly, shuddering, and I knew that, though he had raped me, it was actually I who had conquered him.

PART II
ROGER
1718

Chapter 15

Every night after that Roger took me. All the nights, through weeks, months, a year, two years. He took me with angry passion at first, later with hot passion. Never with the tenderness, the beginning of love, for which I yearned. There was the heat, the eagerness, and I began to feel that, buried within him, lay the love for which I hungered, even though he himself didn't know it, even though he still, sometimes, muttered "Genevieve," in his sleep. As for myself, I knew every inch of his dear and beloved body, worshipped and cherished it, lived only to adore, to come eagerly into his arms.

Frequently he had me put on the blue dress and the pearls. It was then he told me of his school days, of the pranks he and his friends had played. Nothing more. He refused to let me speak of my own past. It was as though he wanted to keep me at arm's length except for the moment when, filled with need, he bedded me.

Time passed. We sailed in convoy with *Crossbones* and *Rover,* taking prize after prize. I worked hard, became a strong, able seaman. No one suspected I was a woman. I fought at Roger's side when we overhauled a prize, killing when I must, belittling my aversion with the fact that it was for Roger.

Our life, between forays, was the sea, the tropic, balmy air, the open sky, the vastness of water with its myriad, changing colors, its unpredictable moods. Always, there were the nights with Roger, whose body spoke of love, but whose lips never uttered the word.

This saddened me less as time went on, for I knew, with my intuition, that he loved me, unaware though he was. Many nights, behind our locked door, I spent the evening with him in one of the lovely gowns he continued to bring. He gave me pearl earrings and a finger-ring set with a big, glowing pearl.

I was almost content. We had a sort of marriage. Our home—the sea—was peopled with schooners, sloops, frigates, men-o-war. We attacked our prizes and took them, every one. When a man-o-war gave chase we fled, swift as the wind which filled our sails, easily outrunning them, free again to rove and plunder. From various ports, Roger sent money to his creditors in London.

It was late afternoon when a convoy of four privateers attacked our three.

"Why do they want us?" I asked Roger, while he fastened on his personal arms. "We don't have cargo."

"They don't know that. They're all schooners, may be after our fast sloops."

"Why don't you make a run for it?" I asked. "If they can't overtake us, there's no reason to kill."

He gave me a straight look. "You still don't like the killing?"

"Of course not!"

"Nor I. But I also don't like to run. It's not for me alone to say. If Fox and Mixer want to fight, I'm staying with them."

I was thrusting my pistol into my waistband when he stopped me. "Stay below this time," he ordered.

"But why? I always . . ."

"I don't want you topside, not with four of them to deal with. Do as I say, Mary."

Without another word or look he went striding out.

I was so disappointed and angry I shook. I'd proven myself, over and over, as a seaman and pirate! Now, when we were outnumbered and every hand was needed, I had to stay in the cabin as though I were a child!

Almost immediately the cannon fire began. First the shot across the bow of each of our convoy, followed by the answering fire from the three sloops. The broadsides began, continued as I'd never heard them do. Roger was on the gundeck, battling four schooners armed with roaring cannons, and he'd forbidden me to be at his side!

I almost defied him. I almost rushed out of the cabin, up the companionhead, and straight to him. But then I remembered the firmness of his order and did not.

Skull dived down one swell, up another. I had to sit on the edge of my berth and hang onto the post. There was a continual boom of cannon from our deck, an unceasing rattle of musket fire, undoubtedly directed at pirates in longboats making for our vessel. I clung harder to the post, not only to steady myself, but to keep from rushing to the side of my captain, my love.

He'd ordered me to stay here because this would be a very hot battle. That meant that, even if he didn't love me, he did feel concern. Further, if I appeared on deck, it might distract him so he'd fail to shout a vital order or fire a shot which might save his life. One glance at me—it would take a bullet or a knife no longer than that to find its way into his heart.

The fighting went on for an hour, perhaps more. Finally, just as I was at the point of going to him regardless of anything, *Skull* shuddered as a cannon ball crashed into her. This was followed by the splintering of wood. Oh, God! I thought. Did they get Roger, along with the mast?

I rushed to the foot of the companionhead. There was much activity above. *Skull* was changing course, beating away from the scene of battle. Only Roger could change course this fast! He'd tried to teach Vannice, and even me, and we'd failed. This meant that he was alive! I went weak from relief. Further, *Skull* was making a run for it. She was using her beautiful speed, damaged though she certainly must be.

I peered about, straining for a glimpse of Roger. I

couldn't see him. I saw two wounded, three dead. But Roger would be topside, at the helm. I hastened up there, looked toward the helm and there he was, the great, red sleeves of his shirt billowing. He was sweeping the horizon with his glass. I looked in every direction, and couldn't make out the shape of any vessel in the thick gray dusk.

Vannice passed, on his way to the bow. I called out to him. He stopped, glared at me.

"Captain said you was below. That you had belly-ache."

"But it's all over now!"

"The hell it is! We got to find a place for repairs!"

"Where are the others?"

"Made a run for it. We got separated, and the Captain says he's keepin' it that way. You'd better get your belly-ache below. He's not in a good mood."

Reluctantly, I went back to the cabin.

To fill time, I lighted the lamps, went through Roger's clothes, both the ones he'd worn in the old days, and the pirate garments. I thought about the wounded men, but had seen others of the crew carry them below and knew they'd be tended. I examined all the things Roger had bought for me—the blue dress and the pearls; the green dress, the white one.

I longed to be in his arms, to exchange kisses, to find glory together on the berth. Bit by bit, I dreamed, as I conquered him at the end, clasped in my arms and within my body, I'd waken that sleeping love and it would grow because I would tend it. Oh, so lovingly, I would tend it!

At long last I felt the drag of the anchor. I opened the door and listened. The men's voices drifted to me, carrying the tone of success.

I was waiting, naked but for a dressing gown, when at last Roger entered the cabin. There was weariness on his face. But no blood—thank God, no blood! He stood for an instant and looked at me, an expression of blankness covering the weariness.

I smiled. Naturally and with all my heart, because I was so happy just to be near him. "Welcome back, darling," I murmured. "Oh, welcome!"

"You . . . stayed here. You did what I told you."

"Not quite, darling. After it was over, after we were running, I came on deck. For a moment only. When I knew you were safe, I came back."

He took me in his arms. He held me—for the first time—with genuine tenderness, laid his cheek on my hair. "We could all have been killed this time, Mary. Thank God you stayed below. Thank God I still have you!"

This tenderness, the giving thanks, stunned me.

"Then you're not . . . angry?"

"No, Mary. I just want you, all of you, right now!"

This time, after throwing aside the dressing gown, I helped him undress. I landed on the berth with a little bounce and opened to him—eager for love. He took me, then—for the first time—with open tenderness, with love, though no word was spoken. Even so, it came to pass that, in the act of love, he revealed that he did love me. One day he, too, would know this, oh, he would! The soaring delight came to us; the victory, at last, was evenly shared.

We lay entwined. *Skull* moved at anchor, rocking us as though we were in a cradle.

"Where are we?" I asked idly, although it didn't matter. I was with him, in his arms, he loved me; nothing else was of consequence.

"Vannice found a cove among some islands. We're well-hidden. We need a lot of repair. One of our masts is broken, and we've got damage to the hull. We've got dead to bury. And two men to nurse. We'll be three short of our seventy."

"Vannice said you'll not rejoin Fox and Mixer."

"Right. I'll take my own prizes now."

"Won't they look for us?"

"Unlikely. Lonesome for them?" he teased.

I opened to him, offering myself, and he took me again. At the end he moaned, his voice blending with mine, making a music, the two of us cradled in *Skull* at some unknown island.

"This is another world, Mary," he said. "A beautiful, dangerous world filled with riches for the taking."

"You mean . . . without Fox and Mixer."

"That's right."

"You like this world, don't you, darling?"

"It's exciting, filled with challenge and action. I have to take advantage of it, and return to England a man of wealth."

I stroked his cheek, ran one finger along that scar on his brow. "Why, darling . . . why must you be so rich? You've never talked about it."

"It's for Courtney. Established by my grandfather. My father came into the inheritance, and he . . ."

I waited. When he didn't continue, I encouraged him. "What happened, darling?"

"My father was very . . . dashing. All the women were after him, and when they paused to catch a breath, he was in pursuit of them. He squandered the family resources, which were extensive. Everything he could get his hands on went for high living, women's finery, travel, jewels, gambling. In short, my present financial condition has forced me to admit that my charming, exciting father was a wastrel. My heritage is Courtney . . . the London house and the country estates . . . but all so heavily mortgaged that only drastic action can save them in the eight years I've been granted to raise the money."

"Would being captain of a merchantman have done it?"

"Perhaps. I thought of privateering, as I've said, but had no funds with which to get my own sloop. I managed to borrow enough to invest in the cargo *The Hague* carried, and would have collected one-third of the profit. That was the pattern I meant to follow."

"Then you turned pirate."

"With a better chance at fortune. Now, alone, I'll go for the best prizes and all I take will be mine."

"But the danger!"

"I'll be out of debt faster. And with a fortune."

"What will happen if you can't pay the debts?"

"I'll pay. I won't lose Courtney. I'll risk anything, go to any lengths."

I caught my breath. I'd only just succeeded in winning his tenderness, his deep, unconscious love, and he was practically saying he'd die, if need be, to save Courtney. I wondered, miserably, if that other girl was waiting for him.

I whispered, "Darling . . . who is Genevieve?"

He stiffened. "Where did you get that name?"

"You called for her long ago, when you were ill. Is she . . . your sister?"

"I have no sister, If I did, God knows I'd want her to love a man for himself. Not make conditions . . . bring this sum, that sum, and put it at my feet and I'll marry you."

"Shh," I soothed, heartsore. Despite unknowingly loving me, he still loved that selfish girl. They'd quarreled over money and parted in anger. But I knew— ah, how well—the blows love can survive. Once Roger got his pirate gold, he'd go to Genevieve and lay the world at her feet. Unless I, who now lay in his arms, could hold him with a love that desired not one gold piece.

"What about you, Mary?" he asked gently. "Did you tell the truth, so long ago, when you were brought to me, a stowaway?"

"Part of the truth. Later . . . you wouldn't let me speak."

"Speak now, then," he whispered and stroked my hair.

This I proceeded to do, lying in his embrace, my voice quick and soft. I explained why my mother had dressed me as a boy to make the visits to my grandmother, why the masquerade continued even after I went to live with her. I told how she'd educated me, how, after her death, Sir Cecil had inherited. Whispering, I told of my kinsman's vile treatment, how he'd robbed me of virginity and demanded that I be his mistress—and his love-lad. I described how he'd plotted, had me arrested, how Ryan and Clarke had taken me away and raped me. I recounted how I'd escaped, tried to get taken aboard one ship, then crept aboard *The Hague* and stowed away.

"Karl found me, brought me to you."

Thank God, I had the wit not to confess my love-making with Karl! I sensed, close in Roger's arms, feeling the beat of his heart, that, though he'd muttered profanely over Sir Cecil and the others, he'd take a different view of my going of my own will into Karl's arms.

One day, when he knows he loves me, I vowed, I'll tell him about Karl. I wanted no secrets from this man of my heart, wanted to live no lie with him.

Chapter 16

The rest of the night was spent in love, but the word was never spoken. I ached to whisper, "I love you, darling, love you!" But I dared not. To perform the act of love, with love, was enough. Anything more might drive him from me.

We dressed together as pirates. He watched as I clubbed my hair.

"It's a damned shame," he said.

"What is?"

"That you can't . . . only evenings, when we're alone."

"Yes," I agreed, smiling. Evenings, if I had my way, I'd spend naked in the berth with him.

"While the ship's under repair, Mary, we'll eat with the crew. You won't cook."

"What will I do?"

"Sew canvas . . . half a dozen things. Like the crew."

"Aye, sir," I smiled.

He smiled back, and my heart seemed to get on its toes and dance.

The cove Vannice had found was shallow, filled with the bluest water I'd seen. The island was quite large, very sandy, with a growth of trees and bushes unfamiliar to me. Roger sent out a scouting party to see if it were inhabited.

Next, Skull's spars were sent down. Most of her gear was carried ashore. Long lines were strung from her masts to trees. Then, as our men strained at the pulleys, the ship was hauled over on her side in shallow water.

The men set to work, myself with them, hacking off barnacles and digging out a wood-boring worm called teredo. The sloop's bottom was so bad that some of her planks and a few of her timbers had to be replaced.

Roger sent other men scouting up a little river, where they discovered that a battered shallop had come to anchor and been deserted. She was deteriorating badly. The pirates slipped up to her in a longboat, went aboard and, finding no crew or sign of recent use, managed to sail her, damaged though she was, to our cove, her parts to be used for Skull.

I scraped our vessel's bottom until my clothes stuck to me and my arms and back ached. There was a crick in my neck, which I ignored. The men were all working equally hard and sweating heavily.

Roger was everywhere, giving orders, scraping, digging out teredos, holding planks in place, hammering. His red outfit turned dark with perspiration, and his hair grew wet. I was proud to see that he worked harder and faster and better than anyone.

Downer had lugged utensils and supplies ashore. He built a fire and cooked a noon meal. Roger and I sat apart from the others.

I gazed at Skull, lying on her side like some wounded sea creature, the broken mast not yet replaced, gaps showing where planks must be set in. How could they ever make her seaworthy enough to overhaul a prize, take to her heels and run, if need be?

"Roger," I said, "have them convert *Skull* back to *The Hague*."

"What the hell for?"

"Well, you're not commissioned . . ."

"I can't be. There are many in the same circumstances. What notion have you got in that red head now? Here I am, making ready to take the booty I must take, and you want me to reconvert *Skull!* And sail her back to her owners, I suppose?"

"Yes, Roger . . . oh, yes!"

"And lose Courtney?"

"No. Follow your original plan. The safe one."

"It wasn't very damned safe when Fox and Mixer saw us."

"That won't happen again! And you'll get your share of money from cargo . . ."

"Not after I lost what I borrowed for the first voyage! No. I'd have only captain's pay. What've you got against privateering, anyway? You've been a pirate yourself for quite a while!"

"Don't you see? You were almost killed when Fox and Mixer . . . If you persist in running the seas, robbing and killing . . ."

"I don't kill unless forced, Mary."

"But there is killing, nearly every time!"

"Part of the life."

Suddenly I was angry. He wanted to risk his fine self. He knew he might be killed, and he meant to continue. No matter how sensibly I pointed out the foolhardiness, he meant to go right ahead and get himself a fortune, at the risk of his life.

'You're even stealing a ship!" I flared. "You're basing everything on theft and danger!"

"I'll return the sloop to her owner one day. With enough payment to reimburse him for her use. If you don't want to associate with a pirate, if you hold yourself too good for the life . . ."

"It's not that!" I cried. "Can't you see . . . can't you understand?"

He glared at me.

All I could do was sit with clenched fingers, holding back my true reason. *Can't you see that I love you, adore every inch of your stubborn body?* I ached to cry. *Don't you know that if you're killed, if you die, there'll be nothing left in the world for me, nothing at all?*

"I don't enjoy quarreling with women, especially you," he said. "Let's stop it . . . agreed? You think one way, I think another. But we don't have to be enemies over it."

"Of course not," I murmured.

I could never be enemy to this man. I could only love him, throw my body between him and a pirate bullet, knife the heart's blood from any man who came at him. I'd follow this man into hell, the place ruled by the Devil, just to be with him.

We slept apart that night and the nights that followed, slept ashore, wrapped in blankets. Roger posted sentries, though the need was slight, the island being uninhabited. The shallop remained a mystery; it was odd her deserting crew hadn't burned her.

I was miserable, sleeping ashore. I longed to creep into Roger's arms, but couldn't. I missed his kisses, his lovemaking, the way his breath struck my cheek as he slept.

The third morning at dawn, Vannice, standing on a dune, called, "Vessel in sight! She's makin' way for us!"

Chapter 17

The vessel looked like a moving sunbeam on the morning ocean. She was painted bright yellow, flew a black flag, and she carried guns. She gave a one-shot salute.

"She's friendly," Roger said.

Since *Skull* was on her side and unable to return a like salute, he ordered Vannice to get off a musket shot, which he did.

We waited. The yellow ship, a sloop, came nearer, her rail lined with pirates. We could make out the yellow hornet on her flag, read her name.

"*Yellow Hornet*," I murmured.

"That's Calico Jack Rackham!" Vannice exclaimed. "She's always had the black flag, but the yellow paint's new! Calico's a friend, Captain, sir. His crew'll help us get *Skull* back in service."

"Tell me about Calico Jack," Roger said.

"People call him Calico because he wears calico breeches and shirts. Says he wouldn't be caught in nothing else."

Yellow Hornet dropped anchor, longboats were lowered and came rowing to us. The Captain, dressed in blue-figured, yellow calico with a green sash, was first ashore. Perhaps forty, he had dull brown hair, a big nose and a tall, bull-like build.

Behind him came a pirate in drabber garb. This one was past his mid-twenties, with red hair, a nose which flared at the nostrils, and a strong, slim build.

Roger stepped to greet them. I followed, expecting him to order me to fall back, but he didn't. He'd for-

gotten me. Illogically, I wished he'd remembered, even
if it meant I would have to stay behind.

He shook hands with Calico Jack. "My mate told
me who you are," he said, then introduced himself.

Calico's vivid gray eyes stabbed about until they
landed on Vannice. He shook hands with the mate.

The pirate who had followed him ashore now moved
in and said to Roger, "This's Bonny, my mate. Got a
firm hand and a pirate's mind." The gray eyes leapt
to my hair, and his thin lips, rimming a big mouth,
went into a grin. "I see you've got a red-head aboard,
too."

Did Roger hesitate? No, I decided. He'd only
glanced from the flame of my hair to the duller red
of Bonny's, which was also worn clubbed. He said,
"This is Red, my cabin boy."

I regarded Calico thoughtfully. I began to feel an
aversion to him and the more I gazed, the stronger it
grew.

The *Hornet* crew came ashore and mixed with ours.
We four—Roger and myself, Calico and Bonny, stood
apart.

"I've heard rumors," Calico said.

"Speak," Roger said, and motioned Vannice over.

"Conditions are getting dangerous for us pirates."
Roger nodded.

"And they're worsening. Captain Woodes Rogers—
you've heard of him?"

"I have."

"Gossip has it that within the year he'll come to
New Providence as governor. That he'll have orders
to clean out the pirates so all Bahama waters'll be safe
for British merchantmen."

Roger considered.

"Damn them high-ups!" Vannice muttered. "First
they commission privateers, and then they talk about
chasin' them out so they'll starve!"

"They say after he comes he'll publish the King's
Proclamation to pardon all pirates who'll surrender
before September."

"That's seven months off!" snorted Vannice. "It may be given up before then. But I know the thing to do, if you'll let me speak, Captain, sir."

"Speak," Roger said.

"We plunder all we can in these months. Then, if the time comes—brings a governor—we can anchor at one of the islands and let him think we've surrendered. It'll give us time to look at the situation and get our ships into top shape."

"That's the idea I've got!" declared Calico.

"And in the meantime," Roger said quietly, "we're peaceable fellows, readying our vessels for what?"

I sighed in relief. At first I'd feared he liked the idea of deceiving the governor, but now I knew he didn't. But then I realized, with sinking heart, that he'd join in if he must, that he'd do it for money, for Genevieve.

"They'll play into our hands," Calico declared. "By that time, with piracy more dangerous than ever, they'll give us protection while we make ourselves stronger!"

Now I really didn't trust Calico. He was a deceiver, a conniver. Greed, and greed alone, inspired him. At least Roger, should he outwit the British Governor, had a vital reason for doing so.

"I'll help with *Skull*," Calico promised. "Then we can go look things over, ahead of time. *Hornet* can sail for New Providence first and *Skull* a few days later, so it won't look like we're partners. Which we ain't."

"Nor apt to be," Roger said. "I take my own prizes."

"Same here. Only way I'd join forces'd be for some unheard-of prize, and even then I'd think twice."

By evening the two crews got *Skull* afloat. This meant we could live aboard again though there remained much to do before we could sail.

Roger made love to me hungrily. Twice we came together, twice lay entwined in silence.

"What is it, Mary?" he asked finally.

Carefully, I spoke of my fears for his safety. "Especially now, darling, when the government is going to hound pirates."

He chuckled. "Some pirates will turn pirate-hunter! Don't worry, Mary. Once *Skull's* ready, she'll outrun everything on the ocean."

I said no more. So he'd made his decision. My only consolation was that I'd be at his side. If he took his prize and ran with the booty, I'd be with him. Or if, in the future, some government vessel overhauled us, I'd go with him into death. The important thing was never to be parted from him. He was my heart, my soul.

I pressed my lips to his. He took me still again, with new hunger, even with haste. And my love rose, budded, and blossomed, sweeping me almost to unconsciousness.

The next day was so muggy and hot I could scarcely endure it. The sun was a yellow lid, searing everything, even those who sought the shade and tried to cool themselves a bit. I washed Roger's clothing and my own, spread it on bushes, my mind going perversely to the fast little river which emptied into our cove.

If only I could have a real bath! If only I could plunge into cold, fresh water! Well, I was a pirate, and pirates are daring. I gazed around, watched the sweating, laboring men as they swarmed over *Skull*. A few were diving into the cove, swimming a bit, though heavily, in their clothes, then clambering out, pulling on their boots and returning to work.

Roger and Calico were on *Skull*, Bonny with them. All were busy, unaware of me. On impulse, I slipped into a stand of trees and away, following the river upstream until I could no longer hear the shouts of the pirates or the sound of their hammers. Even then I plodded on for at least another half-mile.

Then, only the promise of cool water in mind, I went behind some bushes and undressed. I ran to the stream and dove. It was so icy it took my breath. I surfaced, jumped upward so the water fell away from my breasts like an icy scarf, went under again, surfaced, jumped. Life sang through me.

It was then I heard the laugh. I looked up, startled. There, on the river bank, that head with the red hair thrown back, was Bonny, mate of the *Hornet!*

"Don't move!" Bonny called.

Terrified, I stood in water to my shoulders.

"Go away!" I called. "You've no right here!"

"As much as you! Watch!"

Frightened, I realized there was threat in his tone. But it was excited threat, amused, commanding. Not evil. Well, maybe this man took his sexual encounters with humor; maybe laughter was woven into his passion.

"Watch!" he called.

Icy water holding me, frozen with apprehension, I stared up at him. First he pulled off his boots. Then he got out of the sash and breeches.

I shivered. He must mean to take me, standing up, right in the water! But that was unnatural, impossible!

Now the shirt came off, was flung aside. I gasped, one cold, dripping hand going to my mouth. Bonny wore a breast-binder almost exactly like my own! Swiftly he unfastened it, dropped it, hustled out of his underdrawers.

"Now!" Bonny cried. "What do you think?"

My breath was lost somewhere down in the water. I could only stare. For on the bank of the river stood not a man, but a woman with full, big-nippled breasts, a slim, sweetly curved body and beautiful, shapely legs!

She came into the water, smiling. As she neared, it rose to her shoulders, for we were of nearly the same height. Her light brown eyes were dancing, her red eyebrows lifted.

"You . . . you're . . . !" I stammered.

She laughed again, a purely feminine sound.

"We both are!" she teased. "What's your name, truly?"

"M-Mary. Mary Read."

"I'm Anne Bonny, wife to Calico. None of our men know. That superstition."

I nodded, wide-eyed.

"Are you married to Roger?" she asked.

I shook my head.

"No harm. By the looks of you, he'll marry you."

My relief was tremendous.

"How did you happen to come upriver?" I asked.

"Same reason you did. I was hot as hell, the men were all busy, so I came far enough up for safety. And found you!"

She began to splash water at me, I splashed back, and we spent a delightful time playing, swimming, dressing, becoming friends. I told her about the lovely clothes and the pearls Roger had bought me. She confided that Calico had also bought her finery and a diamond but the only time she could wear them was when they were in their cabin at night.

"Like us!" I cried. "I love it . . . and hate it."

"I hate men's garb, too, Mary. But pirating's the best way to get a real fortune. Then we can retire and I can dress as I please. When we get to Nassau, we'll have our men take us ashore! We can leave the ships as pirates, take our clothes along and change ashore, and the crews'll never know, think we're town women!"

"Calico!" I exclaimed suddenly.

"He'll have to know about you, and Roger about me but they'll keep their mouths shut. Oh, Mary . . . it's so *good* to have a woman friend! Think what fun . . . we'll pretend to be pirate friends. And all the time we're women, each in love with her man!"

"Yes," I breathed, "Oh, yes!"

Chapter 18

We gloried in friendship, Anne and I. Careful to behave as men in the presence of others, when we could be alone we indulged in chatter like any two women, talking about clothes by the hour.

Calico would grin and nod to me, and I'd nod back. I found myself liking him less, even as I liked Anne more. Somehow I couldn't trust him, even if he was her husband, even if she did adore him.

When *Skull* had been repaired so that she could sail, *Hornet* put out for Nassau, leaving us to wait our turn. As we lay together the first night, I confided Anne Bonny's true sex to Roger, who was amazed, then began to chuckle. Then he quieted and became angry at the way I'd discovered Anne's identity, informing me heatedly that it could well have been a pirate who had caught me in the river.

"You would have been raped," he said flatly. "And through your own fault."

"But it didn't happen, darling! I know it was wrong of me, but now I've a woman friend! She's told Calico about me, and we'd like it, Roger, if the two of you will take us out in Nassau. Dressed in our gowns and jewels."

He refused instantly, pointing out the obvious objections. When I explained Anne's plan, along with her contention that any crew we met would think their captains were out with women of the town, he did listen.

And did, at last, after much persuasion, reluctantly agree.

It wasn't until we'd been anchored at Nassau for two days that the outing came to pass. I made my dress and other things into a bundle, the pearls in the middle. We went ashore separately, Calico first then, after a while, Anne. Roger and I followed the same pattern.

Calico had hired rooms at a shabby inn, and it was here that Anne and I dressed. Roger stayed with me, watching, and when I was finished, my hair falling in curls, I bemoaned the fact that I had no pins with which to dress it.

"Why pins?" he asked.

"I'd like to wear it high tonight."

"I prefer it this way," he said. "Hold out your hand, Mary."

I did so, and he laid a small, silken purse in it. "There's enough gold," he said, "to buy your way out of any trouble, should we become separated. Not that I expect any such thing to happen."

We joined our companions. We made striking couples, Roger in his red pirate clothes, Calico in bright orange calico with black hornets and a green sash. I wore the newest dress Roger had bought me—thin, silky velvet in aquamarine, my pearl necklace, dangling earrings, and finger-ring.

Anne was stately, her hair high, beautiful in a golden dress which melted into the tender brown of her eyes. She was smiling, gentle, nothing like the brusque mate of *Hornet*.

As for me, I felt like a real woman at last. Never before had I appeared in public dressed so, and I glowed with the wonder of it. I saw the warmth in Roger's eyes as he looked at me. He smiled as I'd never seen him smile.

I was in a delirium of happiness. This was the way I wanted to feel, was born to feel—beautiful, feminine, winsome. This was my birthright, which fate had doomed me to forfeit, forcing me to live as a man.

Half-drunk with at last being woman, with the gold Roger had given me, there rose in me a new sense of release—and possibility. I could slip away from the club for which we were bound, take passage on some vessel sailing at dawn, and remain a woman.

Then Calico said Anne and I were impossible to recognize as erstwhile crewmen, hair or no hair. Roger agreed, chuckled, gazed at me with utter warmth, and I knew that I'd not slip away.

That had been a dream, a flash of madness. I had, momentarily, glimpsed what I thought was freedom. Now, abruptly, I returned to the knowledge that the only womanhood possible to me was with Roger Courtney, pirate.

At table, waiting for our meal, the two men looked around. The club was well patronized, but they announced that no crewmen from our vessels were among those present.

"Prices are too high for 'em," Calico said.

Then they began to speak together seriously. I touched Anne's hand, she stopped her chatter, and we listened to our men.

They were discussing a British merchantman, *The Jasper*, which, laden with a cargo of gold bars, was soon setting sail for Havana. Calico had got the information from one of the newly arrived privateers.

I saw Roger's eyes go keen, studied the way he leaned across the table, his eagerness to catch every word. Apprehension sliced through me. Then came a wisp of relief. *Skull* still lacked repair. It would be impossible for Roger to go after this prize, regardless of its value.

"March fifteenth," Calico said, "and this is March first. Don't get the idea that . . . She's to have a man-o-war as convoy. It'd be impossible to take her."

"Not if you and I joined together."

Roger, who wanted no partner, suggesting that Calico come in with him! Protests came to my lips, but I held them back.

They talked on. All my joy in the evening vanished as Roger insisted he'd have *Skull* in top shape within a week. "I'll even add a couple of days to that, and make it in time," he declared.

"I'm stayin' out of it," Calico said. "I'm not havin' *Hornet* shot up by no man-o-war."

"You're . . . afraid?"

"Damn right! Any privateer's afraid of a man-o-war."

They spoke no more of *The Jasper* as we dined and danced, but Roger spoke of nothing else once Anne and I had changed back to seagarb and we'd returned to our ships.

"I'm going after that prize, Mary," he said.

We were undressing. I hung my breeches and shirt on a chair. My heart was beating so hard it shook me.

"Well, Mary . . . aren't you going to say anything?"

"I can't say anything you want to hear, darling."

"What do you mean by that?"

"I agree with Calico. It's too dangerous. Privateers always run from a man-o-war. This *Jasper* . . . all that gold. Even if three or four privateers . . ."

"Bosh! All it takes is a surprise rush in the dark. My crew'll vote for it, wait and see!"

"Roger! How *can* you go against an armed merchantman and a man-o-war with only ten guns and seventy in the crew?"

"Because I must. This one prize will let me quit privateering. With that gold, I'll have enough."

"Roger, you mustn't . . . you can't!"

We quarreled bitterly. He said unforgivable things to me, and I to him, but we both knew they were said in anger. We exhausted ourselves with the quarrel, and when he finally took me it was with fierce bitterness. Still, my love rose and I touched glory.

Roger was determined. He had every cannon overhauled, every pistol and musket cleaned and oiled, every knife and cutlass honed. When anyone commented on his zeal, he replied that he didn't want his crew idle. He'd decided, when Calico turned him down, not to speak of his upcoming foray.

I confided in Anne as we stood on the dock. I told her that Roger's crew had voted to take the gold-laden *Jasper*. He was going to give every man a generous share, and they were all as keen to go after it as Roger himself.

"All we do is quarrel about it," I told Anne. "I've got to stop him! He'll be killed! Some way, I've got to keep him from sailing!"

"You can't damage the vessel itself. You'd be caught."

"If only I could . . . oh, tie him up! Anything to keep him from sailing in time to overhaul that ship!"

She looked thoughtful. "Time. That's it, Mary!"

"But I don't know how to get the time."

"I do, lovey. Drug him. Opium."

I gasped. "Isn't that dangerous?"

"Not if you're careful."

"But where can I get opium?"

She leaned close. "I've got some even Calico doesn't know about. When I can't sleep, I drop a bit into a glass of water and drink it. Sleep fine and deep. I'll give you some. Put it in spicy food to hide the taste of the drops. They'll keep him from running into sure death."

"And if he finds out?"

"Do you want the drops or not, lovey?"

With aching heart, I nodded.

I stared out at the sea, which had been our life for two wonderful years. And I wanted, now that he was bent on this mission to certain death, only for our wonderful sea life never to end.

The evening we were due to sail, I put the contents of the vial Anne had given to me into a hot, peppery sauce Roger loved. By the time I came back to the cabin after washing dishes, he was stretched out on my berth, fully clothed.

"Do you want me to undess now?" I asked. I was engulfed in shame.

"Did . . . you . . . say . . . something?"

My heart tore. I'd done this to him. I, whom he trusted, who would give my life for him. I'd drugged him because I loved him!

"Should I undress?" I repeated.

"N-no." His eyes drifted shut. ". . . nap . . ."

He was asleep, breathing heavily.

I sat at the table, quivering. At that moment, when he was in his drugged sleep, I would have undone my act if it had been possible. Already it was too late. I had betrayed my love, interfered with his man's work. I rocked back and forth, praying that he wouldn't send me away when he found out, praying that he would forgive me.

Later, in accordance with my plan, I went to Vannice.

"The Captain sent me," I said. "He's decided to sail at dawn."

"Why didn't he tell me himself?"

"He was tired. He's asleep."

"Aye, that he mentioned, being sleepy. He said a nap would do it."

"He's changed sailing time," I lied wildly.

By ship's lantern, I saw the mate scowl. For a moment, I thought he was going to the cabin, to speak to Roger himself, as he should. Then, angry, he muttered, "He's the Captain. I'll tell the crew." He walked away, anger in every move.

It was noon when Roger woke. I'd had to deal with Vannice, who was now walking the deck. All the crewmen looked surly. I was twice as nervous now that he'd find Roger drugged. I sat on the edge of the berth, stroking Roger's brow, trying to rouse him, anxious to make certain he was all right.

He sat up, held his head in his hands, lifted it with a jerk. He sprang to his feet, rushed to a porthole, looked into the dazzle of sun.

"What time is it?" he demanded.

I told him.

"What the hell? Why aren't we at sea?"

I told him that, too, my voice very small, but steady. I told him everything, even about the opium, though not where I had got it.

His face went hard. The white line stood around his lips. His eyes were hot blue.

"You little . . . hussy! Knowing what that prize meant to me, knowing how close I had to cut the time . . ."

"Roger, please! With a man-o-war and an armed merchantman . . . Can't you see . . . Can't you understand, even yet?"

"I do see, and I understand one thing," he said, his teeth clenched. "It is at this point that you and I part company. Take your dresses, take your pearls, take the money I gave you, take all your pirate clothes, and get off *Skull! Now!*"

"Roger . . . you can't mean it . . . please!"

"Five minutes. *Skull's* sailing. If I put on full sail, I may still overhaul . . . move!"

I couldn't pack, not with him watching me. I couldn't even get the little purse, but went running out of the cabin sobbing, listening, listening for him to call me back, but no call came.

I stood ashore, my only possession the pirate outfit I wore, and watched *Skull* put out to sea. Her white sails filled and she went scuttling quickly over the noonday water, running to certain doom. He was gone. Without a word of farewell, without one kind glance, Roger Courtney had sailed out of my life.

PART III
NAT CROSS
1718

Chapter 19

Anne stood with me, watching *Skull* turn in to a white speck on the horizon. Had it not been for our disguises, I knew her arm would be around me. Calico's crew was watching also, shaking their heads and muttering words like "suicide."

"What will I do?" I murmured to Anne. "Where can I go?"

"Aboard *Hornet* right now," she declared. "I've got extra pirate clothes, and we're of a size."

"But Calico . . . will he give me a berth?"

"I'll see that he does. We've never had a cabin boy because we needed our privacy. But you'd have to sleep with the crew."

"That I've done before," I replied lifelessly. That was the way I felt . . . that I'd died. With Roger gone, thrown out of my life, I may as well have died.

Calico, when Anne took me to him, was reluctant, shifty-eyed. "I don't know," he quibbled.

"Red's a top cabin boy and can cook," Anne argued. "And none of our crew know she's a woman."

"That don't tell them why Courtney left Red behind. I'd need a sound reason to convince 'em, or they'd make it hell for Red."

Anne was quick with a solution. "Tell them Red quit. He can take it from there . . . say there's no sense running straight into death like Roger's doing. They feel that way themselves. They'll believe that Red does, too."

And so it worked out. I became cabin boy for Calico Jack and his mate, Bonny. I cooked their meals.

Their cook was even surlier than Downer, but his cooking was above criticism. I held my tongue, did my galley chores as fast and well as I could, got out. I worked as seaman in addition to my cabin duties. The crew treated me well enough, though no man offered me real friendship. I kept myself withdrawn to prevent any intimacy. My only friend was Anne, and we couldn't so much as chat because of the difference in rank.

My mind, furthermore, was filled with Roger. Would he, after all I'd done to prevent it, sight his prize and overhaul it? Would he be killed . . . was he dead even now?

A week after Roger sailed, the sloop *Sea Wolf* dropped anchor near *Hornet*. Calico and Anne went running to greet her captain. I followed behind the crewmen who also moved in that direction, not because I was curious, but to fill a bit of the void in which I now existed.

Calico shook hands with a sunny-haired tall man in black breeches, white shirt with full sleeves, and gold sash. Then Bonny was shaking hands, and the young captain—he looked to be just past his mid-twenties—embraced her in man-like fashion, then embraced Calico.

I wondered if he knew Anne was a woman. His crew came ashore and mingled with Calico's crew. So they were all old friends! Anne motioned me over, smiling.

"We've got a crew member you haven't met, Nat," she said. "Cabin boy and able seaman. He cooks for Calico and me. George Read. Known as Red. Red, this is Captain Nat Cross."

A warm, hard hand encompassed mine. I looked up into light blue eyes over which blond bold brows arched, at a nose which was handsome, though a bit full.

"Red it is indeed!" he laughed. His voice was sunny. His lips were well-shaped, nicely colored, and kind.

He was broad at shoulder, slim at hip. Like Roger, I thought. His chin was pronounced, even stubborn. He wore his hair short, half-covering his ears, and I couldn't help noting again what a sunny yellow it was.

His nature matched his appearance, for he kept smiling at me. Then he turned to members of our crew who approached with confidence, and began to shake their hands. It was like a homecoming.

He took the evening meal in the cabin with Calico and Bonny. This was a near-replica of the cabin on *Skull,* though not as fine.

More than once, as they ate, I saw Nat Cross looking at me—at my hair, my pirate garb, my mouth. I was drawn to him in a friendly way. Even so, I had to keep my chin stiff, my mind on serving. Otherwise, my thoughts would fly to Roger, my eyes would cloud, and there was the ever-possible danger that my lips might tremble.

I heard their table conversation, of course. It was evident that Nat Cross was American and proud of it.

"Are you going to surrender, if the time comes?" Calico asked. "Quit pirating?"

"Me . . . quit?" Nat laughed. "Calico, I'm surprised at you! I've still got a piece to go before I settle down."

"You still mean to buy property," said Anne.

"That's right, Anne-honey," Nat said.

I heard him speak Anne's name with surprise and shock.

"Nat!" she gasped, indicating me.

Those light blue eyes went stricken, then they concentrated on my mouth, wandered to my shirt front which, thanks to breast-binder and fullness of the shirt itself, made it impossible for the keenest eye to discover the truth.

"Sorry," he muttered. "I wouldn't give you away for any money, Calico. If you want to take me apart, go ahead. I've never been a man to let things slip, but I've sure done it now."

"Oh, hush!" cried Anne. "Red knows I'm Calico's wife! He isn't telling! We're still just as we were!"

"It can't stay like this," Calico said.

Nat's eyes were on me again, puzzled.

"I put store by our friendship," he said. "Since before I was a witness to your marriage."

"And you seem to admire our cabin boy," Calico said abruptly. "I notice you keep looking at Red."

I had noticed this; that was why I'd comforted myself about breast-binder and shirt. Now the blond captain smiled right at me. He had a nice smile, nicer every time I saw it. If only it were Roger smiling at me with such warmth, Roger watching my lips!

"Sure I look at him," Nat Cross agreed. "That hair. And he can really cook!"

"Have you got a cabin boy?" Calico asked.

"No. Never needed one."

"Red's yours for the taking."

I held my breath. I'd been right to sense a falseness in Calico's behavior when Anne talked him into giving me a berth.

Nat Cross openly looked me over, from my clubbed, brilliant hair to the toes of my boots. He looked long at my lips. Alarm raged in me. Did he suspect, could he possibly see what no one else had so much as thought of?

"Why, Calico?" Nat asked. "Why do you want me to take Red? Truth, now."

"Truth is, Red's a woman. I'm riskin' enough to have Anne aboard. If the men ever found out I've got one female not to mention *two* . . . aboard *Hornet*—hell itself'd break loose!"

"*Calico!*" Anne cried.

My heart stopped. I'd been betrayed by my own benefactor. I felt lost and alone, Roger gone from me and now two hard years of effort passing as a seaman spent for nothing.

"Nat's close-mouthed," Calico said.

"I slipped up tonight."

"It come from the bottom of your mind. I been

watchin'. You wasn't able to keep your eyes off of Red. No need for your crew to know she's a woman. Keep her in your cabin a lot, the way Courtney did."

"Courtney?"

"English. *The Skull*. He threw her off because she drugged him to keep him from tryin' to overhaul *The Jasper*."

Nat gave a low whistle, eyed me. "You must have been crazy about the man to do that."

I couldn't speak; could only stand there. Anything I might say would put Roger in a bad light, make him appear to be foolhardy, and that he was not. Determined, brave, running a calculated risk—he was all those things, but nothing less.

"Her name's Mary Read," Calico added.

"I'll take her. But only if she's willing."

"What do you say, Red?" urged Calico.

I looked at Anne. There was tenderness about her. "Calico's right, lovey. Nat's a fine captain. You can't do better than sign on with him."

My look went to Nat Cross. His eyes were steady, waiting, kind. They were also assessing. He was a young, healthy man; in my experience all men wanted one thing of a comely woman. How could I go into Nat's arms . . . any man's arms . . . after Roger? Roger, who had deserted me, shattered my heart, left me standing alone and unprotected while he sailed away.

For the first time, resentment tinged my hurt.

"What do you say, Mary?" Nat asked.

Spurred by need, by hurt, and by that scrap of resentment toward Roger, drawn by Nat's open nature, I made my decision. "I'll go with you," I said.

So it was settled.

Numb, I collected my gear. Numb, I went aboard *Sea Wolf*.

Nat introduced me to various crewman as cabin boy. He took me into the galley, where a wiry, mean-looking little man was goading his helper.

"This is Powell," Red told me. "Powell, meet Red.

He's my cabin boy and will be cooking my meals."

"My cookin's not good enough?" demanded Powell.

"It's the best. Red's got galley tricks of his own. He'll relieve you of making special dishes, cut down on your work."

Powell surely had an eye for his own benefit, for now he changed tone. "Aye, sir. It will ease off my work. But nobody gets in my way," he warned me.

"Aye," I agreed, wondering if he was going to be harder to work with than Downer. To do him justice, Downer had calmed some when he saw I kept out of his way. I'd do the same with Powell.

Nat introduced me to his mate, Lee Sully, a man of forty, browner from the sun than any man aboard. We spoke briefly, then Nat and I continued toward the cabin.

We went down the companionhead and along a short passage. "My cabin," Nat said. "You'll bunk in here. Sully's got his own cabin."

He opened the door and I stepped inside, clutching my bundle of clothing.

This cabin was larger than the others. The wood was teak with high polish, which it would be my duty to maintain. But only, I determined, looking at the cabinets and the curtained berths, until I save enough money to make it on my own.

Nat opened a drawer. "You can keep your things in here."

I untied my bundle, folded my extra set of clothes, laid them inside. The drawer still looked almost empty.

"No dresses?" Nat asked, and I could tell he was surprised.

"Why would I have dresses? I'm supposed to be a man."

"Anne has dresses. This Courtney fellow . . ."

"Roger. Lord Roger Courtney."

Nat gave me a keen look. "You shared his berth?"

I lifted my chin, nodded.

"Didn't he buy you any pretties?"

" 'Pretties?' "

"Dresses . . . jewelry."

"Certainly he did. I left them on *Skull*."

"Wanted no reminders. Or to be beholden."

"That's right." I held my chin steady.

"I can understand that."

"Can you, Captain?"

"Nat. When we're alone, call me Nat. Captain before the others."

"Whatever you say. Nat."

"Sit on the lower berth, Mary."

I did so, gladly. My knees were about to buckle. The premonition that he meant to bed me here and now shot through me. How could I endure that? Even with such a clean, sun-warm, friendly man?

He stood resting his fingertips on the table. The lamps made the sunlight of his hair dance with brightness. Except for Roger, I realized with a start, he was the most handsome man I'd ever seen.

"I've got a thing to say to you, Mary," he began, tone very warm, very gentle. "I understand that you think your life is ruined because Courtney . . . Lord Courtney . . . sailed away and left you. Anne told me. I can understand how you must feel. You drugged him in an effort to save his life, and he kicked you in the face."

"No!" I cried. "He isn't like that! He's . . ."

"Stop it, Mary. I've had women who . . . A person gets over it, you know. He just does. I've been through it. I've found a way to take out the first sting, and I'm going to teach it to you."

"W-what is it?"

"You replace the one you lost. Next day, if possible."

"No . . . !"

"But you're going to, Mary." He smiled, and there was the sunny kindness, but also that hungry look a man could get. "Mary the Red," he drawled. "That's what the pirate world would call you if you came out in the open. And they'd forget their crazy superstition."

I stared. What an amazing fellow! What would he do next?

I soon found out.

"Get undressed, Mary, and into that lower. Cover yourself. I'll turn my back."

He did so, promptly. Breath sobbing dryly, trapped —again—I took off my clothes and laid them on the deck at the foot of the berth, then got in, not covering myself. Guilty, because of Roger, that this was happening, I was nevertheless strangely drawn to Nat, grateful for his taking me aboard.

He turned. His face tightened. "I ain't going to do a thing you don't . . . in your heart . . . want done, Mary," he said.

He took off his clothes.

"Must the lamps be so bright?" I asked.

He turned them low. In the glimmer I studied his naked body, how strong and lithe and perfectly formed it was. I felt no dread of him, held no resentment over what he'd said about Roger. I knew, and was glad, that I was turning to his warmth as a flower does to the sun.

He came onto the berth. Willingly, because he was comfort, because he gave promise of friendship, I received him. The berth was so narrow that our naked bodies pressed from shoulder, down legs, to feet. I could smell his flesh.

"Now," he murmured, "is this bad?"

"Mmm," I responded, helpless under the feel of him. At the same time, I was achingly aware of how similar it had been with Roger, yet how different. Then, I'd been in the depths of love. Now I was reaching for a friend, for tenderness and comfort so cleanly available. Then, slowly, came those sweet, familiar feelings of my renegade body.

"I've been without this too long," Nat said. "I'd thought that, here in port, I'd find me a clean girl. I never hoped it'd be someone perfect."

"Nat, Nat."

I nestled closer. I needed to forget, even for an hour.

As though he'd read my thoughts, Nat murmured, "I'm going to wipe Courtney right out of you."

He enveloped my lips with his own. It was a long, tender kiss, and I returned it fully, grateful for its comfort. He held me, treasuring my lips, one hand coming to my breast, cupping and caressing, and my head seemed to float. I moaned, very low, a whisper. He laughed, a breath of laughter, and his fingers wandered my body, which tingled in every spot on which they lingered.

"Mary the Red," he whispered. "I was drawn to you even when I thought you was a lad. I even wished you was a girl."

"I . . . wondered. I . . . noticed."

He lifted himself, then lowered himself onto me. He kept kissing me—that enveloping, tender kiss—and my arms crept around him, pulling him closer. I was burning with feelings I'd thought I'd never know again.

He came into me, began to move in a leisurely way, tasting my body with his own, using it as a treasured extension of himself. I seemed to be drifting in the sky, far up, billows of rapture sweeping me further and further from memory, from the world, and I was aware of only this man. Within that glory of drifting, he shuddered long and deeply, his teeth holding the side of my neck. And I cried out, clamping my legs around him, and went flying into indescribable ecstasy.

Chapter 20

Sea Wolf sailed the tropical waters. Again, my life was ship and sea, pursuing prize after prize, fighting at my captain's side, killing when I must. The crew accepted me; I was careful to make no real friends, content that they assumed I was a man. I worked very hard, discharging my duties as cabin boy, cook, and able seaman.

Time went flying past: days, weeks, months. I postponed jumping ship, wanting my wages to grow into a substantial amount. Besides, my liking for Nat had deepened into affection. His feeling for me had rapidly become love, but the only time he spoke of it was during the act of passion.

I'd brooded, at first, over Roger's fate. Then, after Nat told me that Roger had become the most feared privateer along the South American coast, I knew that he was alive. But he hadn't taken *The Jasper* with her gold, or he'd no longer be a pirate. After this news of him, I made a practice of scanning the horizon on the chance he might again enter these waters, but never did I sight *Skull*.

At night, in our cabin, Nat and I made love. Then we talked for hours, exchanging life stories. He told of a large family of brothers and sisters, of a farm outside New York, and how he hated that work. He told of his decision to be a privateer and how he'd got a respectable businessman to put up the money for *Sea Wolf*. He'd taken many prizes and paid back the man with interest, and was now owner as well as Captain.

In return, I related to him all the things which had

happened to me. I even told him how I'd traded my body to Karl on *The Hague* in return for secrecy, food, and water. Nat accepted it all, comforted me with his body and his understanding. Sometimes I was almost happy.

Our life flowed excitingly. A feeling of peace, which I'd known only with my mother, came into me. But I was not truly at peace, would never be, until I could live openly—and only—as a woman.

My admiration and affection for Nat grew. He was an able captain. When seas were rough, waves towering, he overcame every difficulty. He was ever on the watch, whether beating along the sea to some port to sell booty taken, or searching for the next prize, he was infallible; when privateers turned pirate-hunters tried to overhaul us, he outran them with ease. He seemed casual about this, but I was ever fearful that one of the English Governor's vessels—he was now established at New Providence Island to clean out these waters and make them safe for British commerce —would overhaul and defeat us.

Nat laughed and kissed me when I spoke of this in private. And he continued to ply the seas, his flag— white, with a black, stalking wolf on it—standing out in the wind.

I almost came to dislike life at sea, the longing to live as a woman throbbed so strongly in me. I dreamed, once, that I was married to Roger, and woke in the morning with a hurting disappointment. If it hadn't been for the nights with Nat, for the comfort he wrapped me in, I should have been miserable.

One night, after a year had passed, Nat became talkative. This wasn't rare. I knew he liked to talk, but I had little to say because of Roger, because of my attacks of wanting to jump ship, and Nat didn't often impose conversation.

But this time he did.

"I'm going to hunt a special prize," he said. "I'd like to get some pretty girls, along with other booty."

This was so shocking I cried out. "Girls! What would you do with girls?"

"Sell 'em, what else? A real beauty brings . . ."

"Where? Where can you sell girls?"

"Brothels . . . Havana . . . Caracas."

"That's inhuman!"

"But it pays."

"Have you actually done it?"

"A number of times."

"What about the superstition . . . a woman on a pirate ship?"

"They ain't women then . . . they're booty."

"I suppose that's what you mean to do with me!"

"I don't know where you got such a notion, Mary." He smiled. And I couldn't read the smile.

"I got it because you said beautiful girls . . ."

"Especially English girls. Don't leave that out."

"You didn't put it in!"

"I'm doing it now."

"You said they bring a lot of money! And you've said I'm beautiful!"

"You are that."

"Lying or not, you've told me I am! And I'm English, and you've got me in your power!"

He began to chuckle.

It was when he did that—when he *chuckled,* knowing I was disturbed—that I snapped out of my doldrums. I made up my mind on the spot. I'd never brood again. I'd keep Roger completely out of my mind and watch for every chance to jump ship.

We took another prize. I fought at Nat's side. Piracy had gotten into my blood more than I'd thought, for this time the old exhilaration rose in me, and I wielded my knife as lustily as any. I cut down two men. I saw they were wounded only, and a gladness for them flooded me. They were downed; I'd bested them. But they would live.

When the prize surrendered, I went below and cleaned myself up. Soon I'd have to cook Nat's noon meal.

He came in as I was clubbing my hair, he was disheveled, but grinning. "This prize was the easiest one I've ever taken," he said. "One shot across her bow . . . a little knife work. Loaded with silk. Some gold. Her captain even had his crew help me ferry the stuff. I thought he was going to break down in tears when I told him to be on his way."

"You seem pleased with your booty."

"More than pleased."

"That must mean you got some girls."

He laughed. "Not this time. I'll go to Caracas to sell this. If I'm lucky, we'll sight a slaver, and I can take my pick of girls. And the strongest bucks."

"And really sell them? Human flesh?"

He grinned. "Don't worry about them, little Mary. The girls are well cared for, well treated, as carefully as I treat you. Better than you in some ways, because they're given beautiful dresses and jewels. And the bucks are well cared for because they're needed to help with the crops."

His manner, more than his words, struck terror into me. It shouted that, though I'd not been taken as booty, he would eventually sell me.

In the next hour of lovemaking, he almost swept that fear out of me. But afterward, lying replete in his arms, the feeling of safety and warmth became slowly tinged by cold fear.

Chapter 21

We anchored too far offshore from Caracas to run out a plank. The booty had to be ferried ashore, which meant I couldn't just walk off *Wolf* and lose myself until she sailed.

Nat refused to let me go in a longboat. He looked so grim about it I was convinced he knew I meant to jump ship.

After he'd gone ashore, I approached Sully, the mate. He was directing the lading of boats, shouting orders, cursing. He didn't hear me when I spoke his name, even loudly. He was really cursing four rough fellows, his sun-brown skin dark with rage, brown eyes snapping, hair standing in the wind. He was the very picture of wrath, and I almost faltered, then stepped right in front of him.

"Sully . . . sir!" I said loudly. "A word."

"What the hell you want?"

I daren't tell him I wanted to go ashore. But I had my answer ready. "I'll help lade, sir. And unload, on the dock."

"Get out of our way! The Captain, he wants to get in and out of here fast. Don't like the place."

"I know that, sir. That's why I'm ready to help," I lied.

"He said nothin' to me 'bout you."

"He told me, sir. Ordered me," I insisted.

"Answer's no!" he snarled. "Captain's ashore, I can't let you help without him tellin' me di-rect. Yer the cabin boy."

"And a seaman."

"Only when the Captain says."

"But he told me—"

He shoved me aside. I staggered, caught my balance. The four men Sully had been cursing laughed.

I backed away, but I wasn't giving up. I couldn't get on a boat now because Sully was personally, under orders from Nat, seeing to the lading. I'd wait until he had less to do before I approached him again.

This I did. "If you won't let me work, sir," I said, "I'd like to go ashore on the next boat."

"What the hell for?"

"To see Caracas. To step foot on new soil."

"You trying to jump ship?"

I swallowed. "No, sir. If I wanted to quit, I'd tell the Captain."

"Get away from me!" snapped the mate. "Don't bother me again, or I'll bust yer gut!"

Bested, because I rarely fought lest I betray myself, I turned away. I stood at the rail and watched the activity in the harbor and along the waterfront.

Tiring of this, I waited in the cabin for Nat. I'd just combed and reclubbed my hair when he came in. He had a small package in one hand.

"What's this about you trying to go ashore?" he asked.

I whirled, looked into his face. I'd never seen it so sober, so almost cold.

"I offered to work. Didn't Sully tell you that?"

"And more. That you said I ordered it. Why did you lie, Mary?"

To confess was out of the question. He could so easily hustle me ashore and sell me. I had to keep on with the lie.

"I wanted to go so much, Nat. I wanted to see women. Dressed as women. To see how they fix their hair, and the new fashions."

It wasn't a complete lie. I did want those things. But beyond them, I wanted freedom.

"Why didn't you tell *me* you wanted to go ashore?"

"Why didn't you ask me if I'd like to go?"

"Because this stop was for business only. To unlade, to ferry, get my money, and be gone. To have you wandering about port ogling fashions would only delay us."

I glared at him, suddenly trembling with rage over my lost opportunity.

"Why did you lie, Mary?" he pressed, unable to dismiss what I'd done. "Have I been cruel? Are you afraid of me, afraid to ask for anything . . . anything at all? Why?"

"Because!"

"There has to be a reason."

"Because I knew you wouldn't let me go!"

"Have you stopped to think it wouldn't be safe for you to wander alone in a place like Caracas? Aside from being dressed as a pirate, and with that hair, which draws attention, believe me, you're a woman . . ."

"No one can tell that!"

He eyed me narrowly. "N-no. But I've noticed a man here and there stealing looks. And that first night, on *Hornet,* I kept looking. Something about you kept pulling my attention. It can happen again, especially if you're alone. It can lead to trouble. In the future you can, as before, go with me. Never by yourself. And never lie to me again."

There was nothing I could do but accept his decree. But in the future, once ashore, when he wasn't looking, I'd slip away. I'd hide so he'd never find me.

"I brought you a gift," he said. He extended the package.

His sunny warmth was back, showering me. I told myself I was insane to think he'd sell me to a brothel. Obviously, he'd accepted my stated reason for wanting to go ashore today. He'd keep me on as a cabin boy, seaman, berth-mate, of course he would. He'd even brought me a gift. Yet, even as I opened it, I still couldn't be sure.

The gift was in a narrow sandalwood box. Inside lay an intricately carved, delicate, folding fan of sandalwood. I opened the fan and gazed at it, lips apart, breathing its strong, delicious fragrance.

"Like it?" he asked.

"Oh, Nat! It's lovely!" I waved it gently, and its odor filled the cabin.

"I'd have bought you a dress, latest fashion, if there'd been the time. Those pirate-hunters . . ."

"I know, Nat. I understand."

"You can't possibly know how much I want to see you in a dress," he said, his smile gone. "At times I wonder if I ever will . . . if the time'll come."

"Will it, Nat?"

"Of course. Maybe in Havana."

Havana, a city in which he meant to sell girls! Maybe he bought finery for the girls he put up for sale, made them beautiful so they'd bring a higher price!

That night, in his arms, breathing the lingering aroma of the fan, I was transported beyond any other time. And the feeling came again that, if he could be trusted, and if I were given time, I might come to love him. Though never with the reckless passion I'd held, still held, for Roger.

I clung to him. "Again, Nat," I whispered. "Please . . . !"

We kissed, long and tenderly. Our tongues kissed, winding together. He explored my body with infinite care; I explored his. I was tingling all over. He was moaning. The long, glorious touching made us so eager we were both trembling.

We made love furiously, threw ourselves into our passion as we'd never done. I pretended to fight him, and he pretended to subdue me, rougher than he'd ever been, rolling, bruising, penetrating while I, in turn, twisted and clasped and struggled until, at the end, we melded in long, shaken glory.

He held me silently, lifting himself, after a time, to kiss every inch of my body, lips tender on the bruises, brushing my nipples, warm and moist in the hollow of my neck. Time passed thus, and he entered me still again, slowly and with reverence, giving himself to me, accepting what I gave. I knew then that he truly loved me, loved me as a man loves the woman of his life, that he'd never sell me, and I was both joyful and saddened.

If there'd never been Roger—but there had been, still was. For Nat I held warmth and gentleness, truly and deeply liked him. I sighed. Slept.

Some days later, we sighted a pirate-chaser and had to make a run for it, not easily losing our pursuer. Nat laughed about this in a sober manner, but when the same thing happened again, he grew thoughtful.

That night, after I'd washed dishes and returned to the cabin, he was so solemn he didn't look like himself. "Things are getting pretty hot," he said. "I've been doing some thinking."

"You mean those sloops that gave chase?"

He nodded. "I've come to a decision. We're making for Nassau. I'm going to take advantage of the government decree. I've considered it this whole year, since you and I have been together. I'm not a coward, but I'm also not foolhardy. I don't want *Wolf* shot up or taken from me. And I want to get into a position where I can give you the womanly things you deserve."

Wonder took me. "You'll obey the decree?"

"That I will. I'm not a dedicated pirate like Calico. I hope you don't think that."

"I don't," I murmured. And remembered how intent Roger had been on piracy.

Chapter 22

Anchored at Nassau, Nat gave his crew generous shore leave. I wanted to go, to take another look at the place, though I knew from being here with Roger that it wasn't big enough for me to jump ship and escape Nat.

"Be patient for a few days," he told me. "I'll take you around all you want. Right now, I've got a lot of business to transact."

Well, he did have business, that I knew. He had to report to the Governor, for one thing. I wondered how he'd make a living, if he had funds to pay his crew without turning pirate-hunter. He wanted property. I sighed. Property had been at the root of Roger's aspirations, too.

Maybe I'd be in Nat's way, now that his life was changing. Maybe I should just walk off *Wolf*—Sully was ashore most of the time, hence had no orders to watch me—and hunt for work as a man. Perhaps with one of the fishing boats. I dismissed that, unhappily. There was no future in it and if I stayed here, the place being small, I'd have to talk it out with Nat and win his agreement.

For three days he was ashore from dawn to dark. A couple of times he brought local men to the *Wolf* and they walked her over, inspecting her. I could only assume that they were from the Governor and this was a formality.

I tried to fill the time. I polished wood, pressed clothes, read in Nat's books about the sea. They didn't hold my interest, because I was anxious to learn what he'd accomplished and how things were to be.

By the time he returned on the third night, laden with packages, I was pacing the deck. Comfortable as the sloop was, I'd begun to feel I was in prison—my pirate garb was a prison, everything about my life was a prison. Again I worried about whether Nat would sell me, if he could sell me, here in Nassau. I'd almost dismissed that idea, but now it returned to torment me.

He pierced me with one look as he came aboard. His grin vanished.

"To the cabin, Red," he ordered for the benefit of nearby crewmen. "Put these things away."

I followed him down to the cabin. He dropped the packages on the table, gave me another penetrating look.

"What's wrong, Mary?"

"N-nothing."

"The hell there ain't! I've got a pretty good notion. You're sick of bein' a man, sick to the bone. Ain't that right?"

Miserable, crushing back tears, I nodded.

"I smelled that out from the first," he said. "It's got stronger. We're putting an end to it. Here and now. Open them up." He gestured at the packages.

Excited, I opened package after package. There were two dresses—one thin, red velvet with lace, the other silky white cotton sprigged with tiny black flowers. There were chemises, silk stockings, dainty slippers, even lace gloves.

Tears were standing in my eyes. Both he and Roger had done this, bringing me gifts.

"Nat . . . oh, Nat!" I breathed.

"Hold them to you. See if they fit."

I did as he said. They were almost as perfect as the things Roger had chosen. The slippers, too.

"Did he . . . Courtney . . . ?"

"Yes, Nat. Yes, he did."

"Where could you wear 'em?"

"In the cabin."

"It won't be like that now."

"Why won't it, Nat?"

"You thinking of that superstition pirates have?"

"Of course. Oh, I thank you, Nat. But in the cabin's the only way . . ."

"No it ain't. I've been real busy, Mary, these days. I'm not a pirate any more, and neither are you. It ain't going to matter a damn when the crew finds out you're a woman."

"*Nat!*" This was so quick, so stunning. "Are you going to be a pirate-chaser?"

"Hell, no. I've sold *Wolf* to the government. *She'll* chase pirates. I've talked to the crew. They're all for it. Sully's to be captain."

"What will you do, Nat? Did *Wolf* bring enough to buy property?"

"She did, and I've got more money, remember, from prizes. I'm getting my property at once."

"Where?"

"Right here in Nassau. I've bought a building to make into a club. There'll be income from that for as good a living as anybody'd need. For man and wife, Mary."

My heart lunged. He'd been gone many hours for three days. He'd quit being a pirate, sold his vessel, bought a building for a club, all in that short time. Had he also found a wife?

Breathless, stammering, I managed to get all this into words. He heard me through, face sunny, light blue eyes holding dots of sunlight.

"I found me a wife a year ago, Mary," he replied, going right to my last—and most pressing—question. "She was cabin boy for Calico Jack, and I was lucky enough to get her to sign on with me."

I felt my eyes widen, knowing that they were also more deeply black. I tried to speak, couldn't. I tried to feel anger that he was telling me, not asking, that I'd been chosen for his wife, but couldn't.

"You're the only woman I ever asked to marry me," he said. "And for a damned good reason. You're the only one I've ever loved. And I've waited, tried to let time pass, to help you get over Courtney."

I tried to respond, but my voice wouldn't come. I wanted to say he hadn't asked me, even yet, had only told.

"I know," he said. "You've still got Courtney on your mind."

"N-not the same as at first," I managed at last. "I . . . *like* you Nat, truly like you. And more. I'm *fond* of you. We have fun together, and in bed it . . . it's wonderful."

"But you don't love me. Not yet."

Miserable, I shook my head.

"Marry me. What you feel suits me. I can wait for the love."

"I can't! Please, Nat!"

The sunniness left him. "Don't feel sad, Mary. I hoped . . . But I knew you might answer this way. So I've got another thing to ask, and I don't see how you can turn me down on it. This club'll be for Nassau folks . . . travelers . . . the better pirates . . . the curious. There'll be good cooking and music, and a gambling room. Pretty girls to serve the meals and run the games. No brothel. What the girls do that way must be outside, away from the club. My idea was for my wife to be my partner. That still holds, whether you marry me or not. Be my partner, fifty-fifty."

"Y-you make me an offer like that? After . . . No, Nat! It wouldn't be fair! Besides, I haven't any money! And I can't let you give me a free partnership!"

He got a teasing look. "Who said anything about free?" he demanded gaily. "I need you. Need a beautiful hostess. You can pay me your half out of your share of the profits. How does that strike you?"

"It's still too generous, Nat." My heart was beating so. I glanced at the heaps of velvet and lace, of cotton and satin on table, chairs, even on the berths. Nat didn't miss the glance.

"This is your chance, Mary. With Courtney, you could dress in secret as a woman. Tonight you can take off men's clothes forever. You can be the beautiful woman God made you, and live that way the rest of your life. The club will make that possible. You can marry any man you like, if you want to marry at all."

Tears sprang down my cheeks before I could stop them. Nat took me into his arms, loosened my hair, and ran his fingers through it, murmuring, "Cry all you want, darling. Everything has been a shock to you. I'm an oaf for blurting it out! I should have . . ."

"You should have done exactly what you d-did!" I sobbed. How could I refuse open-hearted, loving Nat anything? I nestled into his arms, liking him so much, so dearly, longing for affection to flare into the blaze of love. But it didn't. There was only the safety, the contentment, the affection, the respect. Nothing more. To marry him would be to cheat him.

"Can I really pay my half from my share of profit?" I whispered.

"Sure you can. It'll take time. And I warn you. I'll be after you to marry me."

"It isn't right for me to take advantage . . ." I began to sob bitterly, mourning that I couldn't force the love he so desired.

"It's right if I suggest it myself," he said, giving me a little shake. "Behave yourself, darling! It's settled. From tonight on you live as woman, you're full partner in our *Pirate Club,* I'm your suitor and . . ." He broke off, looked troubled.

"What's wrong?" I cried. "Did I say something, do something . . . ? Oh Nat, I'd never, in this world, mean to hurt you!"

"It was that word I used, 'suitor.' I'll be that, but how about 'lover'? Will you cut me off when you're a woman? When you're full partner, and your own boss?"

I began to laugh and cry at the same time. He was so dear, so lovable! Why didn't my unruly heart give him what he so deserved?

"Nat!" I choked. "That part will never change!"

He carried me to the berth, tossed aside the finery,

tenderly removed my pirate garb. When I would have helped, he protested.

"I'm man making you into woman. With my own hands."

So I let him. And I began to feel woman as he drew off the breeches I'd never again have to put on, the hated breast-binder. We made love sweetly, for a very long time. And then we lay and murmured plans for the club, for being together.

It was late by the time we'd dressed.

I wore the red velvet and the red slippers. They fit almost as though they'd been made for me. I brushed my hair and let it spring and curl, coming to rest on my shoulders.

"You're a lady," Nat said, "a real lady. The most beautiful one in the world."

"And you're a gentleman, sir." I laughed.

He looked very handsome in dark breeches and coat and white, ruffled shirt.

"Where are we going?" I asked. Then, teasing: "Or are we staying in the cabin?"

He laughed.

"Don't forget. Tonight a woman is born. Mary Read. We're going to a club called *Midnight*. It's the best one here. Until we open the *Pirate Club*. We're going to sup there, lean back in our chairs with easy conscience, a gentleman and his lady out for pleasure."

It wasn't until we were crossing the plank, the crew members on deck staring, that I truly appreciated openly being woman. The men gaped, recognized me, then looked away. This rough sort of respect made me proud as I walked, fingers on the arm of a gentleman, my skirts swirling above my toes. No need to stride like a man; no need to jut my chin or pitch my voice low. I was free . . . free at last!

"You didn't tell the men?" I murmured.

"Sully. One or two. I think they've all heard."

I drew a happy, quivering breath.

Ashore, we went toward a cluster of lights where

people were moving about. Nat's coat was a rich brown and above it, when we passed under a light, his sunny hair glistened.

When we reached the *Midnight,* having lived as a man, I felt uncertain how to conduct myself as we entered. Nat sensed this. As Roger had done on that long ago occasion, in a different club, Nat placed his fingers under my elbow, and guided me into a large, music-filled room. It was decorated in blue and yellow, with bare-topped tables. People sat at the tables, quite a few couples among them.

Nat found us a table against the wall, pulled out a chair, for me. This gesture made me feel exquisitely feminine, as did the fact that he murmured, "My beautiful one!" before he took his own seat across from me.

The music boomed suddenly. The musicians played enthusiastically. They were all black and played very loudly.

"Our music will be quieter," Nat said.

I nodded.

"Our club will be . . . 'elegant' is the word, I reckon," he went on, and again I nodded. I knew the refined, subdued tone he wanted, for I'd spent years in that sort of household. In this area, my help would be a real asset.

A waiter came to take our order.

"Ale for me," Nat told him. "Water for the lady. And your best meal."

"We got nothing but chicken."

"Then bring the best of the chicken. And the best of what goes with it."

I began to notice, and was instantly embarrassed, that people at other tables were glancing at us. My cheeks grew hot. I began to wonder if my hair looked unfashionable.

"There ain't no call for you to blush," Nat said.

"But people are staring!" I whispered, afraid now to look up, even at Nat. At the same time I did realize that my embarrassment was a feminine feeling, and my cheeks went hotter.

Nat chuckled. "They're looking because you're a natural beauty, Mary Read. So relax. This is one of the things you've got to get used to. They're looking with respect, that much I know. If they wasn't . . ."

His jaw clenched.

"Maybe it's the dress. It's so beautiful anyone would look, I suppose."

"It's you *in* the dress. Far as beauty goes, you're the only woman here. Every man in the place is jealous of me."

"I don't see why," I whispered. And I didn't. I knew I looked good, of course, but that I was so much out of the ordinary seemed incredible.

"You're the only stunning woman here," Nat insisted. "It's teaching me something."

I looked at him in query.

"When we open our club," he explained, "you're to wear red only. This exact shade of red, though you'll have many gowns . . . a dozen . . . more. It's just right with your hair. And then there's what the pirates are sure to call you."

"What's that?"

"They already call you Red. Now, when they find out you're a woman, they're bound to call you Mary the Red. You wait and see."

I smiled into his eyes, inwardly tremulous, my fingers not quite steady as I lifted my water glass. For the first time in my adult life I felt cared for, absolutely protected. I felt womanly, dependent on the man who loved her and would let no harm or insult touch her. It was the most delicious feeling. Even the water in my glass was evidence of Nat's concern; he knew how I hated alcohol, that I'd forced myself to drink with the crew to strengthen my masquerade.

We were eating our chicken when I saw a bull-like, finely dressed man of fifty or more making for our table. He was suave and polished. His hair was black, straight, and gave off a blue sheen. He had a strong, hooked nose on which thick, wide eyebrows met, giving the impression that he was frowning, which he was not, for the very red, thick lips under the black moustache were smiling. The smile emphasized the big chin and called attention to the fact that all his features were big and handsome. But repellent.

Nat stood up as this man stopped at our table. They shook hands. Nat smiled as they greeted each other, but only briefly, his expression then going cooler than I'd often seen it.

"Cross!" the fellow exclaimed in a thick, arrogant tone. "You haven't been in Havana recently!"

"No," Nat replied. Then, as the man looked boldly at me, he added, "This is Señor Pablo Gómez y Herrera . . . Miss Mary Read."

I murmured. Gómez bowed. "An honor Señorita," he said in that curiously fat voice. "I've not seen Cross in the company of such a lovely woman before. May I join you for a drink?"

"Certainly," Nat agreed stiffly. He motioned to a waiter, who brought a chair and held it so the Cuban could sit down. Then he hurried to the bar with Gómez's order.

From the manner of both the waiter and Gómez, I felt that the Cuban was a man of importance. His open, bold assessment of me drew my look to his as helplessly as though he were a snake charmer and I the snake. His eyes were very black—a flat, bottomless black. One would never be able to read, from those frightening eyes, the true thoughts behind them.

If there *was* truth in him. If there was anything in him but evil. Try as I would to smile and be gracious, to reply to his charming remarks, I had to force myself because I was filled by the conviction that he really was evil, that there wasn't a good, honest bone in his arrogant, foreign body.

"Cross and I do business together," he told me. "I'm an importer-exporter."

So. He did business with pirates, dealt in stolen goods!

"Señor Gómez is an important man in Havana, in Cuba itself," Nat said expressionlessly. "It's an honor that he has joined us."

Well, maybe Nat *was* a pirate! I thought hotly. But he'd been a pirate openly; he hadn't lived a double life!

Gómez, being so important, had to lead a false life. Undoubtedly he operated as a legitimate importer-exporter, yet actually had dealings with all sorts of pirates. He'd conduct legitimate business too, of course, to maintain respectability. To maintain importance he'd need to appear, publicly, as a gentleman.

I knew it wasn't fair of me to be so certain he was evil, but everything about him impressed me that way, and I shrank inwardly from him. And gave thanks that Nat was open and honest. Gómez professed to have come to Nassau on vacation. Nat accepted this, but I didn't. I suspected him of being here on a deal of some kind, perhaps to buy one of the privateers, hire his own captain and crew, and set them to piracy!

I looked at the two men, comparing them. Nat was like the warm, glowing sun. He was going to become a legitimate business man. Gómez was darkness itself. No matter how sternly I reflected that maybe I felt this way because he was a foreigner—so dark and scarcely taking those eyes off me—and wouldn't feel so if I knew him better. But I didn't want to know him better. The whole time he sat with us, wave after wave of aversion swept over me.

I was enormously relieved when he left, very glad that Nat hadn't told him we were going to open our own club. I began to chatter about the club, mostly to wash the Cuban out of my mind.

"I'd like to have Powell for our cook, Nat," I babbled.

"Powell? He's a ship's cook."

"And a good one. Once he cooked in a good place, quite a good one. And he learned some of my dishes.

I'd like to try him for the club. If he'll come, and if Sully . . ."

"Sully can get another cook. Powell . . . I think he'd be glad to work for us. If he can treat you right."

"He treats me very well now. We're friends, really."

Nat grinned. "You little charmer! Then it's as good as settled. Now, little Mary the Red, finish your chicken!"

We had dessert, danced, laughed. Still, despite our happiness, I couldn't forget Gómez. I was feverishly anxious, back in our cabin, to go into Nat's strong, young, clean arms. And there I finally forgot the suave, black-browed Cuban who had nearly ruined my evening, forgot so completely that he entered my mind no more.

PART IV
NASSAU
1719

Chapter 23

Nat let me decorate *Pirate Club* to my own taste, and I threw myself into the task happily. There were four big, airy rooms in the building, which Nat paid for in gold from the sale of *Sea Wolf*. The biggest room, at the front, I chose for the dining salon,

I found a man of artistic bent who first painted the board walls of the salon a misty green then, with his brush, decorated each painted wall. One bore a running stream, complete with waterfall, and looked so real I felt like dabbling my hand in the water. Another wall was covered with palm trees and beach looking out over a sun-sparkled, empty ocean. The third was a waterfront scene with white-sailed sloops at anchor in the foreground, others running with full sails in the distance. The fourth wall showed a half-wild, colorful flower garden with hibiscus of every shade and yellow, cuplike blossoms among them.

The floor I left bare. It was of fine, hard wood and took a high polish for dancing. The bar curved in front of the palm and ocean scene and was painted a misty gray-green. Crystal chandeliers held candles for elegant, subdued light, the tables were round, draped to the floor in white. The china, crystal and silver I got from merchant vessels were of the best quality. At one end of the bar a small, raised platform was ready for the musicians.

I finally hired Powell to run the kitchen.

"I still don't see why," Nat said, this being the only point on which he gave argument. "I know, you're to do as you please. But I thought you'd try for a chef, particular as you are about everything else, inside and out. Even adding the flower gardens with benches and paths. And Powell's surly as hell."

"He was a good cook when he had to feed eighty crewmen three times a day," I repeated firmly. "I ate the food and so did you until I came aboard. It was always good, sometimes exceptional. Given a free hand, he'll serve the best food in Nassau, and he won't be surly. As for a chef . . . I suppose you mean French . . . surely you've heard how impossible *they* are, so temperamental there's no getting along with them."

Nat smiled, flung his hands apart.

He was pleased that I had the walls of his gaming room painted white with only a tinge of green, and had chosen mahogany for the gaming tables. They gleamed richly and were truly beautiful with their polished wood and deep green cloth tops.

"You're spending every cent I get my hands on!" he declared. "But the results! I never believed, once, how fine our place could really be!"

Suddenly I was overwhelmed by guilt. I'd been feeling so free and happy, dressing as a woman, living like a woman, doing feminine things, that I hadn't thought too seriously about what I must be spending.

"I don't mean to use all your money!" I cried. "I'd better slow down! We could end up with a fine establishment on our hands, no customers, and not get back one speck of the money! I don't want to ruin you!"

He only laughed and kissed me. "With such splendor, with pretty girls in the dining salon and the gaming room . . . with you as hostess . . . we can't fail!" he declared.

"Maybe Nassau isn't big enough to support . . ."

He pulled me into his arms and kissed my fears away.

At his insistence, I continued to furnish the place. The room which served as our bedchamber, I kept simple, merely having the walls painted and installing bed, dresser, and two chairs drawn to either side of a reading table. This would be our home. After the club began to show profit, I planned to convert it into a luxury chamber. Right now, the more substantial funds had to go for the kitchen, which Powell was outfitting.

There had to be, further, a reserve to pay Powell and one helper, and others. We needed three waitresses, three girls in the gaming room, a bartender-cashier and a three-piece combination for music. All told, Nat and I counted up that, with ourselves, we'd have a total of fourteen to run the club.

We gazed at each other, impressed.

"We sure as hell have got to make this thing pay!" Nat said.

My voice was unsteady. "M-maybe if we emphasize that Mary the Red theme, it'll help."

He frowned.

"It might bring people in, Nat."

"Undoubtedly. But now that the time is here . . . I don't like it."

"But it's right, Nat! In a way . . . well, I'll be living the truth. Living both as the woman I am, and, by admitting my identity, the woman I have been! I think it would make me feel better, honestly."

"I want you to feel natural. If you don't . . ."

"But I do! Nat, you're the first human being who has made it possible for me to live as a woman, to feel natural at last! I only wish . . ." I bit my lip, unable to say I wished I could love him.

He understood. I could see it in his eyes.

"I'll like the Mary the Red reputation," I said honestly. "I've . . . well, on the street, I've heard people whisper, 'That's Mary the Red,' and it didn't hurt, it didn't bother me. It's . . . cleansing. There's nothing bad about it, not any more!"

And so it was settled.

Our club was an overnight success. On opening night, Nassau citizens and visitors to the town flocked to us, dined, danced, and the gentlemen spent freely in the gaming room. Pirates, who were frequenting

Nassau almost as much as ever, put on their best breeches and silk shirts along with their best manners, and came. The ladies were elegant in their long gowns, their impeccably dressed escorts attentive and refined.

Wearing my flaming red and the diamond earrings Nat had surprised me with, I met so many people, smiled and chatted with them—my heart beating madly—that I became, indeed, Mary the Red, the living legend. I was a bit dizzy with it all.

I moved from table to table. My gown was slit to midcalf, showing the embroidered clocks on the sides of my silk stockings. All the men eyed me, but with respect, and even the women were gracious.

One lady of forty, gowned in dove velvet, uttered what the other ladies weren't bold enough to say. "Mary the Red," she murmured. "Welcome. Stay just the way you are. It's a pleasure simply to look at you!"

She held out her hand, and I took it. We smiled together. I wished I might know her well, that we might be friends, but that wasn't possible. She was the sort who would associate with the Governor's wife, not the female partner of a club.

All six of the girls I'd chosen to work for us were exquisite, dainty, light-eyed blonds. They wore identical gowns of pale gold silk, the color of faint sunlight. I thought, as they moved among the tables, that they looked like fragile sunbeams. The diners seemed almost as impressed with them as they were with me, and I was delighted.

I'd never been busier. Certainly I'd never enjoyed such a sense of accomplishment. However, as the days passed into weeks and the weeks into months, even though we made substantial profits from the opening night on, I began to feel a vague premonition of disaster. As more time passed, the feeling persisted, no matter how firmly I pushed it away.

During these months Nat made love to me almost every morning just before dawn, after the club was closed. I sensed the deepening of his love, and knew that I was growing fonder of him. But when he asked me to marry him, as he did frequently, I couldn't bring myself to accept. My renegade heart still reached out for Roger.

Hurt by my latest refusal, one morning as the sun rose, he showed anger for the first time. "You're not the only woman in the world, or in the club!" he exclaimed. "I'm a man used to going after what he wants. And getting it. I know. I offered you partnership without obligation, and that stands. But I still want you, always will. Oh, hell!"

He rolled away from me, to the far side of the bed. After a while he slept, but I lay awake for hours. Before I dozed off, I'd come to a kind of decision. I was going to consider marrying Nat.

I fell asleep, with a sweet sense of peace.

The very next dawn, instead of joining me in our bedroom, he escorted Alice, one of the gaming room girls, through the entrance and away. I knew he'd gone to her room and, though it was my own fault, this saddened me. He didn't come back until it was time for the men to clean the rooms and the girls to get the tables ready. He behaved as though he'd done nothing more important than go to the shops.

At first Alice avoided me, then suddenly asked to speak to me in private. I took her to the bedchamber, knowing Nat was occupied in changing the gaming tables around.

"Sit down, Alice," I said, myself sinking into a chair.

She perched nervously on the arm of Nat's chair and gazed at me, her eyes wide and frightened. Her face was delicate, heart-shaped, and there was a sweetness to her rose-tinged lips that was very appealing. Her breasts, in the low-cut gown, showed almost half to the nipples, very white and enticing.

I sighed. Wondered how it felt to be so daintily colored, so blond. It seemed to me that the blaze of my hair was almost indecent compared to her pale beauty. She was like a lovely doll.

"What did you want, Alice?" I asked gently.

"About t-taking Nat to my room."

I managed a reassuring smile. "Knowing Nat," I told her, "it wasn't you who took him. It was the other way around."

A pulse fluttered in her throat.

"Don't feel so badly, Alice," I said. "I don't blame you. Or him."

"Oh, you mustn't blame him, Mary! I . . . let him . . ."

"I suppose you did."

"It shouldn't have happened! I like you . . . I don't want to hurt you. All of us girls like you . . . b-but when Nat starts smiling and teasing and . . ."

She broke off, almost weeping.

"He's hard to resist," I finished for her.

"If you won't d-dismiss me this time . . ."

"Of course I won't dismiss you, Alice. Wait." I held up my hand when she would have spoken. "Don't make any promises you'll not be able to keep. You or the other girls, either. Nat . . . well, in a manner of which you don't know, what happened was caused by something between him and myself."

I knew, as I spoke, that I was obliquely giving permission for all the girls in the establishment to be intimate with Nat. But it was a thing he would do himself if he chose, whether I wanted it or not.

"Then you don't h-hate me?" quavered Alice.

I studied her. I should hate her. She'd lain in Nat's arms, taken his body into her own. They'd experienced together the joy which, until now, had been mine and his alone. But I knew the reason. I knew the hurt in this man who hungered and yearned for me as his wife. It was impossible for me to resent Alice, much less hate her. She'd gone to her room with other men. And when the boss himself—

"You're not to blame," I assured her. "I have no reason to hate you. Now, go back and finish what you need to do before people begin to arrive. We'll forget this ever happened."

She scurried away. She hadn't promised it wouldn't happen again. Perhaps, I reflected, because she knew she really couldn't resist Nat. All the girls were half in love with him. I had noticed this and had been comfortably amused, being too busy with my club duties to give it thought.

I knew Nat hadn't gone with Alice to get revenge on me. Revenge wasn't in his nature. He'd gone out of pique. He would come back to me.

Which he did, the moment the night's business ended and the club was locked. We made no mention of where he'd been twenty-four hours ago. He made love to me tenderly.

But his absences became more frequent. He always came back to me. We never spoke of the situation. I believed, sadly, that he'd always return, knew that it was my fault he strayed from girl to girl. If and when I could tell him I'd be his wife, he'd leave the girls to the occasional man they permitted to accompany them to their rooms.

The club made more and more money. Each month, when Nat tried to give me half the profit, I refused to take it. "Use it to pay on my half of the investment," I insisted. He'd look thoughtful, search my black, upturned eyes, nod.

His nights with Alice and the other girls became less frequent. One morning, after he'd made love to me, murmuring his love, he lay holding me.

"You're not jealous of our blonds, are you, Mary?"

"No, Nat."

"And they're all on friendly terms with you even though . . ."

"Yes, Nat. Dear Nat. They're good girls. Every one of them."

"And you don't . . . care."

"I do care, Nat. But I understand. I have no right to complain. Or object."

"It's that . . . I get disturbed because . . . First thing I know, there I am, with Alice or Norma or Margie or one of them. It doesn't matter which. But you're my only love, Mary the Red, Mary the Beautiful."

I nestled closer. I almost, though I was held back at the last instant by that premonition which tormented me yet, told him I'd marry him. Almost.

That evening Calico Jack and Anne Bonny—dressed as pirates—came walking into the club just as the girls were setting the tables. It had been so long since I'd seen Anne that I gave a little cry, restrained myself from embracing her, and shook hands decorously with both.

"Nat!" I called. "Come see who's here!"

Calico was wearing a red calico shirt, yellow-figured breeches, and green sash. He waited for Nat, who came rushing, and they shook hands, clapping each other on the shoulder. Then he did the same with Anne.

I stood beaming at them. I still had no real trust in Calico even if he had given me a berth when I needed it. Anne had pushed him into it, anyhow; he'd got rid of me as fast as he could. Ah, Anne! It was impossible to tell, from her appearance or from our behavior, that she was a woman, my dear friend.

I longed to talk with her about Nat, woman to woman, to get her opinion on whether I'd be unfair to marry him. Maybe she could even tell me whether what I felt for him was really wife-love. And what I'd felt for Roger was a madness.

The four of us sat at a table, talking excitedly, the men sipping wine, Anne and myself water. She, too, disliked alcohol, though she had to drink her share of it.

"Lovey, I'm so happy you can live as woman," she murmured. "You were the handsomest lad who ever went to sea, but now . . . Well, if I really was . . . what everybody thinks I am . . . I'd be after you to marry me!"

I laughed. Nat and Calico laughed, too. "When're you going to settle down so this woman of yours can *be* a woman, Calico?" Nat asked, his hand on mine.

"When I'm chased off the waters. I wanted to quit once, but she talked me out of it. She's a handsome woman, and I'll like to show her off when the time comes. Right now, I'm tricking the Governor . . . pretendin' to comply . . . makin' repairs but I'm goin' to chase prizes, not pirates. Let them other fellows, layin' off some of these islands around, try to make a livin' fishin' . . . it's not for me."

"Calico's got pirate blood or I couldn't have talked him into going on," Anne said. "Until we get really rich. What matters is that we're together. I'll dress woman one day."

We sat in silence for a while.

Calico broke it. "That Englishman, the one you was with, Mary," he said. "I've pieced out the full story on him."

I stopped breathing. My ears began to sing. Was Calico going to say that Roger was dead? Oh, dear God, was he?

Nat's hand tightened on mine. "Tell her, Calico," he said.

Bless him, he knew I couldn't even speak.

"You've not heard nothin'?"

"I didn't ask," Nat replied. "Didn't care to know. But now . . . out with it and done."

"You must of heard he didn't overhaul *The Jasper,* Mary. The one you drugged him over. He'd have missed her anyhow. She sailed a week before schedule."

I leaned forward, impatient for more.

Calico's eyes narrowed. "He's held to be the most dangerous, most hunted pirate on the high seas today."

I let my breath out slowly. All the old, mad love swept me, streaked with bitter sadness because I knew Roger hated me.

The talk veered to other matters, and gradually I regained my composure. Calico and Anne stayed until just before it was time for me to dress to greet our diners, promising themselves to come for an evening soon.

At dawn Nat told me he was sailing to Havana to see about hiring a couple of pretty señoritas for the club. I managed to hide any surprise. He was going because of the information about Roger, I was certain of it!

When accused, he admitted this.

"Sure," he said. "You were with Courtney . . . how long . . . two years?"

"A-almost," I whispered.

"And you've been with me close to two years. With me trying to . . . Hell, if you don't have to see me every time you look up, maybe you can get things lined up in your mind. Whether you want to live with a memory or marry someone on the spot, ready and willing."

"Is that an ultimatum?" I asked, unsteadily.

"Of course not. Now look here, don't go to cryin'. It's just what I said, nothin' more. And if you still don't want to marry me after you've done some private thinking . . . or ever . . . I'll make do with things as they are. And count myself damned lucky."

My heart twisted. That Roger, leagues away and hating me, if he gave me a thought, should hurt Nat so! Nat, filled with love for me—Oh, I didn't know what I thought! I was confused, loving Roger with a fire which would not go out, fonder of Nat by the day! And now he was leaving, to give foolish me a chance to get over what was troubling me. And underneath all this, still lay that gnawing premonition of trouble, something dire and even dangerous, tormenting me.

Nat sailed at noon.

Listlessly, that night I made ready to greet the people who would soon be crowding the club. When they did, I met them at the door, led them to a table, summoned a waitress, chatted a bit if they were so inclined.

At about eleven, two exceptionaly rough looking pirates, the sort we seldom drew, entered the dining salon. As I led them to a remote table, we passed Nell and Jenny, kitchen-bound with empty trays, and the fellows reached out and tried to paw the girls.

"The table is here, gentlemen," I said, uneasy.

"Who-ee!" chortled the short, powerful, unkempt

one, a fellow in his forties. His garb was clean enough but, with his untidy tan hair and beard, his slits of eyes, he looked dirty. He had muscles in his arms and legs that stood out like rope.

"I beg your pardon?" I asked him coolly. "Do you prefer a table or the bar?"

"Look ut whut we got here, Horse!" snorted the pirate. "Ex-cuse me, Mary the Red . . . fine lady-whore . . . we're off'n a privateer an' gonna be in port fer a spell. Our captain's gonna turn pirate-chaser. Now that we've saw them wenches, we'll spend our time here tonight. Call me Bull. That's my name, 'cause I'm stronger'n any bull." He roared, laughing.

The diners at a nearby table glanced up, away.

The second pirate, a fraction taller than Bull, but very similar to him, so much so I wondered if they were brothers or whether it was pirate life that made them alike, roared, too. "Table, Mary the Red! Give us a table an' whiskey an' grub an' them wenches an' give us yer attention, or we'll take yer fancy place apart!"

I forced a smile. "There'll be no need for that gentlemen. Our girls will give you excellent service, as will my partner, Nat Cross."

There. Maybe they didn't know Nat had sailed. I wanted them to think I had a man behind me.

Something, either my civil words or the tone I used, calmed them and they followed Jenny to a table when I summoned her. As I turned away, they were giving their drink order.

Later, I saw them eating and drinking heartily. After that they danced with each of the waitresses— we allowed this when lone men came into the club and the girls had time—and, though they were loud enough that some of the better class people glanced at them occasionally, they caused no trouble.

There was an uncomfortable moment when the two of them approached me as I was speaking to our music leader.

Bull did the talking.

"We bin havin' a good time," he said. "Yer girls kin dance fine. Now we want to dance with the main one."

I glanced about, pretending not to understand. Bull put an end to this. "We want to dance with you," he growled. "Don't play innocent with us, lady-whore!"

"I'm so sorry," I told them evenly, with a smile. "I'm not permitted to dance. My partner requires that I keep an eye on the service at all times."

Bull's eyebrows shot erect. So did Horse's.

"Whut's wrong with us?" Bull demanded. "We're knew far an' wide. Bull an' Horse. Full brothers. Not to be crossed."

"Nothing's wrong with you," I said. "I truly don't dance with anyone."

Bull laughed, wide teeth rimming his huge mouth. "Yer girls do more'n dance! That right, Horse?" He gave his brother a poke in the ribs. Horse returned the poke, and they guffawed.

Relieved that they'd begun to treat the incident as a big joke, I held my anger and smiled as sweetly as possible. When they got their mirth under control, Bull chortled, "We got the rest of our night took, Mary the Red! An' well took!" They swaggered back to their table, watching Margie and Nell who, apparently, had agreed to go with them. For a price.

I knew that if Nat were here, he'd get the beasts out. Jim, the bartender, would try it now, as well as the musicians. I caught Jim's eye and he looked questioningly at me, but I shook my head slightly. For him to ask the brothers to leave would spark a fight, and we wanted nothing like that here.

The night ended peaceably.

The days and evenings which followed passed quietly. Calico and Anne, both in pirate dress, came to dine. Bull and Horse didn't return, though I knew they were still meeting Margie and Nell after hours.

I found myself missing Nat. I could do none of the constructive thinking about him I should have been. Even though he was probably sporting with girls in Havana, I looked forward to his return, to his love.

When he arrived, he brought no new girls.

"I decided against those dark-haired ones," he said. "We'll keep to our blonds, with you the red-head set off by 'em."

Our coming together that dawn was sweet and intense. Nat told me he hadn't touched a woman the whole time he was away.

"I take it," he finished, "that things are the same between us? You ain't ready to change nothin'?"

Almost, I whispered the words he longed to hear. But the knowledge that Roger lived and sailed the seas held me back. Knowing that all was ended with him, still I couldn't give Nat definite word, not yet. So I snuggled close, tempting, until he took me and we grasped our usual joy.

Three days later, one of the pirates who frequented our gaming tables brought astounding word. That sought-for privateer, *The Skull,* captained by Lord Roger Courtney, had boldly dropped anchor at Nassau, and her crew was coming ashore!

Chapter 24

I waited. The day passed. Roger didn't come. He'd know I was here, couldn't miss it. *Pirate Club,* with Mary the Red as hostess and co-owner, had become more than locally famous.

Nat heard the news shortly after I did. I could tell when he knew from the reserved manner in which he spoke, from his unusual quiet, from the absence of his ready smile. But there was no comfort I could give; I was in such turmoil I didn't know how I could get through my duties tonight.

I wore my most elegant red gown and the diamond earrings. I clasped the new diamond pendant Nat had brought from Havana around my neck. It glittered and flashed in the nest of lace at the top of my tight, figure-revealing bodice.

"I heard Courtney dropped anchor here," Nat said at last, watching me dress.

"I heard, too."

"Just . . . Hell, when you see him, don't forget that I'm even alive," he said.

"I could never forget you, Nat."

He was silent. Then, as though the question were pulled from him he asked, "Or . . . what we are to each other . . . and what I want for us?"

"I'll forget none of it, Nat," I promised.

He wanted to say more, did not. I longed to say more, dared not. I'd been on the verge of promising to marry him for some time, true, but that was when I thought Roger was lost to me. Now he was here, in Nassau. Now I needed more time. Time to see Roger, to find out whether the rage of love was real—and whether he wanted me—or if the safe, warm, friendly, trusting emotion I carried for Nat was the true one. I needed time, too, to make certain I'd not hurt Nat when there might be no need.

The diners began to arrive. I was glad that Nat's duties kept him in the gaming room. I controlled my expression sternly each time someone entered the salon, my heart burning that this time—surely this time—it would be Roger.

It was in this state that I saw the square-built, freckled, tanned pirate appear in the entrance and stand, eyes deliberately searching the salon. My heart lunged, for I recognized him before he found me, and went running to him, hands out.

"Karl!" I cried. "Oh, Karl! I thought . . . you were lost overboard during that hurricane! We all . . ."

He held my hands, his face as warm with smiles as his hands with coursing blood. "I got hold of some drifting timbers, got picked up after about twenty hours by a small privateer. Now I'm back on *Skull*. I didn't even know if you'd recognize me."

"Recognize you!" I chided, drawing him to a corner table. "I owe everything to you, Karl!"

I'd forgotten nothing—how he'd discovered me, a stowaway on the sloop then called *The Hague,* how he'd hidden me in the hold, fed me, brought water, explained about ships, got me taken on as cabin boy by Roger. Nor had I forgotten how I'd tried to repay him—my first friend—with my favors, and how I'd responded to him repeatedly. I hadn't forgotten that he'd fallen in love with me, at least a little.

I was so happy he'd been rescued, that he lived, that I was actually with him, I could have wept. He smiled at me again, and then I did weep a little.

"Now, look!" he exclaimed. "This is a happy time! And if you got any idea that anybody . . . even the Captain . . . will ever know about us . . ."

"Of course I haven't, Karl! It's just that I'm so *happy* you're alive, that I'm actually looking at you!"

He grinned, leaned back in his chair, looked around.

"Quite a place you and Cross got. Really fine."

I nodded. So. He knew about Nat. As would Roger. Well, why not? My being a pirate on *Sea Wolf,* being Nat's partner in the club, was widely known. That we were also lovers was obvious.

I smiled, took Karl's hand. "Are you hungry?"

"No . . . ate aboard."

"Then come." I tugged at his hand, led him into the gaming room and directly to Alice. "This is our lovliest girl," I said. "Alice . . . Karl van Buskirk from the days when I was a pirate, a very new one. I've a feeling that if he plays your table, he'll have a lucky night."

Alice understood instantly. She gave me the hint of a wink. Then, with honest liking, she told Karl, "If you are lucky, I expect you to entertain me when I'm through work."

Karl's light brown eyes flickered. He grinned.

"That'd be top luck!" He glanced at me, eyes full of understanding. "Thanks, Mary."

As the night wore on, I still watched for Roger. I went into the gaming room now and then to see how Karl was faring, and could tell that Alice was being very clever. I saw that Nat was aware of this and I took him aside and told him who Karl was, and he nodded.

The other players called Karl lucky, but he didn't win much at a time. He lost now and again, but the dice were often in his favor. He was pleased and, as his winnings slowly grew, he became happy and relaxed. Even his fellow players, some of whom were winning, others losing, caught his excitement and were pleased to see him do well.

"Break the bank!" they began to urge, but Karl only laughed. I smiled, knowing that Alice would never let that happen, knowing too, that Karl would stop playing first.

It was after eleven when he turned away, considerably richer than when he'd arrived. He laughed when other players said now his luck would pass to them, winked at Alice, put his winnings into his sash.

I walked outside with him.

"Alice told me where to find her room," he said. "But if you think . . ."

"Alice liked you. Don't disappoint her, Karl."

"I don't want you to think I'd rather have her, Mary. You're way out of my reach now, but I remember how it was. I'll not forget."

"I won't either, Karl. But things *are* different."

He looked at me half-sadly in the moonlight. Then he grinned. "You didn't have to give me a lucky night."

"I don't know what you're talking about."

"I saw Alice wink. I have my share of luck with dice, but not like tonight. I could have won on my own."

"I wanted to make sure."

"Why, Mary?"

"Once you were my only friend. Tonight I could make a friendly gesture of my own. You'll really like Alice, too. Who knows . . . you'll need a wife one day, and Alice . . . she'll make some man a really good wife!"

Our hands met, pressed, and we parted.

I went back inside. Most of the diners had gone and the activity now centered in the gaming room. A few latecomers straggled in for supper, and the trio struck up. The girls hastened to the tables.

Only then did Nat seek me out. "Van Buskirk," he said. "I recall the name. He's the one you told me about when you stowed away."

"Yes, Nat."

"Why didn't you introduce us?"

"To avoid embarrassment for both of you."

"I have no objection to what you were to him. Or against Courtney, for that matter. Only that he deserted you."

"But I drugged him, Nat!"

"I don't want to talk about it. Did he show up?"

"No. And I don't think he will."

He grunted. "That's the one thing to be thankful for." He went back to the gaming room.

But less than an hour later, at midnight, I looked up and saw Roger come through the entrance. He stood there, handsome, erect, cold-faced, richly clad in dark breeches and coat. My knees went weak.

But I went to him. As hostess it was my duty to greet each arrival, seat him at a good table, make him welcome, summon a waitress. I stopped before him, aflame with his nearness.

"Roger," I murmured.

He was silent.

My look flew to him. The white line stood deep around his lips; the very blue eyes were frozen on mine. That auburn hair was worn the same, but gleamed, surely, with more lustre. His patrician features had refined and grown sharper and stronger.

Looking at him was like gazing at a marble statue. My heart rocked.

"D-do you wish to sup?" I managed. "Or to game?"

"I've supped. I never game. I do my gambling on the sea."

I couldn't think of what to say. Between unsteady knees and rocking heart, it was all I could do to stand, to force a smile to remain on my lips. Always, before, the smile had been natural, but not now, dear God not now, faced with this man for whom I'd lay down life, for whom I'd walk through fire.

"I'll sit at a table with you," he said. "If you'll join me in a glass of wine, a sip only."

He remembered that I hated even wine!

I led to the most remote table. Nell took our order, brought it promptly. We hadn't spoken. When she'd left and he'd touched his lips to wine, Roger spoke.

"You've become incredibly beautiful."

I didn't know whether this was compliment or accusation.

"P-perhaps the . . . clothes."

"Doubtless they contribute, but there's more. These two years have enriched your beauty."

I went into utter, inward chaos. He remembered how many years it had been! He insisted—let it be accusation—that I'd grown beautiful! Surely, oh surely there was, behind the frozen manner, some remnant of warmth for me, some drop of love!

And then he destroyed that hope, giving the impression that he was vindictive and heartless though I knew this wasn't so. "You're very lovely . . . Mary the Red. Your fame has traveled the seas. But your selfishness, your ruthlessness, overwhelm the beauty and make it into ugliness."

"B-because I drugged you?"

He nodded.

"I did it because I loved you! Because you were heading into certain death!"

He made a sharp motion.

"You surely know I couldn't have overhauled *The Jasper* in any event."

I knew. I could have been with him these years!

"I heard," I said now, "but not for months. I didn't know whether you were dead or alive!"

"Now you know. Also that I'm still a privateer."

"They'll take you . . . you're wanted!"

"I'll discuss taking advantage of the Governor's hospitality and stop privateering. I may even chase a few pirates. Things have gone well. Another year, and I'll be on my estates. Even less."

"Roger! How wonderful!"

Then dread struck me. Back in England, would he seek out Genevieve? Did they plan to marry?

"You've done well for yourself," he said. "You have a partner."

"Yes. Nat Cross. He . . . when . . ."

"I quite understand," he said from clenched teeth. "He was there. You took advantage."

"You don't understand the first thing!" I flamed. "You abandoned me, Calico Jack gave me a berth, and then Nat . . ."

"He's an upstanding partner, I'm sure." Again that white line, near-hatred. No, it was hatred full-fledged! This man had cradled me in his arms, had kissed me, put his body into mine and together we'd soared almost to heaven. He had made love to me not with passion alone, but love. And now, that love had become hatred.

"Why did you come here?" I asked miserably.

"To see for myself. To see that Mary the Red is really you."

His words cut like knives.

"And now . . . what have you seen, Roger?"

"That you're like a flame, in that gown. That you are Mary the Red. That you're well . . . situated.

Right then my indecision about Nat came to an end. I resolved to tell him at once—tonight—that I'd marry him. Then, on the heels of decision, that premonition of disaster set in to torment me. Could it mean that something terrible was going to happen to Roger? For love clung in my stubborn heart despite his hatred. I'm lucky to have Nat, dear and wonderful Nat, I thought, and pushed the feeling of an evil to come firmly out of mind.

Roger stood, his wine finished. He made a small, stiff bow. "I understand the food here is remarkable," he said. "I'll come here one night."

And then he was gone. And I was trembling.

Almost immediately the two rough pirates, Bull and Horse, came in. Their walk had to be exaggerated to maintain a semblance of balance, they were so drunk. For the moment the salon was empty except for myself and the help, so I went to meet them, and managed to get them to leave before Nat found out they were here. He'd told me never to admit them again.

"It's not quite time for the girls to get off," I told them. "If you'd care to wait in the gardens . . ."

"Hell, no!" Bull interrupted. "We come to dance with Mary the Red!" he announced, thrusting his face at mine. "Ye can't say the other customers'll get jealous, 'cause they ain't none. We ain't goin' to be put off with them wenches this time. We're dancin' with you!"

One thought filled me. To avoid trouble. I saw Jenny about to slip into the gaming room to Nat, saw Jim move to leave his bar, and the musicians come to attention. With a quick motion I stopped them all.

I'd been through much worse than a mere dance with bullies. I'd get it over with, send them on their way before Nat knew. I nodded to the musicians, and they struck up a lively tune.

"Dancing only," I warned, stepping out of their reach. "If you want girls . . ."

"Done had girls!" Horse boasted. "We aim to dance with Mary the Red once, an' all hell ain't goin' to stop us!"

I went into Bull's arms first. He clutched me tight and began lumbering to the music. He stank of sweat, tobacco, whiskey. I held my breath as long as I could, then drew in air and held it again. He wasn't a bad dancer, even drunk. He talked constantly, boasting of the fights he'd been in, the duels, the booty he and Horse had taken.

I could hardly believe my turn with him was over when the music stopped. Then Horse grabbed me, the trio played, and it was the same thing over again. Horse boasted of how many women he'd charmed and showed signs of trying to describe what he'd done to them.

This I put a stop to by asking him to hum the tune with me as we danced. Thinking my request humorous, he began to hum. His foul breath hit me full-face, grew worse when he tried to sing the words, which he did in gusts.

At last it was over. Before they could insist on a second dance, I thanked them and suggested that they go to the bar for a free drink. Jim, straight-faced and proper, poured their drinks and, when the pirates weren't looking, dropped a bit of powder in each.

Once they'd downed the whiskey, they reeled to the door and out. I went shakily to the bar.

"What did you put in those drinks, Jim?"

"Opium. They'll go to sleep the minute they hit their berths. Maybe before. We'll have no trouble from them. They'll never suspect . . . they've drunk themselves into stupors before."

I didn't tell Nat what had happened, even after we were in our room. I did tell him of Roger's arrival, our conversation, and Roger's statement that he'd be back to dine.

"I don't think he'll really come," I said. "You needn't worry about him . . . the man hates me."

"But you, Mary? What about you?"

"I'm glad he hasn't been captured or killed. He still —disturbs me. But I'll never marry him."

We undressed in silence. We got into bed. Nat took me into his arms, but not for the usual lovemaking. Instead, he stroked my hair tenderly, stroked my

cheeks, drew one fingertip along my brow, down my
nose, and lightly over my lips. Almost, I whispered
that I was ready to be his wife.

Not yet, that uncanny premonition warned, not yet.

Chapter 25

We were giving a ball at the club, a supper affair,
which we planned to establish as a yearly event. We'd
been preparing for months. Nat had ordered a new
red gown for me from London, a diamond bracelet,
and a finger-ring with a big diamond to wear along
with my earrings and pendant.

The gaming room would be closed for the evening,
and all six of our blonds would serve the dining
tables. I'd had new gowns ordered for them, all identical and in the pale yellow, but of finer silk and
trimmed with costly lace. Jim had new black silk
breeches and satin coat, and the men in the music
trio were to be dressed the same.

The doors of the club weren't open to the public
this one night. Attendance was by invitation only. The
Governor was invited, lesser officials, all the leading
men of the town, and their ladies. A few ex-pirates
were included. Karl van Buskirk, Calico Jack, and
Anne Bonny were among those given invitations.

It was Nat who suggested that we invite Roger,
said to be converting his vessel to pirate-chaser, and
his mate, Vannice. I was undressing for bed when he
mentioned it, and stopped, surprised.

"You don't want Roger here, Nat."

"I prefer having him to excluding him. I'm not jealous of the man, Mary. I come near to hating him

because he treated you so badly. If you don't mind
him being among the rest of the folks, I want it."

I gazed at him, puzzled.

"Don't you see, Mary? We're asking the other 'respectable' pirate captains. Courtney's been getting
acquainted in Nassau. I don't want folks speculating
as to why he's not here. I want this affair to be a
success all the way."

"Then we'll invite him," I agreed. "Probably he'll
come for the same reason we're including him."

I held my tone even, so that Nat wouldn't sense my
inner turmoil. Personally, I never wanted to see
Roger Courtney again. It was too painful. I wished
he'd take *Skull* and sail right back to England, not
make Nassau his headquarters, even for a while. This
way, I'd have to see him at times, know how he hated
me, torment myself that it was his presence which
was keeping me from telling Nat I'd be proud and
happy to marry him.

On the night of the ball, Nat and I—he in rich tan,
I in flame and diamonds—stood at the door to welcome our guests. The trio played a subdued, melodi-
ous background of music. The guests were escorted
by our blonds to tables draped with new white
damask, a-glitter with glass and silver.

Calico and Anne arrived in silk pirate outfits—
Calico's orange, Anne's blue. She looked more handsome than I'd ever seen her as a man.

Roger, Vannice, and Karl, in dark, well-cut garb,
were the last pirates to arrive. I introduced them to
Nat, then they followed Margie to a table. I watched
them go, crushing the unnerving effect which Roger,
looking so handsome and aloof, had exerted upon me.

"It's perfect," I murmured to Nat, looking out over
the salon at the tables where the cream of Nassau
society and the ex-pirate world alike laughed and
murmured. And Roger. He really had come. I realized, now, that I would have felt hurt if he hadn't
attended, regardless of how stiffly he conducted him-

self. At least he was here. He was seeing me in my most beautiful gown, adorned with Nat's diamonds, my hair dressed high, creating a new look of elegance.

"I can see why women are drawn to Courtney," Nat muttered. He and Roger had only nodded when introduced. "Now. If you'll see to our guests . . . Jim'll help . . . there's a new young lady in town I've invited to be my partner for the evening."

I nodded, stricken. It was nothing new for him to seek out other women. But for him to escort one to our ball, to have kept it a secret until now, to be her official table partner, was a shock.

I'd assumed that, in any interval of freedom, Nat and I would be together. I'd counted on it, wanting Roger to see that if he didn't want my company, someone else did. Now I'd be partnerless at my own ball.

By the time Nat returned, a stunning, black-haired beauty on his arm, dinner had begun and the guests were exclaiming over the salad Powell and I had created. Head up, smiling, I went to Nat as he and his companion entered.

The girl was perhaps eighteen to my twenty-five, slim, but enticingly curved. She was a bit taller than Nat, a study in black and white, Her shining black hair was pulled to the top of her head, a diamond clasp just under the graceful knot. Her eyes were as black as my own, her skin very white, features like carved marble, set off with red, perfect lips. Diamonds glittered at her ears, on her fingers, and a diamond necklace flashed on her neck, set against the rich black silk of her gown.

She smiled at me. I smiled back, liking her, but disturbed. How could Nat leave *this* beauty to return to me—if she wanted him?

"Señorita Juanita Martinez y Lopez, Miss Mary Read," Nat introduced us. "Juanita is in Nassau with her father, who has come on business. He didn't feel well enough to attend tonight . . . and it was an eleventh hour invitation . . . but has entrusted us with his daughter for the evening."

I murmured politely and escorted them to the table I'd reserved for Nat and myself. Making a graceful excuse, I left them and wandered about, making certain that all the guests were faultlessly served.

Inevitably, I arrived at the table occupied by Roger, Vannice, and Karl.

"This food is the best," Vannice said. "And the club is beautiful."

"Thank you, sir. For ordinary nights, there's a gaming room, of course. Outside, we have gardens people think are very nice, too."

"Gardens," Roger said. "Will you show them to me?"

Our eyes locked. For an instant, I saw a blaze in his. Then they were cold, deep blue. He rose.

"Now?" I exclaimed. "You're not half through . . ."

"If you'll excuse me," he said to Vannice and Karl. They nodded, faces blank.

Roger offered his arm. I placed my hand on it. The lights caught the diamond on my finger and it flashed. His arm stiffened.

Outside, we followed stepping stones through the walled gardens. We wandered paths in silence, passing hibiscus, winding through trees where were set, at intervals, stone benches. The music faded, throbbed like a whisper from the stars above.

He stopped at a bench under the palm trees. "Shall we sit?"

I sank to the bench, my hand slipping off his arm and into my lap. He took his place beside me, so closely our thighs were all but touching.

Why had he brought me here? To reproach me further? To—? But no, he'd never apologize, ask my forgiveness.

"I've been thinking," he said. "Nat Cross. Are you getting married, or . . . ?"

"It's none of your business, Roger Courtney!" I cried, unable to keep the ache out of my voice, the

pain, the futility of speaking with him at all. Whatever we'd had together—and heaven knew it had
been an interlude on his part, a total giving on mine
—was ended.

"*Are* you marrying Cross?" he persisted.

"We . . . have no such plans."

"Because you don't want it, or because he . . . ?"

"Oh, why do you keep at me?" I half-wept. "He'd
marry me tomorrow!"

Or he would have, before he discovered the lovely
Juanita. Miserably, I thought how I'd hate Nat's marrying her; even more miserably, I wanted to get away
from Roger now, this minute, before he hurt me
afresh. Yet, against my will, my truant heart kept me
with him.

The far-away music throbbed.

"Mary." His voice was hoarse, words torn from
him. "In spite of the way I spoke before, I . . . God
help me! I love you!"

My ears rang. My breath caught.

"No," I whispered. "I don't believe . . . can't
believe."

"All the time we've been parted, I've tried to hate
you. I've tortured myself with memories. Of how I
made you strip and act like a man to make myself
resist you. The bath . . . the hell it was to resist . . .
I kept telling myself you were a bad woman because
you let me make love to you, that you did it only
for my silence as to your true sex."

I waited, throbbing with that music from the stars.
"So. Being without you was torture. I heard you were
Mary the Red of Nassau. I sailed here to find out.
Then, when I saw you, I treated you . . . I had to
leave. I told myself I didn't love you, asked myself
what man could love a woman who . . . Tonight I
came to finish the job, to rid myself of you. But when
I saw your wonderful beauty still again, with good-
ness shining through, I admitted the truth. At last."

"Roger . . . oh, Roger!"

His arms came around me with hunger. His lips

encompassed mine, and we kissed as we'd done so often in the past. But this was sweeter. It was reunion, with love acknowledged. Lips clinging, I waited for him to ask me to be his wife, to say we'd return to England together.

"Come away with me, darling," he murmured. "Now I have you back, *Skull* will continue as privateer until I've finished. Come be my cabin boy . . . my pirate . . . my beloved! Sail the seas with me, capture the prizes! Live in my arms forever!"

He was kissing me again, and I was ready to go where he went, do what he fancied. To be with him. And he'd said forever.

"Will you, sweet darling?" he whispered against my lips.

"Yes!" I whispered back. A question stirred, but there was no need to ask. He'd said forever. Of course he'd take me to England! Of course we'd be married! That I'd have to dress as pirate again for a time, live as a pirate, carried no weight. The time would be short, and I'd be with Roger.

"Two days, Mary. Can you be ready?"

"Of course!" I murmured, bemused.

I thought of Nat and a wisp of sadness went through me. This was wiped out by Roger's next kiss.

We continued to kiss, tenderly at first, then with growing passion.

It was Roger who stopped. "No more. Not until you break with Cross. Not until you're back on *Skull*."

I let him draw me up, walk me back to the salon. I was in absolute turmoil. Yesterday, I'd been on the verge of telling Nat . . . dear Nat . . . that I'd be his wife. Tonight I must tell him I was going back to Roger.

When we were inside, I put a smile on my lips, walked with Roger back to the table where Vannice and Karl still sat. They'd finished dinner. Roger said he must get back to *Skull*, and Vannice said he'd go along. Karl decided to stay on. The others bade me goodnight, passed Nat, who was dancing with Juanita, and left.

In an effort to calm myself, I danced with Karl, then with two guests, chatting and smiling, remembering not a word of what we said. Outwardly, I was in control. Inwardly there was torment over the hurt I was going to inflict on Nat. Nat, who loved me deeply, who had thrown away my pirate garb, had made it possible for me to live as a woman.

A flicker of uncertainty stirred, was gone.

I trusted Roger. He'd come to Nassau, searching for me. I did love Nat, with fondness and liking, but Roger I loved with all the same fire and passion. Hard as it would be, it was necessary that I tell Nat and try to make him understand.

All the while, he danced with Juanita. I wished he would fall in love with her, but knew better. I'd seen him behave this way, out of pique, before. And now he had reason. Roger was in Nassau, Nat knew how I'd once felt about him, and must have seen me go into the gardens with him. I sighed, watching his dear face.

Unexpectedly, at this moment, there came a clamor at the entrance. I glanced over; my hand flew to my throat. There stood Bull and Horse. I'd been so thankful they hadn't come into the club again, and now they were shouldering into the private ball, to which they hadn't been invited.

They weren't drunk, though they'd been drinking.

"Lookut that wench with black hair!" Horse roared.

Every head, even those of the dancers, turned. A few broke step, then caught the rhythm and danced on. Nat steered Juanita further from the entrance, dancing, mouth grim.

"I aim to dance with 'er!" bellowed Bull.

Jim started for the entrance at the same time I did. Nat was making his excuses to Juanita as I passed them, and I motioned him not to leave her. He frowned, resumed dancing, but kept his gaze on the ruffians.

Before either Jim or myself had gone three steps, the brothers, walking abreast, had ploughed through the dancers on the floor, bumping them. "Private party, huh?" Bull bellowed as they came.

"Private, hell!" roared Horse. "Out'n our way. My brother, he aims to dance with the black-headed 'un!"

Nat thrust Juanita behind himself and stood spraddle-legged, ready for the oncoming brothers. His face was as expressionless as rock. I'd never seen it that way. His sunny nature might never have existed.

"You're right on one point," he said as the two surged to a halt in front of him. "This is a private ball. For invited guests only."

"Don't fergit we're pirates!" shouted Horse. "We don't wait to be asked nowhere! We're both goin' to dance with that black-headed wench, an' after that . . ."

Nat's hand flew out, slapped the shouting Horse across the mouth. "Choose your second," he said murderously. "And your weapon. I'll meet you on the beach, beyond our gardens, at dawn!"

"Hell fire an' damnation!" roared Bull, convulsed with laughter. "The Gaw-damned fool'd dare my brother to a *duel!* Not a man-fight, but a gentleman's duel!"

The music had stopped. The dancers melted from the floor. The raucous laughter cut off. The room throbbed with silence. I stiffened my knees. *Nat* to fight that pirate who was more beast than human?

Then Horse began to guffaw. "A duel!" he shouted. "Makes a nice change!"

"I'll be yer second!" yelled Bull.

"I take pistols!" screamed Horse in delight.

Chapter 26

The brothers swaggered to the entrance. Here, they stopped to shout an invitation to all present to watch the duel.

"See how a pirate wipes a gambler off'n earth!" Horse bragged. "C'mon, Bull! I want to get the pistols oiled up! An' give Cross time to rest . . . his last livin' rest!"

Laughing uproariously, they left. The sounds from them became less loud, then faded into distance. Nat held out his hands to our guests.

"Please," he said, tone warm and sunny as usual though I, who knew him so well, detected strain, "don't leave! There's a second dessert to come, and a singing trio . . . three of our lovely girls! And more dancing. Until dawn, as things were planned!"

He gestured to the musicians, who began to play, then turned to Juanita and they began to dance again. Slowly, the stunned guests did as he'd requested. But of course, I thought proudly. They were that kind of people. Civilized. Gallant. I danced again with Karl, who made no comment, but shook his head when I looked into his eyes.

While Juanita was dancing with Karl, I motioned Nat to follow me into the gardens. Because it was the most secluded, I led him to the bench where earlier I'd sat with Roger.

"Are you insane, Nat Cross?" I demanded. "You can't fight a duel with that . . . animal!"

"And why not?"

"Because you haven't got a chance against him! He's used to killing, to . . ."

"I've done a bit of killing, Mary."

"But with knife and cutlass! You're not expert with the pistol, you know you're not!"

"I've got to be now."

"It's too big a risk! I've seen you with the pistol . . . you're as apt to miss as hit! Oh, *why* did you give him choice of weapons?"

"That's the proper way. You challenge, and you give the other fellow choice of weapon."

"Why must you fight for Juanita, to begin with?"

"It ain't for her. It's for our club. For you and I."

I put both hands on his arm. "Please, Nat . . . please don't fight this duel!"

"I've got to."

"The club isn't worth it! You're going to stand on that beach with a pistol in your hand and run the risk of that animal putting a bullet through your heart! Go to him right now. Hunt him down. Beat him up with your fists, or take a beating, if you must, but please . . . no duel . . . please!"

"You don't challenge a man, then take it back."

"But this isn't a real duel!" I pleaded. "This isn't a point of honor between gentlemen! It's . . . foolhardy . . . to dignify that low pirate with a challenge! And over a girl you hardly know!"

"It ain't Juanita, I told you that. It was the insult of that scum breaking into our ball, struttin' up to me and taking charge! I'm either the man-half of this establishment, or I'm a coward. I'd have done the same if the girl had been Alice or Marge or any of them!"

"Nat . . . I . . . forbid you to fight this duel!"

"Sorry, darling," he said, put his arms around me, and gave me a quick, warm kiss. I kissed him back, trying desperately to persuade him even when words had failed.

He drew me up from the bench. "To our guests. It's dancing until dawn!"

I walked reluctantly beside him, casting about for some argument, anything to persuade him to call off the duel. As though he knew, he put his arm around me, pressed.

"I can't make your mind easy about the duel," he said. "But I can about Juanita. I brought her here to make you jealous. Silly fool. You just ain't the jealous kind."

"I did think you might become devoted to her," I confessed. I sighed. I still had to tell him I was leaving with Roger, but this was not the time. I would wait until after the duel.

"I'm taking Juanita to her father, then coming back." he said as we reached the entrance. "Think you can manage alone?"

We stepped inside. I looked around, nodded. The music was playing, the guests were having the second dessert, many were dancing. It was as if the episode of the pirates had never been.

Karl was at the bar, an untouched whiskey in front of him. As soon as Nat and Juanita had left, I caught Karl's eye and he joined me at his table.

He held my chair. I sat down, and in that instant the way to save Nat hit me. Only I needed help. And here was rough, kind Karl who had always helped me when I needed it.

"Karl," I said, "I need you."

"Just tell me what you want, Mary."

"It's Nat. He can't fight that duel. We can't let him!"

Karl shook his head, its sun-dusty hair so neatly combed. "He's askin' for certain death if he ain't expert with the pistol. Both them brutes . . . Bull an' Horse . . . are the best I ever seen."

"You've watched them?" I could hardly breathe.

"At targets. For money. They never missed, always won."

"Karl, I can't let Nat die! If you . . . will you lend me your roughest pirate clothes?"

"Well, sure. But I don't see what that's got to do with . . ."

"Please, Karl! And don't ask me to explain! Just bring me the clothes and then, if you will, come with me!"

He frowned. "When?"

"Now. As fast as you can get to *Skull* and back. And bring two sashes!"

He hesitated. I didn't say another word, but gazed at him, my black, tear-filled eyes pleading for me. At this moment I couldn't have uttered a sensible word if Nat were to die in the next heartbeat.

"I can stay right with you, Mary?"

I nodded.

"Every minute?"

The tears spilled over. I brushed them away, nodded. Only then did he go.

Nat returned, but when I tried to corner him and plead again, he shook his head and lost himself among the guests, telling me to do the same. Indeed, so intent was he on keeping away from me, that when Karl appeared at the entrance, I was able to slip outside unnoticed.

I hurried him into the gardens.

"You brought everything?"

"Even boots. I 'borrowed' them off the galley boy. He was asleep. Mine are so big you'd not be able to walk. Remember?"

"I remember," I whispered. He'd outfitted me on *Skull* when she was still *The Hague* and I was a stowaway. Now he was outfitting me again.

Winding through the garden, now moonlit, we came to the windows of the bedchamber. They were open to the sweet night air.

"Wait here," I whispered. "Stand watch. I'll not be long!"

He helped me through a window, handed in the clothing. Hurriedly, I locked the door lest Nat come in, stripped off my diamonds, put them in a drawer, pulled off my clothes to the skin.

Hating their very touch, I put on rough breeches and a white, full-sleeved shirt. There was no breast-binder now, but the shirt was large and made full, so there was no hint of breast. I put on the men's stockings, tugged on the boots, and they were almost a perfect fit. I put one sash around my waist. The other, which was yellow, I wound around my head as some pirates did, making certain that no hair showed, not even at the nape.

I took one long moment before the full-length mirror Nat had bought for me. I stood with feet apart, like a man. I squared shoulders and jaw, hardened chin and eyes. I flexed my throat, recalling that the voice which now came forth must be low-pitched like that of a man.

I stared at myself, man again. Shuddered. I, who had dressed woman, lived woman, was again what I'd been for so many years—a female masquerading as a man. Never, not even when I was a tiny girl, had I hated men's clothing as I did now.

Yet it was the only way.

I strode to the window, flung a leg over the sill, dropped to the ground. Karl, who had stepped forward to catch me, let his arms fall.

He whistled softly.

"Well?" I asked, man-low.

"If I didn't know better," he whispered, "I'd stake my life!"

"On what?"

"Stand here. Where both moon and lamp hit you."

I moved to where he said.

He studied me closely. "I would. I'd stake my life," he repeated. "That you're a pirate. One I never saw before."

"Not Red, the cabin boy, the young pirate?"

"Not him. You're taller . . . stronger . . . wear a turban. Nobody'll know you." He shook his head. "You're not only a man again, but you're a different man."

This was what I needed to know.

"Let's go," I said.

"Where to?" he muttered as we went through the gardens.

"Midnight Club. Hurry!"

"Won't Nat miss you?"

"I don't think so. I'm supposed to be mixing with the guests. That's what he's doing, too."

Now we were moving along the city's dark streets. I was half-running, my legs feeling undressed without the full skirts to which I'd grown accustomed.

Karl protested every step, trying to find out why I was going to the *Midnight,* saying I should have stayed at my ball, that the hour was very late. I didn't even listen.

We entered the *Midnight* which, despite the guests at *Pirate Club,* was crowded. Karl, hand on my arm, trying to hold me back, had no choice but to follow, for I pulled against him. Inside, because we were supposed to be two men, he had to let go my arm, muttering.

"This is a bad place tonight," he said. "All the worst elment is here. I don't see why . . ."

I swept my glance about, skimming over those at tables, those moving about the dance floor, and others lined two-deep at the bar. A bellowing laughter rose from a clot of pirates there, and I looked more closely. Sure enough, in their midst were Bull and Horse Brambant.

I pushed through the crowd to them. Karl, protesting, grabbed at my arm, but I jerked away and shouldered between the brothers, holding a mean and aggressive expression on my face. I pounded the bar and yelled for whiskey.

The men nearest turned to stare. Bull and Horse bristled. I shot each of them a hard look which aggravated them further. I saw that, though drinking, they were far from being drunk. Which meant, I knew with a lurch of heart, that they were keeping sober for the duel.

"Who ye think ye are?" demanded Horse.

"Stranger to me," growled Bull. "Whut vessel ye off of?"

"None of yer business," I snarled, put my shoulder to his and shoved. "Move over! I need room!"

"That right?" howled Bull. "Watch out . . . my brother's a dangerous fella . . . both of us is!"

I wrenched free of Karl, who had clamped a hand on each of my shoulders. I aimed the opposite shoulder and jabbed Horse, again demanding room. "When I drink, I need space!" I boomed, surprising myself with my own male voice.

Karl grabbed my shoulders again, and this time I really had to jerk to free myself. It angered me a bit that he permitted me to get free, knowing that he could handle me easily. I was angered, not because he let go, but because it lowered Karl in the estimation of the onlookers, and I knew him to be a better man than any of them.

And onlookers there were. They drew around us, jammed together, reaching halfway to the door. They were laughing, throwing comments, pushing.

"Don't back down, stranger!" shouted a voice.

"Don't take no shove from no newcomer, Horse!" yelled another.

"Tell yer name, stranger!" shouted one.

" 'Dueler!' " I boomed, using the first thing that came to mind. " 'Dueler,' and fer good reason!"

Bull and Horse shoved their glowering faces at me, lips back, teeth stained and dirty. They looked, literally, like great, snarling animals. I stiffened, glowered.

"Don't b'lieve it, hey?" I challenged.

"Never heard 'bout no Dueler!" Horse growled. "Only me! I'm the Dueler, I am!"

"Yer sayin' I'm not the 'Dueler?' " I demanded.

"I'm sayin' it!" he brayed. "To yer teeth!"

Steeling myself, I slapped him across the mouth. The sound cracked. "The Dueler don't take no insult from no man!" I bellowed. "I demand satisfaction, here an' now!"

Horse lunged for me; Bull yanked him back.

"Yer gonna get satisfaction an' then some!" he grated.

"Yeh!" Horse agreed. "Here an' now! On the beach!"

"Name yer weapon!" I returned.

"Knives," Horse said promptly. "I'm killin' with pistols at dawn. Knives fer now."

"I'm his second!" Bull yelled.

"I'm 'Dueler's' second!" Karl shouted.

"Fifteen minutes!" Bull yelled. "On that strip behind *Pirate Club!*" He gestured, including everyone. "Yer all invited!" he bellowed. "Yer gonna see my brother win two duels . . . one now, t'other at dawn!"

Karl hustled me out of the gaping, swearing, shouting crowd. When we were well away, hurrying toward the designated spot, he began to say everything he could to persuade me not to fight the duel, but I was not swayed.

"You haven't got a chance, Mary! If he'd named pistols . . . but knives!"

"I was surprised about knives," I replied. "And relieved. I can shoot, yes. But my fencing instructor said I was professional with both rapier and knife."

"But these bastards are killers!"

"I've killed with the knife, Karl."

He said no more, but I could feel his concern grow.

By the time we arrived at the strip of sand, so had the gathering from the *Midnight.* The guests were spilling out of our club, drawn by the noise of the others, the shouts and uproar. The groups came to a halt, the *Midnight* people on the city side, our guests on the club side of the beach, separated from each other.

Karl and I stood on the beach between two tall palms. The full moon showered light over trees, beach, people.

Nat came hurrying to us. He gave me a glance. There was no recognition.

"What's going on?" he demanded. "Why are you and . . ." He gave me a second, keener look, puzzled, but still not knowing me. "Who is this fellow?" he asked Karl.

"I'm the Dueler," I said promptly, before Karl could speak.

"He's goin' to fight Horse Brambant with knives," Karl said.

Nat stared. "What's *your* quarrel with Horse?" he asked.

"He wouldn't give me standin' room at the *Midnight*. He insulted me 'bout duelin'. I'll learn him! If he lives to remember!"

Nat was looking at me searchingly, almost suspiciously.

"Cross," Karl exclaimed low, "it's Mary!"

Nat gave me another probing look, shook his head. "No. A resemblance only. This ain't Mary. She's all woman. This fellow's tough . . . he ain't got a drop of humanity in him!"

"Ask her. She won't lie, not to you."

Nat scowled, stepped close. "I've got my own way. Stand still . . . I ain't going to overstep myself."

He sniffed the air at my head, then thrust one finger into the side of my turban, touching my hair. He dropped his hand, swore. "What's behind this?"

"It started because he wouldn't give me room at the bar," I replied. "He insulted me and I challenged him."

"I don't mean that, damn it! Why did you dress like this and go to *Midnight?*"

"M-maybe I just felt like it! Maybe I get t-tired of dressing like a woman!"

"If this is about Juanita, I told you . . ."

"It's not that!"

"Mary," Karl said, "maybe you'll hate me the rest of your life, but I had to speak up. And now I've got to say more." Before I could protest, he rushed on. "Cross, she provoked this duel. She thinks she can stop your duel. Thinks, I suppose, that she can at least wound Horse so he can't fight."

Fiercely, Nat forbade me to proceed with my duel.

Point blank, I refused to be swayed. I could hardly keep my chin from trembling, but I did.

"I'll tell them you're a woman, and stop the duel!" he threatened.

"You do that," I threatened right back, using the first weapon that came to mind, "and I'll leave you!"

The words sickened me. Duel or no duel, I was going to leave Nat for Roger. My threat was a lie and, if he gave in to it, a betrayal. But I had to do it.

He stood mute, staring at me.

"I'm good with knives," I reminded him. "That's what we're using."

"Horse is an animal. You're a woman."

"Nat, if you keep me from this, I'll not only leave you, but I'll find a way to get rid of Horse before dawn. And that would mean facing Bull at the same time, and he'd finish me if Horse didn't!"

"I can tie you up. Gag you."

"And afterward I'd still leave."

We both fell mute.

His unspoken question beat between us. Why, Mary . . . because you love me? And I couldn't answer the question because of Roger.

Dimly, in the argument and confusion, I recognized that my premonition of evil had been valid. It was here; it was upon us.

"Please," Nat said. "Don't, Mary."

"The answer is no. I've got to."

It wasn't my threats or my determination or Nat's inclination which prevented him from stopping me, but the press of onlookers as Horse and Bull tromped out over the sand to us. It was the closing in of people. It was the mood of blood-thirst which gripped them.

Those from *Midnight* halted at the north edge of the beach. Our guests clustered at the south end. All were silent as death.

Even then Nat would have laid his hand on me, but Karl stopped him. "Cross," he said, "stand back. Her mind's made up."

Nat hesitated, face like stone. He turned, walked to

the edge of our crowd, but I sensed he meant to interfere if Horse became a certain danger to me. I saw
Calico and Anne Bonny draw close to him. A row behind them, I glimpsed Roger. A flash of apprehension
took me that he might see through my disguise, but I
made myself go on.

Bull and Horse stopped in front of us. Bull, acting
for his brother, gave me the choice of knives. They
were a matched pair, handles of carved wood, blades
murderous, sharp, pointed, glinting. I studied them,
took the one I thought would fit my hand, and it did.
Horse took the other one.

Our seconds stood us back to back, our hands hanging, knives pointing at the sand. Karl squeezed my
shoulders, let go.

It was Bull who counted out the paces. "One . . .
two . . . five . . . seven . . . " to the awful end. Sand
moved and slid under my boots; I could hear the
sound it made.

The counting ended.

We whirled, sand spraying, knives at the ready.
Slowly, every sense alert, I moved toward Horse.
Slowly, head drawn between his big shoulders, knife
low, he moved toward me.

Slowly, oh so slowly, the distance between us lessened.

Now I could see his evil face, see the grin that was
no grin, but a baring of teeth. I pressed my lips together, eyes keen on that other knife, that burly, powerful body.

We were within reach of each other.

We circled.

Horse lunged, blade swishing through air. Simulta-
neously, I danced to the side, parried. Our blades
clashed, the sound ringing on the silence—the unbreathing, deadly silence. Again we circled, eyes slit.
We thrust, leapt apart, parried. Again our blades rang
together and we danced aside and back.

I was aware of the silent onlookers. The *Midnight*
crowd was on the side of the pirates, I knew. The

guests, I hoped, were on my side, though they didn't know my identity.

I was constantly on the move—approaching, retreating, circling. The cool night breeze fanned my blazing face, gave me courage, added to my wariness, my patience. I felt neither male nor female, but only a being who had to fight for Nat's life.

Now I took—and held—the offensive, not daring to wait, lest Horse take it. He feinted and, as I parried, he gave a tremendous lunge and his blade sliced along my leg, above the boot. I felt only numbness as I leapt backward, then sprang at him again, circling, ever circling.

I could hear his loud, feral breathing as we thrust. Once I sank my knife into his shoulder, and while I was wresting it out of his rocky muscle, took the point of his knife along the ribs, feeling instant wetness.

We drew apart, both bleeding.

Silence, unbreathing silence from the onlookers.

We crouched, advanced, eyes set.

Sand dragged at my boots, yet I moved well. Horse came at me fast, knife aimed for my heart. I whipped my blade under and up, deflecting his with a clash. We danced, bleeding, ready. Again he made for the heart, definitely on the offensive now, and again I shot my blade under his and this time, as his arm flew up, the tip of his knife caught my turban, ripped it away, and my hair tumbled, blazing, under moonlight.

A low cry, a sort of anguished moan, went up from both crowds.

Horse and I crouched. Worked ever nearer, intent on the kill. We went for each other in the same instant. I brought my blade up under his yet again. Fast, even as he was in mid-lunge, I pulled back my arm, drove straight for the heart with all my strength. The knife went in to the hilt. He stayed on his feet for an instant, eyes staring, and then staggered backward a step and fell, face to the moon.

Chapter 27

I stood in my tracks, the sea breeze whipping my hair across my face, and trembled. Bull raced to his fallen brother, knelt over him. Karl and Nat reached me at the same time but, though I was shaking, I wouldn't let them support me.

Bull sprang to his feet.

"He's dead . . . Horse's dead!" he howled.

The knowledge pierced my own heart like a knife. I'd hoped only to wound, to incapacitate, not to kill. Not even when, in desperation, I aimed for the heart.

Bull thrust his face into mine as though he'd gone mad. "It's you! Whore-bitch! You kilt Horse! Dressin' like a man . . . !" He swung nose-to-nose with Nat. "You 'us the one he wus to fight the duel with!" He struck Nat across the mouth with the back of his hand. "I'm challengin' you to fight me in place of Horse . . . him not able . . . an' it bein' yer woman's fault! Here an' now, an' with pistols, like Horse wanted!"

"Nat!" I screamed. *"No!"*

I tried to hold his arm, but he shook loose, pushed me away so hard I almost fell to the sand. Calico and Anne came to me, pulled me back a few paces.

Both crowds were murmuring now. The whole thing became a nightmare. It went on and on. Some murderous looking pirate shouted that he'd be Bull's second; Karl stood beside Nat and declared he'd serve him in that capacity. Pistols were brought, Nat was given his choice, but scarcely glanced at them, seeming to take the first one he touched.

Nat and Bull were placed back to back. Karl counted

the paces. They went so slowly, so very slowly. I struggled to run after them, but Calico and Anne held me in a vise. Moonlight showered on the white sand, on the palms, on the separate groups, on the dead Horse where someone had dragged him and left him.

Karl shouted out the last number.

Nat and Bull whirled, pulled trigger. The shots cracked out, rode the breeze, and were gone as both men dropped.

Concentrated gasps went up from the onlookers. I tore free, and ran limping and bleeding, to Nat. As I dropped to the sand beside him, Bull's second growled that Bull was dead, shot through the heart.

Karl was leaning over Nat. I pushed him aside and gathered Nat into my arms.

He gazed up at me. "Mary . . . my Mary?"

"Yes, Nat."

"You're all right . . . didn't get . . . ?"

"No, darling . . . I'm fine."

"You . . . really . . . you called me . . ."

"Darling. And I mean it, Nat."

"If only . . ." His voice was low, so frighteningly low.

I realized, vaguely, that the onlookers had gathered in, was aware of those from *Midnight,* from our club, Calico and Anne, even Roger. But still I was oblivious, all my being centered on the dear one in my arms.

"If only what, my darling?" I murmured.

" . . . you could have . . . married . . . me. Mrs. . . . Nat . . . Cross."

In pirate garb, hair flowing, I cradled him, held him tenderly. He looked up at me with a ghost of sunny smile. He was frighteningly pale, and I brushed the sunny hair gently, rested my hand along his cheek. It felt cool.

I glanced at Karl. He gave a tiny shake of his head. In the same glance I saw tears glint in Anne's eyes, and soberness on Calico.

Nat moaned, just a breath. I tightened my arms around him.

". . . been handsome . . . like him . . ." he breathed.

I realized he was talking about Roger. I stroked his hair. "I'm your partner, darling . . . more. I've been waiting for the right moment to tell you I'll be your wife, that I love you in my own way. I'm telling you now, that we're going to love each other . . ."

"Mary!" There was panic in him.

"I'm right here, Nat."

"Where are . . . you, Mary?"

"Holding you, darling."

"Where's the moon . . . I can't see . . ."

"Darling . . . the moon . . ."

". . . stars . . . bright . . . hide the moon. No . . . one star . . . black . . . your eyes . . . Mary . . . black . . ."

I kissed his dear cheek softly.

"Mary . . . stay . . ."

"I'll be here, darling. I'll hold you."

He lifted his arms heavily, got them around me, held on with surprising strength. He stared up toward me, unseeing. He shuddered. Blood trickled from his mouth.

I held him just as he was, loving him more than I'd ever loved him, and when he shuddered again, I kissed his lips, long and tenderly.

"You . . . kissed . . . " he breathed.

"I love you. Have loved you all the time."

"Love . . . Mary-love . . ."

The sunny look touched his face. He tried to speak again, but his lips wouldn't really move. He held me with that uncanny strength. The sunniness touched him again, vanished. I kissed him again on lips which could no longer speak, but moved beneath my kiss, then stilled. His arms dropped away from me to the sand. I held him to me, swaying him ever so gently, as tears covered my cheeks and went down my neck.

We buried him at sunup. Karl thought Nat would want to sleep under the palm tree where I'd held him and spoken of love, and I agreed. I never knew where Horse and Bull were taken.

Tomorrow I was due to sail with Roger. Heartsore, feeling untrue to Nat, yet gripped with the old love for Roger, I wondered if he'd agree to delay our sailing—and our reunion—for a week. In that time I'd overcome the first shock of Nat's death and either sell the club or leave it in the hands of an agent to sell.

Roger hadn't come to me yet, but I knew he would. His gentleman's instinct would be to give me time. Even so, I longed for the comfort of his presence.

Finally I sent Jim to *Skull* with a note.

It was an hour before Roger came. I received him in the gardens, wearing a dress, but this had no meaning now.

The first thing I noticed was how cold he looked. But then he would be reserved at such a time; it was his nature, his training.

We sat on the bench where we'd kissed and made plans. Today he sat at one end, I at the other. I didn't want it otherwise. Because of Nat.

"You know about Nat," I said. "You were there."

"I was there."

His tone was so sharp I watched him in alarm. His eyes were the coldest blue I'd ever seen them, the line around his lips whiter.

"R-Roger," I stammered. "Tomorrow's the day . . . I thought . . ." I broke off. His expression was so icy it seemed to creep into my throat and freeze my words.

"You thought a suitable time should pass."

"I . . . yes."

Because, put baldly, that was the truth.

"I got your note. But I was coming here in any event. I have a few things to say before I sail."

"B-before *you* . . . ?"

"Exactly. I've known of your association with Cross, as you are aware. But I placed the blame for it on myself, not on you, because I did leave you stranded and he offered protection. I forgave that. I didn't like it, but I accepted."

"Thank you, Roger," I whispered.

My blood was racing. Apprehension seethed in my veins.

"I was sincere about our sailing together. However. I was standing very close when Cross . . . I heard everything he said to you, everything you said to him."

My heart twisted; twisted again.

Once with love and grief for Nat; once with love and need for Roger.

I sensed the deep hurt beneath Roger's anger.

"I did love Nat," I said honestly. "But not as I love you."

His eyes went even more glacial. "You dueled to save Cross . . . everybody in Nassau knows it . . . you held him in your arms, your lips on his as he died. I must have been out of my mind to come to Nassau because I heard you were here. I must have been mad to think that a blood-thirsty minx could ever . . . I came here this morning, Mary the Red, to tell you our plans are canceled. I'm sailing at noon. This time, however, I'm not leaving you at the mercy of others. You have the club . . . and some priceless diamonds. You'll pick up another man in no time. No time at all."

I parted my lips to explain, but he cut me off with a chopping gesture. He got to his feet and went striding away.

"Roger!" I screamed. *"Roger!"*

He disappeared among the trees.

He was gone. Finally and implacably gone. Nat was gone. I had nothing, nothing at all. I had no love. I sank onto the bench and wept.

Chapter 28

But I did have someone, I realized, after Roger had sailed. Again there was Anne Bonny, to whom I could turn in my grief. She understood about Nat and she understood about Roger. She was ready to help me in any way.

And there was someone else.

I'd wandered into the gardens later that day, unable to remain in the lovely establishment Nat and I had created. It wouldn't be open for business tonight, maybe not tomorrow night. I wished it never had to open again.

I sat on the bench where earlier I'd sat with Roger. I gazed numbly into space.

"Mary," said a voice right in front of me.

It was Karl. My lips fell apart. I stared.

"D-did *Skull* put back?" I asked, not daring to hope Roger had relented.

Karl nodded his head, every freckle standing out on his solemn face. "I stayed behind. You need somebody."

"Oh, Karl . . . Karl!" I murmured, grateful, remembering that once he'd loved me, fearing that some love might linger yet.

"I stayed as friend only, fond friend," he said. "In the old days . . . I loved you then . . . still do, in a way. But it's a friend's love. I'm just somebody for you to have now. Maybe I can learn to do what . . . well, what Cross did in the gaming room. Help you run the place."

Tears sprang to my eyes, and I didn't mind that

Karl saw. I trembled with relief, with the first bit of security since the duels. Out of tragedy and grief had come a strong man, a staunch ally on whom I could depend.

"Thank you, Karl," I said, blinking away the tears. "I know you could run the gaming room. But I can't bear to keep the club. I'm going to sell it and leave Nassau."

"It makes no difference. Where you go, I go. What you do, I do. Until you're settled."

I reached my hand to him, and he took it in both his big, hard, safe hands. He held it for a long moment, his warmth coming into me and with it, strength.

"I'll go find me a room," he said. "I'll come back later, when you feel more like talkin'. And you can tell me what you want to do."

I nodded, trying to smile. He did smile, and left.

With Karl, in late afternoon, I went to Calico Jack and Anne on *Yellow Hornet*. Karl had no idea Anne was a woman and of course I didn't tell him. *Hornet's* refurbishing was completed and the vessel was ready to sail. I knew that Calico had no intention of honoring his word to the Governor, that he wasn't going to chase pirates, but prizes.

"I want to sign onto *Hornet*, Calico," I said. "I need to get away from this place."

"That goes for me, too," Karl said.

Calico scowled. "You I'll take, van Buskirk," he said. "But not you, Red. It can't be. Everybody knows you're a woman now, and that pirate superstition hasn't changed."

"Our crew knows she's a damned good seaman, sir," Anne put in, going formal because of Karl. Her jaw was sticking out.

Karl walked away, thoughtfully leaving us to our discussion. This enabled Anne to speak her mind, which she proceeded to do.

"That superstition is . . . look how long I've been aboard without anything happening, not even the crew finding out I'm a woman! Look how long Mary was aboard *Skull* and *Sea Wolf!* You're the captain. Just tell them how it's going to be!"

They argued hotly. Anne won, finally, with a threat. "If you don't let Mary sign on, then I'm going to let the crew know *I'm* a woman! And you'll have real trouble, maybe even have to chase pirates!"

This continued for an hour.

At last Calico gave in. He laid down conditions. I was not to let Karl know Anne was a woman. I must change my appearance as a pirate—dye my hair black and dress more flamboyantly and fight harder than before when taking a prize so the crew would believe I was a man. I agreed. My aversion to him grew, despite the fact that, for the second time, he was giving me a berth on *Hornet*.

When Karl and I were alone I told him of my new disguise. He returned to the argument we'd had before approaching Calico.

"I understand you wantin' to leave Nassau, what with Nat . . . and Courtney leavin'," he said. "But not you livin' pirate again. It's a kind of craziness in you, Mary. It'd be better if we go someplace . . . Havana, Caracas, Mexico . . . and you take up woman-life again."

I couldn't explain to him, tell him that everything in me yearned to cling to Anne, my only woman friend, that I wanted to be with her right now. Guilt filled me that I must keep her sex from him, that I was unable to give him any explanation whatsoever.

"It is a kind of craziness," I admitted. "I've got to get it out of me, and this is the only way. For now. Believe me, Karl."

Privately I nourished the hope we'd sight *Skull* one day. I accepted that Roger was finished with me, but yearned, hoping in spite of myself, to explain to him about Nat and have him understand.

My hated new pirate disguise was a success. With my hair cropped short and dyed black as my eyes, my voice a tone lower, and wearing nothing but black

—breeches, shirt, sash, boots—I bore no resemblance to the erstwhile "Red." Inwardly, I longed for my beloved skirts, for my jewels, for my own flaming hair. But I dared not think thus, lest it mar my new identity. I lengthened my stride, gulped down whiskey with the men.

Never did any of them show suspicion. I was accepted as Weed—simply Weed, crewman. To strengthen my disguise, I now cursed along with any man, even had a fight with a pirate from another vessel, picking one who wasn't too burly for me to handle. I managed to knock him unconscious, ignored my bleeding knuckles, tossed back a drink, cursed in victory.

The wounds I'd suffered in the duel had healed. I bore a scar on the leg Horse had knifed, one that would never leave. It would always be a reminder of Nat. Of Roger to whom, one day before I lived woman again, I must explain.

When Anne and I could steal a moment, she laughed at my escapades. "You're the toughest pirate on *Hornet* outside of Calico!" she declared. "Take care you don't forget how to be a woman!"

As if I ever could! As if I'd ever cease longing for silk against my skin, the swish of skirts about my ankles! As if I'd forget the tenderness with Nat, whom I mourned, or the fire with Roger, for whose ship I kept unceasing watch.

We roved the waters—Jamaica, Cuba, all the islands. Fox and Mixer were anchored at small islands off New Providence, trying to make their living as fishermen. We ventured to Caracas and went boldly along the coast of South America. Here I kept keen watch for *Skull,* never sighting her, and listened avidly in the dives at every port, hearing no word of her.

Calico had now grown dangerous. He spoke of himself as the terror of the Indies. More than once I saw him snap his jewel-laden fingers at the very idea of any interference with his ever-building success.

We captured prize after prize. I fought harder,

killed more, according to my agreement to bolster my disguise. We were pursued by pirate-chasers, by men-o-war and outran them, every one. Calico was posted as the most-wanted pirate among the British islands in the Caribbean, not only for his exploits, but because he deceived the Governor and ran away from New Providence, refusing to do as he'd agreed and take the King's pardon.

I saved all the gold Calico paid me, as did Karl. The gold I'd received from the sale of the club, a substantial amount, was packed in a sea chest in the hold of our vessel. My diamonds were also in the chest. I was now a wealthy woman.

I could leave the sea at any time, establish myself as a woman in any place. Karl would follow me, make himself a life wherever I might go.

We discussed it. He suggested that we settle in Havana, that being a beautiful, prosperous city. I longed to agree, to stop the pirating and killing at once, but the far chance that we might one day find *Skull* made me delay.

Finally, Karl began to insist. "There's no reason for you to keep on like this, Mary. Now is the time to go. You're not going to see Courtney again, no matter how long you watch!"

I glanced at him, surprised. I hadn't dreamed he'd notice. Holding my gaze, he nodded.

"I want to see you established," he told me. "Even married to the right man. Then I'll think about taking a wife. Even have a family and a business. We've got to break away from *Hornet* before things get too rough."

I almost agreed. But I couldn't quite yet leave the sea, desert the waters where, even tomorrow, we could sight *Skull*. Because I kept only the one secret—Anne —from Karl, I admitted this.

"We'll stay for one more prize, then," he said.

"And then I'll go, Karl. I promise."

We overhauled *The Kingston,* a large British vessel,

put some of our crew aboard her and moored both her and *Hornet* off a remote, rarely visited islet near Jamaica. Here Calico ordered tents put up on shore and, as this was being done, set others to unloading the prize.

There was a great deal of merchandise—silks, ivory, laces and linens, ingots of gold, and kegs and casks of gem stones. There were casks of jewels set in heavy, beaten gold. Soon the decks of *Hornet* were lumbered with goods, half the crew were carousing ashore, the cannons remained unloaded, having all been fired during the taking of the merchantman.

Karl and I were carrying jewel chests into *Hornet's* hold. Others of the crew pushed and jostled as they moved about. Karl muttered something, and I drew close to hear what he meant for my ears only.

"See that turtle sloop . . . when we was on deck?"

"No!" I whispered. And wondered, Have I missed *Skull* the same way?"

"I've got to warn Calico," Karl said.

"The sloop's gone, isn't it?"

"I'm going to tell him. He needs to know. Come along. We'll tell him we're leaving *Hornet,* too. He won't care; he'll be glad enough to get rid of you."

As soon as we'd placed the chest we had in hand, we made our way to Calico and Anne, at the bow. Calico's fingers were aflash with new jewels, and he was scooping his fingers into a keg of rubies, emeralds, diamonds, pearls, letting the stones trickle and fall back. Anne had on a diamond ring, which she returned to the keg as we came up. Both she and Calico thought it best that she, as mate, not wear jewels.

Karl told Calico about the turtle sloop.

Calico waved it aside. "I seen it. Turtles is all they think about. That wasn't no pirate-chaser. Go ahead . . . get the booty loaded . . . leave other matters to me."

We turned away, Karl not mentioning the fact that he and I were going to quit *Hornet.* "He's in no frame of mind for that," Karl said. "We'll leave when we drop anchor in port, wherever that is. I don't like him ignoring that sloop."

We worked on.

It was dusk when two well-armed sloops bore down on us. They fired across our bow, then across the bow of our prize. Calico was utterly unprepared to fight. The decks were still cluttered with stolen goods, more than half the crew were now carousing ashore among the tents, and the cannons were still unloaded.

Karl and I were aboard the *Hornet*. We saw Calico signal some of his crew; they made for the longboat with him and rowed for shore. Anne, who had gone below to hide away that diamond ring she'd taken a fancy to, and which Calico had said she could keep, was left behind, as were Karl and myself.

The three of us, along with some twenty crew still aboard, made ready with pistol, musket, knives. I saw the longboat near shore, remembering how I'd always felt a distrust of Calico.

Most of the attacking forces followed Calico and his men ashore and, after running them down in short order, brought them back. The crew among the tents being, almost to a man, drunk, offered no resistance.

Those of us aboard fought. But these crewmen were as drunk as the others. Consequently, Karl, Anne, and myself were the only defenders left. We fought savagely, bringing down our men, wounding them only until we, the last to be taken, were overpowered.

All of us were brought to Port Royal, in Jamaica, for trial. We spent two days and nights in a dirty jail cell. I'd stayed with Karl and Anne when we were captured, and the three of us were together now. There were seven other crewmen with us, cursing drunkenly at first, then soberly and in seething rage and fear when the whiskey wore off. They spent most of their time berating Calico, who was in another cell, for their situation. Anne, who stayed close to me at all times, stiffened, but she kept silent.

Karl, too, said nothing. But he was always beside

me. Time dragged. The food was poor, the water we were given to drink was covered with scum, and the cells stank from the many others who'd been locked in before us.

Chapter 29

It was a relief when the trial began. It was held in a large, plain room with benches facing the judge. Every pirate from *Hornet,* was manacled and made to stand along the sides of the courtroom. When we were all in place, we made a living, murderous-looking wall of prisoners.

Anne Bonny was the first one called to the stand.

"Your name?"

"Bonny. Anne Bonny, sire."

"That's a woman's name. Anne."

"I am a woman, sire."

An almost imperceptible sense of shock ran through the pirates lining the room. I could feel it actually tingle from Karl's fingers into mine, for he was touching my hand as we stood.

"A woman . . . living as a pirate?"

"Aye, sire."

"Robbing and fighting and killing? You knew you'd hang."

"Aye. sire. But with your indulgence . . ."

"Speak out!"

"I plead my belly, sire."

The courtroom went deathly still. Tears sprang to my eyes. I gazed at Anne, willing my love toward her. She was a pitiful sight, to all appearances a man pleading his belly to win the mercy of the court.

The judge stared, unblinking.

"For when do you plead your belly?"

"In six months, sire. Even my husband . . . Calico Jack . . . doesn't know."

Silence.

"Sire."

"Speak, woman."

"There is another woman. I plead her belly also."

"Who is this woman?"

"Weed, sire. She's known as Weed."

Karl's hand gripped mine, hard.

I caught a glimpse of Calico. His face was murderous.

"Step down, woman."

My head in a whirl, I heard the next witness, a pirate, called to the stand. He was named Atchison, one I'd never liked, and he was now obviously both frightened and enraged. When my time came, I wondered, should I say that Anne was wrong about my belly? Or should I accept whatever advantage that might give me? Had I escaped hanging in London only to hang in Port Royal?

I began to listen to Atchison's testimony, and stood numb as he gave damaging evidence against Anne and myself, under oath, for his own possible good.

"In action," he said, "fightin' to take a prize, no man on *Hornet* was bloodthirstier than Weed . . . as we knowed one of these women. Or Bonny, as we knowed the other one."

The next lying pirate testified: "When women prisoners wus took, when they wus at close quarters, nobody kept the deck but these two women pirates. Weed, she cursed at us that went below decks an' yelled fer us to come up an' fight women prisoners. An' when we didn't stir, she fired her pistols down among us once, killin' one an' woundin' another."

Crew member after crew member, witnesses by the dozen, gave the same lying testimony about Anne and myself. How can they believe this will save them? I wondered. Then I sensed the reason. It had to do with that superstition against having women aboard a pirate ship. They really thought Anne and I had brought this misfortune upon them, and they wanted to see us hang for it.

My name was called. I walked to the stand.

I freely admitted to my disguise. By now I'd heard so many witnesses, so many lies, listened to ridiculous accusations that the trial had become a blur.

"Do you plead your belly?"

I firmed my chin. "Anne Bonny doesn't lie," I answered, to protect her. Let my own fate fall where it might.

"What is your true name?"

"Mary Read, sire."

"Why did you turn pirate?"

"I had no home. I was a stowaway."

"Were you dressed as a man at the time?"

"Yes, sire."

"Why?"

"To . . . disguise myself."

"Were you discovered aboard?"

"I was discovered and taken to the Captain. He gave me a berth as cabin boy."

"Captain's name?"

"R-Roger Courtney, sire. Lord Roger Courtney."

"What vessel?"

"*The Hague,* sire."

"Courtney turned pirate."

"Yes, sire."

On it went and on, the questions coming at me fast; it was torture to answer with honesty, yet conceal facets of my life which had nothing to do with this trial. Such as my time with Nat.

At last I was told to step down.

Calico was called next.

"Your name?"

"Jack Rackham."

"Known as what?"

"Calico Jack."

"You ran away from New Providence?"

"You might say that, yes."

"You refused to honor the King's pardon?"

"It was the woman made me do that."

"What woman?"

"Anne Bonny . . . my wife."

"Why did you have women, dressed as men, aboard?"

"First it was my wife. Insisted on bein' aboard. She even talked me out of retirin' from privateerin' at one time. I done it to please her."

"What about the other woman . . . Mary Read?"

"When she first come aboard my vessel," Calico lied, "I thought she was a young man of good family. I asked what pleasure she could find as a pirate, where her life was always in danger of musket and cutlass. And not only that, but she'd be sure of death if she was took alive, like now. She said that as to hangin', it was no great hardship. Otherwise, she said, except for the hangin', every young fellow'd turn pirate."

"So you took her on, disguised as a man?"

"Bonny. My wife. She done it."

Unbelieving, I listened as Calico betrayed his wife, lied about her, about me, his one object being to save his own neck. And after him came more crewmen, all lying, to the last man.

Karl testified. He admitted he knew I was a woman, stated that he hadn't known Anne's true sex. He swore that I'd committed none of the atrocities of which the others had accused me. He stated that I had been planning, when *Hornet* was bested, to quit privateering for good.

The long, tedious lying did, at last, come to an end. Anne and I were moved to a cell by ourselves. We scarcely talked, but clung together. She begged me not to be angry over what she'd pled for my belly, and I thanked her for doing it. Sometimes we wept. Though she never spoke against Calico, I knew her heart was broken that he'd betrayed her.

The trial ground on for two more days. Calico, in spite of turning state's evidence, was sentenced to meet his fate at the end of a rope at Gallow's Point, along with most of his crew.

Karl, because he'd been with Calico a comparatively short time and none had lied about him or accused him of any atrocity, was released. Anne was set free because of her belly. Miraculously I, too, was released even though, when recalled to the stand, I'd stated I didn't know whether or not I could plead my belly, and was ordered to look after Anne until she should be delivered of hers. A few pirates were released and ordered to leave the island as were Anne, Karl, and myself.

The officials returned to me the money from the sale of the club, of which I told them after the trial, and all my diamonds. They confiscated all the gold I'd received from Calico from the taking of prizes. Anne lost her money, as did Karl, but that was of no matter. We were free.

The day we sailed for Havana, I wept. The three of us, Anne and I still dressed as pirates, were standing at the rail, watching Port Royal grow smaller. It was execution day for Calico. As I wept, Anne, who'd refused to stay for the grisly event, remained dry-eyed.

"I'm sorry he came to this end," she said. "But if he'd fought like a man that last day instead of running, he need not have been hanged like a dog."

PART V

HAVANA

1720

Chapter 30

Karl took airy, high-ceilinged rooms for us in a Havana hotel. The city, as we drove along the tree-lined, plaza-studded streets, was the most gracious I'd ever seen. The air held the same caressing, soft warmth I'd grown accustomed to at sea, and the feeling came to me that it should be possible to find contentment in these beautiful surroundings.

We dined in the living room of Anne's and my suite, doing so because she and I didn't want to appear in the dining room dressed as pirates. Nor should Karl, for that matter.

"We've got plans to make anyway," I told them.

Both were well pleased at staying in the suite, and we enjoyed our dinner and basked in our freedom. When we were sipping tiny cups of coffee, I spoke frankly to them.

"We three have been partners, haven't we?" I began.

"Not exactly, lovey," Anne replied.

"I've quite a lot of money now," I pressed on. "I'm going to divide it . . . the money from the club and from the diamonds . . . three ways. One part for each of us."

"You paid our boat fare, that's enough!" cried Anne.

"I'll get work. We'll not be penniless," said Karl.

I argued back. They protested, talking at the same time, and for a moment wouldn't let me continue. Smiling, close to tears, I waved aside all they said.

"I've given serious thought to this," I cried. "Please . . . hear me through!"

They subsided, ready to spring back into protest.

"We've each got to have something to give us a start in a new life," I insisted, "and this will do it. I'm not 'giving' you the money any more than Nat 'gave' me the club partnership."

"He gave you the diamonds," Anne said. "So don't try to dress it up."

"All right," I surrendered. "I want to *give* each of you one-third of what I have. Because you're my friends, the only friends I have in all the world, and I love you. You, Karl, are penniless because you left *Skull* and signed on *Hornet* to protect me. And you, Anne, are penniless, because . . ."

"Because I talked Calico into not retiring."

"You befriended me. When I was destitute. You talked Calico into giving me a berth. If you don't say 'yes,' both of you, I'll be completely miserable!" My lips trembled, and I couldn't stop a tear from stealing down each cheek. "Please . . . dear, dear friends!"

Anne's arms came around me. "All right, lovey. I'll take mine, and thank you. I've done some thinking about my baby, meant to talk to . . . Anyhow. If it won't hurt your feelings, lovey, my dream has been to have any child I might bear in France. My mother lives there and the child will have a home and love and . . . because of you . . . security. Later, I'll get work in a shop and conserve my money."

"It's a wonderful plan!" I cried.

I turned my gaze questioningly on Karl. He nodded, but with a certain grimness. "If you'll heed whatever advice I'm able to give you until you marry," he said. "It may not be the best advice, but it'll be my best. And if you'll call on me for anything whatever."

I kissed them both, laughing and half-teasing, but serious along with it. I informed Karl that I'd like for him to do a real service the very next day. He agreed, not even waiting to hear what it was.

"First, if you'll get the diamonds valued. All of them. And sell them for me when the time is right. We want the best price."

"Of course," he said.

"Next, get yourself outfitted in the latest fashion. You'll have some gold. We're not pirates now, and you can't go on the streets dressed as a pirate. Nor can Anne and I."

"We'll have to," Anne pointed out. "To get to the shops."

"And have sales ladies faint when two men come in and want to leave dressed as women?" I laughed.

Anne caught the humor of the situation and doubled with laughter. This delighted me, for she'd been quietly grieving over Calico, regardless of what she said about him.

"I don't see how you'll manage," Karl said.

Anne's eyes met mine, and we went into helpless glee.

"D-don't you, now?" I gasped, finally. "Here is what you must do, Karl, our darling friend! After you've outfitted ourself, you'll leave the diamonds to be valued. Then you'll go to the shops for ladies and buy a complete outfit . . . from the skin out . . . for each of your two dear 'sisters' who, though not twins, have a birthday only a week apart and you wish to surprise them."

"I can't do that!" Karl yelped. "I never . . ."

"You never did, but now you are!" I cried gaily.

"We'll give you our measurements, and we'll tell you what materials and colors we prefer. The sales ladies will show you the latest fashions."

Karl sat looking at us unhappily.

"And the day after *that*," I went on, "we'll dress in what you've bought and do the rest of our shopping ourselves! All you'll have to do then is get rid of all the pirate clothes and keep after the sale of the diamonds."

At last, after much persuasion, drawing outlines of our feet on paper, carefully writing down measurements and lengths of skirts, we overwhelmed a most reluctant Karl, who promised to undertake our errand. He folded the sheets of paper and stowed them in his sash.

"I wouldn't do this for no other . . ."

"Yes, you will!" I teased. "For that wife you'll find! Oh, Karl . . . get one of these dark-haired señoritas! They're the loveliest creatures in the world!"

"I wouldn't mind," he admitted. "But I'd like your help then, Mary. One thing she's got to have. Eyes like yours. As black as yours. And as shining."

Impulsively, I put my arms around him, kissed him on the bridge of the nose. This, I knew, was the last time Karl would even hint of that old love, the one he'd begun to feel for me on *The Hague.* It was my duty, I inwardly vowed, to help him find his black-eyed girl as soon as possible, so he'd transfer that buried love to her, whole and complete.

Three days later, Anne and I were completely outfitted with new, fashionable gowns, hats, and accessories. This time, as I donned skirts, I determined never again, for any reason, to put on men's garb. I gloried afresh in the naturalness of skirts and fitted bodices, soft fabrics, delicate lace and ribbons.

Anne helped me to bleach my hair from black, then dye it red. We got it almost to its natural shade. To hide its shortness, I bought a red wig the exact color of the dyed hair. This I would use until my own hair grew long enough so I could dress it properly.

Finally, when I was settled in an apartment and Karl had opened his bake-shop and was living in rooms behind it, Anne packed her new clothes, bade us a tearful goodbye, and sailed for France. I'd had small, discreet cards printed, announcing my availability as hairdresser to ladies in the comfort and privacy of their own homes.

Karl didn't approve of this venture at first, saying I had enough to live on and insisting that he was going to repay me from the proceeds of his shop, which would give me income. I finally convinced him that I wanted not only to earn money but to be occupied, meet people, and make friends. It was then he took some of my printed cards to pass out, hoping to bring me work.

It was Saturday afternoon. I sat in my tiny sitting room, papers strewn over the table before me. Going over the figures repeatedly, I could not deny what they had told me. Though my spending had been modest, I'd taken in barely enough to pay for my apartment and food. I dared not use any of my remaining principal, which wasn't large.

I made the sheets of figures into a neat stack. I could earn a living if I continued as hairdresser. I'd learned to speak Spanish, as had Karl. If I went from fine house to fine house six or even seven days a week, I could remain solvent. Karl had begun to make a profit, but I hid my troubles from him and refused to take so much as a peso, no matter how he argued.

Now, after four months, I had to admit that hairdressing was not going to be a success after all, because my clients had steadily left me. I had to find another way to make a living.

I'd been losing customers and was unable to replace them. Somehow, word had spread that I'd operated a gambling club in Nassau and had been jailed and tried for piracy. The fine ladies I'd served now considered me a bad woman and were spoiling my business.

I told myself not to resent them. But I did want to *show* them that I couldn't be beaten. And I would show them. Somehow, I'd bring them to my feet.

Already a plan lay in my mind. It was completely selfish, and I wasn't sure I could go through with it. One thing, however, I was firm about. I'd be no victim, not in Havana. Those days were gone. I was taking my future into my own hands.

In pursuit of this, I had an engagement for this very evening, and I would turn it to my advantage and ultimate triumph. Thus decided, I dressed in white, piling my hair, which had grown quite long, extra high and fastening it with a silver clasp above the nape. The clasp had been given to me by tonight's escort, Mario Hernandez y Silva, a handsome youth of twenty-two, whom I'd met while dressing his sister's hair.

He'd come in to watch and tease.

He'd remained to feast his dark Latin eyes on me and talk, warmly, charmingly. He insisted on seeing me to my apartment, pleaded for me to go for a drive with him next day, to dine with him the following night at one of the exclusive private clubs.

I'd been thinking of marriage. At first I considered Mario too young. Then I examined the advantages of marriage to him, of which he began to hint with fervor. I could make him happy, that I knew. I was even fond of him, a ghost of the fondness I'd held for Nat.

He made no improper advances, was completely honorable. The stature I'd gain, married to him, was impressive. The Hernandez family had lived in Havana for generations. They were wealthy, owned jewelry establishments; there were titles. They were social leaders.

Even so, I felt reluctant about seeing Mario, much less marrying him. He was only three years younger than myself, but the unsavory events in my life made me feel older than I was. Also, he was young for his age. Young and gay and teasing until he met me, then deadly serious and intense.

Tonight he wore dark-rose velvet which made his hair blacker, his eyes fully as black as my own, his Latin skin more olive. He smiled at me with red lips, but he was preoccupied; the small crease above his nose betrayed that.

His eyes devoured me in my glittering white.

"Mary!" he breathed, gazing speechlessly.

Getting him to propose was going to be very easy. He was so youthful, so innocently in love, that he had no defense. I wasn't happy over what I meant to do, but I was determined to make him happy.

"You're the most beautiful girl in the world, Mary!" he said intensely.

" 'Woman,' Mario. One who is gossiped about."

"Girl . . . woman . . . querida . . . darling!" he murmured, and kissed my hand.

I sighed. "Mario . . . Mario! No more. At least until we've dined? Please?"

Silently, in agreement, he put another lingering kiss on my hand.

He took me to the most exclusive private club in the city. The ladies were elegantly dressed, but none more so than myself. Some former clients who had dropped me, glanced up surprised, when they saw my escort. The gentlemen were as fashionable as the ladies; they looked at me keenly; one or two of them stared. Mario muttered, half-irritated, half-proud that I was creating a small sensation.

He seated me at the table to which we were shown, sat across from me. He began to chat, lightly, eyes serious, and I studied his handsome face, tried not to see the love in those eyes, and decided that I would, indeed, go through with it. Tonight he would propose. And I would accept. My past, which one day I would confide in him, would never harm him because my future was going to be irreproachable. Nat was gone. Roger was gone. I would be a faithful and willing wife to Mario.

When we married, he would disappoint a girl who loved him, but I pushed this fact sternly out of mind. Life had taught me, at last, that I must look out for myself. The girl in question, being both titled and wealthy as well as beautiful and very young, could easily find a husband.

As I smiled and chatted with my escort, I happened to look up. A man in black velvet passed our table, and as he turned his head toward us, his dead black eyes stared at my face, then he continued on his way.

My pulse raced.

I didn't know whether he remembered me, but I

hadn't forgotten him. He was the bull-thick, evil-eyed man I'd met in Nassau with Nat. The one who looked even more evil than Sir Cecil. Had he recognized me? Would he inform the Hernandez family that I really had been, at one time, the intimate of pirates? Would he ruin my bright chance?

Chapter 31

"That," Mario remarked, "is the wealthiest, most powerful man in Havana."

"Indeed?" I murmured.

"Not inherited wealth. He's an importer-exporter. Really is. But it's rumored that he also has dealings with unsavory people, and it is in that area he finds his greatest profit."

"Pirates?" I asked boldly, watching for a sign that Mario may have heard gossip about myself.

He shrugged. "I wouldn't doubt it. All the girls try to marry him, though. He has the biggest, most elaborate home in Havana, in all Cuba. And he's worth millions. In a way you can't blame the girls, or their mothers. The one who marries him will be rich beyond imagination, and social leader of the entire city."

This gave me pause.

"How does he resist these beauties?" I asked idly.

"My sister says none of them please him. That he needs a special kind of woman."

"Do you know him, Mario?"

"But of course. Everyone knows Señor Gómez."

In that instant, I made my decision. I hadn't lost my aversion for Gómez. Not at all. But if any woman was a match for him it was myself, an ex-pirate. It was I, who had sailed the seas and taken booty, who had dueled in moonlight and killed my opponent in a duel. If anyone could handle Gómez, it was I. And he had the wealth, the power I was determined to get. That I had considered marrying poor Mario now seemed ridiculous.

"I wish to meet this man," I said. "Bring him to me, por favor."

"But Mary . . . ! He's not fit . . . !"

"I'll not speak another word to you, otherwise!"

Reluctantly, he stood up. Protest showed in every step he made for Gómez's table. When he arrived there, the multi-millionaire rose and bowed. He listened to Mario, inclined his head, and the two of them came to me.

Mario introduced us.

Those dead-black eyes thrust at mine. The thick red lips under the moustache formed a knowing smile.

"Indeed, Mario, it is kind of you to present me," Gómez purred, his thick voice dripping suave arrogance. "I was about to risk intruding when you came to me." He looked me over as he might a piece of merchandise, and I knew he recognized me. "A privilege," he continued. "You remind me," he added, "of a woman pirate I once met who later became known as Mary the Red."

I lifted my chin. I didn't know whether he was going to expose me, or was simply baiting me. Suddenly, his motive didn't trouble me at all. So he knew. He was a hard man. I was an experienced woman. I met his eyes full on, gave no sign of perturbation.

"Indeed?" I countered.

"If it's not an intrusion," he said, "I should be happy to join you at dinner. If you'll be my guests."

"Now?" asked Mario.

"Ahora, Señor."

Mario glanced at me. This I saw out of the corner of my eye, for I was still battling Gómez's look. I nodded, and Mario hesitantly accepted.

Gómez sat down. He ordered an elaborate meal. His

strong, hooked nose looked like a weapon. His heavy lips smiled and spoke with arrogance, his voice fatter, oilier. "Greedy," the word fled through me. "Lascivious."

But my intentions remained firm.

He was, I discovered, a superb conversationalist. Though I loathed him, I found myself laughing along with Mario, at some of his anecdotes. And I didn't fail to notice that the fine ladies at other tables, two of whom had dismissed me as a hairdresser, were stealing awed looks my way.

Mario sulked. I gave him attention, and he brightened. Gómez's lips moved in a peculiar smile. His eyes got bolder. By the time dinner ended, he seemed to have made a decision, for he was purposeful and almost impatient as he bade us goodnight.

Mario grumbled all the way back to my apartment. I soothed him, but not too much. I wanted to hold off his marriage proposal.

I wanted to see what Pablo Gómez would do next.

I paid a visit to Karl's shop early the following morning. It smelled deliciously of freshly baked bread and cakes. Karl was surprised to see me but happy, and when I told him I had a matter to discuss, took me into his tiny office and shut the door. He gave me the only chair, a straight wooden seat he used at the table to keep his books, and sat himself on the edge of the table.

"What is it, Mary?" he asked. "It must be important to bring you here so early."

I told him about Gómez. In Nassau and in Havana.

"I've heard of him, Mary. He's the most notorious rascal alive."

"And the richest."

"He has a bad reputation about women."

"I've got a reputation about men."

"That's different. He's the most powerful man here. He's out of your reach."

"Not from the way he looked at me last night."

"As if you were for sale?"

I nodded. "You've said I should marry, Karl."

"The right man, yes. Even young Hernandez. But better, one like Nat. Or Courtney. One you could . . ."

"Love? Love doesn't exist for me now. I want money and position. I prefer to marry a powerful man. I'll take what I get with him. And deal with it."

"Forget Gómez," Karl insisted. "He's a bad one with women. There's talk . . . really bad, understand?" He broke off. "If you've got your mind made up you can't love again, take Hernandez, do. At least there's nothing . . . peculiar about him. And he worships you."

"You haven't even met him, Karl."

"I've made inquiries. Seen him with you in a carriage. Even at that distance, it was plain that he's mad for you."

I sprang up, hugged him fondly. "I'll have to do things my own way, dear friend," I murmured. "But thank you for the . . . warning . . . And be my friend, forever!"

Who do you think you are? I asked myself as I walked all the way home. If you capture that filthy but rich and powerful prize, you'll have to work to get him. You'll have to plan and plot. It can't be done in two meetings—one introduction in Nassau and one dinner in Havana.

Breathtakingly, it seemed I wouldn't have to plot immediately. As I came to my apartment, I saw a fine black carriage, drawn by blooded horses, in front of the house.

Two uniformed men perched on the driver's seat. One of them jumped down, opened the carriage and stood aside. Out stepped Pablo Gómez, resplendent in dark brown. He swept me a bow.

"Mary the Red," he murmured. "I've waited."

I met his eyes straight-on. So it was to be war! There could be no other reason for him to call me by my pirate name. He knew all about me. What, then, was he doing in front of my dwelling?

My lips tightened.

He smiled, that rich smile.

I remained sober. If he thought I was in the market to be his mistress, even his toy for a day or a week, his arrogance was due a real blow.

"My intentions," he said, eyes slitted, "are honorable. I know your mettle, admire it. I've come to take you to see my home. It is a house which no woman, other than servants, has ever been permitted to enter. I'm doing you the honor to let you be the first."

My heart raced. I'd piqued his interest! He might be lying about his intentions, but if so I hardly thought he'd rape me, like Ryan and Clarke in London. A determined refusal would be enough to stop this arrogant man desired by so many women.

I said nothing.

"You don't chatter," he commented. "I hate a woman who chatters. And you don't ask questions. You haven't so much as spoken. Now I . . . request . . . a reply. Do you wish to inspect my house and all it holds?"

"Yes," I said simply.

He handed me into the carriage. I settled my skirts, composed myself. He got in, keeping a proper distance between us.

The carriage started and, as it rolled along street after street, past the many beflowered plazas, he pointed out important estates surrounded by walls, flowering bushes, and trees. He spoke of the importance of the men and women who lived in them. We passed several to which I'd gone to dress the lady's hair but I didn't speak of this.

"My home is the finest in Havana," he said. "I believe you will agree."

I inclined my head coolly. He smiled. If I can win him, I thought, I'll give him value received.

I thought of what it would mean to go to bed with this man. He wasn't filthy from lack of bathing, as Ryan and Clarke in the hidey-hole. He had an inner, unidentified filth.

With him I'd have absolute luxury; to let him use

my body was fair exchange. *If* it was a marriage he offered. I'd told Karl I was experienced now. Dear God, how experienced I'd become! Sternly, I refused to let myself dwell on others who had known my body, wouldn't admit the existence of the word "love."

The carriage turned onto a graveled, winding, tree-lined drive. I glimpsed formal gardens, each one different and more beautiful than the last. There were clipped hedges, flowering trees, walls covered with yellow blossoms. There were flowering bushes, a sun dial here, a piece of statuary there, a fountain in another spot, spilling into a flashing pool.

"Oh!" I gasped as the carriage rounded a bend and the house came into view. It was immense, the central part three-storied, with a two-storied wing on either side and one running out at the back. It was built of such pure white marble that it sparkled like a great jewel set down in a vast nest of green, ruffled with flowers.

"Like it?" Gómez asked.

"It's exquisite! Who designed it?"

"I did. I created it in my mind, then put it on paper and had it built. House, gardens, everything."

My gaze turned to wonder. That such a reputedly ruthless and, to me, loathsome man would create this utter beauty! But had he, really? With the bad reputation Karl insisted on, with that fabulous wealth, much of which I knew to be ill-gotten—would he tell the truth?

Yes, I decided, looking at that hook-nose, the shining moustache, the arrogant mouth. He wouldn't lower himself to lie about the house.

On impulse I asked, "What were you doing in Nassau that time?"

"Dealing with pirates."

I'd been right. He might conceal personal evil. But once caught, he'd not lie. He had a strength, and with that strength he had won riches and power.

He showed me through the house. The rooms were spacious, the ceilings high, the floor of decorative tile.

The windows were barred with iron as were all Havana windows, and the glass portion folded back inside the rooms, gracefully, as my sandalwood fan had done.

The furnishings were airy, painted white, delicately upholstered. French. The chandeliers were crystal. Each piece of furniture, each vase or painting or bowl of flowers, enhanced the jewel-like interior.

Finally we stood together in the entrance foyer. The stairway curved, painted white, seeming to float upward, behind us.

"Is anything missing?" he asked.

"Servants only. I haven't seen one."

"I dismissed them for the day. So we could be alone."

"I see."

"You like my home, Mary the Red?"

"I think it must be the most beautiful in the world."

"And I . . . ?"

"Please make your meaning clear, Señor Gómez."

" 'Pablo.' Do you find me presentable?"

Deliberately, I looked him over. If it hadn't been for the aura of evil, he would have been almost handsome.

"You are presentable, Pablo."

"I don't intimidate you."

"No."

"Have you considered that you should be . . . frightened?"

"No. And I shan't be."

"You could get hurt."

"I can look out for myself."

"Yes. You want money."

"Lots of money. And absolute security."

"Luxury."

"All I can get. And position and diamonds."

"Splendid. I have a business proposition for you."

"Business, Pablo?"

"As you see, I need a wife to complete my house. To entertain for me. To solidify my social position."

I waited. I wasn't going to say it for him. His proposal, every drop of it, had to come from his lips.

"It will be a sensible arrangement."

"Explain, please."

"I want a wife, but not in the usual sense. I don't want love and roses and moonlight. That would be extremely boring to a man of my nature. I want this house to be the social center of Havana, my wife to deport herself as a lady, yet have the strength to be a social dictator. I want her to be seen with me at various functions."

"And in private?"

"Not what you might fear. I realize that you're a passionate young woman and have certain needs. I'll satisfy them, within reason. I want you to bear me a son. You'll put mettle into him, along with my iron. One son only."

He fell silent.

"And if people gossip about Mary the Red?"

"I'll quash it."

We fell silent. I considered the evil I'd felt in him at Nassau, considered Karl's advice. I decided I could handle the proposition.

We both fell silent.

I thought of bearing his child, determined to train out any evil he might inherit from this man. He would inherit from me, from my blood line, too.

"That's the whole thing," Pablo said now. "You'll live as I said. I have affairs in the city and will come and go. You, Mary the Red, a woman with courage, will have everything a woman could want."

This was too easy. It was happening too fast. It was, indeed, a business proposition. A cold-blooded marriage of convenience on both sides. I felt that he despised me as much as I despised him. Well, isn't that what you want? I asked myself. You planned to get him, and now he's offering himself—to a point. I thought of Mario, of a marriage in which there would have been, at least, love and fondness.

The silence lengthened.

"What do you say, Mary the Red?"

"I accept."

"We'll be married within the hour."

"An *hour?*" I cried, all my coolness gone.

"Why wait? I've got a special permit."

I thought of Mario again.

"I . . . I'll need to write a note. To Mario."

"Ah. Let him understand this is final. I don't want him hanging about."

He took me to a writing desk, and I dashed off a brief note, assuring Mario of my fondness, telling him, as kindly as possible, that circumstances had arisen which had changed my life.

Though I strove to make the note kind, it was cruel. My comfort was that Mario, being young and good-natured, would find another girl. Perhaps he'd return to the lovely one he'd been wooing before he met me.

I wrote a note to Karl, too, telling him the news. In it I promised to see him soon, and invited him to call and see my new home.

The marriage took place in an official building downtown. I still wore the simple dress I'd put on that morning to go to Karl's bake-shop. What a wedding gown! I thought to myself. And for my first and only marriage!

It was mid-afternoon when we got into the carriage. I was ravenous.

"Can we have something to eat, Pablo?" I asked. "I had an early breakfast. and not much of that."

"Food can wait. We have an important task ahead."

I didn't argue, but leaned back in the seat and watched the lovely Havana buildings and plazas and greenery flow past. It was quite some time before we arrived back at the marble mansion.

Pablo took me directly to the east wing, the entire top floor of which constituted our marital suite. He ripped the satin bed cover down.

"Take off your clothes," he ordered.

We both undressed, moving fast. I flung myself onto the sheets, open to him, telling myself not to shrink, not to withhold. Cruelly, he grabbed me and, yanking me against his thick body, encompassed my mouth with his own.

He took me roughly, briefly.

I felt no response whatsoever.

When he had finished he left me, and I didn't see him for twenty-four hours.

Chapter 32

We dined together the next evening. Pablo looked as suave and pleased with himself as ever.

I didn't mention his unexplained absence. This was part of our bargain. Besides, I'd not give him the satisfaction. Let him assume I thought it normal for a bridegroom to leave his bride, abandon her, for so long.

Not that I cared. I had no desire for his company or his lovemaking. I suspected that he had a mistress, one he had no intention of giving up.

I was wearing a long, fitted white gown. My only ornament was the silver clasp in my hair. Pablo studied me minutely, smiling that red smile.

"Tomorrow," he said, "I'll visit my jeweler. You need Spanish combs, silver with diamonds. Also earrings, a necklace, a pair of bracelets, a wedding ring, and another ring with a large stone. I prefer diamonds. And I prefer that you wear white at all times. You'll be stunning in white, with the white fire of diamonds, the sheen of silver, the white skin, and flame of hair. Agreed?"

"Yes," I said honestly. "White and diamonds are my favorites."

"I admire your taste. I'm happy to indulge it. For my own pride as well."

"It's generous of you, Pablo."

"It's part of our bargain. There'll be other diamonds . . . tiaras, pendants. Matching rings. Bracelets that reach halfway up your arms. What I select today is only a beginning."

I nodded. The thought of so many gems was pleasing. Moreover, they were necessary to the life Pablo meant to live.

"Your first duty," he said now, "is to staff the house. Make any changes you see fit."

I inclined my head. I'd met the housekeeper, Señora Rosa Bori, and liked her. She was a sturdy, proper, black-haired woman in her mid-forties. She'd introduced herself promptly, had a pretty maid serve my breakfast, and later paraded the servants she'd engaged, introducing them by name. They were all young, lovely, black-eyed, gentle of manner.

But they seemed to be frightened.

I mentioned this when they'd gone.

"It is the master, Señora," Rosa said. "They fear the master."

I couldn't possibly ask her the reason for their fear. Pablo was my husband; I owed him loyalty. So I smiled.

"They needn't be afraid, Rosa," I said. "They'll be under my supervision now, getting their orders through you. It's more comfortable for servants when the household is run by the mistress."

The next evening, as Pablo and I sat in the elegant little salon of our suite, I told him I'd decided to keep on the present staff. He looked complacent.

I gazed about, my eyes lingering on the painting on one wall. "It's all very beautiful to me," I said, "but strange. Soon I hope to think of it as my own."

Pablo said, "Mí casa es su casa . . . my house is your house. It is important that you feel this. Wives of men with whom I deal and know at the clubs will be coming to call. It's my wish that you tell them we'll give a ball a month from now. To introduce you formally to society."

My throat went dry. One month! Such a brief time in which to produce the sort of function Pablo would expect. Yet it was no imposition, merely a facet of our agreement.

"The time is short," I told him, "but it will be done."

"Of that I'm confident. You've proved your mettle, Mary the Red. This is easy in comparison."

He was right, after a fashion.

However, I found myself busier, with every moment taken for planning, making decisions as to decorations, a new gown for the ball, other gowns for receiving guests who would call, and invitations, than I'd ever been either as a pirate or hostess at *Pirate Club*. In pirate days, life had been rough and violent, but there had been days on end when we sailed the calm seas. Running the club had eventually fallen into a routine and, though I was busy, I had hours to myself.

Now in preparation for the upcoming ball, which must eclipse anything ever given in Havana, I was personally writing invitations and sketching designs for floral arrangements which had to be discussed with the florist. The whole house was to be bedecked with white roses. I had to audition musicians for the many small orchestras which were to be scattered through the house and gardens, so that the whole estate breathed not only the scent of roses, but the pulse of music. There were discussions with Señora Bori concerning food to be served, endless fittings for the gowns, interviews with girls, one of whom I'd select for my personal maid. And there was a daily influx of ladies and their daughters who came to call, and with them so many names—Sanchez, Molino, Carranza—I grew dizzy with names and faces, all of them important. They were all exquisitely dressed, extremely beautiful. They sipped coffee in my salon, nibbled tall, light cake, chatted, and smiled. Some of my former clients called; they pretended, and I didn't hint otherwise, that we were old friends. All their eyes were on me constantly—some friendly, even admiring, others curious, many speculative, envious or even resentful.

The resentment was understandable. And the dislike. Probably every girl had wanted Pablo, his wealth and position, for herself. Certainly their mothers had wanted it for them. Instead, a stranger they'd never heard of—unless in a scandalous vein— had won him, and was the recipient of all for which they had yearned and schemed. I wonder how they would have behaved if he'd left them on the wedding day, not to return for twenty-four hours, what they would do if he continued this behavior, as he was doing.

Personally, I was relieved. On the nights he did visit my bedroom, I endured his onslaught, never feeling response, my only emotion being relief when he departed. It was a curious, unnatural life pattern, but he laid it down and I followed it, content with what I received in return. I was living as a woman. My time was filled with womanly activity. Some day I'd have a child to fill my heart. Still, I missed being a woman with Nat. I felt the loss of that bright promise of fulfillment I'd held when Roger declared his love for me. I don't *feel* full woman, I admitted sadly, because I don't love.

With all my tasks and interruptions, it was two weeks before I found a personal maid. Señora Bori escorted her into my small salon, introduced her, and departed.

The girl's name was Elena Chavez and she was a beauty; quite small, not two inches over five feet, perfectly formed. She had soft, natural features and a sweet, smiling mouth. Her hair was dark and shining, her eyes as black as my own.

Seeing those eyes, I thought of Karl. Perhaps—but

that was leaping ahead at something which might not come to pass.

"You're from Jamaica?" I asked, the very word bringing back those unhappy days when I was on trial there.

"Sí, Señora. I've been in Havana six weeks."

"You have a Spanish name."

"Sí. My grandmother had a Cuban father."

I questioned her, liking her better every moment. She was twenty, had served as maid to a Jamaican lady since the age of eighteen. She'd wanted to see a bit of the world, so had come to Havana.

"Do you have a sweetheart, Elena?" I couldn't keep my thoughts away from Karl.

"Oh, no, Señora!"

I smiled. "It won't be long until you do have. I don't see how you've escaped this long."

Suddenly she laughed, her cheeks breaking out in dimples. Then, remembering her place, she sobered. "Forgive me, Señora. I had not meant to laugh."

"I'll want you to laugh, to be my friend, Elena!" I exclaimed. From that moment. I felt affection for this girl.

"I'm to be your maid, Señora?" she gasped.

"And my companion! Señora Bori says you've been educated."

"I love to read!"

"I love it also. As soon as the ball we're giving is over, I'll order books. We have a library, but my husband hasn't collected many books yet, and the ones he has are in Spanish. I shall add English books and newspapers, though I think we'll have a tutor so we can improve our Spanish. Or do you know the language?"

"A bit, Señora. But not to read."

"It's settled! And we're to be friends . . . agreed?"

"Oh, sí . . . please!"

"When we're alone, you're to call me Mary."

Her eyes widened, shone.

"I'm almost as new to Havana as you are, Elena.

I have only one friend, Karl van Buskirk, whom I'd like you to meet. But I also need a woman friend."

"But of course! All women need such!"

So it was settled between us. I stole time from my preparations for the ball and wrote away for English books and newspapers so they'd arrive as soon as possible.

When Pablo first saw Elena, I found that he approved my choice. "I congratulate you," he commented when we were alone. "I know real beauty. I couldn't have found a maid for you to excel this one."

Once or twice, when he came into our suite and Elena was there, his flat black eyes lingered along her figure, his mouth lay quiet, but he was entirely proper in his manner. Elena, however, looked frightened. This gave me an uneasy feeling, which I dismissed. Pablo was too class-conscious to make advances to his wife's maid. If anything, he was mentally comparing Elena's beauty to that of the mistress I was positive he kept hidden away.

During one of Pablo's absences, I sent a messenger to Karl with a note in which I asked him to call within the hour if convenient. I then asked Elena to wear her yellow cotton dress, a color which transformed her into a gorgeous, flower-like being. I dressed her hair myself, drawing it up onto her head, finishing it with a cascade of curls. I decided against adding one of my ornaments. It would mar her natural, glowing beauty.

All the while she protested, teasing me to let her know why we were dressing her up, reminding me that we should be working on some facet of the ball. I laughed, refused to answer questions, promised only a surprise which I hoped she'd like, until she gave in helplessly, laughing with me.

We were in the small downstairs salon when Karl arrived. He looked solid and prosperous in dark breeches and light coat, his sun-dusty hair neatly combed. I advanced to him, hands out.

He held them warmly. "Mary," he murmured. He

gave me a probing look, seemed briefly troubled. "How are things for you, Mary?"

"Everything is all right, Karl," I said.

He understood all the unspoken facts. He knew that I had no love for Pablo, but that I had the wealth and luxury for which I'd bargained. He knew I couldn't be said to be happy, but that I had no reason not to continue in my present situation. And I understood that he still cherished for me that ghost of love, and that this would never quite end.

Happily, believing there was a chance that he might find a new love, I led him to Elena. "Elena Chavez, this is my friend, Karl van Buskirk. He owns a bake-shop. Karl, Elena is my close friend and companion."

Their eyes came together, didn't part. As in a daze, she rose from her chair, offered her hand. He took it and didn't let go.

"Elena's from Jamaica, Karl," I told him.

"From Port Royal?" he asked, and I knew he feared she might realize we'd been on trial there.

"From a village," she replied. "I was maid in a big hacienda." She made no move to recover her hand.

"I . . ." Karl blurted. "You . . . we . . ."

"I know what!" I cried delightedly. "Elena, take Karl through the gardens! You'll find things to say!"

They did as I urged. It was in this manner, and at first sight, they fell in love. Love made Elena glow, heightened her beauty.

Now, when he was at home, I saw Pablo taking secret looks at her. But of course it meant nothing, I told myself. We hadn't been married a month; the ball was still to be held. He'd never risk a scandal.

Elena made no secret of her love for Karl.

"He wants to be married right away," she confided, "but I won't."

"Why not? I'll get another maid. You'll be my best friend."

"I'll marry him in one year," she declared. "He

has agreed. I'll get my wedding things, teach your new maid to care for you, and while I do this, Karl will have built for us a house with five rooms. I am to select the furniture."

I was happy to keep Elena so long even though the way Pablo kept sliding glances at her troubled me increasingly. His manner was impeccable, and I decided that, because I knew evil was in him, it didn't mean he intended to ruin Elena.

The ball was a complete success. Pablo was attentive, the adoring bridegroom. He held my hand, stroked my arm, even kissed me on the cheek as we danced. He left my side only when each of us was obliged to dance with a guest.

My planning and work had been worthwhile. The house was a bower of roses, roses in every room. The house throbbed with music, the gardens pulsed with it, and paper lanterns glowed along every path, lighting every bench.

There were two hundred guests. The women were dressed in the finest the world had to offer. Their jewels and tall Spanish combs glittered.

My own gown was of white, glittering fabric, and I wore the diamond tiara Pablo had bought especially for it. I felt overloaded with diamonds, but he insisted that I wear the collection—tiara, necklace, earrings, twin bracelets, two rings. Given my own preference, I would have worn only my wedding ring, a flashing circlet of diamonds. That, with my flaming hair and the gown—which was itself a jewel—would have been enough.

More than one man that night told me I was the most strikingly beautiful woman he'd ever seen. This troubled me. Despite the life into which I'd been forced, in which I'd stayed for love, first of Roger, then affection for Nat, I was easily disturbed by extravagant compliments.

"He's a lusty hombre, your husband," some of my partners said. "I envy him. But then, he's Pablo

Gómez. He'll get what he wants . . . one way or another."

These remarks confirmed what Karl had told me: that Pablo had a reputation, that he wasn't admired, despite his wealth and power.

I wondered, wryly, what all the fine people would do were they to discover that the bride of Pablo Gómez had indeed been a pirate and a club hostess. That she'd been ravished by the grossest, filthiest beasts alive.

Karl didn't attend the ball, though I invited him.

"When Elena and I are married," he promised. "Then we'll both come to your affairs. But not until she can be a guest."

I'd accepted this sadly. I dared not invite Elena now. I knew, without ever having seen one, what a rage Pablo would go into over that.

At last the ball was over. Pablo complimented me on its perfection, informed me we must give two such affairs each year.

As time passed, Elena and I grew very close. We read the books and newspapers which came, exchanged many confidences. I did not, however, tell her of my past, saying only that Karl and I had met on shipboard and that I'd been educated by tutors in England. She knew nothing of my pirate days. I told Karl, I'd confide in her after they were married, telling her everything except for our own brief affair. To this, Karl agreed.

"I don't want to lie to her, Mary," he said. "But it would hurt her, and there's no need for that. She's to be loved and protected to the best of my power."

I smiled sadly, nodded. I, too, loved Elena.

Pablo and I attended many functions. Though he continued to disappear, he never failed to escort me and caress me affectionately in public, or to bring me some new jewel. We gave dinners, intimate dances and musical evenings, and always he was present, a charming host. He took me sexually at intervals, always roughly and fast, never rousing my passion.

Elena and I began to study Spanish seriously. For the moment, the only English I read was the London newspapers. I read every word in every newspaper, seeking any mention of Roger. Though I was married, secure in high social life, and wealthy beyond description, it was Roger for whom I longed. I still grieved, quietly, for Nat. But it was Roger who burned in my heart.

At last I found a tiny mention in a newspaper. It said that Lord Roger Courtney was presently residing at the family country estate. I began to tremble, the paper shaking in my hands. Elena, engrossed in a book, didn't notice.

I breathed carefully, not wanting her to notice me. Roger was safe! Oh, thank God, he was safe! He was no longer a privateer. He'd attained that for which he'd risked his life for so long! Now he could enjoy what was his due both by inheritance and personal effort!

I excused myself to Elena, slipped out of the library, and went up to my personal salon. Here, at my desk, I wrote out a paid statement for that same newspaper. It was an announcement of the marriage of Miss Mary Read, formerly of London, to Pablo Gómez y Herrera, of Havana, Cuba. I hoped that Roger would see the announcement and know that I too was well-situated. I sent a special messenger to post the announcement, and enclosed more than enough payment for its printing.

Chapter 33

A month later, when Elena brought my breakfast tray one morning, as she insisted on doing, she walked with a limp. She looked pale, and there were dark smudges under her eyes.

"What's wrong?" I asked.

"Nothing, Mary. I'm a bit tired, I guess."

"You're limping!"

She set the tray across my lap, adjusted the pillows behind me. There were bruises on her arms.

She saw me looking at them.

"I . . . stubbed my toe," she said, and I knew she was trying to lie, a thing she simply couldn't do convincingly.

"Your arms are bruised and you've dark places under your eyes!" I insisted. "Elena, you've got to tell me what happened!"

"I . . . fell."

"When? Where did you fall?"

"Last night. Going down the kitchen steps. Then I c couldn't sleep."

I stared at her in disbelief.

"Did you and Karl have a quarrel?"

"Mary! Karl would never . . . ! We never quarrel. Besides, I didn't see him last night."

There. That had the ring of truth.

Further, Karl would never be rough with a woman, least of all Elena.

"Please, darling," I begged, "tell me what happened! Don't think I might be angry. I'll never be angry with you!"

Plead though I did, she only repeated the unconvincing lies she'd already told me. I commanded, half-weeping in my anxiety, that she look me in the eye and when she did manage that and I begged again for her to confide in me, she only gazed back in a manner which could only be described as apprehensive. It was then her bruises reminded me of those which Pablo sometimes left on me during his brutal efforts to beget a son.

Knowing Pablo hadn't been at home last night, I questioned her anew. "Was there a prowler, Elena? Did he . . . ?"

"No, Mary! No prowler!"

The ring of truth again.

"You *must* tell me, Elena! I'm your friend, we're like sisters!"

She began to sob. "Please, Mary! No more . . . please!"

I couldn't go on tormenting her. "If it ever happens again," I asked, "will you talk?"

She gazed at me miserably, half-nodded.

"What will you tell Karl about those bruises?"

"I'll not see him until Friday," she quavered. "I'll wear long sleeves."

I tried to eat my breakfast, couldn't.

Pablo, the thought returned again and again. But Pablo had been gone last night, and the night before that.

All day, when I thought she wasn't aware, I studied Elena. She did limp. She tried to hide it but couldn't quite succeed. The few times I caught her face unguarded, there was such sadness, such terror, that I had to bite my lips to keep from questioning her again.

Another month passed.

Elena looked herself, except for a fleet expression of sadness when Karl was mentioned. I decided that whatever had happened to her was indeed bad, that she didn't want Karl to know. For if he knew, he'd be so enraged he might harm or even kill the one who had assailed her.

I was now convinced, due to her manner, that she'd been raped. I considered telling her my own experiences, but decided that might add to her burden. To my relief, she continued to see Karl and went along with the marriage plans.

During this time, Pablo ceased looking at Elena and used me twice to beget a son. I began to pray that I'd never bring a child of his into the world, infect a helpless baby with his evil seed. As usual, after these occasions, he would disappear for two or three days, reappear for some social event, then disappear again.

Then came the morning when Elena crept into my bedroom holding herself erect with visible effort. There was a lurid mark along her shoulder where her dress fell away before she could prevent it, and another across her right cheek. Her lips were pale.

I sprang out of bed, ran to her, put my arms around her, got her into a chair. I knelt, took her hand in mine, felt dampness, looked down. Her knuckles were bleeding.

This time there would be no lying.

"Elena," I murmured, and held her in my arms.

She sobbed, her dear body quivering.

"Tell me, darling . . . this time, tell me."

". . . ruin your life . . . !" she sobbed.

"Nothing has ever ruined my life, Elena. Speak, don't be afraid. Tell me now, while we're alone!"

"N-nobody saw me come in! He t-took me there in the night and when he l-left, I got away! He s-said he was going to his m-mistress!"

I could make no sense out of what she said or who 'he' was. Yet a still, far sense whispered the identity, and I wasn't shocked.

I stroked her hair. "Who did this to you?"

"S-Señor Pablo!" The name jerked out on a tremendous sob. "Downtown . . . dungeon . . . g-girls!" She began to wail softly, collapsed in my arms.

I got her onto my bed, brought water and bathed

her cuts and bruises. There were red welts around both ankles and both wrists. There was a welt across her throat, the mark of teeth on her neck.

"Oh, Mary," she sobbed, "the other time I didn't . . . it happened in the garden. But last night . . . that dungeon . . . those girls . . . the *things* he has there! He was d-drunk when he l-left and I slipped out behind him . . . he didn't know. Mary, you're not safe with him, no woman is! Karl mustn't know . . . he'd go after your husband . . . he'd be m-murdered . . ."

I tried to question her more specifically, but she went into frenzied sobbing and I could get nothing more from her. I made up my mind then.

"He's gone to his mistress now?"

She nodded.

"And the girls are in this . . . dungeon?"

"Y-yes."

"Stop crying, dear," I said. "I'm going to see what this is all about. I know you're hurt and shaken, but you've got to take me to that dungeon right now!"

Chapter 34

Our destination was across the city. Elena, terribly frightened, refused to tell me where we were going. "You'll s-see," she said, and that was all I could get from her.

We went by hired carriage, which I dismissed on Elena's instructions. We stood together on a deserted, shabby street lined with great, old stone buildings which looked like warehouses.

"This way," Elena murmured and guided me around the corner, then down a gloomy stair cut through rock. As we descended, a musty smell caused me to press my handkerchief to my nose.

At the foot of the steps a massive, iron-studded door barred our way. Beside the door stood a strong, coarse man, his black hair and swarthy skin very dark in the cavern-like spot. He was armed, a pistol being thrust into the waist of his breeches.

"Nobody allowed here," he growled.

"Is this the place?" I whispered to Elena.

She nodded.

"These premises belong to Señor Gómez," I told the guard. "I'm Señora Gómez. I'm here at his request," I finished, wanting to get the lie out convincingly.

"El Señor didn't tell me."

"My husband never confides in servants," I said coolly. "What is your name?"

"Pic."

"You're to unlock this door. My maid and I are to go inside. You are to remain here. Let no one else in. When we leave, you may lock the door."

"This is not El Señor's custom."

"His custom has changed! If you don't admit us at once, if you don't follow my orders, I promise you my husband will deal with you!"

Inwardly I was trembling. Everything hinged on whether this fellow believed me. I stood firm, let him glower, and frowned sternly back. Only then did he turn, sullenly, unlock the door, open it.

I stepped briskly inside, having no idea of what I was going to find. The door swung shut. Elena clung to my hand, moved as I moved.

We were in a satin and velvet bedchamber. It was windowless, lit by deep red glass wall-lamps. Everything was red, rich, and glowing, from the carpet to the velvet hangings covering every inch of what must be stone walls, through the velvet chairs and bed hangings.

"Does he keep it lighted all the time?" I whispered.

Elena nodded, eyes enormous. "I think so."

"Is this where he brought you, where . . . ?"

"Beyond. In here."

She parted some hangings and we stepped through. I stopped abruptly, crying out softly as the chamber and what it held struck me. This was a small room, all damp stone and dimly lit by iron lamps.

Hanging suspended on each wall, feet above floor level, spread-eagled, a heavy iron chain on each wrist and ankle, was a girl. All were young, beautiful, naked, bruised, cut, marked with long welts. They seemed to be unconscious, for they hung from their chains. One of them was bleeding at the mouth. Another moaned, a breath of agony.

"He . . . does this . . . Elena?"

Surely not, I thought. Not Pablo, not my husband, not even him!

"Yes," Elena whispered.

"Where did he get them? Who are they?"

"They're quadroons, from Jamaica. When they . . . wear out . . . he replaces them."

"What does he . . . why?" I gazed at the battered girls in horror.

"Look at the walls, Mary. This is the way he . . . enjoys himself . . . as a man. There are others like him."

I swept a look over the walls. Hanging from iron hooks were lengths of chain and rope, iron manacles, leather whips, straps, knives. A banana-shaped piece of polished wood lay on a shelf, a mysterious, frightening object which made me shudder, though I had no concept of its use.

"Has he . . . done any of this to you, Elena?"

"Not yet. Just the bruises and a whip. I fought him. He thought that was amusing. But he said . . ."

"What did he say?" I demanded, shaking.

What monster had I married, who would use his wife to beget a son, to impress society and grace his home, leave her to abuse helpless girls in some unknown, unnatural manner to satisfy his lust? Who further kept a mistress for who knew what practices? Who would even lay hand on Elena, my friend.

"He said that . . . next time . . . he'd use all the implements on me. And I'd have to let him, or he'd have Karl thrown into Morro Castle Prison."

Silently I cursed myself for telling Pablo about Elena and Karl.

"On what charge?" I demanded.

"He can arrange a charge!"

"Not now, he can't! Help me, Elena! We've got to free these girls, get them out of here! Where are the keys to the chains?"

"No keys. The chains are hooked in such a way the girls can't . . . see?" She unfastened an ankle chain and I ran to her and helped with all the chains and we lowered the first girl to the floor. She moaned and struggled to a sitting position. When I saw how young she was—not over fourteen—my outrage grew and I couldn't work fast enough to help Elena free the others.

"How can we take them out naked?" I cried. "Elena, go home . . . bring dresses, anything!"

"No need," she said and ran into the bedchamber.

Now all four girls were conscious. They began to weep and plead with me to save them. They called Pablo Devil and Satan.

Elena came running with silk robes, and we put these on the girls.

"Go to the street . . . get a carriage!" I cried.

At first Elena shrank, then left. The guard, I willed, wouldn't interfere.

"How have you gotten food and water?" I asked one of the girls, who was now up and walking about, limping.

"The guard."

"Help me get the other girls on their feet!" I urged. "We've got to get away before we're caught!"

After what seemed an eternity, Elena came back. She had a carriage waiting. The guard had disappeared. "To tell your husband, I know it!" she gasped.

"Take the girls home with you," I said. "Put them on the third floor. Tend their wounds and have Señora Bori give you food and drink for them."

"But the other servants, Mary!"

"To hell with the servants!"

"Where are you going, Mary?"

"To the law. To expose this."

"Your husband . . . he'll kill you!"

"I hardly think so. Hurry, Elena! I want to get everything arranged before . . . *hurry*, darling!"

The man I saw, the one in charge of police, was under Pablo's control. That I could tell before I'd been with him ten minutes.

"Señora Gómez," he said smoothly, his shiny black mustache moving. "This is a most serious charge, no? It isn't our custom to permit a wife to speak against her husband. Not without witnesses, and even then . . ." He spread his hands.

"But I have a witness! My maid . . ."

His shoulders lifted. "A servant, Señora."

I glared at him. "Are you telling me that you'll permit a man to hold girls prisoner, to . . . torture them . . . and do nothing about it?"

"Señora. Your husband is the most powerful man in our city. And your own position . . . you must consider that, Señora. To bring dissension into your home, to disturb your fine marriage, that alone is enough to inspire me to protect you from the shame which you in your womanly outrage . . . It is understandable, perhaps, but foolish. For men will be men, Señora."

Only then did I consider what this meant to my own life. I determined on the spot to leave Pablo, to get a divorce and, with it, money for my needs. Some of the money I would use to care for the girls, to get them started in decent lives.

There was no point in talking to this police officer. I stood.

He sprang to his feet. "Señora. I shan't speak of this interview to your husband. My advice . . ."

"Is to let him abuse as many girls as he wishes?"

"No. I shall warn him. Let him know that his . . . er . . . arrangements have come to my ear. Advise him to discontinue. This, I assure you, he will comply with. He'll not want word of it to get about. He'll protect himself."

I nodded, lifted my chin, sailed out.

Arriving home, I let the driver help me from the carriage, paid the fare, went running to the front door. My thought was to get upstairs to Elena and the girls.

Señora Bori met me just inside.

"There is a gentleman waiting for you," she said. "He insisted on waiting. He's in the library."

Impatient, because I was in such a hurry to see the girls before I must face Pablo, I went quickly to the library. I opened the door.

The tall man standing at one book-lined wall turned.

I caught hold of the door jamb to keep from falling.

It was Roger.

He wasn't in England, across the sea.

He was here. In Havana, in this room!

Chapter 35

He came to me, hands out. I'd never seen him so handsome, so vibrant.

I gave my hands into his, felt their warmth and strength, my own raging blood. We stood thus what may have been one moment or many, his blue, blue eyes sinking into the black and wondering depths of my own, drowning themselves.

"I saw the notice about your marriage in the newspaper," he said at last. "I came on the fastest ship. Pray God I'm in time!"

"But I'm already married. I have been for . . ."

"That's why I came, my darling. You couldn't know what you've married. You, so innocent . . ."

"Don't forget what I've been. My experience . . ."

"Experience that was forced on you, that you had to force yourself to endure that you might survive. That's over, can't stand between us. I know it all."

"You don't know about Karl," I whispered.

"Karl?"

"Karl van Buskirk. He was my only friend when I was a stowaway. He . . . I . . ."

The white line appeared around his lips, vanished.

"That, too, is past," he said.

"He's still my dear friend. He's going to marry Elena, my companion and dearest woman friend."

I wondered why I was chattering about Karl. Elena needed me with the girls. But I had to make certain that Roger no longer hated me. I'd gotten myself into the most deplorable condition yet, but all I wanted, this instant, was for Roger's wonderful kindness to continue.

"Why did you come?" I asked.

"Because you married Gómez. Because I know how evil he is. He's a legend along the South American coast. I had a mate from Jamaica whose sister . . . Gómez got hold of her. She escaped, but she'd lost her beauty, and her mind."

I stared at him, almost trembling.

He'd known, when I didn't, what beast I'd married! He'd come swiftly to me. What did he mean to do? How could he stop Pablo when even the most important at the police would give only a warning?

I stammered out the question, thinking he'd never be able to understand what I meant, but he did. "I have a few connections in Havana myself," he said. "Has Gómez harmed you, Mary?"

"No, Roger. Only young girls. And Elena."

Grimly he said, "I need witnesses."

"I'm a witness!"

"A wife isn't considered . . ."

"There's Elena, my companion, highly intelligent! We went there, to the dungeon where he k-kept the girls! We've got four girls upstairs in this house! All bruised and cut and . . ."

"That's enough!" he exclaimed. "They're living evidence. I'll get a hearing. I don't know what will happen to Gómez, but you'll be freed of him, if you want to be."

I stared in wonder, in birth of hope. "Of course I want it, Roger!"

"Darling," he whispered; took me into his arms, and it was a homecoming. I was safe, absolutely content. Nothing else existed.

The first we knew that we weren't alone was when a hand grabbed my shoulder, whirled me, and a fist slammed my jaw. I crashed to the floor, heard Pablo's curse, saw Roger move to come in behind him.

"Where are they?" shouted my husband, no sign of drunkeness about him. "Where are my quadroons? Where did you take them?"

"How do I know?" I cried, giving Roger needed time.

"I'll kick you in the mouth if you don't talk! It cost Pic an eye, but he talked! After I went back to my joy-spot and my girls were gone! Indeed he talked!"

Roger jumped him from behind, knees straddling Pablo's torso, arms clamped around his neck, boring into his windpipe. I scrambled up and dived headlong for Pablo's ankles, throwing him off balance, bringing them both to the floor, Roger holding Pablo mercilessly, crushing his neck.

Pablo gave a mighty twist, lunged to his feet and bellowed. "Nissi . . . Carlos!" At the same time, he smashed his fist into Roger's nose just as he, too, regained his stance.

Roger hit the floor so hard his head bounced. Pablo was in a half-crouch and this time I threw myself vigorously against his buttocks, throwing him off balance, flooring him.

I struggled up fast, hampered by my skirts. Roger

and Pablo were already on their feet, crouched, circling. Pablo kicked viciously, his boot catching Roger under the chin. Roger staggered backward, brought up against the book shelves, and books fell.

It was in the next breath, with Pablo leaping for Roger, myself in motion to grab Pablo's knees, that the blood of pirate days rose again in my veins. Exhilaration sparkled. I was a living rage to fight with my man, to fight for Roger.

As I hurled myself against Pablo's knees, toppling him, two hulking figures burst into the room. I got an impression of brute strength, then only a blur as they hurtled at Roger.

He moved like lightning, as the pirate-Roger of old had done. He brought the edge of one hard, practiced hand down on the back of one fellow's neck, kicked the other in the belly.

The first one dropped like an ox. The second doubled, clutching his middle. Pablo, ready now, backed a couple of steps and then, head down, rushed at Roger.

He leapt aside, drove his fist into the small of Pablo's back as he went staggering past. Pablo roared curses. His fallen ruffians scrambled up, sprang for Roger.

I went for them headlong. Pablo jumped in front of me, and I took his fist in my eye. I grabbed his wrist with both hands, sank my teeth into it. He bellowed, wrenched free, slugged me on the side of the head, and once more I was on the carpet.

I couldn't see what was happening as I fought my skirts. My head roared, feeling as though it were split. Again I clambered to my feet. I heard blows, grunts, curses; in that manner I knew they hadn't bested Roger.

My eyes were glazed. I blinked furiously, pushed my fallen hair back, tried to focus on the melée. A blur of motion appeared between the door and the murderously fighting men. A voice that could only be Karl's gave one shout. A fleet thanks to God whipped through me and, with a shake of the head, my vision cleared.

Karl was fighting both of Pablo's men. He was bigger than they were, but they were two against one. Roger and Pablo were side-stepping, each with hands locked around the other's throat. Roger's face was red, eyes staring; Pablo's face was livid, flat black eyes popping.

Panting, I tore off my dress and petticoats. Running free in chemise and underdrawers, I jumped onto Pablo's back, buried my fingers in his hair and pulled as hard as I could. His head came slowly back; Roger's grip on him didn't lessen, nor did Pablo's on Roger.

Letting go his hair, I ground a thumb into each of his eyes, digging mercilessly. I meant to blind him and I would have done it, but sudden, not-to-be-reached hands grabbed my shoulders and peeled me off Pablo as though I were the skin of a grape. The hands hurled me aside. I crashed into the desk, felt a thump of pain course my shoulder.

Still panting, each breath a knife, leaning helplessly against the desk, I saw Roger bear Pablo to the floor, saw that my husband had lost consciousness. Roger let go, sprang up and threw himself into Karl's unequal fight. Karl was on his knees, unable to get up from under the battering Pablo's men were giving him.

Again, injured shoulder or not, I used my pirate body as a weapon. I shot across the room, attacked one of the beasts, hooked my arm around his neck and began to dig into his windpipe. Hanging onto him, I knew Karl had chopped his remaining opponent across the head, and that the fellow was unconscious.

The one in my grip twisted, wrenched my shoulder, but I hung on. Karl hurtled to us, drove a fist into the scoundrel's face, another into his groin, and the man yelped, cursed, lay still.

Roger and Karl lifted me, lowered me to sit on the couch.

"The . . . police . . ." I gasped. "Have . . . to come . . . now."

And they would have to. Roger had every right to charge Pablo with assault. He, an English Lord, had come to call and had been attacked and forced to fight for his life.

"My best friend is with the police," Karl said. "I sent for him when Elena's messenger gave me her note."

"You . . . got here . . . so fast!"

"I met him on my way to see Elena. Mendoza and others will be here any minute."

I tried to draw a deeper breath, winced.

Roger was at my side instantly. "You're hurt! Where is it, my darling?"

"It's only my shoulder. It'll be . . . fine."

He drew my head carefully to his own shoulder, held me.

Thus it was that Señora Bori, when she dared look into the room, having herself sent for police, found her mistress in the arms of the strange Englishman, wearing only her chemise and underdrawers, hair down and tangled, jaw turning purple and one eye swelling shut.

She had just covered me with a robe when Mendoza and the others arrived. One officer was named Silva, another Perez-Guerra. They, unlike their superior earlier in the day, were extremely interested in everything I had to say. They promptly put the three half-conscious men, Pablo among them, in irons and, promising to send other officers to interview Elena and the other girls, took the prisoners away.

Chapter 36

Elena now appeared and went straight into Karl's arms. Señora Bori murmured and departed.

"My gratitude," Roger said to Karl.

"It was nothing."

They exchanged a deep look. I knew they were thinking of the time when I had been a stowaway and had given Karl my body in return for protection. When the look ended they were silent, but there was a feeling of respect in the room.

"Karl," Elena said, "he kept girls in a dungeon. Mary had me bring them here. I'll have to go to them."

Shock at the extent of Pablo's evil showed on Karl. It was fortunate for Pablo that Karl hadn't known how he'd abused Elena. With Pablo in custody, she'd have time to explain that my husband had whipped and struck her, but nothing more. While we waited for the carriage, one of the girls had told us, sobbing, that Pablo got his satisfaction from abuse, and had never taken them as man takes woman.

He'd taken me, but roughly. Not for pleasure, but for the begetting of a son. Undoubtedly he had perverse ways with his mistress. He was the vilest man alive.

After Elena and Karl left, Roger and I stayed on the couch, happy just to be together. Soon he insisted that we call a doctor for my shoulder.

"There'll be one for the girls," I said. "He can tend

to me later. This is what I really need . . . to be with
you."

"I've missed you so, my darling," he said. "Twice
I deserted you. Once because you drugged me . . ."

"I did it because I loved you."

"I know. To save my life. Then I left after the
duels . . ."

"You were hurt, Roger. I hurt you."

"Angry, too. When I asked you to come away with
me that time in the garden, I meant we'd be married
in England. Then I heard you tell Cross you loved
him, that you'd marry him. When he was dying. So . . .
my damnable temper took over and I left."

"Not temper, darling. Cause. I'd even killed a man
for him. Even now, you know I'm besmirched . . ."

"Never! Life has put you through the crucible.
You're as pure as the moment you were born. You'll
always be pure. It's all over now."

"Not until you really understand, darling. I did love
Nat. Not as I love you, with every bit of myself. I
loved him more deeply than a friend, but quietly, and
I really had decided to marry him. Until you came
back, and then I all but forgot him. Then, when he
was dying . . ." I looked into Roger's face anxiously.

The white line showed, faded.

"I understand, Mary. I don't like it. But I can see
that Cross loved you . . . God, what man wouldn't . . .
I'm glad you comforted him in the end. And with
truth."

"Thank you, darling," I whispered. "Pablo didn't
love me, nor I him. It was business between us. I
thought you were lost to me. So. I was to be his hostess
and produce one son. In return I was to have position
and luxury."

Roger nodded grimly.

"What will they do to him, Roger?"

"He'll buy his way out of it. But the scandal will
ruin his position and take away much of his power.
He'll never be important again."

"The girls upstairs . . ."

"We'll find them an apartment, leave them in Elena's care. I'll give Karl money so they can establish themselves. You're not to worry about another thing."

Held so tenderly in his arms, hearing him tell how things were to be from now on, a delicious feeling came over me. Slowly, I recognized it for what it was.

Furiously, all my life, I'd striven to be a woman. At first, I'd thought that wearing dresses, living openly as woman, was the answer. With Nat, I'd come closer to my goal, for Nat had enriched me with love. But it was only now, as I sat reunited with Roger, that my dream was coming true. I let my arms creep around his neck, nuzzled into it, shoulder hurting, and remained.

I marveled at being here at last, marveled at my growth from lad to woman. In spite of everything, I'd moved to this moment, becoming stronger and stronger as I progressed from being my grandmother's "boy," to sexual toy for any man who could get his hands on me, to pirate, to club hostess, to villain's showpiece, to the woman I was now: unafraid, loving, and beloved.

Roger's lips came to mine. We kissed long and purely, with endless love. "We'll get you a divorce," he murmured. "Then we'll marry, and you will at last be my wife, Lady Mary Courtney."

Now, at this moment, dressed in a soft blue gown chosen by Roger, we are on the high seas, enroute to England. Roger returned *Skull* to her rightful owners and paid them well for her use. He restored his estates and has given much to charity. In London, he'll see that any charges Sir Cecil made against me are dismissed.

We stayed in Havana only long enough to see Karl and Elena married, then left the city where Pablo now walks the streets a free man. But one from whom I am free, whom I will forget.

Roger is waiting for me on the upper deck. I must go to him, for we don't like to be parted for even a moment. And, of course, we have all our future to plan as this great vessel carries us into our life.

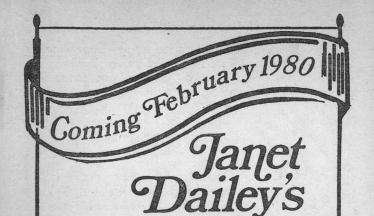

Coming February 1980

Janet
Dailey's

THE ROGUE

A strong-willed and beautiful
young woman, the father and son who
love her, and the legendary
Ghost Horse of the Plains that ignites
the passions of all three—it is an
uneasy trio which sets out to track
down the pure white stallion.
Diana likes the boy, but she loves the
man...with a white hot passion
they've disguised as hate for ten years!
Watch for THE ROGUE, wherever you
buy paperbacks.

OCKET BOOKS

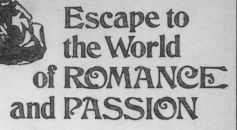

Escape to the World of ROMANCE and PASSION

Romantic novels take you far away— deep into a past that is glittering and magical, to distant shores and exotic capitals. Rapturous love lives forever in the pages of these bestselling historical romances from Pocket Books.

____81961	BELOVED ENEMY Amanda York	$1.95
____82320	DAUGHTER OF THE FLAME Julia Grice	$2.50
____81817	DIOSA Charles Rigdon	$1.95
____82251	DULCIE BLIGH Gail Clark	$1.95
____82014	FAR-OFF RHAPSODY Anne Marie Sheridan	$1.95
____80944	FORBIDDEN RITES Joan Bagnel	$2.25
____81845	JEWEL OF THE SEAS Ellen Argo	$2.25
____82273	LORD OF KESTLE MOUNT Joan Hunter	$1.95
____81919	MARIE Margot Arnold	$2.50
____81043	TAME THE RISING TIDE Virginia Morgan	$2.25
____81135	TARTAR Franklin Proud	$2.50
____81486	VALLAMONT Pamela Gayle	$2.25

POCKET BOOKS
Department HRO
1230 Avenue of the Americas
New York, N.Y. 10020

Please send me the books I have checked above. I am enclosing $_____
(please add 50¢ to cover postage and handling for each order, N.Y.S. and N.Y.C.
residents please add appropriate sales tax). Send check or money order—no
cash or C.O.D.s please. Allow up to six weeks for delivery.

NAME_____

ADDRESS_____

CITY_____ STATE/ZIP_____

HRO 5-79